REQUESTS and DEDICATIONS

BY ELISE LEVINE

FICTION

Requests and Dedications (2003)

SHORT STORIES

Driving Men Mad (1995)

REQUESTS and DEDICATIONS

ELISE LEVINE

M&S

National Library of Canada Cataloguing in Publication

Levine, Elise, 1959–
Requests and dedications / Elise Levine.

ISBN 0-7710-5277-4

I. Title.

PS8573.E9647R47 2003 C813'.54 C2002-905908-9
PR9199.3.L4675R47 2003

We acknowledge the financial support of the Government of Canada through the Book Publishing Industry Development Program and that of the Government of Ontario through the Ontario Media Development Corporation's Ontario Book Initiative. We further acknowledge the support of the Canada Council for the Arts and the Ontario Arts Council for our publishing program.

This is a work of fiction. Names, characters, places, and incidents either are the products of the author's imagination or are used fictitiously.

Book design by Terri Nimmo
Typeset in Bembo by M&S, Toronto
Printed and bound in Canada

McClelland & Stewart Ltd.
The Canadian Publishers
481 University Avenue
Toronto, Ontario
M5G 2E9
www.mcclelland.com

1 2 3 4 5 07 06 05 04 03

David

"Is it only love
that makes a place?"

— EAVAN BOLAND

contents

PROLOGUE

First came the merry-go-round, smeary yellow on a damp afternoon, then a parade in which the morning sunshine spun a filigree of golden horses. Memories like sno-cones, jewel-toned cups of flavoured ice. A tall bunny in a tuxedo and top hat, a miracle carrot-peeler. A woman in a floral-print dress with full pleated skirt leaning over from the waist, head floating above in an aureole of pink cotton candy, the warmth of sugared breath. And once, at a schoolyard fair, a ride on a pony called Pickles. Look mom – no hands!

Now, on this November afternoon, my thirty-seven-year-old arms deliciously overburdened with stuffed animals, tin belt buckles, plastic lampshades – having stormed the kiosks, driven by a nearly boundless love of sour-cream fudge and guaranteed never-to-chip fingernail polish – it's still me all right, the queen of par-tay. No point making sense. You live your life and that's that. It's a credo that's got me this far – I've only just begun to realize the good times can't last forever.

What the?

Walker refuses to notice me, and my practised sneer goes to waste. Instead he keeps whistling, pursing his thin wormy lips, gazing into the rafters and down at the hay-wisped concrete floor. He checks over his fleshy shoulders once or twice then shrugs, shaking his head as if to say, What can you do? His whistle is high and soft, a wooing sigh with little rolls and flutters, notes ascending then curling over the top like tiny waves, the scrolled song folding over on itself like the folds of his own decadently wrinkled skin. The horse beside him pays scant attention, flicking its bony head up and down, tapping the ground with its front hooves in boredom.

Must be losing it, Walker, the horse's groom says.

Sitting on an overturned steel bucket next to the horse's rump, he's a gnomish man, short and wiry with an oversized head and an off-centre mouth, a sneaky, ventriloquist's voice. Impossible to guess his age. He raises his buggy eyebrows and winks at me, leering. I smile icily, just in case, though Walker doesn't seem to notice.

The horse stiffens and spreads its back legs. When the pee comes Walker holds his hands palm out and looks upward. The groom scrambles forward onto his knees, upends his makeshift perch, rocks back onto his heels.

Crouching low to aim the bucket, he grudgingly shakes his head and squeaks, Still the best, my man.

Then off he trundles, taking the sample to the makeshift veterinarian's office where it will be tested for illegal substances.

My guy – the official whistler at the Royal Winter Fair. He stands with his arms crossed over his massive belly, not quite looking at me.

Want something? he says.

After all these years we save our expressions of interest for the late harvest of prize-winning pumpkins in exhibits A and B, admit to a longing only for blue-ribbon peaches-and-cream corn, admire only the glass jars gleaming with orange-blossom honey stacked in pyramids on the mezzanine floor. And this armload of toys and trinkets I won at the plastic rifle range? Where is the pleasure, the panties-in-a-knot pleasure? The cheap darlings only remind me of what we no longer feel – gifted, extraordinary in each other's presence. That once upon a time we were the main fucking attraction.

All this stuff! My arms are killing me. I can see the apple-cider vendor in his white peaked hat watching from his stand at the end of the aisle – checking out my high-heeled boots and pouffy hair, my tight, lace-thonged ass in skinny jeans as I stand in relief against Walker – but he can forget it, nothing to see here, folks, nothing but no-show as I turn and walk away.

Where is she, Mimi? Walker booms out after me.

Terrific. *This* is how I have to win his attention? Somewhere along the way I lost his porky twelve-year-old daughter. I last saw Jena in the Coliseum, at the opposite end of the fair buildings, filling up on cream puffs, skipping from one butter sculpture to the next, oohing and aahing with slack-jawed abandon. Why should I be the one to keep track of her? I'm *busy*.

Any guesses? he says. Because otherwise this could take me a while.

Fine by me, I say over my back. I won't hold my breath.

Along the mazy aisles of stalls in the horse palace, packs of lanky teenage girls – all pouty anorexic attitude with their pointy Wonderbra'd breasts, their J. Crew cargo pants and baby tees, their barn jackets tossed carelessly on bales of hay, one looking-good, hip-chick posse – snack on California rolls and guzzle Evian, time out from braiding the manes and tails of their pedigreed hunters. A Jack Russell and a miniature schnauzer sniff each other in front of a team of men yoking the massive, blinkered Carlsberg Clydesdales to a green-and-gold wagon. Between this crowded centre and the security-patrolled outer aisles that house the international show jumpers – those priciest of the pricey – lie a few rows of mostly empty stalls.

Here's one that's occupied – a seven-foot-square box stuffed with trunks and cots and folding lawn chairs, Walker's plaid Markham Co-op work shirts and greasy, horse-shitty jeans in a pile in a corner. Carefully hung on a makeshift clothes rack, the snow-white breeches and leather field boots, handmade in England, that belong to his niece, Tanis, beneath which lies Jena's scatter of half-eaten bags of Doritos and Cheezies, wincingly sweet beer nuts, empty cans of Mountain Dew.

I toe open the door, stand at the threshold, fling my junk to the floor. Hope you break a leg, you bastard! I can dream, can't I?

Then I turn back into the dusty light filtering three storeys through the precious dreck of the crowds, the high-stepping hackney ponies, the taffy apples and silver harnesses and hoof goo.

In the practice ring Tanis works Walker's best horse, really just a so-so creature with little talent and a flawed conformation. Not to mention borderline lame half the time. Lodged in the saddle like a boulder of determination, face closed as a fist, Tanis herself isn't much to look at. Unpronounced overbite – nothing to write home about – with a slight lean to the front teeth. Average in height and weight. Hair a stick-in-the-mud brown I've practically begged her to let me lighten – a little colour can work wonders for a girl. Average in school, is what her report cards have stated for years. A sourpuss, is what her teachers have called her since fourth grade. But her rage – average? they might as well have branded her forehead – makes her something to watch. Witness the way she sometimes treats her cousin – sheer torture.

Put it up, Tanis barks at the ring attendant when she takes the straight, single bar, now up to a shocking six feet.

Each time she makes her pass there's the short bunched

gallop before the toss into air, then the hanging second when the horse shakes loose of gravity's boring hold. *Put it up.* The ring attendant shakes his head, but does what she tells him.

Wish I could do that, but oh well.

Some of these rich prissy girls with horses so much better than themselves – horses they don't deserve – are watching Tanis tough out jump after jump. Take that! I'm thinking as I look around at the perfectly straight noses, the knifing glint of expensive metallic mouths.

So I miss what happens. The casual misstep, a moment's easy hesitation when the dumb beast loses faith – balk or go? – and crunches into the bar, hits the ground, and rolls over. When I look, the horse is down and Tanis is nowhere to be seen.

Falling is percussive, sound stunned from the body. My first time Walker stood over me in dim outline and I could hardly hear him yell, You fucked up, as I began to black out, a cartoon whoosh! as I spun down the drain. I found that under the earth the horses are thunder that bring the dead to sound – a tonal clash in black and white, a jazzy scherzo in reverse. I heard temple blocks and crotales, exotics rung out by rickety bone-fingers. Fucked up! It only took the first fall to know there was no going forward from there.

The horse stumbles to its feet. I can see Tanis now, on the ground, rolled over on her left side. Walker pushes into the ring and takes the dazed horse by the reins.

You okay? he shouts.

He looks as if he's seen a ghost, right up until the gate at the top of the ring swings open and the paramedics rush in with a stretcher.

In a few minutes Walker will lead the horse back to its stall. He'll remove the tack, slip the halter on, lead the horse back out, and walk off the sweat. He'll take care of things, do what has to be done – I've seen this before. Later, much later when the fuss has died down, he'll sit on a bale of hay with his big head in his hands.

Christ, he'll say, lord jesus fuck me to tears.

(Because at moments like these he feels certain of his relationship to god, who seems, in Walker's sappy brain, to bear a curious yet unmistakable resemblance to his mother, Rose – how many times have I watched him gaze with soulful devotion at the hand-tinted photo he *so* predictably keeps by the side of his bed? A transplanted New Brunswicker with a wooden stare, she died when Walker was eleven.)

Then, with a start, he'll lift his head from his hands and, rising from his prickly seat, wonder aloud if he should call the police.

Jena, he'll say.

Come off it, Walker, I'll tell him. Sometimes there are more important things to worry about.

Dirt and dust from the practice ring's floor, the oiled dirt with its ancient earthy smell, rise like smoke. It's hard to see anything from where I sit craning my long neck in the hushed stands. Somewhere in the distance, from the main fair building where along the crowded aisles there are back bacon on kaiser buns and wild-rice risotto – ticky-tack kitchen gadgets and catcalls and dollars – a calliope snores into action, house sparrows flit above the mezzanine, and pigeons click in the rafters.

But for now, here, there is only the blackness rich as velvet, a bitter chocolate thickening the tongue.

Curtains.

I

1

CAVALCADE

We tie the fat girl up. Her face is caked with barnyard crap but surprisingly unalarmed. Tears glide from her as if she were naturally inclined, gifted from above. We threaten to bury her alive if she tells, we wave a stick in front of her face and for the first time in my seventeen-year-old life – here in the heady, hay-stinky shade – everything is control and clarity, the arrest of relations. Suzanne stands beside me, tall and thin in her platform sneakers and boot-cut jeans, the tight orange baby tee with the word *suck* printed in white. Her skin is sweat-shiny, eyes open wide, and I feel a secret power arise like armies. Beneath us the pink lardy bundle wets herself in the straw.

Jena, we say, as tears tick from her like clockwork. Don't you dare tell.

Girls go! In the white Explorer's wake a creamy dust laps the dirt road. The radio's cranked, the windows down all the way, the air conditioning turned full blast. We cross Highway 7, go up past Bloomington Road, turn back the way we came, stop at the bridge. Suzanne's hottie dressage instructor flipped her Jeep over the guardrail one night last spring, snapped her neck in the Rouge riverbed and died. A month later her Rhodesian Ridgeback died too, ripple-ribbed and lovesick. O silence, Camels dangling from the sides of our mouths. Tiny sparks of water fly off the rocks below us. When the dark sugar of a country wailer starts I lean forward to really pump up the volume: you, me, she is his. A bright waltz blithering about whirligig nights, a tall tale of sunshine and no regrets.

Too hick, Tanis, Suzanne says, and I bump the sound back.

We make a left past hayfields and red brick farmhouses then a right at the mall then another right, into nerve system central of the new subdivision, pinging among its circular drives and cul-de-sacs, its fake Tudor and Georgian mansions, its baby weeping willows and black maples – none more than five feet high – limp and useless against the smoggy apeshit heat.

In Suzanne's darkened bedroom: iMac-topped cherry desk, cherry armoire and sleigh bed with pale Laurens, ecru matelasse cover, and blond cashmere toss pillows. The vanity on which two bottles of Tangerine Wavelength Fruitopia bead with water. The room is scentless and huge, Miele-groomed, the sci-fi and comic-book collections cascading from the floor-to-ceiling bookcases the only messy gesture.

I lie stomach down on the bed, stroking Suzanne's Goddess polish in aqua Miriamne – "Peace be in my thoughts, my words and in my actions," the bottle reads – across my nails while the Sony across the room dishes a dusty: Marilyn Manson zipping through a sticky black tunnel on a pig, lip-synching "Sweet Dreams Are Made of These." Close my eyes, and a light like video, blindingly neural, splashes against my lids and somewhere down the hall in her father's teak-lined study, sitting in his Eames rip-off lounger at his Eames rip-off desk, privacy-obsessed Suzanne lisps secrets into a phone, fogging the Lexan with a beautiful code I imagine endlessly helixing.

I wait for my nails to dry – feel like I'm in drag! – they dry, I get up from the bed and go to the window, draw up the whipped-cream Duettes. Suzanne's mom, slender as a model in a zebra-striped swimsuit, stands on the cedar pool deck among the array of wrought-iron tables and teak chaise longues, the terracotta urns of impatiens and pansies. She stretches a white bathing cap over her hair, adjusts a pair of tinted goggles, and dives into the pool, parting the flawless turquoise as she laps through chlorine. I wander over to the vanity and try another Goddess selection, Psyche in baby pink. "I bask in my own opulence; I belong to myself." Swab away, masking the old colour.

Suzanne appears in the doorway. She yanks at her crisp black hair. A natural white-blonde, her usually porcelain-pale face is flushed, a rosy dab at either side of her downy lower jaw.

Oh my god, she says breathlessly, baring her excellent orthodonticized teeth. My day has been so out of control.

Yeah, I say. Tell me.

Above us the ceiling fan spins and spins. When I look in the doorway again Suzanne is gone.

In the hallway, down the sand-toned Berbered stairs. Three-foot-tall glazed pots grouped on the landing. Stepped in descending order, black and white photographs: nudes yielding to the rippling skin of desert landscapes which in turn yield to cityscapes of Paris and New York.

On the first floor, in the very French Provincial breakfast nook, at the antique pine table set with Provencal-patterned placemats and napkins, Suzanne stokes a late light lunch of muesli and soy milk. To the left, in the kitchen, copper pans hang from a ceiling rack over the butcher-block island. Above the granite counters, above the maple cupboards, the walls seem to be a picture of eternity itself in a *trompe l'oeil* of turtledoves and trailing ivy.

I'm just deciding to help myself to some cereal and join Suzanne at the table – she's so intent on chowing she won't even notice – when her mother, wrapped in a white terry robe, slides open the glass door behind the breakfast nook and steps inside, towelling the short blonde hair at the nape of her neck with a plush white towel. She tenses when she sees us.

Ah, she says. The Deficits. I see the ADDs have put in an appearance.

Suzanne's mother is the director of the Dream a Dream Village north of Stouffville, a special community – a country club! – of braindeads and legless wonders and mongos, the slow set out there in the woods humping trees and each other night and day: lush libidos, according to Suzanne, who has a part-time summer job driving the Dream a Dream van. Forced to work, having failed half her classes this past year at school, twice a week she carts a load of crips and ids to softball practice and picnics. In between she studies algebra, biology, and French with a tutor. *And* her Nazi parents sold her horse, took away her cellphone for the summer – can you believe?

Suzanne's mother pulls her bathing cap out of a pocket in her robe and bounces it on the table. She stares at it for maybe ten seconds. When she looks at Suzanne again it's with an expression of bewildered hopelessness.

Eating again? she says. My god, where do you girls put it all?

Suzanne keeps eating, rucking her spoon around the bowl, dividing and subdividing the cereal into increasingly smaller bites she sucks at more than chews.

Suzanne, the mom says. I'm talking to you. You're, my god, seventeen now! When I was your age.

Suzanne erupts in a strangled laugh and soy milk ejects through her nostrils, too gross.

Suzanne's mother looks disgusted.

When you're done with your face, fix your hair, she snaps at Suzanne – who stares at her mother blankly while mopping her chin with a napkin.

The woman turns to me, exasperation and dismay in the straight-line set of her mouth.

And while you're at it, fix *yours*! she says.

She reaches across the table and grabs the keys to the Explorer.

Suzanne, her mother says to her. Am I talking to myself? What am I saying?

Suzanne freezes. Her mother hefts the keys in her hand, spikes them at Suzanne's head. Suzanne's elbow flies up in an intercept arabesque, knocking the keys to the floor. Suzanne's father, vice-prez of a pharmaceutical company, is away again on business, so it's the mother-daughter show as usual: no biggie.

Like, you could've hurt me, Suzanne bleats.

Like, I feel for you, but when you're finished stuffing, you can take your little friend back home.

I wait for Suzanne in the marble foyer while she hurls oats in the upstairs guest bathroom, the one with the navy-blue ribbed-silk wallpaper and mirrored ceiling. A make-work project for the twice-weekly cleaners. When Suzanne's done she'll scrub her hands and nails with Bulgari soap, go down the hall to her own bathroom and carefully Sonicare her teeth. To kill time, I slap the brass tits of the reclining nude sculpture next to the front door. On the wall across from her hangs a huge blown-up colour photograph: an Ute-something, an airy taupe and mauve tumble, a dreamy pixellated spill beyond which the baby grand gleams in the living room and, beyond that, another hallway with a black granite and white marble floor. Altogether a neat clippered effect, some uncluttering of the mind.

Outside on the patterned brick drive there is only the smothering heat. We get in the Explorer and go, this time no air, just the windows down. At first the streets are long fields, and later the fields are grassy blanks, sunburnt, unremembering as wrong answers on a geography test. We smoke, say nothing all the way.

Ten minutes later, two-thirty, we pull up to Walker's again, yo-yos. A killdeer worries the tall weeds at the edge of the dirt drive. Suzanne eases the Explorer past the large sign – MACLAREN'S STABLES in black lettering – and pulls ahead of the dusty white Monte Carlo parked beside the house. The car has long scrapes the length of the driver's side from which rust holes frill like starfish. Sun stings the pocked windshield, and fine cracks web the passenger's side. The back right-hand passenger window is missing. Both bumpers hang low and loose, jerry-rigged to the car with bungee cords.

Nice, she says.

That was fresh, I say. No really. How original.

Fine, she says. Give me something to work with.

No can do, I say, looking around me.

On a slight rise of newly mown lawn ringed by tall maple trees, the house itself is tidy, a well-maintained two-storey red brick built around the turn of the century. The house faces west, and around the back – facing east, off the kitchen and barely visible from the front, revealed only by part of an aluminum-sided wall – is the apartment Walker added ten years ago in which my mother, Joy, and I live with Joy's best friend, Mimi. For which the two women pay Walker rent and hydro, clean for him, cook sometimes too. One door of the apartment leads to a single-step back exit, another takes you straight into

Walker's kitchen with its Ontario pine pressback chair, its broken-armed oak Windsor, its plaid vinyl and aluminum chairs – chairs like a collection of mismatched buttons. Walker's kitchen also has two exits: the one into our apartment, the other to his porch and triple steps onto the drive.

On the other side of the drive, lying south of us, is a white-fenced paddock, also ringed by maples, in which a couple of boarders' horses stand sleepily. Only one of Walker's two Ford trucks is parked in front of the first of the two barns farther to the east behind the house.

He's not back yet, I say. You wanna?

Suzanne cuts the engine and there is a moment of perfect stillness, sorry heat. Then whoa! Joy cannonades from Walker's kitchen, herky-jerks across the porch, and pounds down the grey-blue wooden steps.

Flap-yap! she goes, saying – something.

I consider my mother's mouth, behold burnt-orange lipstick, her rigid, killer-blonde bob. In the surrounding trees the heat bugs start up, electrically shrilling.

Suzanne takes a final drag of her cigarette and flicks it out the window. She turns the key in the ignition and the engine catches like that.

See ya, she says. Wouldn't wanna be ya.

Yeah yeah, I say, opening the door.

Suzanne puts a CD into the player. Before the sound starts I jump, hit the ground hard, jarring my steel-pinned left foot – crip, big dumb crip. I slam the door. Suzanne backs onto the road and is gone. Off to her secrets that over the past few months have seemed more interesting to her than me.

You stupid, Joy squeals.

Her eyelids are paper-thin beneath plucked and darkly pencilled brows, the whites of the eyes clouded with humidity. She backs me up against the Monte Carlo. I catch a glimpse of Jena, the chubbo herself, twelve years old going on two, watching from the shadows on the porch.

Well? Joy says. Explain *this* one.

Right – like I'm robo-girl, operating instructions included! Instead I look back at the porch: Jena is gone. The sky is high and pale and I'm sweating. Joy's mouth works for a few seconds, twisting and pulling, her face red like there's a fishbone caught in her throat. But nothing comes out except her hellaciously stenchy breath – she's so close now I can't turn my head, her hips wide-bodying into mine – and it's like she's going to inhale me when she breathes in again, rehearsing every bad day and shredded luck of her life, this woman who tinders to anger at the slightest provocation. She raises her hands and puts the heel of her palms on my chest, digs in. I hear trees tizzy with wind and, past the blur of Joy's head, branches bobble in the lake of sky. Then I hear Walker's kitchen door open. Joy moves back a foot, drops her head, and crosses her arms.

Nuts, she says.

She looks punched out, exhausted from working Mondays through Saturdays – starting at six in the morning, finishing by two, as she has today – as a cleaning lady at the golf club off Steeles Avenue, a five-minute drive south and west of here. After a couple of seconds she lifts her head slightly toward the house. I look too, waiting for Jena to come forward.

Instead, Mimi. Of the long, thick hair dyed a thrilling red, almost always Scruncheed into a ponytail. She sweeps onto the porch as if into a spotlight, as if she's preparing for a gig at the Drake. Tastefully attired today in very short white-denim cut-offs and white mid-heeled mules, a strappy white tank top with picot trim that shows off her tan. She stays put a moment in the shade, a black vinyl tote slung over her left shoulder, frowning, before prancing down the stairs and onto the drive, ponytail swishing. She smiles broadly now, waves airily in our direction as if to say, Never mind! – whether at us or the swampy weather, who knows. Her long fingernails and matching red lipstick tangle on the fumy breeze of body heat and dust.

Mind? As if! Joy's already got the passenger-side door of the car open. Sticks her big old butt in the air, squeezes in and squares herself in her seat. The handle on the driver's side is missing so Mimi reaches through the window and opens the door. Then she slides in and settles, lightly tapping her fingernails on the steering wheel.

A whippoorwill wind jitters the tall grasses in front of the ditch and the leaves in the trees purl softly. The car engine turns a couple of times before catching. When it does, a song is playing on the radio. Mimi turns up the volume and a tinny noise whirs out the window. She doesn't sing along, though. Must be resting her voice. She leans across Joy and studies me: my cargo shorts are bunched around the tops of my thighs, creased where they cut into my crotch, my loose tank top hangs limp at the neck and my Jogbra's soaked. I feel wasted by bloating, itchy, tender in a dismal sort of way.

Don't encourage her, Joy says wearily.

Mimi arches her left eyebrow and cocks her head to one side – a move I'll practise later tonight in front of the bathroom mirror. The song ends and she bends away to turn the radio down, all dippy deejay nonsense and the hourly news. The wind wilts and the trees are still.

She leans toward me again.

Hey girlfriend, Mimi says, winking. Heard about your recent exploits. Don't you just *rule*.

Her voice is low and scratchy, and lipstick glosses her front teeth when she smiles. Looking good! She must have spent the night in the house with Walker – a man all belly swollen over his Jack Daniel's belt buckle, impressive, somehow, even with his hairy ass crack showing all the time, his jeans so low slung they always seem about to fall to the ground – instead of in the apartment where for the past nine years she's mostly slept on the faded, red velvet fold-out in the living room. Joy and I share the wrought-iron double bed in the cramped bedroom where, lying beside her nightly, back to back, I'm hardly a sleeper at all, more a container, trap of fractured REM: sword-swallower of my mother's snore-splintered exhalations, the ever-wakeful yet reluctant safety net for her death-defying, apnea-spiked sleep.

Even with the radio's volume turned low I can make out the deejay's plummy baritone.

Pile in, bet you don't know what day this is. Your lucky day, you bet. Big Dan here and I tell you, we've got clowns, balloons, free hot dogs. So come on down to Bob's Country Beef, and bring the kids too. While you're here, order a side of freezer beef, on special.

Mimi's still leaning across Joy, looking at me. She winks again.

Thought we might go to DQ for some scrumpdillyish, she says. My treat.

Tell them Big Dan sent you.

In the fields, horses indistinct and grainy in the afternoon light. The cicadas seem to forget to call, their intervals lengthening like shadows. Long since lifted are winter's damp bandages of snow, spring's chilly, lingering frowse. Mimi's all high octane – My god, Joy, laughed till I peed! and Oh that big bastard – as she smokes the car along the dirt road. Joy's yapping high as a kite. On the radio Big Dan's still hawking freezer beef, his voice a twangy chaff. That's right, free hot dogs and Cokes.

Mimi catches my eye in the rear-view mirror and torches a kiss. She takes one hand off the wheel and fluffs her ponytail. In places, curtains of sunlight mixed with dust drape low over the long fields and radio songs flare like signals along the route. Joy sings along, her voice crackling like static. A plane slips through fields of thin cloud and, climbing higher, vaporizes in the sterling sky. Another plane swings low above the car, flattening Mimi's and Joy's voices into fluttering veils of sound. She do, ran too. She up, you too. And Joy's yeast infection – tried this, tried that. Joy, did you never think of trying? Really?

And what do you think, Tanis? Mimi says.

A dog barks in the distance. Mimi hums a tune while a commercial for Zest soap plays on the radio. She-he, the big man ran. And then he said. No way! Walker this, Walker that. A horse. Dog-cow. A red-tailed hawk perched on a fence post. Hurry on down. Walker. Walker.

Just before the Wilsons' farm Mimi suddenly swerves the car then slows and stops. She puts the car in reverse and backs up.

There's another one, she says, pointing out the window. See?

She pulls over and I get out. The air feels cooler here, dry. The sky brightens and turns a clearer blue.

Hurry up, baby, Mimi calls out the window. Haven't got all day.

A snapping turtle. Unusual to see one here this time of year. In the spring the females lay their eggs in the sand by the side of the road, making them easy sport for the four-wheel-drivers.

This one is medium-sized, and even so will weigh a ton. I get it from behind, stabbing at the tail, sweeping it chest height into the air and away from me. A rotten smell seeps from beneath the carapace. Pudgy legs swim frantically in the breeze as it clacks its head around, biting air. I manage to lift it higher, looking toward the car where Mimi and Joy have lit up, their cigarette ashes sparkling out the windows. I can hear them laughing.

Mimi, Joy is saying. You tell that bugger to get off the pot.

Why would I tie myself to him, Joy? Mimi says. Give me one good reason. I did that, it would be game over.

No way! Joy says. It'd be like, touchdown, and then you have the halftime show. That's what it would be like if it were me.

I lug the turtle over to the far side of the ditch where, scared it might tear a chunk out of my leg, I half-drop it on its head. I walk back to the car and get in. As Mimi pulls away I turn around in the back seat to watch the Wilsons' Clydesdales weaving slowly across the light-brown field as they graze, in the increasing distance like rusty beads strung on telephone wire. A hawk floats across the popcorn-cloud sky.

Nearing Highway 7, Mimi waits until the last second to slow down, jumping the car brakes suddenly, scalding dirt and stones like layers of skin from the dry mid-July roads. Wisps of hair curl and lick the back of her long white neck. In the heat her ponytail seems to be losing volume. On the radio Big Dan chatters like windup toy dentures.

I tell you, Thursday's the big draw and someone's going to get lucky, so get out your pen and paper. Ready? Write to Big Dan, your man.

Joy digs out a pen from the bottom of Mimi's tote and scrawls the address on the inside flap of her cigarette package. Mimi turns left onto the highway and accelerates slowly.

Got it? she says.

Joy puts the pen back in the bag.

I wonder, she says, patting the short kiss-curls that extend below the line of her bob at both sides of her cheeks. If he really is. I mean, *Big* Dan? Whoo-eee. Any time, honey! I need to get me some of *that*.

Mimi thumps her left hand on the door.

Knock on wood, she says.

Then she puts her foot down again and we swing past the new housing subdivision. I lean forward, put both hands on top of the bucket seats. The highway shakes and blurs beneath us like a wing and we sway slowly.

As if, I say. What makes you think he'd stoop so low?

Joy exhales sharply, stung – I'm like, *touché*.

As if you have any idea what you're talking about, Joy says, twisting around to rag on me, forcing me to sit back in my seat. As if you'll *ever* know.

She faces forward again, shifts from side to side, elaborately squaring her shoulders.

What's to know? Hype and lies: by way of example, take any summer afternoon on Musselman's Lake, a twenty-minute drive north of here, where Suzanne and I go swimming sometimes, though less often than we used to last year.

We park the Explorer by the side of the road that rings the water, among the Harleys and ancient Trans Ams, the empty beer cartons pitched about the sparse grass. Then we make our way through small clumps of spindly trees and stiff shrubs to the lake itself, strike a path along the brown weedy shore among bodies rimed with greasy water and sweat, moms and dads yelling at each other over gritty macaroni loaf sandwiches while crying kids wander around, Huggies loaded down, and biker guys with bandanas covering their long hair, arms like hams, prise open the jaw of a giant woolly Bouvier, its teeth smacking the slabbed flesh of a Rottweiler – there are always these dogs.

We pick a spot, spread our towels over the pebbled dirt, and lie on our backs, smooth our hands over our hip bones to see how far they jut out, smoke cigarettes bummed from Mimi (which she's nicked from Walker), sit up occasionally to turn the pages of paperback novels translated from the Spanish or French filched from Suzanne's parents.

And each time we look up from our books it's like party on! killer zombies: the glazed, good-time eyes, faces grim, mouths slack. Such a fucking feast of happiness.

That's a good one, all right, Joy says, crossing her arms over her chest, raising her chin to the side window. *That* I'd like to see.

Can you believe it? Almost out of those free hot dogs.

Chrome flashes in the oncoming lane. I shield my eyes. When I put my hand back down Joy is at Mimi's tote again. She fishes out some lipstick, then reaches in and takes out a compact. Concentrating to steady her hands, she re-does her lips, Mimi's frank red on top of her own desperate orange, stretching her mouth like a clown's.

Mimi glances over and laughs.

Joy, she says. It's really you.

At the Dairy Queen in Markham, Joy scoops pineapple sundae with a pink plastic spoon. She's standing beside a Ford pickup in which three men sit. She flirts with the one behind the steering wheel. I keep out of her way, leaning against the car, sucking a rapidly liquefying Oreo Blizzard, coaxing the chunks up the edges of the container with my straw. The driver swears at something Joy says. His gravelly laugh ends in a coughing attack. The other two men eat their burgers in silence, looking down. The driver's left arm heaves out the window. He coughs again, rattling violently, his face and throat red. He tosses a half-eaten Dilly Bar on the ground at Joy's feet.

Jesus, Vince, Joy says loudly. You dirty bugger.

She dribbles pineapple syrup down her front.

Jesus, can't take me anywheres, she says and dabs at her breasts with a napkin.

Need help? Vince says.

I don't think so, she says. The only help I need is the kind you can't afford.

I finish my Blizzard and, woozy from the sugar burn, drift toward the garbage can near the drive-through window around the side of the building. Mimi – who rarely passes up the opportunity to be busy in two places at once – is using the nearby pay phone, putting her hand over the mouthpiece, calling to me.

I can't get through, she says. She's in the bath or something. They're checking for me. Of course, that's what they said when I called from Walker's an hour ago. It's like they *so* do not have their act together.

Mimi's mother is a resident of a shall-we-say *home* in Whitby, about an hour south and east of Markham. Originally from Vancouver (by way of Montreal and Toronto), and exotically well-travelled – *worldly*, Joys calls her – Mimi had only ended up here to be near her senile mother (how her mother landed in the vicinity was anybody's guess, the result of an untethered notion she one day took into her head). That's my story and I'm sticking to it, Mimi liked to say when pressed for details.

I'd never known her to actually visit Whitby though. She made do with weekly, minute-long phone calls, after which she'd be withdrawn for hours – days, months even, it had seemed last winter.

Now Mimi was hanging up.

I'll try her later, she says to me, sighing. When I called from Walker's it was forget it. They must be having trouble with her still. She can be *so* you don't want to know!

She searches in her tote and brings out a loose five.

Maybe we'll go visit her, she says, wincing as if the thought pains her.

She scans my face. I rearrange myself: arms behind my back, right hand gripping the left elbow, cock my head to one side to express support.

What do you think? she says, sounding worried. Would you like that? Her quack says she's been improving lately.

Great, I say. Sure.

You can watch my back, huh? she says.

She picks up the receiver again and starts to place another call.

Hey tiger, she says, giving me the money. Get me something nice?

I've reached the front door of the DQ and have it half-opened when I hear her erupt.

Jena! she shouts. Tell your dad I want to talk to him. Will you just do that for me?

I stay where I am and let the door close. Several customers are looking Mimi's way, curious, smirking.

Really? she says loudly. And when did *she* get there?

She holds the phone a couple of inches away from her head, then presses it once more to her ear, lowers her voice.

Your dad never *mentioned* your mom was coming today, she says. Didn't you let him in on your plans?

Another pause, then Mimi slams the receiver down. She stalks to the front of the building, passes me, and goes inside – forgetting about the five she gave me, as well as the change from Joy's and my orders. I study the front page on a *Star* displayed in a newspaper box. A minute later she emerges holding a regular cone.

Hey pretty lady, a skinny, brittle-looking man eating a hand-dipped by the picnic table calls out.

He has a patchy, day's-old growth of beard, and his head waggles nervously, like a jack-in-the-box.

Mimi ignores him.

Yeah you, he says. It's me, Al. Over here, copper-top.

Mimi still hasn't looked his way. Lipstick quavers at the corners of her mouth. She smooths her damp hair with her free hand and keeps walking. I'm right behind. When she gets to the car she hands me her cone. She shakes the car keys out of her tote.

Joy, she calls across the parking lot. You coming?

But Joy's still carrying on, dodging then grabbing Vince's arm as it snakes back and forth out of the truck window. High above, an airplane blisters the sky.

Like, thank god for friends, Mimi says to me, rolling her eyes.

Al tries again.

Al, he says. From the other night, remember? At the Drake. Christ, you were pretty friendly then.

Mimi's cone caves in the heat. I lick around the edges. Mimi wheels abruptly.

Hey you, she says and winks at me.

Al thinks he's getting somewhere now. He holds up his free hand and waves.

Make my day, he wheedles. Be nice and say hi.

Mimi pulls open the driver's side door.

Like, I'm saying hi! she says to me, huffing.

She gets in and I pass her cone through the open window. Joy's laugh barks across the lot. Silence for several seconds.

Lay off, she cackles.

I'm still standing by the window, so close to Mimi I could easily reach in and touch her, place my hand on her thin shoulder. She's staring straight ahead through the windshield, sweat a beaded choker around her delicate throat.

Hey, where you going? Al calls out. Not leaving me already are you?

Ever since she entered our lives nine years ago, Mimi was the one who tended me – replacing Walker (Joy never had the patience) – when I was home from school, sick with the flu or the mumps, the chicken pox or a bad cold. Jena, sick as well, would be fortressed with Walker in his living room, their TV bleating an idle tattoo through the wall that separated us as I lay on the couch in the apartment.

At first Mimi would bring me beer mugs of stale ginger ale, gently unpeel the wet face towel from my forehead, return, moments later, with a cool fresh one. Later, if I felt well enough to sit up, we'd play Crazy Eights, listen to music or TV reruns in the background, *The Hour of Charm* All-Girl Orchestra (featuring Evelyn and her magic violin) playing their hearts out – for us, I'd think. By eleven in the morning we'd have the first of the Coke floats, Mimi's juiced with rye. Around noon she'd knock on the door connecting the apartment with Walker's kitchen. Either the door wouldn't open, or it would and Walker would appear briefly, hands in the front pockets of his jeans, before soundlessly closing the door again. By one o'clock Mimi would switch to rye and Coke, no ice cream. By two it would be straight rye.

Walker, she'd say occasionally, conversationally.

I'd nod my head and say, Uh-huh.

Three o'clock: cowled together in a blanket, slow-dancing to songs playing on the radio, swaying damply in what I imagined as a perfect forever – never mind I felt worse than before from all the ice cream. Mimi whispering in my ear, the same thing over and over. *That bastard, that bastard*. I'd hold her as tight as I could, as if I could hold the sickness in, contain it somehow with each lovely rotation, press it smaller and smaller into a glittering ball as the fever-talk bubbled us around, the giddy sickness lofting us – until I'd grow dizzy, flush again with fever and nausea, and I'd have to let her go.

Joy coming home late from work at four, putting Mimi in the shower, unfastening her lacy black brassiere, easing her black rayon slip from her slim white hips.

Hey dolly, Joy would say. Don't you worry, I'm here now, honey.

Joy wrapping a towel around her, helping her back into the living room. Joy half-crouched beside the door leading from the apartment to Walker's kitchen, listening. When she hears him she knocks on the door. The door open sesames.

In one of her moods again? Walker says, his high-pitched voice – he'd been rendered permanently nasally from a sinus operation – carrying into the apartment. What do you want me to do about it?

Joy smashes the door shut, Walker's chair scrapes across his kitchen floor.

A little sympathy wouldn't hurt, she yells.

She pounds on the door, Walker shouts something – Women! or, Fuck me! A curse so ordinary it seems wordless.

And Mimi? She always seemed to have come to us from out of nowhere. *Other*-worldly. No more so than now: out cold on the sofa bed, hands curling exquisitely inward like fronds furled in sleep, her face a pale alien flower, Walker's botched voice mantling us all in something like love.

I get in the car, directly behind Mimi. Al walks toward us. He waves in the direction of the back seat, stooping, trying to see inside. He cups a rose-tattooed hand to his mouth. Nausea worms through me. Mimi's still as stone.

That your daughter? Al says. Nice-looking girl. I don't mind, believe me. We all make mistakes a time or two. Believe me, you're so pretty, I don't mind at all.

I can see in the rear-view mirror that Mimi has closed her eyes. When she opens them she turns away from Al to look at me.

Puh-lease, she says in an overbright, strained voice. I just had the worst dream.

I smile, sort of.

Nice try, she says. Not bad. But keep practising.

She faces forward again. She jams her key in the ignition and starts the Monte Carlo, puts it in drive, and begins to chauffeur me to the exit. I sit tall.

Hey Al, she says once we're well past him and there's no way he can hear. Eat my dust, you knob.

She stops before she reaches the road and puts her left turn signal on. She laughs: Joy, redfaced and panting from her sprint across the parking lot, grabs the handle on the front passenger side, gets the door open. She's barely inside with the door shut when Mimi kicks it, and the Monte Carlo roars onto the road.

It takes a second for Joy to catch her balance. She huffs, and then tsks at her feet, reaches down, sits back up to throw a crumpled paper bag with leftover doughnuts – god knows how long it'd been there, stashed on the floor – onto the back seat. It bounces against my leg. She claws inside Mimi's tote, pulls out the lipstick and reapplies it, this time without using a mirror. She smacks her lips together and sticks out her neck to check herself in the rear-view: I can see her top left lip has been rouged higher than the right, and her bottom lip is smudged as if swollen. She reaches into the bag again and pulls out a pair of sunglasses and puts them on. Next she pulls out a scarf printed with West Highland White terriers she once gave to Mimi, having found it one day while cleaning the women's change room at the golf club. She puts the scarf on her head, knotting it under the chin. She sighs heavily, then leans forward and twists the dial on the radio.

The city's classic rock station comes in loud and clear. "Satisfaction" is playing. A blast from Mimi's groupie-girl past.

Your song! Joy says, perking up a little, only to seemingly have a change of heart as she slouches back in the seat, turning her head to the side window.

Maybe it should be *my* song, she says morosely. Why'd we have to leave so soon? I was *this* close to scoring a date.

Mimi doesn't respond. High above the car, the waning sun seems to dissolve like Aspirin. Traffic lights slow us among the car dealerships and Burger Kings. Eventually we're swinging past bushes and uncut grass, weed-choked culverts and abandoned, elm-shadowed farms. When the song ends, the newscast comes on. Mimi is still quiet, carefully eating her cone. With her other hand she lets go of the steering wheel and switches off the radio.

Going, going. A raccoon, a dog. Cat-dog. I sit up in the back seat, feeling better now – at least, up to enjoying the gross-out.

Road pizza, get a whiff, I say.

Joy swivels around to look at me in the back seat: the large black sunglasses are scratched and dusty, and her skin yellows against them.

You stupid, she says.

Give her a break, Mimi says softly.

Joy snorts but says nothing back. She scratches a swollen mosquito bite on her left arm. When she stops, blood prickles up. She fakes a yawn, which makes her jawbone crack, and two seconds later I catch the tail end of some primo halitosis hurricane. Mimi delicately tips the bottom of her cone out the window. She tugs at a limp strand of hair.

Joy, she says, her eyes gone squinty. Remind me to change your cut one of these days. Your colour's a little tired-looking too.

Joy's hand flies up to the scarf.

What's wrong with my 'do? she asks, alarmed. You said it was flattering!

Mimi shrugs, glances to her left out the window, then looks forward through the windshield again. A plane leaches distance from the colourless sky. Above us a skinny thread of mouse dangles from a hawk's beak. The weak breeze stitches a blanket of high-thinning cloud to cloud. Hot air limps past. The fields shrink.

Joy fidgets, crossing, uncrossing her legs. She pats the scarf now and clears her throat, leans an elbow out the window, then pulls it back in again. Already, though it's nowhere near September, goldenrod is blooming in the ditches, fringing the unused fields. Tiger lilies wilt. More goldenrod, its flash wind of pollen in the eye. Mimi puts her left hand to the back of her neck, then piles her ponytail on top of her head and holds it there.

I'm just melting, she says.

More roadkill.

Diablo bones, I say and screak like a crow.

Mimi and Joy ignore me. I try again.

Aw-aww.

Stupid.

Just past the Wilsons' farm Mimi pulls over.

I get out, and the road beneath my feet is smoky with dust. Corn stalks gust in waves against a rusty wire fence. I hear Joy jet air through her nose – as if to say, Not again! – then a crunching sound as Mimi walks behind the car and climbs in the back. The sky is white again, round and milky, edgeless.

I get in the car on the driver's side and adjust the mirrors. I take my time. Although I've had my licence for a year now, I hardly ever get to drive. The women seem tiny as dolls, almost unbreathing, which makes me feel huge, turned inside out, as if beneath my skin there were nothing but weightless blue gases and I were a bulging, vaporous globe.

Joy turns the radio on again, switching back to the country station, clowns and free hot dogs and Cokes.

Tell you what, tomorrow's another scorcher for sure.

I release the emergency and the car slowly rolls forward.

By the way, Joy says. You're on your own with this latest stunt. How many times do I have to tell you? Leave. Jena. Alone.

She laughs nastily, makes a gargling sound in her throat. I glance in the rear-view at Mimi. She's staring at her knees.

You've made your bed, Joy says. Now you're going to have to lie in it.

Only if Walker finds out, I think. That is, if you don't tell him. Because I know Jena won't.

I press my foot to the gas pedal: suck it up, girlie! In a year or two, or three – as long as it takes – I'm out of here, sayo-fucking-nara. Next? Hello sun-blissed moment by moments, lulling breezes cooling my skin. *Soon.* I gently rock the steering wheel from side to side as the sky wheels shapelessly overhead.

I make the turn into the drive.

A boarder's horse grazes in the paddock. The Lucifer, goat brains blunted by twelve-inch horns, abrades himself against the white fence, and one of the dogs lies sleeping between Walker's two trucks parked in front of the first barn.

I take my foot off the gas, the car coasts to a halt. I turn off the radio, the engine.

Mimi and Joy are silent. Wind spooks the trees beside the house. Walker opens his kitchen door.

2

TOUCH AND GO

At night when it's cooler my dead mumma rides out to meet me. Mumma! I'm surprised at how good she's been keeping. She touches a mercury hand to my face and disappears.

Baby, Mimi says when this happens.

She stirs beside me in bed, gently rakes her fingernails over my chest, and in the absence of light her hair cobwebbed against my shoulder, her sleep-clotted voice, confuse me.

She's thin. I roll into her, bitch.

Bony, I whisper.

She says, Oh you, I'll tell you what.

I sit up, wait for my head to clear. Then it's downstairs to the kitchen for a smoke. With each drag my confusion shrinks, becomes a black knuckle easily swallowed by the time the sky brightens. Always takes me a while to get things straight.

Take today.

She sits in the drive with her big red hair, in her boat of a car that eats gas like candy (I should know, I'm the one who pays). With her ridiculous name – Frenchified, part Jew. She is mean to my only daughter. *Yo, dummy.* Like something said on TV. But I myself have heard Jena as we walk the BiWay aisles, announcing T-Fals and $19.99 specials, magazine headlines in large print as we stand in the checkout aisle with socks and girl things, tight fuzzy sweaters and flimsy gold necklaces, rings set with opal, her birthstone – the jujubes and gummi bears. For each my daughter sounds out words and prices, confident in her remedial reading.

From the porch I can see across the drive, past the ancient Monte Carlo to the paddock, where the branches on the maple trees clog in the hot four o'clock wind. A boarder's mare grazes. I can almost hear the snaggle-toothed stand of birch and ash saplings behind my house, the puny leaves ticking slowly, the single, silent alder wind-stripped beside the rusted-out hull of a tits-up truck.

Out back of the barns, behind the indoor arena – in the fields beyond – the flash of killdeer within the sea froth of Queen Anne's lace and daisies, the Rouge River sliding its green poison, emptying forty miles south into Lake Ontario. Sometimes it's snap! what you see not what you get. Last night was great between Mimi and me. And now? Go figure. Women. How do they always know when bad things happen? Which in this case, happens to be Lily. Left only minutes ago, Jena in tow.

Waves of heat shiver from the car, despite its blanket of dust. The two front doors fall open, my sister and her seventeen-year-old kid drop out, hesitate in the drive as if dazed. Kid jacks her head around – Mimi's sitting in the back seat, a strange place for her to be, she loves that junker, would row it broke-down to Neptune and back given half a chance, running her smart yap the whole way – then turns her head back. Everybody's looking nowhere.

Now the kid slinks from the car toward the barns, limping slightly. One of my dogs stops scratching his ears, gets up from his spot in the dirt, and trots amiably alongside her.

Ready, aim, here comes Joy.

Could've been worse. Last time I had the pleasure of Lily's uninvited company she came face to face with Mimi. After, I had to drive for hours in a thin rain so I could chase Mimi down and – un-fucking-believable! – beg her forgiveness. For fucking what?

I found her late that night in the back room of the Drake, just past last call. She was by the washrooms, face slack with beer, hair scraping the sticky table over which she drooped like someone had flung her, the Exit sign above her head like a warning. When I got closer the guy she was with stood uncertainly, tilted away. Somehow I got her outside. She was pale, her face scaled of light. I put my hands on her bare shoulders to steer her to the truck. Her skin was clammy and cold. I wondered what, besides the beer, she'd stuffed into herself – I worried she'd slip past me for good, knew I'd be up the rest of the night, watching, thinking should I run her to ER, would she try to get back at me that way?

I landed her into the passenger seat, scooted around the other side and got in. As I backed from the parking spot she began to cry in woozy, insucking breaths, as if bunches of words were being jammed back inside before they could get out. I wondered if she could hurt herself like that. I swung the truck around and pulled onto the wet road, the rain coming harder now. I thought I could explain.

What am I supposed to do? I said. She's the mother of my child and all. That hoor.

That last I threw in for good measure, thinking it might get me somewhere, but Mimi only cried harder. She has never understood. I've tried to explain – doesn't a girl need her mother? though it's not like I'd ever let Lily take Jena for good – but no way will Mimi deal. Even Jena herself is hard for Mimi to tolerate. She hates to think I had a life before I met her. Vanity! I try to be sympathetic, understand how this might be difficult for a woman used to being the centre of attention – even her crying is some kind of show. Long, hard to see how it will end.

If you have any ideas, I said, you tell me what, because I'd really like to know.

Somewhere between Bloomington Road and Highway 7, I considered putting my fist through the windshield. *How do you like me now?* Then I thought better.

Once in waking and now in my dreams Mumma said, Tomorrow is another day.

Better believe, I remind myself. What choice has a guy got? It's that or the slammer.

So let the dust settle. When I finally step off this porch – and guess what? – all crap breaks loose, I'll do what I can to keep the old lid screwed on tight.

And then it's howdy-fucking-doody time, off to the races – Mimi unleashes herself from the car, starts working that mouth. At least off the bat I learn how she put two and two together.

You can't even tell me yourself! she says. You let Jena do your dirty work for you.

Leave Jena out of this, I say.

Though I remember I did hear the phone ring, faintly in the kitchen, when I was on the drive talking to Lily.

And where do you get *dirty* from? I say. I would hate to be in *your* head.

Prick, she says.

Mimi, I say, trying to be patient – maybe I got off on the wrong foot somehow and I better try another tack. Lily comes here, gets Jena, leaves. Period. No advance warning. I don't know why you even care. A woman of your, should I say, *calibre*, ought to be above such feelings.

Excuse me? she says. Say what? Don't try to butter me up, Walker. You should listen to yourself sometime. *Lily this, Lily that*. You think I'm stupid? *Lily! What a pistol!*

She rolls her eyes and I relax a little.

She must have been some dish, Mimi says, arching her long back.

I roll my eyes too.

Like, back in the day, she says.

I relax even more. Maybe that's the end of it for now. Sometimes that's all there is.

I'm wrong, of course. There's Joy, always fucking Joy.

I think Mimi's entitled to her feelings, Joy says, like she's been watching too much *Oprah* lately. Why can't you respect that? Where are *your* feelings?

Where? I say, and I can feel the pressure building in my head, feel how hard it is to keep from giving a flying fuck in the face of these two, always egging each other on.

At least Mimi's not throwing things, that usually happens inside, whatever's handy, coffee cups and alarm clocks, chairs, once a bag of garbage that broke and guess who had to wash the kitchen floor? There should be a show on the tube about it – a guy doomed from Adam. I could be the star.

They're up my ass! I say. Isn't that what you think?

I jump back a foot as Mimi's bag flaps through the air, dead drops on the topmost porch step. She gets back in the car and wheels that big bomber around, launches it the twenty feet along the drive and a right onto the dirt road, heading north. Whaa! That's the horn on the southbound pickup she just missed hitting. The driver pulls over, leans his head out the window – not only his head but his shoulders, half his thick torso too. He yanks himself back inside, opens his door and out he goes, heading straight for her – at least she's sitting tight, frozen still, trap shut for now, thank fucking god for that.

I walk over Mimi's bag, down the porch steps onto the drive, no way around it.

Hey guy, I call out.

He stops, holds my gaze, gauging. Shrugs his shoulders, walks back to his truck, gets in and shuts the door. He leans out the window again. He laughs.

Hope for your sake she's worth the trouble, he says. You poor jackass.

Then he drives off, while Mimi – who might be crazy but isn't stupid – gives him a good head start in the opposite direction before taking off as well.

What *is* it with her? I'd like to take her apart myself, piece by piece with my bare hands. If I could find out how she works! Then I'd put her back together again, but someplace nobody could bother us. Like, on a mountain. Only there aren't any here. Or I could drive to Florida – make enough money next year, take off for a couple of weeks in the winter. Pink fucking flamingos, pink drinks, my treat. Mimi with tan lines, laugh lines, just the start of them – a long-legged, still good-looking woman. The beach our bed, miles wide. Do what we want and no one to interfere, the whole shebang.

Now you've done it, Joy says.

She's lowered her head, cups her elbows with her vice-versa hands. Does she look bagged. Has since she was little, even before Mumma died, all through the time Mumma was sick and there was nothing anyone could do no matter how hard you wished. Joy's still little, stout. A tough nut.

I am not the enemy, I say. I wish you'd realize that.

Whatever you say, she responds. I'm not going to argue any more. I'm just going to stand quietly aside and let Lily continue to ruin your life.

Exaggerator, I say. There's no ruining! Besides, I'd think you'd know by now that it's my own business.

If that's the case, Joy says, then pauses for effect. Maybe you could keep out of mine from now on. I've never done any worse for myself than you have with *that* mistake of a woman.

I go up the steps onto the porch, open my kitchen door.

We're even-Steven, Walker, Joy continues. Especially if you take into account our useless daughters. The trouble they get into over each other. I don't understand why you hang on to Jena. Why *not* let Lily take her?

I close the door behind me and lock it. Take a few seconds to calm down, then unlock the door and open it.

Joy's sitting on the porch rummaging furiously through Mimi's bag. Joy looks like she's playing dress-up, playing as if afraid she'll never get her fill. She doesn't seem to notice I'm here, the empty dirt drive, the sleepy horse in the paddock behind her, the sleepy drone of wind through the maples. A syrupy heat. A feeling like this has been going on for ages.

Then I see her kid, standing by the barns, watching. She puts her hands in her shorts pockets and walks toward the house. *That* gets Joy's attention. She looks behind her, sees me standing in the doorway.

Great, Joy says. Just what we need now. You have no idea, Walker. You are so stuck in your own little world, you can't see past the end of your nose, same as always. My god how they fight! As recent as this morning when you were out.

The kid stops, looks at her mother. Looks at me, then away.

I am not clueless, I say.

Then I go back inside my kitchen which is like an oven, shut the door.

I get the bottle down from the cupboard above the stove, and an old Mason jar, only one I've got, that's been kicking around for years. Later I'll nuke three or four frozen dinners for myself, dine out with Mr. Swanson – how I prefer to eat anyway, like a snake, one big meal and I don't have to worry about the small ones, probably that's why my gut looks the way it does.

For now I settle with pouring the drink. I knock it back straight – damn! if it isn't hot too – hold the empty jar up.

Earlier when I was at Ray's – smoking a sweaty cigarette as I leaned against a Vise-Grip in his Quonset hut, a Vornado blasting mid-afternoon air at the metal-shelf-lined walls brimming with gaskets and fan belts, filling hoses, stainless-steel adaptors – where racing bike and car parts crested and troughed on the concrete floor and, off to one side, awash in a debris of crumbling newspaper and ancient, cat-pee-reeking tarps, floated a majestic cream-coloured Studebaker that hadn't run in years, if ever, and ants hilled over half-eaten cheese danishes from, oh, say yesterday, day before, day before that, and –

Shouldn't you be allowed to speak what's on your mind? he was saying – noodling his long, grey-streaked beard through his fingers. Fuck the thought police. They want us to piss our freedom away to foreigners. What *I* don't get is, why people are so willing to do just that.

I'd been there since noon, shooting the shit – which consisted of me watching Ray nod his bald on the top, long-haired on the sides head, straighten over a rebuilt car battery, stroke his beard, cross his wiry arms, and rest his elbows on the coffee-stained workbench as he riffed his opinions.

Nobody but nobody is as entertaining or enlightening as Ray, who has theories – which have to do with secret government plots – as a person might have a profession or an expensive set of golf clubs. He always finds a way to cut through the mumbo-jumbo, judge what's right and what's wrong. Not bad for a guy who's never had a social insurance number or a bank account in his own name, never paid taxes. An unlicenced mechanic, under-the-table cash only. A talker to boot. Always reading these books and brochures. When you're flat bored, Ray's is *the* place to go.

Problem is, I was also thinking, once you get there, you can only listen to him so much – it's like there's a meter running on the whole experience. His notions can make it hard to get out of bed in the morning, make you wonder, Why bother? When for one, I've got the horses, and two, some part-time roofing to keep me going – not to mention maybe three, a little something on my mind about my indoor arena that I was there to discuss, once I was ready to try to get a word in edgewise.

I fingered some wing nuts mounded in a plastic tray, dragged some more on my smoke, waiting for his latest spiel to konk out.

Yeah, I'm with you, I said when it did – because I wasn't *quite* up to talking about myself yet, and I liked to have one or two things I could say to jump-start him with. And what I *really* don't get, is why you can buy a car that goes two hundred clicks an hour when you're only allowed to do eighty, a hundred tops.

I paused, waiting on Ray's refrain. I'm not *learned* or anything – that's Ray's department – but sometimes just being with the guy could make you feel that smart.

I hear you, good buddy, he said. Part of the plan. They've got us by the yin-yang and there's nothing we can do. May as well lie down and never get up again.

I opened the back door of the Quonset hut and flicked my cigarette butt outside. The hut fronted Ray's property. Farther along the dirt drive I could see Renata, packed into a fancy lawn chair in front of the bungalow, its windows covered in plastic sheets to ward off both summer heat and winter cold. She waved absently in my direction – woman has never really liked me that much. Next to the house and almost as big – bulky, twenty-feet high, the lengthy near-vertical slope of its boom-sway cables lank from lack of work, the massive claw of its shovel half-sunk in dirt – sat the excavator, a 1952 Bucyrus Erie from South Milwaukee, the reason I'd come today. I wanted it so I could build myself a new arena.

The machine had been Ray's inheritance, originally purchased by his grandfather so almost three generations could earn a living clearing out foundations for new buildings – this was before the big contractors started pulling in all the jobs. I've seen the family photo albums tended by Renata, the pictures of Ray at five in a cowboy outfit, pointing a toy pistol out of the cab. Ray's two older brothers – long since disappeared out west – hanging upside down from the boom, mooning each other. Ray and Renata at seventeen, perched on the edge of the backhoe, arms looped around each other's waist, smiling goofily, Renata already knocked up and on her way to becoming this fleshy, silent woman with straw-coloured hair still worn in braids like an old hippie chick.

(Baby turned out wrong – fell out of his high chair onto the floor when he was two, hit his head. They never had another. Five days a week Renata lumps herself and the slobbery man-boy, must be thirty years old now, into the old station wagon. She drops him off at the funny farm in Stouffville, then continues on to Unionville, where she sells gingham pincushions and fancy wreaths tied with red ribbon that you see on the doors of heritage-home renos and executive ranch-styles. Unlike coin-operated Ray, she gets paid by cheque – those from her job, those from the government due to the *offspring* – depositing them in her own account. I know because I sometimes run into her at the bank in Markham. We don't talk long. She's got the swamp creature waiting in the station wagon, wetly bumping around in the back like an empty wash bucket. At least he seems happy, gibbering away. Doesn't know any better. No expectations or nothing.)

I looked back inside the hut.

Ray had picked up a broom and was sweeping the few pockets of clear floor space, his narrow head still bobbing back and forth on his scrawny neck as if he were agreeing with the arguments he set up in his mind. Hell of a busy guy. I could hardly keep track of him – the odd-jobber, the fixer. Poking the floor with his broom, stirring the junk, sweeping and nodding in the middle of this mess of parts as if the voodoo of his outlaw thoughts could somehow pull the rinky-dink pieces together, make them whole. Must be how he stays so skinny, racing along the threads of his thoughts day and night. Who knew what really went with what, how things connected – if they did at all? When he felt like it – just for kicks – maybe Ray was an unfixer, like a spiteful elf. Padding his pockets, staying ahead by keeping you in the dark. Meanwhile the once bright-yellow excavator sits out back and rusts from lack of use, blushing for shame.

I pushed the back door of the Quonset hut open wider, stepped outside onto the crinkly brown grass. The treetops surrounding the Erie buzzed with insects, sounded like a fridge about to go on the fritz.

Ray, I said sharply, to get his attention.

I tipped my head toward the giant, complicated-looking machine. It rested on two thick treads. On the right-hand side, the arm of the backhoe rose from a square section that topped a swivel. On the left-hand side sat the cab, which looked like a castle turret. Inside that cab – and did I know! Ray had shown me and it was impressive – there were all the gear sticks. You had to learn, and somehow remember, what each was for.

What do you want for it? I said. How much do you figure?

Ray stopped sweeping, and looked at me in surprise. He looked back down and prodded some scraps with the broom. Then he put both his hands on the top of the broom handle and rested his chin. I wasn't exactly sure yet how I'd start off trying to explain, and I was a little nervous.

People want fancy-schmancy these days, I said – taking the plunge. *Heated* arenas. And with plumbing for bathrooms, and glassed-in, indoor viewing areas. That's what people want.

Yeah, and that's *their* fucking problem, he said.

Nope, I said. It's fucking mine.

He stopped leaning on the broom handle. Now he tossed it back and forth from hand to hand, a little game he was making for himself.

Ray, I said. Not to step on your feelings or anything. But that machine's not doing *you* any good.

He stopped with the broom and stood in silence, some internal pressure jamming his jaw shut. When he did speak, it was to the ground.

Well, I hate to mention this, he said. Since you don't seem to be asking for my two cents about your little home-improvement plans. But, buddy, think about it! It's not like you can even read, and this lean machine's got a manual the size of the fucking bible. Way beyond you. I mean, I hate to state the obvious, but that seems to be the position you're putting me in.

He chuckled, and started back in with the sweeping, then stopped and lifted an elbow, pointing it at me.

Mr. Moneybags here, he said.

Ray, I said. Don't make this something it's not.

Like what? he said.

Nothing against you, I said. But I don't want to sit on my fifty-fucking-three-year-old duff all day every day and complain.

He stood stiffly, not a peep. Then he relaxed into movement and leaned the broom against one of the shelves.

Jesus, he said. You're something, really something. Only I don't know what. All you have to do is ask, and you can borrow it.

Sure. But Ray would have to service it first, in his own sweet time. And the money stables that had been bleeding me dry of my best boarders for the past couple of years would only get richer. And I am way past sick to puking over the kick in the head I get every time I see my own stalls sitting empty, and know the business I'd built from the ground up is going to stinking rot. I have to get ahead, or I'd lose everything I called my own.

I walked toward my truck. The stiff dry grass crackled like glass beneath my feet.

On your way then, are you? he called out. Don't work too hard, buddy, okay?

I clenched my fists and almost started back toward him.

Instead, I got in the truck. By the time I slammed the door I no longer felt angry. It was July, it was hot, I was tired, it was almost three-thirty in the afternoon and what had I accomplished? I wanted to go home and have a shower, a drink, unwind. Re-lax! As people get older, they become more of who they really are. Ray was solid, nothing but Ray, more Ray more of the time. I guessed I was just me.

Ten minutes later I got back from Ray's to see Lily shooting out of my drive.

I barely managed to pull over onto the edge of the ditch and wait for her to stomp on the brakes. Her car mashed to a stop, stones and dirt flying from the road, hitting my truck. We faced off, me trying to turn in and her desperate to haul out, nothing unusual about that. I noticed her old car was looking pretty good – a fish-flash of metallic light blue, the quicksilver shock of a newly minted quarter found in the dirt. Must have dropped big bucks on a new paint job. I sat there trying to think of all the ways she might have managed that, when she finally gave in and backed up, craning her neck to see out the rear window. Once she was back on the drive and there was room, I drove past her to the first barn and parked. Mimi's car was gone, that was some relief – and no sign of Joy or Tanis. By the time I got out of my truck and shut the door Lily was still backing up, coming at me in reverse.

She pulled alongside and stopped, her frizzy blonde hair like a gigantic burr inside the car. Before, when we were together, she was a brunette. I could see her hands perched on the steering wheel, still small and delicate. *Petite*, she used to call them, trying to *edumacate* me. She used to smooth cream on them each night – I remember the sucking sound as she rubbed the lotion in – then pull on a pair of white cotton gloves. How she slept, as if in a bed of roses. Me lying in that bed beside her, breathing easy, for the first time in my life until then, what I could remember of Mumma no longer heavy, lifting instead, rising like a light to hum there between us. Listen carefully, a word – *family*.

Lily cut the engine and glared.

Looking for a good time? I said.

She allowed herself a cat smile.

You are so full of shit, she said. Do you know that? Do you know how full of shit you really are?

I thought, Well, okay. Compared to *some* people, not very.

I took a step closer to the car, flicked a spot above the door handle, leaned over and peered inside. Folds of green plaid – her grampie's favourite shirt, stuffed and sewn into a cushion to give her an extra couple of inches in height when she drove

– peeked jauntily from between her legs. I looked higher. Wattles starting to slop below her jawline. Around the edges of her low-cut T-shirt wrinkles webbed her still-loaded cleavage.

Heading out? I said.

You bet I am, she said. I can't stand it another second. I'll leave it for you to talk to your daughter. I'm at my wits' end! While you were goofing off somewhere, your Terminator niece was whaling away at her, and now she's feeling sorry for herself. And can she mope.

Kids, I said.

Yeah, she said. I know! It's like, you have to let them do what they're going to do. You can't baby them forever, because they'll get spoiled if you fuss over them too much. But in the meantime, they'll drive you crazy.

Right you are, I said. You are so right on.

Crazy's not the word! she said.

She bent her arm and rested her elbow on the window ledge of her car door, settling in, enjoying herself – trying the thought of being a good, caring mother on for size. Glad to be of service, I felt like saying, teeth bared.

I straightened and leaned my hip against the car door, stroked my hand over the paint, then moved away a step as if to see better – I bet it cost her. She was watching me closely. I could tell she was proud.

I stepped forward and stroked the car again, shook my head pityingly.

Could've had Ray do it cheaper, I said. He'd have done a nice job too.

I pursed my lips, let my gaze drift above the car roof. Swallows flopped like bats about the treetops. I mimicked their sound, a soft chitter I have down pat. Without having to look, I could tell Lily was staring ahead, down the drive and out to the road, away, her little body vibrating as if she were a trout caught on a line. Then she smacked her tiny hands on the steering wheel, and the spell broke.

If it's over, then why do you *engage* with her? Mimi always screams. Leave her be.

Can't, won't. The trick is knowing to quit while I'm ahead.

You shit, Lily said, gagging the words from her mouth.

Nothing I hadn't heard before – say, ten years ago? At any rate, it was a clean April morning. Blue sky, a kick to the air when I opened the kitchen door – that first hit of earth smell that lets you know the hard ground's opening up. I was puttering around, fixing coffee after feeding Jena, wondering if I should cook breakfast for myself or not.

I spent a few minutes looking for the frying pan. I'd just found it, back of the cupboard beneath the kitchen sink, when the phone rang. I picked up, and for the first time in the two years since she left me to raise our baby on my own, it was her, the ex. Lily.

How are you? she said.

How I am – at first, a blank pool. Then ripples, things I'm remembering – all she wrecked to ratshit when she left me for some Stallone-stud and in those first grief-sunk days after I swore I would waste her, never mind the consequences.

How I spent years getting a grip, deep-sixing how I felt – I had a daughter to think of, had to put my socks on everyday.

Lily tried again.

How *are* you? she said. You don't understand English any more?

I said, What do you mean, how am I? What kind of fucking question is that?

What I said, she said, and started crying.

I don't deserve this, I thought. I decided to wait it out, and after a minute or two (not long enough!) she was telling me she was in Scarborough, in one of those eastern suburb high-rises off Brimley Road – I was imagining a dusty, poured-concrete tower, cinder-block walls, stained carpet, particle-board furniture.

Brace yourself, she said, snuffling. I'm, how do I say? *With child*.

Congratulations! I said. *You*.

I took the phone receiver away from my ear. Pow! I banged it against the kitchen table.

I put the phone back to my ear.

And you're calling, why? I managed to say after a couple of seconds.

I'm in a state, she said. You jerk-off. I didn't know who else to call. Something's *wrong*.

As in, Don't ask, women stuff.

Can't you come get me? she said. I need to go to East General. I don't have enough for a cab. Please.

The sound of my voice when I heard it next surprised me. I wasn't even sure what each word meant. Then it was my turn to wait for a reply, but it never came. She hung up. The dark smell came in the kitchen again, fluxing through the screen door, tangling on a current of wind. Under the smell bobbed something small and gristly, so crudely bitter, raw as salt, I ground my teeth in disgust, ground them so hard my head hurt.

That's when I *made* it – a permanent turning from the places despair can take you. Damn, that felt good! Mark that day with an X, brand it on my heart. If that makes me a shit-headed bastard, so be it. *I yam what I yam*.

A month later, I heard through Renata that Lily lost the baby. But somehow that wasn't enough for me – each time I see her, I do what I can to get that good feeling back. I mean, since I have to see her anyway because of Jena – no denying Lily and me will always be linked. Part of the past that makes us who we are. And that's what Mimi can't stand – how she's not in that picture.

Lily turned the key in the ignition, ready to leave again.

Just then Jena banged open the kitchen door and shuffled onto the porch, fumbling uncertainly with a small pink duffel bag. The wide-flung door caught her right shoulder on its return arc, and she slumped forward, then turned her head back to look at the door with a shocked, hurt expression. It took her several seconds to collect herself sufficiently enough to continue across the porch – which told me she'd had a time with her cousin, but was doing her best to get over it.

Life's lessons. They were tough on Jena, I knew. But they'd help her grow up right.

Lily sighed and shifted the car gear to neutral, took her foot off the clutch.

Jena began to come down the steps. A large, well-developing girl of twelve, she favours oversized, flaring jeans and untied Nike running shoes, which she assures me is the correct style these days. Nevertheless I could only pray she wouldn't trip in front of her mother. What else could I do, seize my head with my hands, squeeze until the grey stuff popped out, have a smoke? But I was afraid to light up in front of Lily, who's allergic to almost everything.

I glanced at Lily, who had quite the expression on her face. I couldn't help but ask myself, not for the first time, was it really helping Jena to see her mom? Or was packing her off like this only helping me to keep Jena out of Mimi's hair? I hated to think this barbed line of thought. I liked to cut through it, simplify. *A girl needs her mother.* Look at me and Joy. All we missed out on.

And here we have the state of the union, Lily said. What've you been feeding her? I swear that kid's big as a barn.

I kept my mouth shut, smartest thing I could do – by now Jena had made it to the car, and why drag her worse into things? She stood before us, held out her arms, and let her bag chunk to the ground – shot daggers at it with her eyes.

Did you find it or not? Lily snapped.

Jena, hair falling over her face, bent and stabbed at the bag. She tore open the zipper, reached inside, and pulled out her new orange two-piece bathing suit. Green streamers drooped from the bottoms – it was like a kind of hula skirt, I suppose. Just holding it in her hand got her smiling, maybe she was remembering how we argued over it recently in the BiWay, and that as usual she won – and seeing the suit again, here in the driveway, I had to admit it was really something, all right. She thrust it toward her mom, and shook it like a pompom.

Ta-da, she said shyly.

Lily stared, mouth open. A slow cackling *oh* escaped her. She seemed to be putting something together in her mind.

Uh-huh, she said finally. Very nice. Slimming too, I bet.

Jena wasn't quite smiling now. Lily shrugged her shoulders.

Doesn't matter, Lily said. Never mind. For all I care, you can go naked. As long as you cut it out with the long-face business.

I waited until Jena was settled in the car, seatbelt fastened.

Don't drown, I told her. Make that an order. Do not drown.

Daddy, she said, trying not to grin.

Can we go now? Lily said. I mean, are we fucking ready to go?

Then she left, again. Turned out of the drive onto the road in a car almost colourless, a silvery twinge of blue. If I rubbed my eyes and squinted, put my mind to it, nothing in particular, nothing at all.

It's well into evening – eight o'clock, and Mimi's still not back – before I store the bottle away and sit again at my kitchen table. I'll admit I've had a few. There's a rabble of loud sounds from Joy's TV in the apartment. Soon it'll be dark outside. The temperature hasn't dropped. Not a breath of air riffles the yellow sheers in the window. From where I sit I can see into the living room, still lit by the fading sunset. Jena's deaf white cat lies upside down and motionless on the couch, one slatey eye regarding me.

What? I say, the air so humid I'm finding it hard to breathe, the word coming out high pitched, a half-strangled sound.

Is that me? My stomach billows with heat and there's a harsh taste in my mouth, and I remember the stack of frozen dinners in the freezer – but first, another drink, another smoke. Can't hurt. Not any more than it already does. I wonder if Jena's eaten yet. I wonder when she's coming home – now my stomach starts to hurt for real.

Someone testing the porch steps, missing most of the creaks. The kid – Tanis – opens the kitchen door, too carefully, and almost backs up when she sees me. But then she seems to change her mind again, and takes a step forward into the room. She's in her jeans and boots, her chaps – last year's birthday present from yours truly – draped over a shoulder.

Hi, she says quietly.

Smoke? I say, taking a pack of Camels from my shirt pocket.

She shakes her head and pushes her dark hair from her expressionless face, so masklike it's easy to forget the dimpled smile, eyes like navy chips, so deep-set they're striking – you have to look twice, three times to sense how unusual her eyes are. Hands broad, the knuckles strong, knobby like mine. Not tall, but a powerhouse build, a way of carrying herself that reminds you to take her seriously.

Sure? I say.

I light a cigarette.

Good for you, I say, inhaling. I should quit one of these days. Costs too much. Everything does. All the bullshit. If you know what I mean.

Her silence, her way of disappearing into herself before my very eyes, is getting on my nerves.

Well? I say.

Well? she says back.

There an echo in here? I say. What, you coming or going? You need a special invite?

She looks like she has no idea, though with that face of hers she's hard to read. I wonder, Can she read me? I look at the ceiling. From the corner of my eye it seems she's gazing at the table, though I'm not sure, not of anything any more, not even the roof over my trash head.

This or that? She's trying to figure, and it's almost sad, how she's just a kid trying to make her way in the world and no one can help her but herself – some people are like that, have to make their own mistakes. You want to help, but they won't let you, you want to apologize for how unfair things are, but you can't – that's just life, like it or lump it. For a second I think she's going to cry – her poker face has become weak and gooey-looking.

There's some bills here, I say.

She closes the door, walks over to the table. She drops her chaps in a pile on a chair, pulls another one out and sits, reaches for some papers stacked to one side. Beside them is an old jam jar holding a clutch of ballpoint pens. She takes one, and from beneath the jar slides out a chequebook. Unfolds a bill, writes a cheque, pushes it across the table toward me, looking relieved to have an excuse to do something with herself (looking relieved plain and simple, as well she should) – from the time she was in first grade she's liked to help, be involved. Once Jena gets older and gets her confidence she can lend a hand too.

Electricity, Tanis says.

She reaches across the table and passes me the pen. I sign. My stomach is starting to settle. I don't mind the company. I try to think of good times, something to talk about. Suddenly, silence from Joy's apartment. Must have turned the TV off. Then the sound jabbers on again.

Remember Lily's dog? I say. Or were you too young?

The dog, she says. There's? A dog.

That's right, I say. You have just won a million fucking dollars.

Be nice, she says, unfolding another bill.

Black and tan, I say. Mean as snot. Rubman's mare kicked it, broke its jaw? Thing dropped like it was dead. And I said, Lily, you know that dog deserves worse.

Tanis nods her head vaguely.

Really, she says. Pretty funny.

I knock out my cigarette, bark a laugh – neither of which seems to impress her.

Remember that horse I had that went lame? I say. I doped him up so he wouldn't limp for a couple of hours, hauled him to the Stouffville auction? Remember Friday nights there? What we did that time?

Christ, isn't she stubborn? – arms folded across her chest, leaning back in her chair. Not helping me one bit.

What an idea that was, I say. You were this runny-nosed, teary thing, and I put you up there on his back for when they led him into the ring. Which worked. All the awws? I mean, people *cooed*. And me yelling from the back, Don't lean forward or he'll go! Like he was some heavy-duty, serious-shit jumper, would try to take the railing in front of him.

I light another smoke.

Yeah, she says. So?

I'm laughing now.

Those people in front? I say. They jumped from their seats, ran halfway up the aisle. Oh, Jesus!

Something catches in my throat and I cough for a minute. Then I take another drag off my cigarette and continue.

And when the bidding started? Holy shit if that lame sonofabitch didn't go for a thousand, when the meat man could've had him for fifty.

I look at her hard. She's smiling, but not much.

Yeah? she says. Yeah so?

Forgot that one too, did you? I say.

I thrust a finger in the air and wag it at her.

Lesson of the day, I say. Maybe you can try to remember this, might do you some good. There's always something a person can do.

She pushes the chequebook away, drums her fingers on the table, yawns, then raises her arms in the air and stretches.

Like use someone? she says. Like rip someone off?

I think for a moment, smoking. Who told her she was so smart? When here I am, out of the goodness of my fucking heart not breaking her ass.

Where's your sidekick? I say. Wasn't she with you earlier? I thought I saw her this morning. You know, come to think of it, she seems to be making herself scarce altogether lately. What's up with you two? Thought you were joined at the hip. Or something.

She lowers her arms, dangles them at her sides.

Don't know, she says.

Must have a guy. Or something.

It's not like that.

So what's it like? She too rich for your blood? Now that you two are growing older?

She doesn't answer. She still looks big sitting there, blocky, but like a chunk of ice about to melt, disappear with only the smallest puddle to remind you it once was there, and even that would eventually dry up – and who would care? This *kid*. And to think I – well, her mother. Not *much* of a mother. I've stepped up when I could.

I start coughing again, which begins dryly but turns into a wet, loose affair. But I can feel my thoughts still trying to turn sharp.

So you don't know, I say when I'm finished and can speak again. Don't know much, do you?

But then I can't help but feel a little sorry when she pushes out from the table and stands.

Thank you, Mr. Hardass, she says. How long you planning to be like this?

Don't know, I say meekly.

Then I guess that makes two of us, she says.

I can feel my head start to settle, and I feel even better when I see the tease of her smile.

She picks up her chair and places it under the table, lunks over to her chaps and collects them. She thumps outside and down the steps.

Nine o'clock, and am I sloshed. Almost dark out and I decide to leave the house. Both my dogs – both mixes, one a Husky something and the other a Gordon-setter something – are lying on the porch, panting, tapped out from the heat. I take their water bowls inside and refill them, carry them back out again and put them down. The dogs stay put. The arena lights are on – Tanis. I walk over to the first barn, the sound of Joy's TV squabbling at me all the way.

Cool inside, a musty quiet. The roomy box stalls filled with the boarders' quarter horses, their kids' Welsh ponies, and the narrow standing stalls with my ragtag hit-and-miss horses – except for my thoroughbred brood mare when she's about to drop a foal. My few chickens and geese nesting here and there in stray piles of straw. No idea where the goat is – into something no doubt.

Near the tack room I pass a tortoiseshell cat hovering over the carcass of a deer mouse. The cat angles its head and with sombre, surgical ease parts the mouse's flesh, separating a strand of tendon from bone before methodically grooming its paws with a fierce pink tongue – professional services rendered, that's the way to go, nice to see at least one job done right. Though there are always people waiting in line to screw things up – last year around Christmas some of the boarders drove up from the city in their Jap and German cars, set out plastic bowls of Meow Mix, only stopped when I threatened to lock the cats out of the barn for the winter, said, You know what that means, don't you? Coyote kibble. *Rich, squeamish brain-deads.*

I make my way through the first barn to the wood-planked walkway attached to the smaller, second barn, its runt box stalls housing my less well-off boarders' unregistered, bargain whatchamacallems, biting, spitting things – full fucking capacity here. When I get to the end of this barn I pull open the plywood sliding door to the arena, step inside, stop to catch my breath.

It isn't big. *Intimate*, Mimi calls it, a joke. Nowhere near as big as the indoor arenas at the more expensive stables, with their guest viewing areas and snack bars and meeting rooms. But it's big to me. I'd built, roofed, wired it, installed the overhead lights, banged together three sets of standards that along with six cross poles Tanis repaints red and white once a year. Worked – brings me the value-minded boarders happy to use it year-round (which they can't with the outdoor ring in back, too cold and snowy in winter, too muddy in spring). So what if it's not the best arena ever and I'm going to have to build another one – I love the place, still fucking love it, with its corrugated aluminum siding, its oiled dirt and woodshaving floor on which Tanis is now trotting my light-grey thoroughbred toward me.

As they get closer the horse stumbles, and Tanis quickly collects him. When she gets nearer she walks, takes him sideways across the bottom of the arena, coaxes a *passage* from him. Then she turns and canters clockwise to the top of the arena, cuts a downward diagonal through the centre, pushes him through a flying lead change, passing in and out of the lights' sodium glare.

I'm right, and I know she knows, if only she'd let herself admit it. There *are* things you can do. You work with what you have. Sucker might not turn out half bad.

I'm not sentimental. That's the best thing I can say about myself. That I'm a realist. Forget the registered pinto pony, the not-cheap Western gear and fringed outfits, the red Justin cowgirl boots, Jena riding around in front of those panting brats she brought home from school – happened once, twice at the most, kids never came back. Pony mostly ungroomed, turned to pudge in no time. Embarrassing, if I cared – which I don't, you either have it or you don't. Tanis does. She's been at the horses ever since she could walk. Never had her own – she has mine. Like me, easily grasps the mechanics, old school like me too – aggressive, really motors, sometimes bricks it. How you learn, if you live long enough.

I once saw her pull one of the boarders' dull horses down almost on top of her. She'd been earning money schooling it daily, here in my arena – enough money to keep her in clothes, her mother's too much of a tightwad to lay out for even the bare essentials, I mean christ! I came out to watch one day around noon, had just stepped inside the arena to see the horse refuse a jump. Nothing inventive, merely a cold balk that unseated Tanis an inch at the most – but she took that thoughtless dab and dizzied herself up a masterpiece of carelessness for her own self's safety. She wrenched at the reins – slashing the mouth – then reached around with one hand and whaled away at the haunches with her crop. Animal popped up, down, then began a leisurely, *lazy* rear.

Still she kept her feet in the stirrups, kicked the horse's sides, continued to haul on the bit with her hands – balancing herself on its mouth as they towered higher. *That* was a rocking horse! rocking like a pendulum, a measurement of something, fear perhaps, then that fear itself became airborne as she pulled the horse over onto its back and barely managed to fall clean.

Fizz of legs in the dirt-flurried air before the horse rolled over onto its side. Then this vast structure of sinew and reflex, the tongue and groove of the thing, somehow untoppled itself, buckled upward onto its feet – a strange, reverse motion, unnatural-looking, no grace to it. The horse shivering itself out, the loose stirrups and reins slapping the air with sound. The doomed, knowing look on its face. Tanis standing shakily, the same look on her face.

Lucky. At least that time. Last November she was less lucky. Smashed her foot trying to prove something, her *worth*, if that's the word – ego-shit, whatever it is. If that's what she wants I won't stop her – I'm almost curious to see how far she'll push things.

They're walking now at the top of the arena. The horse stumbles again. Again she collects him. I'm breathing okay by now so I make my way to the middle of the ring, my bad knees giving me grief every step of the way. She drops the reins, rests her hands on her thighs. Slips her feet out of the stirrups, moving exaggeratedly in the saddle as he leaves the track, neck drooping, chugging forward. When he reaches me he stops and nudges my chest with his nose, then flippers his head up, shimmies his whole body. Tanis laughs. I tap him on the neck to get him to stop and he rests his muzzle in my hand. I turn him away and step behind. Run my hands down his back right leg, the grey so light it's almost white. I'm hoping as he gets older the colour deepens to charcoal, make him look more dignified. I'm hoping Tanis might show him as a hunter-jumper. If she can calm herself enough.

How's he feel? I say.

A few steps away and I check again.

What is it? she says.

I say, Walk.

The horse starts moving. Tanis puts her feet in the stirrups and gathers the reins, turning counterclockwise onto the track.

Trot, I say, and when they get to the top of the arena I call out, Reverse.

There it is – a shortening of the stride, the tiniest humpy hitch, stutter in the long clean line. I haven't been imagining things. I wave my arm and they drift into the centre again. I can feel my head heat up, the pressure rise, again. Now I'm cold fucking sober, too bad.

Didn't feel anything? I say.

He's short in the back? she says.

He is, I say. You didn't notice before?

She says, Just now, I think.

You think, I say. *Just now.* Should've tried thinking earlier. You're going too far too fast with him.

She takes her feet out of the stirrups and swings off – but I'm already halfway out of the place before she hits the ground and I can say another angry word. I don't want to push it. Not tonight, when it would be too easy to take my troubles out on her.

Back through the barns, into the full dark, a spitting rain, TV laughter and applause broken by spats of silence. Mimi's car is still gone.

I step over the prone, drowsing dogs on my porch, re-enter the house. Another drink? Now there's only quiet from Joy's – that is, until the knocking starts on the door between her apartment and my kitchen. After a minute that stops, then there's a distant slam – Joy's front door, which is in back, behind my house – and not fifteen seconds later I hear her charging up my steps. I open the kitchen door to her upthrust, boiled-looking face, eyes glittering. Her hair is dew-dropped with sweat, clothes blotched with dark spots. Looking past her I see the dogs are settling themselves on the drive.

You rotten –, Joy says, hands on her hips. Poor Mimi!

A grown woman like Mimi can take care of herself, I say, reasonably enough – what I'd like is to ask Joy why she doesn't take better care of her own daughter, but wouldn't that be throwing grease on the fire?

Now Joy gets herself inches from me, face pruney and pinched-up, a twisting, retchy mouth on her before she even speaks another word. I try to head her off at the pass.

She doesn't need you fighting her battles, I say – keeping my voice low and steady. Quit getting involved.

Involved! she sputters. It just *burns* me. Seeing how you allow Lily to do as she pleases.

Not this again, I say, groaning – I know where this is going.

And you stand around and let her! she says, warming to her theme. When *I've* always had to tiptoe behind your back whenever I wanted to see someone. Like you're the police, running a background check on whoever.

Why might that be? I say. Wouldn't have anything to do with you picking a fly-by-nighter for a husband, would it?

You introduced us! she says.

Didn't mean you had to go ahead and marry him, I remind her. Proved I have to protect you from yourself.

You protect *me*, she says bitterly. Never.

Always been this way with Joy and me. Nothing I do for her – and who the hell does she think set her up in that damn apartment? I'd like to know – can ever set her right. A woman so full of misery and dread she makes me feel hard. From that first Ontario June – so unlike the cool New Brunswick ones we left behind (the drunk old man car-crashed to eternity, Mumma free to seek her fortune in the richest of the central provinces) – that ended with a school's out war of water-filled balloons, and a girl's pleated skirt flipped up to reveal white panties flossing a cleft of bum. Even then, when I was eleven – newly big in my body, at large and roaming the dirt roads and old farms south of Stouffville – Joy at six was already beetling her way through life beneath an armour of spite.

She was a scaredy! While all that first summer here, I'm snagging snapping turtles by the tail, and up above me the Rouge riverbank is littered with hissing boys. A summer of dares. I would do anything! And watching me from the higher ground along the path through the fields and into the cedar woods, a crown of giggling girls, Joy slipping, half-sobbing, among them. The boys locked together in chant, *New-fie, New-fie* – all Maritimers the same to them as they urged me on.

Eventually the summer vacation wound down, ran out of steam. One afternoon, alone, tired of poking about with not much to do, I climbed the struts and gridirons of a half-built high-rise. The construction workers had left for the day, stranding cranes and bulldozers across the deserted lot, beached up by the day's swells of heat. I peeled my shirt off and rolled it into a ball, dropped it on the dusty, tractor-tire-slashed ground and ascended, bare skin burning from where it touched hot steel.

Partway up I sat, turned and looked down. Group of freckle-faces gathered in the lot, watching silently, not even goading me this time – I *would* do anything. Joy was there too. I could barely make out her face squeezing tears. I climbed higher and the afternoon dwindled until finally, in ones and twos and threes, kids watching from below straggled home – for dinner, TV, a pre-bed game of catch with good old dad – leaving me in a late light that pulled at my head, pooled at my feet. Even Joy had disappeared. I felt so above everything I didn't care. I stood, lifted my arms above my head, straining to my blistered fingertips, fingerprinting the air itself as the sky deepened to dark blue.

I was – *the Newf.*

Then I saw Mumma on the street below. Shading her face with both hands despite the hour as she crossed into the construction lot, stepping gingerly over the ruts and gullies of the gouged earth. Wind licked the edges of her faded housedress. She was gaunt, seemingly weighed down only by the grubby white sweater she wore like a second skin – she was always cold never mind the heat.

She'd been sick for months, almost ever since we arrived in Ontario, unable to work, clean houses as she used to for a living. Getting by on handouts from neighbours, the Sally Ann – I knew from some of the kids' taunts tossed my way. I fixed sugar sandwiches for supper most nights, careful not to disturb this frail woman who sat in an old green armchair for hours on end. Hours? She could go days not speaking, not drinking the glasses of water I'd bring her each time I was indoors and could hold still long enough to remember. It seemed she could hardly raise her head, recognize I was there. How could I stay inside with her like that? Joy mostly saw to her needs.

But now she was coming to get me.

As I waited I drew my arms back down and wrapped them

around a steel beam, held on tight, stilled every muscle as I watched her brittle approach. When she got closer she dropped her hands and stared into the burdening sky. I couldn't make out the look on her face – couldn't tell what she was thinking, or might have wanted to say.

Cherished, darling son.

Never let go, I love you.

Promise to keep your sister from harm.

Or a scathing curse – moved to it by her suffering condition, aided and abetted by troublemaker me, for wasn't I more trouble than I was worth, disturbing her in her sickness? Not loved. What's the term? *Reviled.* Who knows? And who knows if I wasn't trying to get back at her. Back at her for being sick.

In a daze, I unwrapped my arms from the steel beam I'd been hugging. I shifted closer to the edge of the beam on which I stood and, swaying, threw my arms open.

My rock-a-bye, rock-a-bye baby.

In the treetop.

Still, I couldn't tell – then she turned her back on me and I climbed down, ashamed of myself, followed her home. Twilight narrowing around us as I fell farther and farther behind, scuffing my toes, wondering what I'd seen, if anything. Anything to keep my bearings by. Keep me going in the right direction. That darkness tunnelling closer around us. Mumma disappearing at the far end.

Even now, in memory, that look is like a distant call, word-dust. I strain hard to hear it, but can't.

Now Joy has turned from me and is pouncing down the porch steps and onto the drive. I make like I'm starting after her, and she stops and swings back around. My sister – the righteous face on her. A cleaning lady, like her mother before her.

And what about Jena? I say. What about her right to see Lily?

She should *live* with Lily, Joy says. For the sake of you and Mimi. You don't want to give Jena up. But, Walker, we all have to make sacrifices. You can't just do whatever you want.

I look down at the grey wooden boards of the porch. I look at my feet.

She's right, I think, deciding. You can't. There's always someone on the ground, calling you down from the high places. And if there isn't, there should be.

Before I open the screen door and step inside, I turn again. Joy. I wonder why she can't be the one to reach me. I'm sorry we're strangers – but then, I could feel sorry about a lot of things if I let myself, so I won't.

I wake several hours later. There's knocking on the door between the kitchen and the apartment. I get up from the living-room couch. My head hurts.

I open the door. My sister, gripping her old striped bathrobe across her chest. Her face is white, exhaustion probably. She smells like cleaning solvents, industrial strength, a chemical, nasty kind of clean. I do feel bad for her, a little, okay.

I ask her in but she refuses.

You better go, she says. She won't be in any state to drive, who knows what she might do. Don't let things get worse than they are.

I leave the door open. It's one a.m. by the kitchen clock. I get the truck keys from the mug hook beside the toaster oven. Same toaster oven in the same spot as it was when Lily and I were together.

I say, And what if Lily brings Jena back while I'm gone?

Walker, Joy says sharply. Jena's twelve already. She doesn't need you every waking moment of her life. I'll fix her something to eat and send her to bed.

I say, I'll leave this door unlocked for you.

Then I'm on the porch, lighting a smoke, getting ready to leave. I hear Joy in the kitchen behind me.

I want her in one piece, she says. You hear me? Can you try?

And when I get there, it's just like the last time, no shit, deja fucking vu.

The Drake's parking lot is mostly empty, a few pickups and SUVs, a blue Ford Probe. A frazzle of rain, the clean asphalt air from the cooling effect. I go inside and it's bleak, the mouldy-smelling red carpet and the ashy tables. Some underages watching TV, drinking draft by the half-pint. Two guys throwing darts near the bar. Mimi's in the back, legs up on the chair beside her, three full ashtrays on the table in front of her, sitting with some skinny, coiled prick in a muscle shirt and tight-fitting faded jeans, the kind you buy so pre-bleached they're almost white. He's got long, light-brown hair tied back in a ponytail. She's laughing grimily, a slick-backed, oily sound.

Both of them likely drunk on my money.

I stop at their table and the guy jumps up fast, says to Mimi, Nice talking to you, and leaves.

Hey, she says, lifting her head in confusion, a bloated, fuzzy movement. Where you going?

Then she sees me and her face goes blank. She drags on her cigarette. For the life of me I can't imagine how I could ever have wanted her.

Yeah right, she says, exhaling.

I say, It's time.

She turns her back, finishes her smoke while I stand there waiting. Then she gets up and walks through the bar without stopping to look at me, as if I'm only there by accident, someone she barely knows. Though in the parking lot she seems to think she knows me pretty well – she's crying, everything's my fault, I'm lousy, demeaning, the usuals, the *usual* usuals.

Eventually I get her into the truck. I pull out of the lot onto the road. Clouds wobble and mass in the sky. I slow down and light up a smoke, knock open the no-draft. In places a light fog pearls the road, and the truck slides through a thin varnish of rain. Every time I think she's stopped crying she starts again. I turn onto Bloomington, punch up the high beams, light splashes the far ditch. No one else seems to be on the road tonight.

I could almost hear Ray. *Better watch your back.* Or, *Trust me, it's her kind who pulls the world's strings. First they confuse you, then they control you.*

And I'd always shrug him off, I'd laugh and say, Yeah, well you let me be the judge of that. Give me some credit, there, buddy.

But maybe he'd be right. Nine years thick and thin, I know how good she can make her nonsense look – knew it the first day we met. Early fall. Wasps veiled the crabappled ground. Joy's idea – gets her new gal-pal up on one of the horses. So much about her seemed wrong – but then, I'd never met anyone called Mimi before. Heels and hands up, elbows flapping, body slagged forward – that supple torso, those long legs. Springy red hair and white skin, pulpy lips splayed open in a loopy, off-centre smile. All I could figure was, high maintenance, definitely.

Mistake number one, I opened my mouth. *Keep your hands down.* Forget it – horse ran away with her, dumped her at my feet.

But now she had her audience – if you were looking you were hooked, that was her game. She's head to toe in dirt, and *she's* laughing at *me*, a ripple of notes tickled into half-starts and stops as if she's beginning or ending a song – there's no in-between where you learn who does what to whom, or why.

Just beginnings and endings, each time different, things you can never predict, you get caught up, end christ knows where.

Which is how we fell in together so fast, a whole lot of hoopla that very night, nimble things I'd never done before. Left me feeling red and swollen, delicate to the touch. I felt like I'd been dipped in acid. That singer Jena talks about – Puff Daddy? That's how I felt – like a puffed-up daddy. A glow on, new. Some enchanted evening, huh? How I got cast as the crazy sonofabitch in the show that's her life.

I should have seen it coming – that there'd be no room in that show for *my* past, because that wouldn't be about her then, would it?

The next day I found out she *fronted* (her word) the Drake's house band – really was a singer. I heard her only once though. When she sang, it was as if parts of her, of her and me together – the after-shock, the racked-up grief sounds and sex moans – coiled in her lungs, snaked from her mouth into the microphone. No other way to describe it. Playing us out before the crowd as the band thumped and stuttered its way through cover after cover, every sauced guy in the place watching her, checking out her tits. Her own eyes dark, unrecognizable, hands half-raised in front of her swaying body. I sat alone at a table in the back through two sets, all I could stomach.

I still wake in the night sometimes, imagine her staring at me with that same unreadable look – another look, shades of Mumma – I'm unable to fathom. With it – if I let my mind play – whispers and shrieks, footfall, echoes down the darkened hallways of my house. (Or is it just the wind, a strange night wind that jimmies loose the window frames and door locks?) I can't fall asleep again, not until the darkness outside finally lifts.

What I do know is this – in nine years of shacking up with her (close enough, anyway), never the ordinary, neither the plain nor the simple. At least she mostly keeps away from the horses, thank you fucking lord. Think what might happen! (I know where her old lady's living.) It wears you out – even the best act gets old when one thing always leads to another. Spice of life be damned. You get tired of the nonsense, the surprise drains out of you – besides which, she barely tolerates Jena.

So here's how it adds up. The thrust of the matter is, there's only so much you can take before you think, *Enough* – and then stop, as the mind sort of cliffs out over the thought of how maybe there *isn't* a good goddamn thing you can do.

Where we going? she asks a couple of times between sobs, her voice flukey in a way I used to like.

For a drive, I tell her.

The truck's running smooth. Eventually she falls asleep against the door. A couple of hours, I don't know exactly, and I'm on winding two-lane highway blasted out of granite that looms above the road. Chiselled and pried out of the rock, small lakes and night-emptied tourist towns, pricey places that would be nice to retire in (another joke, and this one's on me).

By the time I get to the town of Bala, with its falls on one side of the highway and Lake Muskoka on the other, I can hardly keep my eyes open. I slow and turn into a picnic area next to the water. I used to come here in the early, good days with Lily. Sit on the grass, eat a packed lunch, smoke, swim, dry in the sun. Lily pregnant with Jena, *expecting*. We used to pretend we belonged.

Still raining. I don't know why we're here, other than that I drove us. Don't know what I thought I'd see beyond the brackish, peat-muddied lake, black as hell even on the brightest day.

I lean my head against the window. On the other side of the road the falls are running low. I can just make out the sound of tumbling water beneath the truck's engine and the percolating sky, the rain drumming the lake, where below – inside, where armies of crayfish advance through the stones and swollen weeds, at war with the waterlogged bass – the dead world feeds silently on itself. That I can picture. That makes sense.

She stirs. Reaches over and with her nails lightly scratches my arm. No way to tell how long she's been awake, what she's been thinking, but given what I've been thinking I'm startled, my hair stands on end, rises in tufts on each pitch of goosepimpled flesh, and the spaces in between.

Suddenly I want to fuck her. Drag her skinny bones all over me. Yank her from the truck, lay her flat on the muddy ground and push her open, slowly rummage through her, then roll her on top of me so I can lift her to my mouth, wrap my arms around her slim hips, and press down. I want the piss-pot stars to come out in the sky so I can shake my fists at them, want what I am to fall away as lightning bolts into my head, busts me up like a building falling down, I want the buildings to fall down.

She's still tickling my arm with her long white fingers, going higher, up my shoulder beneath the sleeve of my shirt.

Inky-dinky spider, she says, not making sense, her voice strangely still and small.

She says, Do you *parlez-vous*?

I can hear Ray again. *Don't let them mess with your head. Get them before they get you.* I think, What if Ray is wrong? Then what would be right?

That you in there? I say.

She doesn't answer. Just begins to give her laugh, the one I like, the one I still like. I realize I have no idea what's coming next.

3

LITTLE RED ROOSTER

I cut the barn lights, cue the settlings, the whuffs and sighs of the bedded-down animals. Rain waffles the roof. I step out onto the drive: Walker, panicking around his lit kitchen – pacing, cradling his block head in his hands, combing his fingers through his wiry hair, stopping to thump the heel of a hand on the side of his head. Man's in a *mood*. So I hopalong like a lame-o through the dark behind the house, up the cracked concrete step, and open the door into the humid, AC-less apartment.

At first Joy doesn't notice me. Then she does: her gaze startles in my direction, her eyes flick back to the sirening TV screen, she gives a crabby shrug. I'm not the one she's waiting for.

What do we do now? she says. I hope this doesn't set her off again, and then we have a repeat of last winter. She's not bulletproof, you know. Any ideas?

Jack, I think, unzipping my rain-splattered, English-style chaps – courtesy of Walker – and dropping them to the living-room floor: for the record, Wonderwoman always lives to see another day when it comes to Lily. I consider sit mode. Reconsider: like I want to cozy up to the momster, well-girded in her grey striped bathrobe, gargoyled on the Goodwill-issue, red velvet fold-out sofa? In profile, she seems like some kind of evolutionary accident, with her fleshy nose hastily cropped in a face simian round, thick, workhorse neck short-fused to wide shoulders. In action even when at rest, a kind of stalled action: stubby, reddened fingers rabidly chomped upon by a thin-lipped, frown-lined mouth. The shellacked hair like a freeze-frame of fur flying.

You going to answer or not? she spits, still not looking at me – like she ever really looks at me!

She ratchets up the volume on the TV. I do a quick disconnect, leg it as best I can to the bathroom. I stand in front of the soap-spotted mirror, peel off my sweat-sloppy, rain-rashed tee. But within seconds Joy follows me in, pointing the TV remote at my head as she crowds me against the sink – she's so in my face I have to lean over backward. Without my shirt on, standing in my well-past needing to be replaced bra and jeans, I feel like an opened tin of something soft and rotten. She throws her arm up as if to strike – I switch to cringe mode – but just as suddenly she lowers it.

You don't care, she says. You're selfish, just like your father. He never cared about anyone but himself either.

A quick tuck and I'm past her, around the corner and into the bedroom. Above the TV din I hear her scuttle back into the living room. I get my boots and jeans off, ease onto the squeaky bed with its scratchy, poly-blend sheets. I wad a pillow between my back and the bumpy iron headboard, reach behind it to finger the peeling wallpaper with its repeating rose pattern on an intricate trellis. I flake off a flower, pop it in my mouth, grind it to a paste between my teeth, swallow. I lean over to the clock radio on the stolen plastic milk crate night table beside the bed, turn it on: spry yips and yodels, souvenirs of nearby places I've only been to like a million times.

Going to take a short break, be back in a jiff! Up next, a special request from Jimmy in Aurora.

Beside the bed is the small window covered by an old yellowed bedsheet. Beyond the window lie Walker's fields – an east finger of the Rouge River probing southeast across them – full of night things: barn owls and deer mice, foxes on tight paws threading the embroidered edges of pine stands. And, when I was younger, timber wolves glimpsed at dusk that hours later would be tapestried into my cry-baby sleep – alien canines bigger to me than behemoths wrapping plush paws around ice dream infants, sipping little girl breaths, boy breaths, stealing the innocent air of abandoned children – this ancient harmonium, pulse of a lullaby world. Lost: the wolves fled, fucked over, vanquished by subdivision upon subdivision as the south-lying city conquers all but the occasional runtish coyote, wily scrap scavenging the local Mini Mart dumpsters.

I lean over again to the milk crate, pick up the book Suzanne loaned me a week ago. One *big* mo-fo.

We'd been standing before the bulky, carefully distressed oak bookcases that anchored one side of her parents' great ark of a bedroom, with its his-and-her Shaker-style dressers against the opposite wall while behind us, a gleaming, black platform bed covered in gauzy beige linens floated Zen-like. Suzanne reached up to a high shelf and hooked one of the many inches-thick volumes bound in leather, very swish. She wrestled it down and swung it at me. The idea was to say we were starting a book club. That way her parents might cut us some slack.

How about *this* bad boy? she said. Get through that, I guarantee my queen mother will be impressed. Besides, it kind of wouldn't hurt you, you know.

Like, close my eyes, try to enjoy it? I said.

You'll never get anywhere, young lady, she said. Not with an attitude like that.

That's the plan, I said. Mock me not. At least I have one.

You bitch, she said. Don't rub it in.

Sitting in bed now with the book, I run my hand over the tooled leather, balance its weight on my thighs, try to recall what I've read of it so far, and fail. Before I open the cover I reach out once more to twist the dial on the radio – stations, stations between stations.

Your lucky day, you bet!

I turn the radio louder – the TV's still clanging away in the living room, where Joy smoulders in her furnace of grievances. Everything – Mimi's cat-scratch problems with Walker, my every move – seeming to remind her of my father.

He'd called one day on the phone when I was eight to rumble and buzz across the puke-box distances, bragging how he'd just arrived in Nashville and spent his last three hundred dollars on a pair of peanut-coloured, lizard-skin shit-kickers. He made it sound like a dare. There was a swallow, glass clinking. More, I thought. Say more.

Going to learn you to shine them, he said and paused.

Then he said, Why don't you put your mommy on.

Joy refused to come to the phone.

Fuck, he said. The fucking. Tell her to send some money.

Walker had introduced them at a Quarterama at the Canadian National Exhibition grounds in Toronto. I can easily imagine Joy's tall, loose-fleshed beau, already coming apart from drink though still dark and handsome, riding and roping his way into her desire to be horse rich as opposed to horse poor as she eyed him in the practice ring of the horse palace – same ring, same palace in which I wrecked my foot last year – that long-standing emporia of cowgirl dreams. Easily imagined, since those dreams framed the edges of the shabby patchwork of complaint and innuendo, the coverlet Joy had tucked me to bed with almost nightly when I was younger.

His father the ace breeder of American saddlebreds: wasn't hard to see Joy – at age thirty-one more than a little long in the tooth – swooning to tales of the austere sweep and shush of the riders' formal black silk habits with their elegant curves and folds, the high-stepping five-gaited horses, the regal, brutal pump of horse blood and old money. The annual Shriners' parade in Fort Worth, Texas: the old man, pillar of the community, riding one of his prized palominos, leading the golden cavalcade along the main street of cow town, a river of golden horses shining for god, the silver bridle and heavily ornamented saddle flashing to beat the band under the mythic Texan noon.

You don't mess with Texas, the wastrel son told Joy, kissed her deeply.

Or do you? he said, nimble fingers lifting her skirt.

Dark and handsome, disinherited, drifting, he knocked her up then rode into the alcoholic sunset, managing to call faithfully on the phone for years – from Cleveland and San Diego, Sitka, Seattle – demanding handouts. He'd slur and swear his way through buckets of vodka, sweet talk her if he wasn't too far gone. His buggered voice a loping continental vernacular, accents and inflections flanging in and out, straddling the emptiness of geography.

What in hell is he doing there? Joy would say after she'd hung up – poor luckless Joy, stuck here in this lacklustre south-central Ontario so far from the Lorettas and Wynonas singing their heads off on the radio, their thin warbling sopranos making her think of an Old Testament veiling of the bride. *Sigh.*

For years Joy would get out the battered *Collins World Atlas* and scan the pages. Eventually she stopped. The atlas lay buried beneath forgotten magazines, late-payment notices, the crayoned pictures it took me years to learn not to bother bringing home from school. By the time he called that day from Music City – the last we spoke – she was fuck-you-mister, he was finito, kaput. So his voice, though it stung my ear with hope, changed nothing – he'd only just hung up on me when Joy started her already familiar poor-me rave: what decent man would ever have her, with a smart-ass daughter – named after Joy's long-dead, never-met paternal grandmother, a rumoured Scottish-born Dutch-Slav mix – a daughter had not exactly so young. Her love – her life! – become a highway to nowhere, a dead end. I was a road sign: you are here, welcome to loserville.

Until, one night within weeks of that call, Joy met Mimi in a bar. With her been-around-the-block allure, it seemed only Mimi could do for Joy what my father once had – intoxicate with stories of a larger, more vivid life, one in which Joy could imagine herself anew. It seemed only Mimi, with her glamour-girl flame, could withstand Joy's hellhound heat. Now Mimi and Joy were close as sisters-in-law. It was like I was Mimi's niece.

I open the book. I've lost my place. I scan forward and backward, confused. I seem to have missed the something someone did to someone, sometime back when. Rain tosses against the window. I turn the radio off.

I lean over the side of the bed, dump my head upside down, looking for my dictionary, swallowed by a bestiary of dust: bunnies, dogs, buffaloes. I mole back into bed, bag o' crap tired, but not wanting to fall asleep yet, wondering who'll end up where tonight. In Mimi's absence I can take over the sofa, let Joy – rough snorer, dream-jumper, hitter of endless pavement – have the bed to herself. Snout to snout, force-fed her snorting breath, her angry heart stamping my chest – my flesh shrinks at the thought of how close to me that woman can get.

Well past one in the morning and Joy's still in the living room. Moments later I hear the TV switch off. Joy goes to the door of Walker's kitchen and knocks. Their voices are so low and smudged I can't make out what they're saying. Walker leaves the house, eventually his truck starts up. Joy doesn't come back into the apartment right away. Probably ransacking her way through Walker's fridge.

I prop an elbow against the dictionary, open the novel, turn to page one, one long haul ahead. I slide through pages, nothing sticks. My flimsy mind folds in like paper cut-outs – the stamp-stamp of a blacksmith's hammer grows louder, nearer, the silhouettes string open in shapes from weird to worse – then I wake to hear Jena and Joy in Walker's kitchen. The face of the clock radio reads two-fifteen.

Auntie Joy? Jena's burbling loudly. And then my mom did this? Auntie Joy, look. Is that funny? Or will daddy be mad? Auntie Joy?

Go on, get out of here, Joy says. Shut that fridge door. Up to bed. I don't want to hear another word. Didn't your mom feed you? Okay, I'll fix you a jelly sandwich. Don't turn your nose up! Beggars can't be choosers. And you better be asleep by the time your dad comes home. Don't give me something else to worry about.

Then I wake to a dim awareness: Joy's stubby leg sweating against my hip, her slithery rayon nightie hiked around her waist. Though it's only five-thirty I get up. In the bathroom, I shower, with a washcloth rub-a-dub as many microbes as I can

– mine, my mother's that have leaked onto me – to extinction. In the bathroom mirror I check out the circles under my eyes. Rationing the clean stuff, I put yesterday's underwear back on, go into the kitchen, angle the last chocolate marshmallow cookie from a crumpled bag: last night's missed dinner. I find a diet Dew in the back of the fridge, take it into the living room, turn on the TV. Religion. I turn the TV off. I go back into the bedroom and grab the jeans and top I wore yesterday, flee before Joy wakes. In the living room I collect my chaps and boots.

I open the unlocked door from the apartment into Walker's kitchen.

Jena, her big mitts in the fridge. She turns around, startled to see me. Her moist mouth opens, and her hands release a carton of milk to the floor.

Stupid lump, I say. Big baby.

She looks at the spilled milk, her face pink. Pure candyass princess, never has to lift a finger. Five years younger than me, but already about ten lifetimes behind – what does she know about anything? She is so deep into dumb I want to pound her.

I'm going to tell my dad, she says.

What is it you're going to tell him? I say. That you're a messy pig?

She grows very still. I hear floorboards creaking above our heads, heavy footsteps rocking down the stairs.

Jena, I whisper. Better clean up fast. I won't tell if you won't.

Walker slumps into the kitchen. His eyes, like Jena's, are puffy and dull – maybe he hasn't been to bed at all. He grunts once in our direction. We watch as he makes two cups of instant coffee, which means Mimi must be upstairs. When he's done he takes them and heads out of the kitchen, back the way he came. Before he's reached the bottom of the stairs I hear Mimi calling to him.

Wahh-ker? Bring me a little nosh? I'm *dying*.

Walker ignores Mimi's request, doesn't return to the kitchen, and it's unlikely Mimi will come down soon – she'd rather do without than be quick to help herself. How many glasses of water, or refills of rye, or magazines left in the bathroom have I fetched her as she lazed on the sofa in the apartment?

That is *so* sweet, she'd trill. Kiss-kiss!

Jena's face remains flushed, a whipped-dog wary. Her pokey, developmentally delayed little breasts lag far behind the plump potsticker middle, the dumpling tum. Really, if she were twenty, thirty pounds lighter she'd be cheerleader pretty – her hair is centre-parted long and blonde, her eyes large and blue, round – popular, at least as she blew her way through the post-football game locker rooms. But how would Walker feel about his angelcake, then?

You spoil her too much, Joy has warned Walker for years. If you gave us a shred of what you give her!

To which Walker replies, Jealous? That's women for you, always green around the gills.

Joy responds by setting her mouth tightly shut and quietly raging.

Standing in front of me in the kitchen, Jena. Her brows start to rise, twin commas – and, and – like she's waiting for the next round of punishment.

I saw a girl her own age push Jena once. She'd been standing by herself, watching me play after-school field hockey, and the girl had materialized from a giggling, egging-on group to thrust a freckled arm hard into Jena's back then run away, the group eddying after her. Jena had regained her footing and stood stock-still. She'd stayed like that to the end of the stick-slashing game – and then I'd hitched a ride home with Suzanne, leaving Jena to re-enter the school and call Walker to get her. Joy had come down hard on me for that.

Want to watch TV? Jena says now, taking me by surprise, since I haven't exactly encouraged her.

Nothing on, I say.

Though secretly I wouldn't mind. Walker's set is about three times the size of Joy's.

We can play with my Nintendo? Jena says.

Maybe, I say. Why don't you fix me some breakfast first? Then we'll see.

I'll make pancakes, she says. I love pancakes. We have syrup. Whipped cream, don't you love whipped cream? Know what I do? Want to see? Tanis? I'll show you?

She rushes to the fridge and pulls out a can of Reddi-Whip.

I hold it in my mouth and press the button? she says. Want to do it too?

You know something? I say. That sounds like more fun than I can handle. But you go ahead without me. Sock it in. It's only six in the fucking morning. Maybe you can pack a few million calories under your belt before noon.

She turns from me, shuts the fridge door, leaving the Reddi-Whip on the kitchen counter. She faces me again. The dark circles under her glassy eyes deepen, trap doors. And then whup! it's like I've lost my footing and down I go, I'm somehow peeping into her damp, cellared head where a soft dough rises, splits, rises again – Fuck, is all I can think, and, Let me not be you.

And then I can't leave Walker's kitchen fast enough, through the door and onto the porch from where I see that last night's rain has stopped, though the sky, foamy with clouds, still threatens.

I take a break from grooming and working three of the boarders' horses (for which I get paid the big bucks, I wish!) to call Suzanne from Walker's kitchen. It's eight o'clock. No sign of Mr. Big – when I left the barn I noticed his truck was gone. Jena's in the living room with the TV on. Joy's probably still asleep, but I play it safe anyway, lock the door from the apartment into the kitchen. I can't stop her from making an entrance, but I can at least slow her down.

The phone rings twice. Suzanne's mother answers.

You again, she says. Fine, then. Fair enough. I'll see if the mademoiselle has arisen yet.

A minute goes by, then another before Suzanne comes to the phone.

Hey, she says.

Your mom so has it in for me, I complain.

Ta-nis, Suzanne warns, then yells, Hang *up*.

The other line clicks dead.

Another slick moment brought to you by Tanis! she says in her best TV announcer's voice. Anyway. I suppose you're calling about yesterday.

Zero repercussions, I say. Want to come over, try to go another round?

Can't make it, she says, sounding bored. You know. Imprisoned by the wicked witch.

There's always matricide, I say.

Too much effort, Suzanne says. Maybe the psych diva is right. I *have* got a serious motivational deficit.

I hear Joy, rapping on the door.

Tanis? she says. Is that you in there? Open up.

Suzanne says, And then there's life on the funny farm.

I can *hear* you, Tanis, Joy says.

I put my hand over the receiver.

Everything's fine, I call to Joy. Go back to bed.

Are they home? Joy says.

Yes, I say. They were, and then they left.

Left?

Ciao, Suzanne says and hangs up, and I head to the barns again, back to the horses, leave Joy alone in the dingy apartment – asking questions of no one – with no exit but the one onto the crumbling step, the weed-laced dirt path.

I lead the third boarder's horse – a bay mare – into the steamy arena and get on. We come around, go around – the schooling, circling, collecting, the knocking down of two piddly sets of cross poles. There's more: I try again, again she whiffs the jumps, I crop her hard, *I'll give you more, all right.*

I get off – whap the ground – and snap the reins, back her into the arena boards. The oblong head flails high. I walk her into the middle of the arena, wait for her to settle down. I leave her standing while I go to one set of cross poles, convert the jump to a single straight bar. I think about it, adjust the pegs, raise the bar. I get back on, ride off into the killer day, barely begun.

Once, all I knew was how badly I wanted that horse toward which, despite my hammy diapers, big-bellied Uncle Walker hoisted me through the cool, shadowed air. *Up you go, he said. Monkey dunk, droopy drawers.*

Outside in the dusty sunlight there was Joy – yacking away at nothing, everything, complaining to the blue jays and common crows, the birch and maple and cedars. The clouds, for all I knew or at that moment cared, for instead here was Walker, easing the effects of Joy's careless carping by giving me what he could, showing me all he had, sharing his delight in his first brood mare – wasn't I his little stinker?

But the horse – the bored, incurious horse – seemed to have seen it all, remained unmoved, if judged by the half-open eyes, unimpressed by my spongy nappies glowing like a puffball moon in the dim barn's nursery twilight. My impossibly short arms outstretched, mutant appendages furiously pumping toward the apple-scented air above me, this oat-branned stratosphere: how I *wanted* that breath to be my breath.

Say hello to Miss Horseyhead. Say, How are you today?

Really I was too young to say anything. Encouraged by my epically proportioned, go-getter uncle, I tried anyway.

Walker's nasal voice, his arms Popeye-wide. He laughs and laughs.

Now that I think of it – years later, another mare's coarse mane brushing my fingers as I grip the soft, waxy reins – I laugh too.

I take the boarder's horse into one last circle, then approach the jump straight on. She refuses. You win, I think – I can't, won't, lift you myself, you're so not worth it – remembering the first time I fell, the last time, all the times in between: I'd come to, shunted back into myself, gasping and wheezing, lungs pleated into accordion folds. A crushing chest pain, no laughing matter. Open up, windbag! Sure I wanted that breath – any breath! – as above me the beamed rafters wheeled. And there I'd go again, sprawled in a confusing spiral, blootered out, spanked, sunk.

Down, out.

What do you know? Looks like we got ourselves a winner today! You feeling like a winner today? Don't forget to tune in tomorrow when we give not one, not two, but three prizes to some lucky listener.

Are you okay, can you hear me? Walker – the instructor, the chider, the in-a-pinch medic – would bray like an ass, like a stick rubbed on a ribbed washing board, a hillbilly phantasm in a comic-book never-never land.

Did he always have to shout? Couldn't he leave me be? Big bastard. Uncle.

If I concentrated, I could hear the precipitately shed horse nearby, the leisurely clink of the bit between his teeth as he waited for me to pick myself up off the ground.

Aw, Walker would say. You're okay. Up and at 'em, kid.

And there I am. *No place like.* Bundled in the oiled arena dirt with its piercing acrid tang – up to my elbows! Sometimes, the times I remember the most, there'd be rain on the aluminum roof – the roof Walker put on years ago with his own hands. He'd have the animal, his latest greatest hopeful, by the reins. They'd stand above me looking down. It was always like this: this triangle, geometry of failure. The ground soggy in places where the rain's come in, and a crude, farting breeze entering through the same chinks in the imperfect joinings.

Even now, on that horseshit wind, this architecture of smell: carved eddies and hollows, roaring places, easeful familiar mazes to which I still return again and again. It is a house. A make-believe house where Walker – Mr. Muddle, too busy trying to work angles that don't include me – tries to convince himself he's mothering me, as an old male cat will a puppy in an interspecies act of faith and hope. Flat-out dumb-luck love.

Will you get a load of that? I'm telling you –

Stick a fork in me. Stinking tired, sore, I leave the barn. It's not yet ten. Walker's truck is back, as is Mimi's car – once-grand junker half an inch short of the graveyard of bad taste. Mimi and Joy are on the porch, laughing and squealing, kicking up their heels, busting some totally duh moves. Joy hoists a small Igloo-brand cooler above her head. Mimi's attempting to twirl a tube of Pringles like a baton: she must have ended pretty tight with Walker last night. I watch for longer than I should, a deflating tire, no get up and go. The sky is growing darker. Walker's dogs are lying under the maples by the paddock, panting, ears swivelled in the direction of the noisy women.

Want to join us? Mimi calls out to me. Come along for the ride?

No way, I think. No *fucking* way.

I'm kind of tired, I say.

No kidding, Mimi says. Look at the circles under your eyes, almost as bad as mine. Craters of the moon. What you need is some quality R&R.

Tanis has work to do, Joy says to Mimi, then, turning to me she says, What about Billie Johnson's mare? Have you taken her out yet?

Joy, Mimi says.

What? Joy says. I'm just saying.

Mimi turns to me.

Don't make me twist your arm, she cajoles. This is maybe a once-in-a-lifetime offer I'm making. Your one and possibly only chance to visit the nuthouse. I'm taking my mother out for a picnic! Come witness the historic event, tell your grandchildren years hence. Seriously though, I'd love for you to come with. You'd be, like, moral support. Your mom here's *slaying* me with her negative attitude. Yeesh! It's enough to make you comatose.

What are you talking about? Joy says. I'm happy! Wasn't I laughing, just now?

Her forehead is raked with lines, mouth set into a downward groove.

See what I mean? Mimi says. Bummer.

Doof, Joy says.

Grab a shower and change, Mimi says to me. We'll wait.

I don't know, I say, feeling cornered. Think this weather's going to hold? Kind of looks like it's going to rain.

Weather, she says. You poor stickler for details. You little miss bore-ing. What, are you going to be an accountant when you grow up? A *dentist* maybe? It's only *weather*. I think somebody needs to loosen up.

That'll be the day, Joy says. No wonder she doesn't have many friends. Even Suzanne doesn't come around so much any more. Well, I never liked her anyway. Too good for herself, if you know what I mean.

I set my chin and look away. The Monte Carlo – not much muscle left inside *that* baby. Then Mimi, still on the porch, catches my eye.

Please, she says, sticking her fingers in her ears.

Guess you're going to be a loner all your life, Joy says.

You *guys*, I say. Too much.

The aforementioned Pringles, a half-dozen Very Berry twist-top wine coolers, Famous Amos chocolate-chip cookies. Gingerly, I pick up an opened bag of baby carrots – slimy wet-looking, several weeks past the sell-before date – lurking beneath the bag of cookies.

This is it? I say from the back seat of the car. This is your idea of a smorgasbord?

I replace the lid on the Igloo. Mimi's driving us under a spitting sky. The wind is up, casting a gritty net through which the car shudders violently.

I never see *you* contributing, Joy says.

The skanky smell of Joy's unwashed clothes wafts from the front seat – at least my ratty underwear is clean, rinsed two days ago in the bathroom sink and hung to dry on the towel rack.

She leans forward and fusses with the dial on the radio, stops when she hits the golden oldies station. Within seconds she's crowing a few words from the chorus of the Rolling Stones' version of "Little Red Rooster" as it tides through the car on a drift of poor reception.

Give it a rest, Joy, Mimi says sharply, shuttling a hand in front of her face as if to dispel a truly rank odour, but Joy keeps at it for several more bars until Mimi turns the radio off.

What bullshit, Mimi says. Some guy bragging about his dick. When you know I hate that. Don't be an idiot.

Joy grows quiet. She glances over her shoulder at me, eyes pinched at the corners. She seems to be beyond exhaustion, about to crash big time.

I'm just trying to have some fun, she says after a minute. Why does everybody but me get to decide what's okay and what's not?

Don't ruin this, Mimi says, her voice dropping. I can't believe how needy you are. Okay, so I'm sorry you feel ignored. I'm sorry you can't take a joke. I haven't seen my mother in how long, she's finally well enough for me to come visit, and now I have to deal with *your* stuff?

Me ruin this? Joy says. It's you! If it were me, you wouldn't know what hit you.

If I could open the door and jump – or roll into a ball on the car floor and sleep and when I wake be someone else, someone smarter or braver, someone with the chops to seriously bail and never look back – I wouldn't have to settle, as I do, for the next best thing: nothing, as if nothing were a faraway place. Not far enough, though: I can still hear Joy and Mimi, their usual ping-pong gibes sounding harsher, more slap-happy than ever before.

All I can do is keep my eyes shut, miserable. So when the car sheers to the oncoming side of the road and beyond, bucks into the low ditch and stops, I think we've barely avoided an accident, that another car or an animal has jumped in front of us and Mimi has swerved to avoid it, that this is why I've struck Joy's seat with my arms thrust forward and bounced back, wrist-sore.

Joy starts to whimper. Mimi turns toward her, and Joy collapses against the side of the door, legs drawn together and raised, hands over her face, boo-hooing at the window.

Mimi puts the car in reverse and, without checking for other vehicles, guns onto the middle of the road and stops. She searches for another station on the radio, starts driving slowly.

Pile in, get your honey buns down here, this special's not going to last forever. In the meantime, how about some Bob Wills and His Texas Playboys?

My wrist feels frozen in a pre-throb – at least it doesn't *look* broken – and my ear's tender where the cooler lid flew up and dinged me. The bag of cookies rests in my lap, and a number of obscenely spent-looking carrots lie strewn here and there. In the front seat, instead of the dopey predictable jokes, the bumper-car child's play, there's this: Joy cowed silly, Mimi smashmouth mean. Cool, I think, too freaking cool.

We drive for a minute or two, the car labouring along, on either side of us the storm-lavendered fields gapped open by the incision of road. I feel as if I've floated out the car window and am trailing behind, dangling upside down by my heels, a sticky, topsy-turvey thrill in the gut.

I look inside the lidless Igloo. Pull out a wine cooler, twist off the top – wrist evidently in functioning order – reach forward and hand it to Mimi.

That's more like it, she says.

She takes a swig and holds it out to Joy, whose face is still in her hands.

Friends? Mimi says.

She drinks again.

Don't tell me that's a no, she says.

Joy rubs her face, sits up, shakes her head. She twists her shoulders and tries to catch my eye. A smile crosses her face and, with it, a look that appears to be a mixture of disbelief and pleasure and admiration, almost – as if she thinks she might have been the good-natured butt of a joke, a really good one, and she wants me of all people to tell her if it's true or not. When she gets no response, she straightens forward again, then reaches over to Mimi and grabs the bottle. She tilts the bottle to her mouth, drinks, passes it back to me.

You crazy bugger, she says to Mimi.

Way to go, Joy, Mimi says. Awright! Ready to kick some booty?

A skipped beat, then Joy thrusts her right hand out the window and slaps the exterior of the car door.

Ready to *roll*, she announces.

She drops her chin to her chest and wags her head as if to some down-deep groove.

Rip it, she says.

Mimi whistles.

Love your lingo, she says. Listen to your mom, Tanis. Isn't she just the best? Where does she come up with these things? Ah-mazing! Dee-vine!

A man grins at me, raises a finger to his lips: ssh, don't tell anyone. He nods: okay? He's sitting on a piano bench about twenty feet from the table at which we're seated. Behind him, perched atop the piano, is a teddy bear. Otherwise, the place seems pretty much deserted. The only other person we've seen in the ten minutes we've been here is the receptionist on the first floor who gave us the once-over before asking if we had an appointment. Upon hearing Mimi's flustered answer – *a say-what?* – she placed a cryptic-sounding phone call, and then mildly directed us to this recreation room one floor above.

The piano is surrounded by large soft-looking cushions in pinks and greens scattered across a rag rug. To the left of the piano is a set of large, sealed windows. Construction-paper pictures are taped to the room's green walls. It's eleven, early for lunch, yet the room smells of the KFC someone has already eaten: on the table next to ours, some of the remnants – greasy bones and small pieces of fatty chicken – protrude from the cardboard box. Beside it, there are squibs of ketchup on grease-stained napkins, and a squashed fry decorates the floor. In the middle of the table is a large plastic water jug holding a bouquet of purple-blue cornflowers.

Ssh, okay?

I nod back vaguely, trying to avoid meeting the piano man's eyes. Three empty chairs from me sit the tanked-up Mimi and Joy. Joy in her pale-blue, poly-cotton blend shirt with sweat-stained underarms and her matching jersy knit shorts, both of which are adorned in places with the residue of yesterday's ice cream sundae. Mimi in her black, tight-fitting cap-sleeved tee and her tight jeans, her scuffed high-heeled red sandals and matching red handbag – a change, at least, from what she wore yesterday. I pull up the collar of my short-sleeved shirt, roll the cuffs an inch and try to crease them. I'm getting cold from the AC. I button the shirt, hiding my tank top. I comb my fingers through my hair. Mimi's placed a pack of pilfered Walker smokes on the table, but they remain untouched. She crosses and uncrosses her legs, folds and refolds her hands.

Suddenly she tips over into Joy.

We look like fucking librarians, she guffaws.

In the middle of the room are three construction-paper and pipe-cleaner mobiles hanging from the ceiling by twine: purple, yellow, orange strips, ends stapled together to make interlocking circles. Some smiley, pie-plate faces above the door.

Joy is snickering, pushing Mimi away.

Straighten up and fly right, she says. Or they'll lock us up too.

Scare-y, Mimi squeals. Oooh.

Mi-mi, Joy says. Can it.

Mimi makes a show of pouting. Then she picks at her nail polish, nips at a cuticle. I look again for the nodding man, and he's gone. Then I see him: he's moved to the table next to us, the one with the KFC box on it. He lifts a hand and waves at me.

Tanis, Mimi says teasingly, only now catching on to the man's presence. I think you've got yourself an admirer.

She throws her shoulders back.

How you doing today? she booms out to him.

Mimi! I hiss, as a young male attendant enters the room and approaches us.

Mimi ignores him.

Aw, she says to me. Just funning with you. Don't go and get all snitty on us.

The attendant stops a couple of feet from our table.

Dr. Lipman would like to speak with you, he says to Mimi. Would you like to come to her office?

Mimi places her hands onto the table, palms down, and leans over them.

Am I going to see my mom or not? she says loudly. This is unreal. We've been sitting here an hour at least. What's the holdup?

The attendant regards her levelly.

This way, he says.

Mimi rises, knocks the empty chair next to her by mistake. She picks up her red bag, slings the strap over her shoulder. The strap slips. She puts it back in place, again it slips.

I am so not amused, she whispers hoarsely.

But when she reaches the attendant she drapes her arm around his shoulders.

Hiya handsome, she says. Where've you been all my life?

He smiles lightly, and walks her from the room.

How long is *this* going to take? Joy says, looking about for something to do.

Now *she* takes an interest in the nodding, waving man.

Look over there, she says. Isn't that sad? He's like a boy trapped in a man's body.

He can hear you! I say under my breath, mortified.

Joy pushes back in her chair and smiles at him pleasantly.

Did you have a nice lunch? she says. A good visit?

Wah! he says excitedly, rocking in his seat. Wah-uh!

His eyes are large and brown, almost too large for his slender, boyish face. He's repositioned his chair so he's now sitting sideways to the table, legs crossed, knees toward us, and we can see his worn moccasins, his bare sticklike ankles that jut above them. Over his shirt and pants he's wearing an untied bathrobe that hangs over the sides of the chair.

That's nice, she says. And did somebody nice bring you those flowers?

Uhh!

She leans over in her chair, squints at the floor near the man's feet.

You didn't make a mess, did you? she says.

She gets up, goes over to him, takes a napkin from the table. Kneels and picks up the squished fry, folds the napkin over, and rubs at the spot on the floor. Stands, puts the napkin in the box, picks up the box, gathers the remaining napkins, takes the garbage to a trash can near the door. She returns to the man, places a hand on his shoulder.

What's your name? she says.

Bob! he says.

Very good, Bobby! she says. What a good boy you are.

She bends over him, pulls his robe shut, reaches for the belt and ties it around him.

Don't want to catch cold, do we? she says.

On the opposite side of the room are two sagging easy chairs and a coffee table on which sits a Monopoly box, a *People* magazine, and a deck of cards. Joy wanders over and picks up the cards. She walks back to Bobby, puts the deck on the table, pulls out a chair beside him and sits. She helps him turn and tuck himself under the table. She picks up the cards and shuffles them. He's nodding all the while.

What is this? I say. Like, the meeting of the minds?

Ignore her, Joy says to her new friend. *She* doesn't know how to have fun.

She deals three hands.

You playing or not? she says to me.

I sit on Bobby's other side. His eyebrows are wispy, his lips like twists of Saran Wrap – someone should get the guy some Chap Stick. Joy and I hold our cards in our hands, but his lie face down on the table in front of him. Joy chooses one for him, turns it over. Two of diamonds.

What are we playing? I say.

She looks at me, then at Bobby.

I think Tanis knows what this is, she says.

I don't. Then I do: the game is from a time I can barely recall, before Walker moved us into the apartment at his place, when Joy and I were on our own together above a laundromat in Whitby, and she was working nearby at a dry cleaners.

Sometimes, though, a wash of colour – the blue couch from the Sally Ann on which we nestled, the rosy walls of the one-room dwelling – swipes through me. With it comes the feel of Joy's arm against mine when that was a good sensation, when her chin would nuzzle the top of my head, her fingers tickle the back of my neck, her smell like a warm soapy bath mixing with the toasty sensation from the flannel PJs she dressed me in. She'd take a card from a worn deck and lay it on my lap, then another, and another, with a story for each: elaborate plots involving salty sailors and saucy barmaids, Yosemite Sam, train conductors and firemen, crones and thieves, Maid Marian and Robin Hood, even the Jolly Green Giant of advertising fame. And a handsome, devil-may-care cowboy who rode off with his lady love's heart.

What correspondences Joy made between the cards and her seemingly inexhaustible cast of characters was never clear, and likely never mattered: this was just something we once did together, a thing forever inexplicable, tales she once told herself, perhaps, when she was young and her mother was sick. Walker off somewhere, all ruckus and romp, leaving Joy alone, having to be her own best company, provide for herself.

And then their mother died: Joy in foster care, Walker somehow dipping beneath the authorities' radar, gone.

How did Joy's fantasy world ever become so unpeopled? I don't remember ever playing once Walker took us in – once he'd surfaced, having bought the house and stable, and built the apartment – and all talk became back-talk with bite marks. It's as if Joy's subjects took one look at gruff Walker, suffered one earful of his clumsy ridicule, and hightailed it for the hills, fanned out along the vast deltas of kingdom come until they vanished, replaced by the trickier, more at-stake world of Walker and Lily and Jena, and now Mimi – to Joy's in-over-her-head, nose-pressed-to-the-window fascination. Totally undignified, like she were Mimi's groupie – fan of the fan *extraordinaire*. Joy never seemed able to get her footing, to know her place, no matter how hard she tried – thanklessly cleaning up after everyone, minding Jena's manners, grudgingly looking after her as well as me when Walker wasn't paying attention, minding Walker even, when she dared, though he wasn't exactly responsive to her ministrations.

Two of diamonds, and Bobby's trembling.

Yah! he goes.

Dude, I say. It's cool, relax yourself.

Joy wiggles impatiently in her seat. Had she even known until now how badly she missed her, if not more innocent, then at least far less complex, fictive pals?

Okay, I say. Give me a sec.

But before I come up with a stitch of a story that Joy can use, Mimi returns, stands a couple of feet into the room, her eyes and nose swollen.

What gives? Joy calls over to Mimi. I thought we were going to see her.

We are not, Mimi says, her voice tight. We are never. Not you. Not me.

She presses the heel of her hand into her eye.

I didn't even see the bitch, she says. My mom's all fucked up. And it's *my* fault? I told that quack to analyze this!

Mimi raises a fist in the air, extends her middle finger, jabs it in the direction from which she just came. I sit up straighter in my seat – even for Mimi, the gesture is crude. Embarrassed, I quickly check to see that we're still alone in the room, that no one is watching us from the hallway.

No one saw. I'm relieved. Then I feel ashamed – a sticky Kleenex feeling in the pit of my stomach, a dull pocking at my temples – for having felt embarrassed by Mimi.

You mean we came all this way for nothing? Joy complains.

Suddenly Mimi tears her bag from her shoulder and dashes it to the ground. The top is open, and a makeup compact clatters out, along with a hairbrush and a jotting of loose coins. She spins around, kicks the purse several feet, and rushes toward the elevator, which is directly outside the room. When she gets there, she pushes the down button and remains facing the door, waiting for it to open.

Joy slaps her cards down, rises from her seat. Bobby returns to his steady, regular nodding.

What? Joy says, kneeling to gather Mimi's scattered belongings. What did I do now?

Twenty minutes later we're pulled over by the side of the road. The three of us are standing outside the car. The hood is up and vapour ricracs from the engine. Thunder anvil-heads toward us as, for long seconds at a time, the chill wind skirls then lets up, then gusts anew, as if powered by giant bellows, the breath of this roiling world. I hug myself with my arms.

Do we even know where we are? Joy says.

And now the rain begins. A steady downpour, dull and heavy, like a thick tarp thrown over the day and its cheap-trick heat that this morning had seemed as if it would never end. We stay put, with not even enough sense to get out of the rain.

A navy-blue Saab convertible, the top up, drives south along the road, toward the city. When it gets closer, the car slows down. The driver swivels his head and stares as he edges past.

The fuck *you* looking at? Mimi snarls after him.

I'm soaked, jeans plastered to my legs, and it feels like I'm encased in cold, rough concrete. I start to shake, grip myself tighter then let go, scared Mimi will notice, scared that I'm scared. *Stop it.* I fix my welling eyes on the raw sky until they film with grey. *Better.*

II

4

THE ODDS

Mist drapes the red- and gold-leaved maples and sumacs, drips from damp-blackened pines. Birches' white skin unpeels. I'm overdressed for the muggy September weather, sweaty in my too-long-in-the-sleeves, Polartec-lined anorak, a last-year's hand-me-down from Suzanne, who's sitting two rows in front of me on the school bus, head to head with another girl. I blow my breath against the window, write my name in the cloud.

The meet: with her toned legs and sinewy torso, her easy balance, her speed, Suzanne flies over the hurdles, airwalks the long jump, wings it down the clay track for the 100 metres. Tendrils of fog laurel the field. I sprint to several respectable finishes. Then it's all over: girls swirl in twos and threes toward the waiting buses.

I bump my hips down the aisle to the back of the bus, retake my seat as a vintage, citrine-coloured Sunbeam Tiger, miniature motorized gem, whisks past, top down: Suzanne's ride-of-late, piloted by our curly-headed, high-cheekboned power-pack of a gym coach, Kendrew – that killer cutie, much beloved by her more *aware* students for her chic-butch smarts. Suzanne is lapping up the attention. I watch the backs of their heads until the fog veils them.

I pull the hood up on my jacket, finger my glands, which seem swollen. Three other girls are on the bus, each seated apart from one another: the leftovers, the unpaired-off, like me, no one to cheer them on at the meet, no one to pick them up. Pathetics. Not even a hi to each other.

The bus drops me off at Walker's. I can hardly make out the end of the drive, the barns. The dogs are nowhere to be seen. The lights are out in the house: no one appears to be home. I sit in the growing dark at his kitchen table, light one of his Camels. I put a hand to my feverish forehead, stare at the table's oilcloth patterned with buttercups and bluebells that dance like motes across the table, flicker like tongues. A low groan from the living room, and I almost pee my pants.

Walker and Mimi, entwined on the sofa.

Guys? I say, standing in the doorway between the kitchen and the living room. What's up?

The TV comes on, the dim room lit by a *Magnum P.I.* rerun, pops and flashes of Hawaiian sun. Mimi raises her head from Walker's, which rests against her shoulder. His arms encircle her hips.

Who wants to know? Mimi says, sounding as if she were a million miles away – she's been like this, inaccessible to all but Walker, lost in sadness since our ill-fated attempt to see her mother in July.

Walker lowers his head to Mimi's thigh. A kiss, then he turns his head to one side and rests it there, her white hand in his hair: a country of two, a place beyond words, borders sealed.

Outside, the fog has become so thick I can't see the barns at all. I take a few steps in their direction, as if slowly swimming toward the outline of shipwrecks, whatever won't float, the broken masts and grinning dead-eyes I saw a picture of once in a magazine.

Blind man's bluff: turn, turn again. Stop: Jena, head down, about ten feet in front of me. She doesn't seem to notice I'm here. She's talking to herself under her breath, sing-songing.

Suckah, she goes. Got no grasp, I ask, who's the suckah now?

A no-brainer, I say. You are.

She stretches her neck to the left, as if she has a crick in it. Then she moves it to the right, holds it, then straightens. A glimmer of a smile frosts her lips. She's got this pink bandana doo-rag tied on her head. Fog blossoms around her.

No, she says gamely. And if you don't know who is, then I'm not going tell.

She's Little Miss Motley in a puffy, dingy white down vest over a pale-yellow sweatshirt, baggy red jeans with white stitching, black quilted sneakers. She looks full, dumpy as a Weeble toy – looks like she'd roll with your punch only to flop back up again, like you could never really lay her low.

Weeble, I say.

No, *you* are, she says.

In Jena's princess room, her roomy room: the princess dresser and desk and bed in white veneer with gold trim, the easter-egg pastels of Teddy and Annie and Toad, the fake quilt-patterned-patches for the drapes, ditto the ruffled sham and bedspread on which her white cat curls. With her own hodge-podge outfit, Jena's almost camouflaged as she sits on her bed – hands on her knees, feet fixed to a brightly hued rug – no moving parts except her twinkly eyes tracking me.

Next to her lies my jacket, which I didn't remove until we got here, not wanting to disturb – if such a thing were possible! – Walker and Mimi, still braided together on the sofa as I followed Jena through the house and up the narrow stairs into this oasis of warm colour, softly illuminated by two white side-table lamps capped with pale-pink shades.

I pick up a yellow plastic ducky-embossed hairbrush from her dresser. I review Jena's reflection in the mirror – eyes shining like she's in heaven, the yutz. As Mimi might say.

Want to play spanky bum? I say.

Her eyes widen. I put the brush back down on the dresser, next to a splay of marbles. Beside a JVC CD player is a tidy stack of Britney and Busta CDs. Also on the dresser: an Olive Garden matchbook – a door prize, probably, from a dinner date with her mom – and a jewellery box, which tinkles when I open it. I take out a pair of dangly beaded earrings, hold them up to my ears in front of the mirror. I put them back in the box, cross the polished wood floor to the window, draw back one of the drapes and look out: white blooms and blows.

I think I have to go to the bathroom, she says apologetically.

So go, I say, drawing the curtains shut. You're excused.

Will you be here when I get back? she asks hesitantly.

If you're lucky, I reply.

Come with me? she pleads.

She slowly turns the door handle, swings open the door. She sticks her head out. The bathroom is beside her bedroom, mere steps into the unlit hallway.

Go, I whisper. *Go.*

Come *in* with me, she whispers back.

The bathroom, I see when she flips the light switch, is very mauve, from the tiles to the painted wood trim to the lilac- and silver-striped wallpaper – decorated recently by Walker, under Jena's priceless direction. I pull open the lavender-coloured shower curtain, wedding-cake-like with plastic lace: guess the home-improvement plan never extended to the chips of soap fused to the ledge of the tub, the numerous bottles of shampoo and conditioner with labels disintegrated.

Jena, I say. Tell me you don't *bathe* in there.

No, she says glumly.

I open the medicine cabinet, poke through the half-finished tubes of toothpaste and packets of razor blades, the bottles of Pepcid and Nyquil and a prescription bottle for Jena, what I recognize as mismatched earrings belonging to Mimi: several sizes of gold-plated hoops.

Jena, sitting on the toilet – her cat, who followed us in, rubbing against her ankles – turns and reaches behind her for a roll of toilet paper sitting on top of the toilet cover. She tears off a couple of squares, drops the roll on the floor. It lands behind the toilet, and the cat pounces and paws it. Jena turns on the seat, looking down, trying to find the roll.

I palm a bottle of Aspirin with codeine, put it in a front pocket of my jeans. Jena gives up on the wayward paper. Though she hasn't peed, she wipes. I snap the medicine cabinet door shut.

You didn't go yet, I say.

I didn't have to, she says.

In the sink, long blonde and red hairs curl around each other, hobnobbing in a fracas of filth. The whole place is in major need of Joy's decontaminating protocols – they should let her at it.

What're these for? I ask, holding up Jena's prescription bottle – its label torn and the type smeared.

She's still sitting on the toilet, the cat purring now in her naked lap. Behind her, on the tank cover, a jar of girlie soaps shaped like seashells, pinks and greens – a sweet ether smell – the jar with a BiWay sticker still on it.

Those are for helping me, she says. Want one?

Do yourself back up, I say – uncapping the bottle, tapping out a med.

I put it in the other front pocket of my jeans.

Don't look, she says.

I wake the next morning in the sofa bed with the flu, bike shorts and tank top sweat-soaked, covers kicked to the floor. I spend most of the day horizontal, and the night.

The following morning, five o'clock, Joy wakes me on her way to work.

Aren't you going to school? she says roughly as she stands over me.

I fall asleep again, rewaken to hear her opening a cupboard in the kitchenette, running water. She returns to the living room. I half sit up. She holds a cloudy glass toward me.

What're you missing? she demands.

Nothing, I say.

Except for a math quiz – free-float of multiple choice like chalk dust suspended in air – I'm primed to flunk.

I take the glass from her, and sip. She bends over, picks the covers off the floor, and drapes them over my legs. I try to pass the glass back but she doesn't budge.

A review, I say. Easy stuff.

No way would she call school to check on me, make appointments to see my teachers, or the principal, or – terror of terrors – one of the feel-you-up, feel-good counsellors. How intimidated she'd been the only occasion she did put in some face time at a school interview, two years ago. We'd sat, side by side, before the metal desk of my home-room teacher – a brusque, brass-ballsy man – Joy nervously twitching her crossed legs, laughing too loudly at all the wrong places, while the teacher huffed at her regarding the urgent matter of my frequent absenteeism.

They always start the year like this, I say smoothly. Nothing new until next month.

She takes the glass from me and puts it on the coffee table. Then, seeming to change her mind, she picks it up again, walks back into the kitchenette. I hear her pour the rest of the water into the sink, the knock when she puts the glass on the counter.

You want me to leave you alone, she calls out wearily. But if I don't care, nobody else will. You're already a year behind. Don't you ever want to graduate?

I'm sick, I say. That's all. Don't I get to be sick?

She appears suddenly in the doorway.

If I called in sick every time I had a little ache or pain, we'd be on welfare, she says. Or on the street.

But you never *get* sick, I rejoin.

Her forehead furrows, and her mouth tugs down at the corners.

Is that what you think? she says.

I won't meet her eyes. I pick at the mouldy-smelling bed cover heaped around my hips.

She takes her coat off the wall peg just inside the living room, shrugs it on.

No rest for the wicked, she says ruefully, under her breath.

Then she squishes in her sneakers across the kitchenette floor – a forlorn sound, sad echo of thousands of days of echoes. I hear the back door open, close. I trudge back into fitful sleep.

Nine-thirty, cabin-fevered – codeined from the Aspirins I stole the day before, all four that were in the bottle, too bad! plus I took Jena's pill as well – I'm entering the first barn when I smack-dab into Walker.

He's carrying a pail containing a couple of inches of a green liquid with a strong iodine smell.

I'm thinking, he says, putting the pail down.

I point at it, nauseated.

What *is* that? I say.

He takes a package of cigarettes out of his work jacket's pocket, taps the package against his free hand – this in lieu of removing a cigarette and lighting up, an act of potential arson he would never commit in the highly flammable barn.

Why should I be doing all the hard work around here? he says – sounding like Joy, give me a break. There's still three stalls that need cleaning.

I don't have to do it, I say.

Not if you're in school, he says.

He puts the pack of smokes away.

I never had anyone to get after me, give me advice, he says. Consider yourself lucky.

He picks up the pail and walks to a nearby stall. He unlatches the door and opens it. The horse stops picking at its hay in the corner and clumps over to him, flattens its ears and swings its head up.

Get back, you fucker, Walker growls, and pushes against the horse with a shoulder, puts his back to it and shoves his way to the corner, where he dumps the contents of the pail into the horse's regular feed.

Leaning heavily into the excited horse now, he musters one last push – the horse retreats enough to let Walker duck out. He latches the door again, watches through the bars as the horse scarfs its breakfast.

Reconstituted, freeze-dried *sea* vegetables, he says, his back still turned to me. Don't laugh. What happens when health nuts own horses. Next we'll be having yoga classes for them.

I can't help but move closer: the scrape of teeth, the flute-like noises of satisfaction – the sense of at-oneness – mesmerize.

Balance their energies, I say.

Yeah, and praise the fucking lord, he says dryly. That too.

We stand shoulder to shoulder, momentarily absorbed.

Still gazing at the horse he says, You look like *you* could use a pick-me-up.

So, the ruler of the roost is worried about me! Like I should be so grateful – he usually has more important matters to concern himself with.

I steal a glance at him. Even in profile I can see that beneath his woolly hair his wide, high forehead is creased, his thin lips pressed together. The nose bulb-shaped, chin asymmetrical. Substantial development in the jowl sector. For all that – for all his bossy bluster – there's something insubstantial about him: the deep eye sockets overhung by the jutting heavy brows suggesting muddled recesses, doubts parallel-pathing firm decisions. Self-sabotage. Weakness.

The semi-literate, I think suddenly – wrenchingly. The orphan.

For a second, the ground cuts away beneath me. To steady myself, I clasp his meaty, generous arm just above the elbow.

I'm all right, I say. Old guy.

I fucking hope so, he says. Don't you be falling apart on me too.

I let go of him. He opens the stall door again, and the horse nickers, steps forward. *Too?* He'd never admit that about himself.

Mimi? I say.

Broaching the subject with Walker – a first – makes me squirm inside, what it must be like to rummage through his shorts drawer, or Mimi's lingerie piles. Embarrassing, maybe treacherous: what if I get caught? In this case, by Mimi – if, that is, Walker says something he shouldn't.

At the same time, I'm all ears, eager for insider knowledge. I straighten my spine, then shrink – at once appalled and fascinated by my own eagerness.

She's taking her mother hard, I say, prompting him. The visit this summer.

I guess, he says, noncommittal.

The horse noses Walker's work shirt. He flattens his hand across the horse's forelock, and the animal calms. Walker cradles the head to his chest – I'm shut out. Conversation over. Dismissed, I think, saluting him angrily in my head.

Outside again, I notice the flawless, end-of-September day, the blue-glass, high-domed sky. Geese V above. None of the horses have been turned out yet, and the paddock is carpeted with sparrows and starlings. Squirrels riddle the trees. Mimi is sitting on the top porch step, sunning herself, smoking, drinking a cup of coffee.

Avoiding her – a residue of guilt from the conversation-that-wasn't clinging to me – I go to the paddock. Feeling spinny, I rest my crossed arms on the fence. I hear the barn door open behind me, and the clop of hooves.

Easy, Walker says. Jesus!

He leads two horses by their halters past me to the paddock gate, opens it, and turns them loose: they loll against each other just inside the gate, close their eyes, appear to fall asleep. Walker, hands in the front pockets of his jeans, not moving. Mimi, leaning back, legs stretched in front of her. My niggling guilt eases.

Lazy day, she calls in a gravelly voice as I near her.

Yeah, I say. Well.

Another ringing endorsement from Miss Congeniality,

she says smartly – upbeat, a way she hasn't seemed since July.

She's wearing a red tank top, white shorty-shorts. Goosebumps bead the fleshy parts of her exposed thighs. A stack of silver-coloured bangles tambourine on her wrist when she lifts a hand to finger-comb her hair, which hangs loose over her bare shoulders. It's as if she hasn't noticed summer has passed, hasn't had her fill yet of sandals and suntan lotion – as if she's picking up where she left off in more carefree times.

She yawns luxuriantly, without covering her mouth.

Wakey-wakey, Mimi, she says out loud to herself.

She glances over at Walker. Then she turns her face toward me again.

Sweetie, she coos. Part of me hates to ask, but do you mind if I give you a little advice?

Can I borrow your car? I say, cutting in – anxious to get Walker off my case. It's urgent.

She taps the ash from her cigarette onto the step beside her.

Missed the bus? she says after a pause – at least she seems to know the school year has started.

I nod. My mouth is cottony.

And Suzanne's not going to run over and pick you up, right? she says.

Nope, I quack.

Like I always say, she says sarcastically. Thank god for friends!

She examines me – face marauded by pimples, my unwashed hair – and her open smile tapers off. She exchanges another look with Walker, who remains by the paddock. My head is swishy and full, like there's a load of laundry inside.

I have a makeup test at eleven, I manage to lie, desperate – not only does Mimi refuse to let Joy take the Monte Carlo, but I've never soloed before. It's really important!

Well! she chirps. If you put it *that* way.

She drags off her cigarette, pulls her legs under her, puts the coffee cup on the step.

You sure you're okay? she says suspiciously, squinting at pants-on-fire me, hiding behind the smoke she's exhaled. Behind the eight ball and all?

I shrug, which she mimics. She sticks the cigarette back in her mouth. A plug of ash breaks free and falls.

Keys are on the kitchen table, she says. Good luck with your test, tiger. Go out there and knock their cocks off!

She sniggers into her hand in a way that seems strangely wrong for her: an off-balance teeter-totter comes to mind, with this crude replacement on one end, and the elegant Mimi I've always known on the other. Right now, crude Mimi's on top.

Again – as I did this summer in the psychiatric home, and as I did only minutes ago in the barn with Walker – I feel embarrassed: by Mimi, and for her.

But this time, I don't feel ashamed. Only unnerved.

If you'll pardon my rock 'n' roll, she says, with a hint of defiant pride – as you might apologize for a deliberately offensive belch.

The ground cartwheels underfoot. I will the sensation to cease. Places to go, you know?

I nick the cushier gravel of the shoulder, nose recklessly sidelong across the culvert and halt.

I relocate my hands at ten and two.

Now I hug the narrow road past the red pines south toward the small church and cemetery by Steeles Avenue – a route I've ridden countlessly on horseback, with Walker when I was much younger, with Suzanne more recently. A quarter-mile more, and I turn off to park in the drive of the church, lay my arm outside the car window, let it hang down the door, listen to the hiss of city traffic along Steeles.

Out there, somewhere not far to the south, lies the zoo. Farther still, downtown, with its Royal Ontario Museum, the planetarium – before it closed for good – with its dark-cave projection theatre, my former best friend, that snob – I see it clearly now, that she'd take any excuse to turn away – agape beside me. The art gallery, *The Nutcracker* at Christmastime, while the marigold school buses wait in a gleaming row along the street.

I adjust the rear-view to see myself.

Brown mop head, unstocked. A place to which none of the learned, tricked-out names for things of awe would ever attach themselves. To which so much – history, French, palling around in the cafeteria at lunchtime – seems to be simply beyond. Close-set dark-blue eyes, circles under them. A dirt-road background.

Looking through the windshield, I can see beyond the church, where, scattered among mature trees, lie the old headstones – grey teeth gnashing the trunks of maples whose coronas flare red, yellow.

A breeze tickles the fine hairs on my arm. I withdraw it from the window. Lean close to the mirror, run my tongue over my parted lips. Closer: a kiss, the mirror breath-blurred. Lean back: a star-fossil.

A car zings past on the road.

I lean back farther still, feel under the waist of my jeans with both hands, finger my stomach hard as my thighs from working horses off the leg. I bring my hands back out, undo the buttons on my shirt, readjust the mirror – pull my bra down. The material is constrictive beneath my breasts, swelling them up and out. I lay my head back against the headrest: in the mirror, I see my muscled throat.

I push against the seat, unzip my jeans, and yank them down, press a hand between my legs, which I open wider until the denim cuts into them. My nipples shrink and roughen, catch on the silky cool September air.

The red church door opens. I freeze. A man steps into the dappled sunlight, tool box in hand. He notices the car, stills to attention. A cardinal, ember-bright, lands on the railing beside him.

Bir-dee? it calls once, twice.

The man shakes his head, shuffles back inside.

Caught. *Stupid*.

I wait a minute. Leaves swish their fancy skirts in the trees above. The fountain grass splashes in the breeze. I put my other hand to my throat and hold it tight, until sunmelt glazes all.

I tighten my grip. Wonder how far I'll go.

Several weeks later, ten at night, I'm making up the sofa bed for myself when I hear the back door fly open. Joy sails backwards through the kitchenette and into the living room, reeling a man in with her, hands on his shoulders.

The golf club staff's annual end-of-season party is in midswing right about now – most of the employees work April through late-October, living off unemployment benefits the remainder of the year – and I've been expecting Joy to down her usual one too many drinks and have to be helped to the door by someone she works with.

But this? Speechless, I let go of the sheet I'm spreading over the mattress, and the sheet billows to the floor.

Joy stops short, as well.

I forgot about you, she says curtly, taking her hands off her victim.

I can't help but gape: he's portly, and the left leg of his

eyeglasses is taped on. He stands awkwardly, hands in his cushy pants pockets.

Let me get us some drinks, Joy says to him. Then we can go into my room.

She flusters away. The man looks at the ceiling, the red shag rug, anything but me, or the half-made bed. He clears his throat several times.

Nice place you've got here, he says in a soft, girlish voice to the blank TV screen.

Thank you, I say. It does the trick.

His hair is blond and curly – permed? Tan pants a couple of shades off his tan windbreaker. He appears to be sporting a pair of no-name sneakers.

I wonder if I should offer him a seat – but do I fold up the bed first, replace the cushions on the sofa?

By any chance are you two ladies related? he says, finally mustering enough nerve to look directly at me – I think, since it's hard to tell for certain, as his eyes don't seem to focus very well behind the lens of his glasses, and the way his mouth moves doesn't quite match his words.

No, I say. Not even remotely.

Joy bustles into the room with two empty tumblers stacked together, and a can of Coke.

Where were we? she says, and herds him into the bedroom.

I watch the late show with the sound turned down. Eventually – nothing to report on the eavesdropping front – I fall asleep. When I wake in the morning they're both gone. The glasses have been rinsed and are sitting to dry in the dish rack.

All day at school, I can't keep my mind off what might have happened. I get home at four, nuke myself some popcorn. When Joy finally shows, I'm onto her fast – but she acts as if nothing has happened as she takes her coat off, as I follow her from the living room and down the hallway to the bathroom.

She shuts the door in my face, and I wait outside. When she comes out I follow her back through the living room and into the kitchenette.

Well? I say.

I thought you'd never ask, she says coyly.

She laces her fingers together behind her neck, arms akimbo, fronting her chest forward. She flutters her eyelashes.

How about that? she says. Your old mom's got herself a guy!

Seriously? I say.

Don't get smart, she says touchily, dropping her arms to her sides.

She turns abruptly and opens the fridge. I peer over her shoulder: there's a brown-leafed head of iceberg lettuce in plastic wrap on the lower shelf. Assorted condiment bottles stored on the inside of the door. Top-shelved Cokes and Sprites.

Hell, she says. We should be dieting anyway. It's a miracle anyone would want to take us on. I mean, look at us. Couple of chunks.

Like mother, like daughter, I say.

Apple didn't fall far from the tree, she says ruefully.

She reaches out, musses my hair. I quickly step away.

Don't, I say.

She sags, looks sadly back into the near-empty fridge, then closes the door. When she faces me again her expression is bright, hard as dry paste.

Two days later I arrive home from school to find Joy in tears in the apartment, Mimi beside her, facing the closed door to Walker's kitchen.

What did you open your mouth for? Mimi's saying loudly.

All I did was ask about him, Walker says from the other side of the door. Don't blame me.

And who'd you ask, anyway? Mimi shouts. Ray?

I hear things, Walker says. Leave it at that. You two want to live in a fantasy world that's your business. But he comes around here again, I'll toss him. I don't want him near my daughter.

Your stupid daughter! Mimi says. *What* is the matter with you?

Mimi calls over to me.

Tanis, she says. *What* is wrong with your uncle? He can't stand to see anybody happy.

Yeah, he says forcefully. And you'd think you'd both be concerned about *her* safety, at the very least! Why don't you think about that for a change? Instead of taking her here and there, catting around with you.

Mimi rattles the doorknob. Locked. She slams her hands twice on the door.

Walker! she yells, exasperated. This has nothing to do with Tanis. She's *fine*.

But he has a good job, Joy plaints – oblivious to all but her own narrow plight. He just started. He's a *manager*.

Joy, Walker says. I *told* you. He just got out of the crowbar motel in Kingston, and you *don't* want to know what he did to get there in the first place. And he's not a manager, he's a fucking dishwasher!

Walker, shut up, Mimi orders. The guy says he's a manager, he's a manager.

I go into the bathroom, lock the door. Turn the shower on, take off my clothes. I hear glass break in the kitchen, Joy yelp, then only the sizzle of the running water as I let it run over me, the eclipse of all else, whiteout – nothing ahead but the coming months darkening, the fog turning to snow and sleet.

When I leave the bathroom, Mimi and Joy are gone. I get my books out of my knapsack, take them to the sofa. In the kitchenette I make a mayo sandwich on white. I take it into the living room, eat it standing up. I go back and make a second – down the hatch that one goes. In the cupboard I find a can of SpaghettiOs. I heat the contents in a small saucepan, put two slices of bread in the toaster. When the slop is hot I pour it over the toast I've laid on a plate, which I proceed to polish off, standing at the counter. Half a can of Coke later, I have to lie down, my stomach a big bollocky thing.

Forget the sofa, I think. Mimi will be back in the apartment with us tonight – now that she's siding with Joy against Walker – for the first time in months.

In the bedroom I undress down to my underwear and crawl into bed beneath the covers. I'll get up in a few minutes, I tell myself, do my homework. But instead I fall asleep, wake in the dark to two masses shifting into the room, Joy giggling and grunting, slurring hard-to-recognize sounds. The shapes sag onto the bed.

Hey, a man says in a deep bass.

He puts a hand on my leg.

What've we got here? he says – I don't recognize his voice, which doesn't seem to belong to the previous night's boyfriend.

That's just –, Joy says. Never mind.

They laugh, rolling into each other. Joy clunks to the floor.

Oh! she says.

The man moves his hand higher up my leg. I grab his thumb, lever back as hard as I can. He doubles over. I throw off the covers, swing from the mattress onto the floor, bound over Joy.

In the kitchenette I open the cutlery drawer.

Feisty, I hear the man say. I *like* it!

Joy? Mimi calls from the living room, surprising me since I didn't hear her return earlier – I must have been crashed.

Tanis? she calls.

Hey, the guy exclaims. You got another one here? Party hearty!

Shut up, you fucking idiot, Mimi snaps out. Tanis, get in here with me.

Suddenly she appears in the kitchenette. She just stands there, looking. Then she comes over to me and shuts the drawer.

Come on to bed with me, she says. It's not worth it to you. I'll kill her myself, tomorrow. So to speak.

I lie awake as long as I can, inhaling her spiced-cider scent while she sleeps with her arm around me, long after the laughing and groaning from the bedroom has ceased. Then I sleep, until I hear the toilet flush in the bathroom, and I reach out and Mimi's gone. She comes back into the living room, sits on the arm of the sofa, lights a cigarette.

You up? she says quietly. Yeah?

I pull the covers tighter under my chin.

She says, It never rains but it pours, huh?

She smooths the covers around the outline of my body. Then she gently pries them from my chin, folds them down neatly over my chest.

Okay, she says. Here's what we'll do. Why don't you beat it for now. Go to Walker's, get something to eat. If you see Walker, keep him occupied. We don't want him to find out. Give me an hour and I'll bust loverboy. Hope to god Walker doesn't see the guy's car!

I fold my hands across my stomach, stretch my toes.

It's sad, it really is, she says. You have to feel for her. But she can't just drag home some low-life and expect us to throw her a bridal shower.

No, I say – as if the word were a taut fishing line reeling back inside me, something floppy with fear on the other end.

She sighs.

I'm partly to blame, she says.

It's not your fault! I say.

I should have forced her to leave with me, she disagrees, shaking her head. But she said she'd get home on her own, call a taxi. She was having a ball! And I've been so. You know. Out of it lately. Not paying much attention to her. I didn't think I had the right to shut her fun down.

She strokes my hair from my forehead.

Bummer, she says. I know she's going to hate me for this. But I'm damned if I do, damned if I don't. The kicker is, it'll never even enter her head that this could end up causing trouble between me and Walker.

She stops with my hair and cups my chin in her palm.

Promise *you'll* never hate me, she breathes. I'd just die.

Frosted Flakes with whole milk, a glass of Tang poured from a gallon-sized pitcher in Walker's fridge. I sit at his kitchen table, lights out. Jena's white cat rubs against my legs, jumps into my lap and lies down, a soft motor idling. I hear water running in the pipes above my head. I finish my cereal.

Walker comes down the stairs and into the kitchen. He doesn't turn the light on. He goes to the fridge and takes out the juice, brings it to the counter, reaches into the cupboard and removes a glass. He pours, drinks. Refills his glass, brings it and the pitcher over to the table and puts them down. He pulls a chair out for himself and sits. The cat jumps out of my lap onto the floor, capers from the room. I reach for the pitcher, take another glass myself.

That'll be a buck-fifty, he says.

I'm running a tab, I say.

Nah, he says. Forget it. On the house.

You are a prince of a human being, I say.

A prince? he says. And here I thought I was the king of the fucking castle.

Now Jena stands in the doorway, still dressed in her blue flannel nightie trimmed with lace at the high neckline. She rubs her bland face, scratches her head. She flips the light switch, and stands blinking.

Nice bed head, I say.

She goes to the fridge and gets out the milk.

If I'd known you were coming, she says, I'd have baked a cake.

Walker's smoking now.

Put the kettle on, he says to Jena.

Five minutes later, steaming coffees before us – Jena on her second Pop-Tart – the car outside the window starts up.

Who the hell's that? Walker says.

He gets out of his chair, leans across the table to get a better look through the window. I hear barking: the dogs are roused.

Fuck me! Walker says, striding to the kitchen door – but as he opens it the car lurches into gear and drives off.

Everything okay in your place? he says, and when I nod he says, Christ, I better go see the horses.

He leaves. Jena takes another bite of her Pop-Tart, chews noisily.

Give me half, I say.

She finishes chewing, swallows.

It's mine, she says. Get your own. *Sorry!* You don't *have* your own.

Cold, rain-besotted days follow. I slip further into myself, sealed shut as a thin envelope: no news here.

Nights, I lie in bed launching ragged knots of breath into the space between my head and the puckered ceiling, unable to sleep, floating on a raft of fear – Joy tossing and turning next to me, snivelling, searching out my feet with hers, flinching each time I draw mine away – at being trapped in a jackhammer anger so intense there's no telling what I might do. So I do nothing.

One morning within a week after the club has closed for the season, Joy's up early – back in business, having lined up several housekeeping jobs in Unionville and Markham.

She curses when the alarm goes off, but quickly shoves her way out of bed and dresses in the underheated air. I've hardly slept, but now she's gone I spread out, drift into hints of dreams broken by Mimi's *Joy!* and Joy's slam of furniture in the living room, Mimi's *what the fucks?* and *aw jeez* and Joy's banging doors open and shut – par for the course ever since Mimi threw Joy's perv out.

When I wake, it's noon: another school day blown off. Steely dread tracks along my spine.

Mimi's not in the apartment, but the sofa bed and bedclothes haven't been put away yet. I burrow in, better acquaint myself with daytime TV, the tidy bouquets of laughter and tears, the talk-talk, the unspooling ribbons of satiny little appetites. Bolstered by the cheery exhortations of no less than three major-hair talk-show divas, for about two seconds I vow to advance alphabetically through the public library shelves according to author's name – then drop the idea, marooned by this lurking thought: I'm stupid, always will be.

Joy doesn't get home until six. She's brought burgers and fries from Wendy's for supper, which mollifies me enough to sit with her and eat in front of the TV, the bedclothes tangled at our feet on the floor.

I saw them this afternoon, she says, food in her mouth. The happy couple.

Go back one, I say. There, no, forward one.

They were getting his truck washed, she says, takes another bite of burger.

On-again, off-again, I say, reaching for some fries, dipping them in ketchup mixed with the hot sauce that's been stored for years in our cupboard. So what. It's just how they are.

Yeah, but you'd think, she says.

I think you expect too much, I say.

I blow my nose in a paper napkin. Joy crumples the wrapper from her burger, dunks it in Wendy's paper bag. She has a dash of mustard at the corner of her mouth.

She's supposed to take my side, she says. She's my friend.

She's his girlfriend, I say. And it's not like she snitched on you. She helped cover your ass!

Oh no she didn't, Joy says. She told him. After all I've done for her!

Stunned – so Mimi *did* tell on Joy? – I pick up the remote. *Naive. Childish.* There are things you don't know, I inform myself.

And another thing, Joy says. I don't like your lip.

Change my mind: put it down, take the garbage from dinner into the kitchenette and trash it before going to the drafty bedroom to sift through my books from school. Which should I choose to prove how little I know? Within minutes, I hear the TV turn off.

Must be nice, Joy is saying.

The TV comes back on. Whistles and cheers, funny stuff. A woman screaming: yes, yes!

Thank god for friends, isn't that what you always say? Joy is saying over the racket.

Joy, Mimi says. We better have this out, once and for all.

I walk past the living room and the women – Mimi standing, Joy scrunched into herself on the sofa, the bedclothes picked off the floor and pulled around her now – don't notice me.

I listen from the kitchenette.

He knew, Mimi is saying. He already knew. What was I supposed to do when he confronted me? Lie and tell him the guy was visiting me? *Tanis?* You brought this on yourself, Joy.

I try the door, let myself in to Walker's kitchen. No one there. I pass through the living room, continue up the stairs.

Jena's door is open, and amber light radiates from her room into the hallway. Inside, she's sitting on the floor, surrounded by pillows – her little ceramic heater going full blast – languidly brushing the hair on a large doll. She glances at me, continues her long, loving strokes. There's a half-eaten pint of butter brickle ice cream sitting beside her on the floor, two spoons sticking out of it. On the doll's red mouth, a creamy smear.

Knock-knock, I say.

Jena looks up groggily, flushes – medicated, I think, remembering her bottle of prescription pills. Holding the brush in her hand, she leans backward and balances on her elbows, with her blocky Fred Flintstone feet moves a large pillow over the floor, positioning it on the opposite side of the doll.

She extracts one of the spoons from the ice cream.

You're supposed to say, Who's there? I say, plopping onto the pillow. What's wrong with you anyway?

She holds the spoon out, and I take it from her. The ice cream is a centreless softness, a sweet thick sleeve.

The next weekend Mimi invites Joy to accompany her to a gig in Bradford, and Joy, after some hesitation, goes: friendship teeteringly resumed, apparently. They leave Friday afternoon. The next morning around ten I hear Walker start up his truck and leave as well.

The apartment is cost-cutting arctic. I shower forever, draining the hot water heater. Once dressed, I let myself into the kitchen. Looking out the window, I see his truck is back. The house, though, is quiet. Assuming he's in the barns, I climb the stairs.

In the bathroom, I check the medicine cabinet. No new codeine. No Jena's prescription.

Jena's bedroom door is shut. I rap my knuckles on it. No answer.

Inside: avenue of stuffed toys and dolls, lined up and grinning at me. The deaf white cat asleep on the bed, unaware of my presence.

I plug in the electric heater, rub my cold, dried-out hands together like kindling, then cross the rug to Jena's dresser, open the top drawer: partially clothed Barbies, tube socks, old birthday cards from Walker, signed in his childlike hand. No pills. Then I hear a creaking from down the hall.

The door to Walker's room isn't quite closed. I stand outside and nudge the door wider: he's on his back in bed, long white blue-veined feet hanging off the edge while a naked woman shucks over his bulk in a brisk uh-huh, uh-huh. He's looking up into her face, lifting her droopy breasts with his hands.

He's smiling.

Jena doesn't get back until around noon the next day, Sunday: first a car tears up the drive, only to scream out and onto the road maybe thirty seconds later – mommie dearest, who can't drop her daughter off fast enough. Then Jena's in the kitchen, sobbing: a not-so-unusual aftermath following a forced visit with Lily.

How *convenient* those visits are for Walker, I think, listening from the apartment.

Don't make me, Jena gasps between hiccups.

Walker's voice is a low rumble.

Daddy, she pleads.

Mimi and Joy arrive home late at night. I'm in bed in the bedroom, and don't get up to greet them. Joy retires shortly after they arrive, and I pretend to be asleep.

But I'm awake most of the night, rolled to the edge of the bed, body rigid for fear of touching snoring Joy, grinding my teeth until I think they might shatter.

In the morning – long after Joy's gone to work – I can't get up. Forget school: I have a stomach ache, a headache, an anything to be excused ache.

Around eleven in the morning Mimi comes to the door with a glass of ginger ale. She's barefoot, wearing a white slip, low cut and trimmed with lace. Her pretty face is makeup smudged.

How about some Crazy Eights? she says. For old times' sake, sweetie?

The ache in my stomach hives off into nausea. I turn on my side.

Want to go to a doctor? she says. Is it really bad? I could run you in.

I close my eyes, press my fingertips to my lids. I hear her leave. A minute later she's back.

You ever want to talk, she says. Dot-dot-dot.

I open my eyes, raise my head, twist my neck around toward her so hard it feels sprained. Her mouth is slack with incomprehension. In her femmy lingerie, with her makeup-blurred face, she suddenly seems faintly ridiculous: someone to whom something terrible has happened, someone who's now a victim – only no one's told her yet.

What? she says. Out with it. Are you in some kind of trouble?

My head feels weighted, nightcapped by metal chains linked and woven. I lie with my back to her again, curl my knees to my chest and bury my head in my arms. Shame a muffler around my neck.

She's silent for a few seconds. Then I hear the dry rustle of her slip.

You are weirding me out, she says, lightly scolding as she tries another tack – though underneath the criticism her voice is warm and reassuring. Don't get funny with me, missy. Because funny so does not become you.

I roll over onto my back and struggle to raise myself to a half-sitting position.

I know, I say mournfully.

All I want right now is for this scene to pass.

She gracefully spans over to buss me on the forehead.

I don't always get you, she says. But who cares? I love you anyway.

Green apples and vanilla: for hours – long after I've heard her let herself in to Walker's kitchen – only the memory of her scent salves.

Walker holds out the keys to one of his trucks, asks me to take a circular saw he'd borrowed back to Ray's. We're in the barn. It's three in the afternoon, and the lights are on. I've just finished with the horses for the day.

His face is ruddy from exertion, streaked with white from the cold. Like a side of pink, salty bacon. Obscene.

I back away from him, but the sweaty funk of the horses – his horse – is on me like a contaminant.

Not talking to me any more? he says. And here I was thinking you might like to drive my truck.

I grudgingly take the keys.

You're welcome, he says. Any time. You don't have to thank me or anything.

The saw in the truck already? I say, scowling.

Loaded up and raring to go, he says, reaching into his back jeans pocket and taking out his wallet, pulling a twenty from it. Give him this too. Tell him I said to buy himself something nice.

He extends the bill toward me.

Maybe you should thank *me*, I say.

Give your head a fucking shake! he says – drawing his arm back, dropping the suddenly forgotten twenty on the ground. And while you're at it, get the bug out of your ass. It's not as if I don't know you've been missing school again, and here I am, out of the goodness of my tender heart turning a blind eye.

You're not the only one! I say hotly.

I saw you. Betrayer. Bastard is right.

The only one what? he says.

When I don't respond he covers his face with his hands. After a couple of seconds he massages his prominent forehead with his nicotine-stained fingers and an image comes to me of a wire-thin filament guttering deep inside, haunting him, everything he is a winding away or toward that one element.

Finally he lowers his hands and whistles a soft descending pattern.

Then he says, Don't push your luck, kid.

He rests his hands on his back, and exhales tiredly.

Right, I say, rolling my eyes.

Fuck me, he mutters, and stoops to retrieve the twenty from the dusty ground – then he holds the bill with both hands and snaps it out, looks at it.

Let's just say, if you keep slacking off, he tells me – this time his voice is patient, determined – I will personally see to it that you take a real job.

Along the road – Walker's pickup hogging the pitted route – the tree branches are almost winter-bare, scratching at the harsh November sky. Patsy and Lucinda on the radio, sad guys called Steve. I kill the sound when I get to Ray's, turn onto his mucky dirt drive and park alongside his Quonset hut, lug the saw from the back of the truck and leave it on the patchy grass outside the hut's door.

Farther down the drive squats Ray's cinder-block bungalow, in the dark afternoon a bluish glow coating the sheets of plastic that cover the living-room window, as if concealing a sound stage for an episode of *The Outer Limits*. Ray's wife's station wagon is gone, but his truck is there.

I start toward Ray's house – shallow mud sucking at my workboots, a rubbery sensation in my gimp ankle – pull my lined jean jacket tight against the cold. I'm shivering by the time I ascend the cracked steps to the screen door, where I can see into the plain hallway lined with stuffed trash bags needing to be taken out. Even with the light flickering down the hallway, the place seems abandoned.

I press the buzzer.

Ray appears, moonlit from the TV, wearing only his snug-fitting Jockeys, goosebumps haloed, glaring at me, gripping a large plastic cup with both hands. Not many years younger than Walker – hard to remember, if all you notice about him is the matted grey beard – and considerably shorter, he offsets his dearth of height by his wiry strength: his legs are finely shaped, the sprung arch of the ham taut and firm, the calves delicate as almonds. A bushy spread of dark hair flares like wings from his groin, framing the damp-looking, shadow-bruised rise of his penis visible beneath his Jockeys.

I look long, casually, taking my time to consider Ray in his underwear – the harmless, familiar Ray I've known for years, with his gassy laugh and pert motions, his bulging peepers giving him the aspect of an intelligent Chihuahua straining with every fibre of its pint-sized self to be human. I have no plan of action in mind, I'm as usual not even thinking anything in particular, and the normalcy of this is comforting as mittens – despite the fact Ray is standing before me in his skivvies.

He shifts his welterweight and continues to look at me.

What do you want? he croaks, his voice like something snared in the nest of his beard while the hallway light curls off his head, smooth as an egg where his hair has long-ago vacated the premises.

I consider his question. But as I continue to look back at him I realize I'm not sure he even recognizes me, given the shape he's in, and with my own uncertainty – who am I, anyway, if I'm so insignificant not even Joe-Shmo here gives me a second thought? *nothing?* – a small finger of resentment begins to poke under my collarbone, tentatively at first, then jabbingly until a blush of anger spreads over me, pools in a miasma around my back by my shoulder blades, lifts me over the wall of everything in my life until now, until everything – Walker, the horses, each precious word I have for the few things I know – drops from me like useless pebbles.

Ray leans an arm on the door frame – displaying deodorant-caked underarm hair – loses his balance, spills some of his drink on himself. Alcohol laces the air. He clutches his cup with both hands again. He's stinko, and I can feel the booze heat rising off him.

I brought your saw back, I say. From Walker? I left it outside your hut.

I reach into my pocket and bring out the twenty Walker gave me, tuck it between my fingers and hold it high.

What, he says. He giving me money too? Then hurry it up, before I freeze my bag off.

I lower my hand, slide the money toward him, point it at his crotch. I'm thinking that, odds are, I've got nothing to lose.

So, Ray, I say, in an exaggerated, slo-mo way, a way I hadn't known my voice could sound – deeper, furred with an oddly lilting burr, jokey and suggestive.

Nice, um, package, I say.

Ray stares, working any number of thoughts over in his head. I stare back, trying to smile in what I hope is an attractive way. Finally, brow perspiring, he lifts an arm and points, as if I were slowly coming into focus.

You, he says.

He gives a low chuckle and sways, unsteady on his feet. He drinks from the plastic cup, and a dribble escapes down his chin and into his beard.

Me, he says.

And you can keep the change, I say.

Was this what I had in mind? The suspenseful spell cracking open – Ray in his drawers crashing through the screen door and slopping after me through the mud as far as Walker's truck?

I can't stop running, though: up the freshly graded road, alongside the stubbled fields. By the time I finally slow, and my breath comes easily, I hear the gurgle of an engine, dip into the neighbouring field, and lie down in a still-hard groove of cold-clenched earth, watch headlights go by. The moon plods into the sky. I wait, Frigidaired, until I figure Ray'll be passed out. Then I stand, aching and brittle, brush the dirt from my clothes, and head back to get Walker's Ford.

I'm like a brick, I think, a brick stuck inside my body: already, dismally, myself. Desperate for signs, symptoms of outbreak like hints of spring – the crampy tilt of axis to pole, the gathering speed.

Not even the first snow yet.

5

SCHOOL OF VELOCITY

You stand outside yourself once, twice in your life, look as hard as you can. Like how – on the third of February, Markham, Ontario – I step onto my snowy drive and think, I am not getting any younger. It's now or never, dumbass.

Before I come inside I stamp the snow from my boots, take them off, leave them on the mat inside my kitchen door. Snow puddles. I remove my coat, hang it on the peg. I get a rag from under the sink and mop up.

When I come in the living room, I see she's waiting. So what if the forecast says weather for days? I don't mind. Got nowhere to go right now anyway.

I get on my knees, lift the blanket caving her lap, serve her for all I'm worth. My mind drifts, tireless. When it's her turn – and I'm stretched on my back on the couch – I notice her ears are like ivory, delicately carved, the lobes beginning to crinkle with wear and age. Sexy.

Afterward, I lift her hair, carefully, from her face. Gently pull her up me. Always, lately, this look of ruin. I'm sorry I had a hand in that.

A tiny pink Mimi pops into my head. She looks sad.

Above her, a tiny spotlit violin, a bow sawing away. Bizarre how the mind works sometimes! I know it's not right, but I can't help but hope for tiny Mimi to curtsey, or start singing.

You always surprise me, I say. No getting bored with you.

The cartoon creature in my head disappears as the real Mimi pushes her head deep into my chest. Refuses to speak. Serves me right.

I stroke her back, the back of her beautiful head. I want to tell her some of my plans, how – no matter what I most regret, like a black polished gem sparkling in my gut, a snide winking mesmerizing my eyes open all night, keeping me awake, guilty as charged – they certainly include her.

You are one sexy lady, I say – but she's already asleep, or maybe she's awake and doesn't care to respond.

I wrap my legs around hers. I reach out an arm, pick the blanket off the floor, do my best to smooth it over us on the couch. She refuses to come upstairs, does her snoozing here instead. Has since early November – when I fell off the wagon, first time ever. Just – someone, a chipped-tooth waitress at the Salonika, could have been anyone. Nothing worth a repeat. Proves I don't always know why I do what I do. Air between the ears.

Mimi and Joy were away for the weekend, trying to patch things up with each other – and with Jena at her mom's, and the kid in the apartment with her books, locked in her own world as usual – there was no reason for Mimi to ever find out. Except that it made me love her harder – how she caught me.

What was *that*? she said, the very next time, right after we did it.

Trying to keep up with you, my sweet, I said – still feeling pretty frisky.

My *sweet*? she said, bristling. That doesn't exactly sound like *you*.

She sat up in bed, narrowed her eyes.

There something you want to get off your chest? she said.

In a way I did want to tell her. Bring her into my feelings in a way she often complains I don't. But I knew she wouldn't want *these* details. (What was her name, anyway? Eleanor? Margaret? Florette?)

Yeah, I groaned, exhaling thickly at the memory – then I caught myself, too late.

Walker? Mimi said, and did she sound cold.

I sat up too, rammed a pillow behind my back. I clasped my hands together.

She looked like she couldn't believe what she was thinking, and fear scurried across her face, which suddenly sagged with age. She looked sick. Then she looked okay. Which sure as hell wasn't how I felt.

You have to take everything apart and destroy, she said flatly.

We sat side by side. No tears. No coming at me tooth and nail, as she would have over the slightest thing with Lily – this was more like the Mimi who's gotten off the phone with her mom, or her mom's doctor. Moody Mimi – my pet name – a shell made of skin, sitting motionless on the couch.

I'd try to reach her – work my way in – as tenderly as I could. That was the only good thing about her being that way. How I'd work free the twist of rust-red hair caught in her mouth, trace a finger over her lips as gently as you would to wake the dead – figuring you had to be careful not to scare them with suddenly being alive again. Mimi varnished with darkness, a dull sheen rising off her, a reflection caused by the glass of my rye gleaming in her hand. I'd seen that darkness in the months my mother was dying. The good thing was this reaching each other in this sad place.

But this time it was my fault – I was the one who set Mimi

off. Like I keep thinking, guilty as charged! Sitting in bed next to her – seeing her quiet, the stuffing knocked out of her – I felt helpless. How I felt when Mumma passed.

Wasn't until we heard Jena's footsteps coming upstairs that Mimi jerked to life on her own – yanked the blanket off the bed with her, wrapped it over her shoulders. She grabbed her clothes in one hand, juggled them and the blanket as she opened the door and raced into the hall and started down the stairs.

God, Jena! she shouted. *Move* it.

I heard Mimi tool across the living-room floor, into the kitchen, through the door into the apartment – and then the soft whumping sound of Jena as she slowly resumed climbing the stairs. She reached the top. Then her footsteps stopped for a minute – did she just evaporate?

The floorboards creaked. Took forever for her to reach her bedroom door. I heard the click – knew she was safe.

That was in November.

Now, three months later – the snow continuing on this cold afternoon, pale freckles against the living-room window – I unwrap my legs from Mimi's, press my hand to the button of muscle where her back meets her ass. She loosens into me, mouth on my chest. The tiny points of her sharp teeth, teasing.

I'll wait her out. Eventually her own pride – isn't that all this is, when you really think about it? the same pride that's preventing her from going crying to Joy like she used to, turns out I'm not the only one with nowhere else to go, so to speak – will stop stinging her, and she can give up on being mad, come up the stairs with me again.

I give a big squeeze.

Hey, I say.

Hey yourself, she says, turning her face to the room – whatever kept her hidden seems to be subsiding, she seems to be slowly coming around again.

I decide not to let on what I've got in mind. A million tricks up her sleeve – I don't know where she comes up with such things – but wait until she sees what *I* have in store, this time next year if all goes well. That Florida vacation, for starters.

Everything's going to be fine.

I cup her to me, hollows and curves. I want her to feel what I feel. Is such a thing possible?

See what you do to me? I say.

I close my eyes. She travels. Her mouth on me – there – again. It's like – god.

I know exactly what I'm going to do.

Outside, the snow continues to continue.

I was in a movie once.

Galloped up a hill on horseback, crested along the narrow stone-cropped ridge – fog machines, a real pissing rain – hurtled down the other side. Riding to someone's rescue, never found out whose. Bits and pieces, need-to-know basis only, that's the bizworks, apparently – only one or two lucky snots pull the strings. But I held on through the worst of it, kept it together – that was me in the lead! if just for a moment – and emerged into the clear, knew for the first time that I could be a lucky snot too.

Mumma had died when I was eleven, Joy got fostered out. I remember this little figure being picked up by the armpits and placed in the back seat of a car parked beside our old house – my sister carried away, crying, while I watched through the cracks of my hiding place in the rundown shed. Didn't know it then, but I wouldn't see her for years.

I'd always been clever with animals, and could listen, take orders. So I hung around the old-timey Markham horse geezers, and in return they fed me, gave me a place to sleep (you could do that then, no sheriffs and aid workers to harass you) and five lousy bucks here and there when they were drunk and feeling big-hearted. Orangemen, cheap Protestant bastards. Owned the world, but wouldn't pay me much to shovel their horse crap. They only loved their annual parades, fife and drum, their bloody alcohol tears – yammering for hours late into the night, talking horses while I leaned on my elbows at their kitchen tables, listening, staring at the neat oilcloths, the buttercups and bluebells identical from house to house.

(Now I've got the same in my kitchen. And those hundred-year-old Ontario pine pressbacks we sat in, painted white or red, thought they were junk, now they're worth a fortune – stripped, they go for three hundred apiece to city people who drive up in their Saabs for some weekend *antiquing*. I've got some of those chairs as well.)

By the time I was fourteen – I was already almost six feet tall, with a Chef Boyardee gut spilling over myself – I was tired of the geezers, always talking *at* me, over me, talking to themselves, really. I started thumbing into Toronto.

That was exciting – the crowds, the drugs and drink, the head shops lining the Yonge Street Mall near Dundas Avenue. The mall's gone now but then it was blocked off to traffic, ped only. Ban the man, Peace Now, etcetera – god, I loved those posters! It was all so far fucking out. I didn't care that the pros on Yonge used to mock me.

And when one Saturday night I split a man's skull open with a lead pipe – happened in the alleyway behind the Gasworks tavern where I slept drunk at night beside a dumpster – it *was* self-defence. Only spent a week in the Don Jail's juvie before a judge – little guy, poindexter Hymie type with glasses, big red honker on him – threw the bum rap out, circumstantials, hearsay, no witnesses. Even so, he took it upon himself to get personal.

Let this be a learning experience, he said sternly. A warning if you will. You think you have friends here?

He laughed, shook his head in mild disbelief – like he was surprised at how naive I was. But also like he wanted to believe in me.

Suddenly I wanted to prove I was worthy, that I understood the joke.

Yes sir, I said. You're right, that's a good one.

And I credit the guy, I smartened up – began to take cash jobs at construction sites, at first a couple of days at a time, then regular when I turned sixteen, what with the building market heating up in the 'burbs, and Markham just starting to be one of them too.

Geezers said, Look who's back.

Through them I heard about the movie, which wasn't really a movie – a TV show, kiddie stuff.

Yeah?

They want extras who can ride.

Yeah so?

Hombre! Wanna make a hundred green?

I remember a week of rain. Then three days during which the ground slithered like something alive and barely beaten down beneath the horses' hooves as we tried to sit our animals between scenes. The Rouge River swollen. Clouds scabbed the sky.

To kill time, the extras – mostly older guys – told stories, jokes slippery as a drunk's mouth, like cash earnings pooled from the truckers' runs from Winnipeg west to Vancouver, up to Kamloops, quick back down and east to Montreal, Trois-Rivières, Fredericton, Truro, the two nights' wild crush in Atlantic City to blow it all.

I began to see it clearly. That there was this disease you

could catch – loneliness – a virus spooling silver-black as a road that ends at the altar of a metal bedframe in a rented room at midnight, each creak of the box springs the memory of an air-brake dip and shush, a thirty-third hour on the road hue. Every small town in between nothing but one long night. Brainpan slamming a woman's soft shoulders into a cinder-block wall, *cow you fucking cow*. No turning back, anything could or might as well happen, and no one to care.

Waiting for my cue, keeping my horse quiet, I swore to myself I would make my little pot of gold, that I would find my sister, put back together what had been broken when Mumma died. A sister – there'd be a wife too. Kids. I'd be steady Freddy.

How do you make a hormone? a guy says.

(Swallow. Think, you fat fucker.)

How?

You pull her tit.

(Heh heh.)

That first afternoon a horse shuddered through a muddy ditch, slid over, and broke its rider's back. The rest of us kept going. *Poor asshole.*

Between takes, a guy says, How do you make a hormone?

(Scratch the balls, try to look older. Swallow.)

How's that?

Don't pay her.

Second afternoon. The hero, dog by his side, stands over the vanquished villain.

Hero to villain. *Think you can afford to let me down, then think again.*

I swore so hard to myself I bit my lip, tasted salt, spat blood.

On the third and last day a sky molten with rain. That really *was* me in the lead! Riding to some bullshit rescue over ground smoking with fog, the rest of the cavalry indistinct as wraiths sliding behind me down the mud-swiped hill.

When my own horse begins to fold under me like a card table, I hold his head up, use the reins to balance him on his mouth, squeeze my legs to push us through the worst of the nightmare, continue across the swale, arc up the other side, the hills in this area rising and rolling like waves as rain turns to silver-needled light and thunder masses – a school of velocity.

It's like I was writ large, for all the world – myself included – to see.

I hold on to Mimi, still the rocking. She creepy-crawls herself around and back up me until we're face to face, and then some.

Bastard, she breathes into my mouth, all her sorrows and fears floating out. See what you do to *me*?

No matter what happens, I won't let her go – it's like the future's here. Almost here. I've got its hot ticket in my head.

Don't know how long we've been asleep. Suddenly Jena's home, I hear her in the kitchen. I should get up, ask her how school was, make her a snack – at twelve she's so young still – all the things I imagine my own mumma might have done had she lived. (Though I did wait until Joy, like me, had a young daughter to support – and I'm the one who introduced Joy to the guy who put the loaf in the oven! – before I really stood up for her.)

Jena comes to the door, looks into the living room. Our eyes meet, even in the dim winter afternoon light. But Mimi's teeth are on me again, and she clings tighter. Jena soundlessly continues by, climbs the stairs. I hear her shut the door to her room.

I nest my face into Mimi's neck.

Then I lift my head. Carefully I press my thumb to her thin line of collarbone.

Bitch, I say. Look what you've done to me now.

I raise my hand. A red thumbprint marks her white skin. She's still open beneath me, mouth and limbs loose and warm, nipples wide plates. I match my thumb to the same spot. This time, I press harder.

Daffodils, Mimi says. *Jonquils.*

I know what they are, I say.

It's nearly April. Her face is swollen, drowsy-looking, like she's just woken from a long sleep. She's brushed her hair nice and put on some lipstick. Took my good scissors out to the flowerbed in front of my place and snipped herself a bouquet. The stalks bleed green onto my kitchen table.

Bring them in to her, she says, nodding at the closed door to Joy's apartment.

Been a winter of spite with *that* woman. She's still so frosted by my thankless efforts to keep her from harmful men that she doesn't seem to notice the roof over her head – the one *I* put there for her!

Me? I say, suddenly annoyed with Mimi. You're the one who always wants to make up.

All this time spent nursing my girlfriend – walking on eggshells for her sake – and she finally comes to her senses and all she can think to do is disturb my peace and quiet? Like I'm going to stand, bouquet in hand, while Joy froths at the mouth in my direction some more? Fuck me.

Mimi picks up the flowers one by one, makes a show of admiring them.

It's not quite noon. I pound another slug of rye into my coffee. Been hitting it hard lately. Why not? I'll dry up once the weather improves. Outside is mud. The mud season. I haven't turned the horses out all week. Spring – who needs it? Jena's upstairs in bed, sick with a cold.

I lift the mug to my mouth. The rye is rich and sinful in the coffee, makes it taste like a sweet dark cake. Devil's food. I take several swallows as Mimi tickles the flowers, their dainty teacup faces, childlike.

I know somebody else who might like those, I say.

Mimi shudders.

Wouldn't hurt you, you know, I grouse – though that's how I feel, cut to the quick. You could try being nice to Jena for a change.

Mimi's lips are flattened into a fake-looking smile. Does she think that's going to keep me wanting to settle down with her? Help wash away my doubts as to her being a good – or even less than outright evil – stepmom to my daughter? Sometimes Mimi's not too bright.

Could even help your case, I say, reaching again for the bottle.

Case, she says, her eyes gone glassy.

Yeah, I say, letting go of the bottle, warming to my theme. Your *situation*. If you were smart –

She stalks to the trash can by the kitchen sink, opens it with one hand, thrusts in her florist's special. Then she takes a glass from the cupboard above the sink, comes over to the table and pours a stiff one, knocks it down neat, standing so her hips are inches from my face and I can smell her, in the place where her jeans make a tight triangle. Back of her hand on her mouth, like a stevedore. A tough cookie. Fuck you. Fuck *this*. Isn't that what she's telling me?

Tanis squints against me in the May sunshine. Her shuttered face.

You got nothing else to do, you come with me, I say, standing my ground.

What do you need me for? she says, looking toward the barn, chucking the heel of a boot against the toe of the other.

I don't *need* you, I say. Don't really want you, either. Guess I'm stuck with you, though, since you don't seem to be too interested in school any more.

Thinks she has me wrapped around her little finger. A free pass on life. I can see it in the way she leans, hands in her pockets, against Mimi's car, the sun on her face. Like she's got all the time in the world. Like nothing matters.

Seems like you're not interested in working, either, I say.

That's not true, she says. The part about working.

Better not be, I say, opening the door to my truck. Consider yourself warned. If you're not going to school, then you should get yourself a real job. And keep on with the horses.

I've let her off the hook too often. Worried about her for months, didn't want to put the pressure on – she got enough of that from Joy through the winter, cooped up inside together like that, it's not right. Joy mean, always thinking the world's against her. For a long time I could excuse the meanness, understand it. But her own kid's almost grown! No excuses now.

None for Tanis, either – if she thinks I'll let her coast through the rest of her life, she's got another think coming. Besides – she doesn't know because I haven't told her yet – I'm about to go pick up the goddamned excavator! Finally, get a start on my new arena. Maybe she'll be impressed by the old uncle, for a change. Surprised. Inspired, even, by the example I'm getting ready to set. So though I do need her to help me with the truck today – drive it back from Ray's for me – I also believe I'm in the end helping her as well.

Won't Mimi be surprised too? Help her get over unfortunate recent events. There'll be that Florida vacation, sure – with a nice rock on her finger. Why not? Bells on her fucking toes, if that's what she wants.

I slam the door shut. Tanis glares for a few seconds at the sign on the truck door, then comes around to the passenger side, puts both hands on the top of the window frame, sticks her head between her raised arms and looks in, scowling.

If only you could see my good intentions, I say.

She brings her eyebrows together.

Take a pill! she exclaims, real snotty. I'm coming. So you can spare me the barf.

You want to get lippy? I ask.

She lowers her hands, clasps them together, and rests them on the lower part of the window frame. Raises her eyes, very angelic-looking.

Nice halo, I tell her. Looks good on you. Maybe you should try keeping it there.

Once we're on the road I notice it really is a pleasant day. Balmy almost, spindrifts of colour from the forsythias in front of people's houses. The trees are budding, and some have started to leaf out.

Anything new on the dance card? I say to Tanis, trying to make conversation.

It's a question I used to ask Joy in the earliest days of our reacquaintance. She was working at a dry cleaners, laundering men's dress shirts, fancy lady dresses. I'd pick her up when her shift was over – that chemical smell stepping into my truck. I'd toss a bag of toffee, tied closed with a ribbon, onto the seat between us, put the truck in gear. She was shy – we were, together – and she never let on about the years in foster care, neither a yea or a nay out of her if you asked were they good or bad.

So I'd ask instead about her day-to-day life. She'd untie the ribbon from the bag, wrap it around a finger, pluck out a candy and put it in her mouth, tell me about Tilda, or Mary – women who starched collars for a living, alongside Joy – as she rolled the words around the sugary chew. Savouring it all, I thought – the toffee, the having tales of friendship to relate, having me there to listen. Not wanting it to end – she'd still be sucking on that same piece by the time I dropped her back at her place! Which happened to be a one-room apartment above a laundromat.

I used to tease her, tell her she should marry a Mr. Clean.

That apartment was Tanis's first home.

A quick glance, and I see the kid's eyes are closed. Her face is pimpled, and she's packed the weight on over the winter. Hair stringy-looking. She turns her head to the window.

No longer on speaking terms? I say to draw her out.

I'm here, she says through clenched teeth. What more do you want?

I ease up on the gas. What *I* want? Suddenly I feel like something's hoovered the air out of me – I felt the same way when, after a month of driving Joy around once a week, one day she announced she'd never liked toffee.

Why'd you keep eating it? I said accusingly.

What choice did I have? she answered – made it sound as if I'd wronged her, like *I* was the reason she'd never gotten what she wanted.

I remember it had been a hot afternoon. I'd started roofing at five in the morning, finished by eleven when the heat was turning my brain to cinders and the danger of stroking out was for real. Even so, I'd gone straight and had my truck washed. Then a close haircut, my scalp sweating against the chill of the barber's scissors.

When I picked her up I was wearing a new shirt. I could feel its sharp creases against my sides, from where it had been folded in its plastic wrapper. The scratchy material itching my skin all over. When she told me, I hardly knew what else to say – couldn't think my way around her logic. In desperation I felt like tearing that shirt from my back, throwing it out the truck window. Putting the little sister out by the side of the road like an unwanted mutt and never seeing her again.

I'd been overreacting – realized it within seconds. There was almond bark, wasn't there? Double-salted licorice. Options, right?

Like I always say to the kid.

In my truck now with Tanis, still fighting for my breath, I touch my foot to the brake.

The problem is, a part of me feels sorry for that young guy driving around with his sister, trying to fill himself and others with hope – only to feel duped in those first few seconds when his good deeds, misunderstood, tumbleweed to bad – hating himself that he was so unsuspecting of how things can turn out. Maybe wondering why he never jumped off the damn building when he had the chance! Part of me is still him.

While I'm thinking like this, driving slowly, a white beamer passes us going the opposite direction, taking up more than its share of the road, almost forcing me into the ditch. I start breathing again, hard – feel like whipping around and following the guy, putting the scare on him. Bumper to fucking bumper, all the way into the city – but then we're already at Ray's, and I turn in, nose down his long drive, past the Quonset hut to the front of his bungalow, where I park and get out.

I'm almost at the side door to Ray's house when I realize Tanis is still in the truck – just as Renata opens up only to disappear back inside, no hi or anything. I try to get the kid's attention – raise my hand in the air, thumb jerking toward the house – but she screws up her face at me, mouths something, then looks the other way. I march back toward the truck, don't have to go too far before she gets out.

What am I supposed to do with her? Buy her toffee – how about a deck of playing cards, like I did for her mother, once? (If I remember correctly, I bought the cards around the time Tanis was born.) Or should I knock her into the middle of next week, hope she's a better person for it?

Get your ass in there, I say.

Fortunately for us both, she does – following several paces behind me until we're in the hall, where she slumps, hands in her pockets.

Hey guy, I call out.

In here, Ray calls from the living room down the hall.

Before I head that way, I poke my head into the kitchen, which is compact and orderly-looking. Renata stands inside with her back to me. Renata takes up a lot of the room.

What's this? I say to her. No peameal bacon and farm-fresh eggs, no homemade waffles with maple syrup tapped from your own trees, steel-cut oatmeal with handpicked huckleberries, ryebread toast dripping just-churned butter?

She turns and glares in my direction – not that a little thing like that's going to stop me!

Not to mention your healthful apple butter, I continue, grinning. Also, your pear butter, rich-in-unsaturates cashew butter, and your live-action yogurt cultures. Heard all about it on TV, make you live forever.

She's wearing a long bathrobe, frayed at the sleeves and hem, that barely covers her. I try not to look – the dragging breasts, the untidy threads of light-brown hair, like a mouse's nest, below the soft hill of belly. Topside, her hair hangs down, unbraided, unbrushed. I hear a noise – like a closet door opening and shutting, and boxes being moved around, and a man's voice, which surprises me at first until I remember –

coming from one of the bedrooms up the hall. Must be the son, talking to people who live in his head.

A joke, I say sheepishly – how could I have forgotten that Renata's never been particularly fond of me?

She turns back around, grabs two plain white mugs out of a cupboard and puts them on the counter, then pours coffee into them from a Black & Decker coffee maker. She takes out a carton of half-and-half and a bowl of sugar from the fridge, puts those beside the coffees. Every couple of seconds I hear the son jawing away.

You can help yourself, she says. Spoons in the dish rack.

She's never been much of a charmer. Kind of rude, in fact. I don't know what *I* ever did to her. Nothing! Nothing a good stiff you-know-what wouldn't fix.

Where's my country breakfast, woman? I say – giving it one last go at making her day. I've got an appetite, Renata. I mean in case you haven't noticed. Appetite for life!

Hardy har har, Renata says, vanishing into the bathroom off the kitchen – for a large woman she moves fast.

Use a coaster with those, she yells from behind the closed door.

I carry the mugs past Tanis, past the two bedrooms, and into the living room, careful not to spill. Ray's standing in front of the brown tweed couch, gazing at the ceiling. I stick my head back into the hall where Tanis still stands glowering. I make a face, and she reluctantly comes to the doorway. Ray sits on his couch, legs spread wide.

Some things I'll never understand, he says to me – he doesn't seem to have noticed the kid's presence.

Aw, get out of town, I say to him, turning away to pass Tanis her coffee – burning my fingers before she agrees to take the mug from me. And here I thought you knew everything.

I face Ray again. He's swinging his legs open and shut, making a thwucking noise with them.

What I don't understand is, why the hell you would want it, he says, face reddening. Especially since it's me who'll end up with the better part of the deal. I mean, I hate crowing about it, but.

Two hundred, seventy-five smackers, I say grandly. Don't I know it.

Abruptly, he jumps up from the couch, walks over to a low wood-veneer shelf behind the TV and crouches down, his back to me.

Let me be honest and tell it to you straight, you might be sorry, he says – rummaging around roughly, slapping pamphlets and stapled-together books on the floor to both sides of him, clearly irritated, as if I've just one-upped him.

I can see this might take a while, what with Ray having to be Ray.

Why are you taking this as if it's personal? I ask, exasperated.

He just stands dumbly, holding the machine's huge manual.

There's the problem right there, buddy, he says. It *is* personal. You should have listened to me all these years. I told you, no point in trying to get ahead. Tax dude'll only scam you for it. Well. I guess I'll just have to keep reminding myself it's *your* problem.

Yeah, I say. And your problem is, I'm buying you out.

Is that right? he says. I guess that's one way of looking at it.

He extends his arms, pointing the manual at me.

Another is, he says. That you might be buying this wreck of a machine from me, but you sure as shit won't know how to run it without this.

Then he calls over to Tanis, who's still standing in the doorway, speaking to her for the first time today.

Here's a nice long beddy-bye story, he says, his eyes strolling over her. You and me could read it together sometime.

At first, I'm not sure I heard him right. But I guess I did, judging by the way Tanis lowers her head and glares at him like a bull about to charge – I half-expect to see steam coming out of her ears, which strikes me as so funny it takes me several seconds to react the way I should.

Ray, I growl.

No offence intended, Walker, he says – smirking as he casts his gaze back at the manual. Besides, it's time to quit dicking around and get serious.

He turns to the first page of the manual and reads aloud.

To the men, he says, who are responsible for the operation, care, and maintenance of Bucyrus Erie excavators.

He flips through the book, shaking his head gravely.

Don't think you won't need my help, he says. Above and beyond me driving it back to your place with you. Because this here's what you're getting yourself in for.

Boom-sway braces, he says. Keep them tight. Lubricate the boom hoist. Here's some stuff about suspension cables.

He looks lost. He turns back to the first page and seems to get his bearings again.

To the men who are responsible, he repeats.

I'm not scared, *Ray*, I tell him.

Just because you can buy me out doesn't mean you're better than me, he says, his eyes searching mine.

Still holding his gaze, I down my coffee, scorching my mouth – but damn if I'm going to let on.

Then I take Tanis's coffee from her and bring the mugs past the bedrooms and into the kitchen.

No sign of Renata. I rinse the mugs and put them in the dish rack to dry. On second thought I pull the spotless blue-striped dishtowel from the fridge door and wipe the mugs before replacing them in the cupboard. I can hear Ray in the hall, putting on his jacket and boots – the side door opening and closing as he leaves the house.

Now Tanis is in the hall again.

Where's the manual? I say, poking my head out of the kitchen, speaking in a hushed voice.

A loud No! sounds from a bedroom.

Thomas, Renata says crossly – Thomas! I think, surprised, only now realizing I never knew the son's name.

I put a finger to my lips. Silence.

He put it back on the shelf, Tanis says.

Get it, I whisper. And keep your fucking voice down. Christ.

Get it yourself! she whispers back loudly, really indignant. I'm only here because you forced me to come. This is –

The bedroom door opens and Renata emerges. Again, not a word of greeting. She proceeds into the living room.

If that's how Ray and Renata want it.

Ray sits hunched beside me in the excavator's cab, giving instructions, tugging his beard, fingering the coarse fur that grows around his neck – hygiene has never been his selling point – and he's jabbering a mile a minute but the Erie's click-clack-ricking along the road swallows his words. Tanis follows us in my truck.

What had Ray been trying to pull, talking to her the way he had, looking her over like she was someone else, someone I'd never seen before? A way to get at me. Something that occurred to him out of the blue. Or something more?

Once again I'm finding it hard to breathe, the pressure's rising in my head – plus it's hot for early May, rumour of corn and sweet peas, summer flat on the heels of spring. *Summer.* After a while the Erie's pendulous gait eases my mind.

But by evening, the excavator is wedged between the dark-blue sky and the even darker earth and Ray is still clapping the jaws. Still not making sense.

You want those cat belts loose, he's saying. But not loose enough to let the lugs on the driving tumbler jump. You pour the waste oil from the engine crankcase on the track-link pins. You follow?

Maybe he's never really made sense, and I've just blindly jerked around after him all these years, trusting him, thinking, What a smart guy! And can he read! It's like I thought if I hung around him long enough, I could too – at least, I could come to know what he knows.

But I see now that maybe I've had it ass backward – the truth is, I've been carrying him. Letting him weigh me down.

Like last fall. We were at Mike Martin's fortieth birthday party, the weekend after Labour Day. Even before we got there, I could sense Ray would be a liability.

A cabinetmaker in Port Perry, Mike gets me word-of-mouth roof-repair jobs sometimes, so it made business sense for Ray and me to go to the party. But what has Ray ever cared about business? He was no-way-Jose for weeks leading up to the big event. That very night I had to stand in his hallway for twenty minutes as he changed his jeans twice, combed and recombed the buggy hair wigging his head, untangled the egg yolk strung in his beard, brushed the dried yellow out, shouted down Renata for not ironing his favourite shirt. I could hear his son, locked up in the room down the hall, shouting back – Loud! he said, Too loud! – and Renata trying to shush him. Ray put the shirt on anyway, and it *was* pretty wrinkled.

Finally he squared his shoulders – really he didn't look so bad – and shrugged on a light-brown jacket, shiny at the elbows and pockets, that looked vaguely familiar. When he opened his front door he stepped back to let me go first.

Oh, after you, I insist! he said mockingly – like we were each other's dates. How romantic. Just you and me and the night.

The party was at the Scugog community centre, just outside Port Perry. About a twenty-minute drive in not much traffic. When we got there, the parking lot was packed, people lingering outside, smoking and talking, drinking from plastic cups, checking beneath each other's van hoods, slapping each other on the back. Inside the centre, a wall of noise from these four-foot-high loudspeakers. Long lineups for the food table. More people crowded together in complicated-looking knots on the dance floor. Ray squeezed ahead of me, heading for the beer. I saw Mike in the middle of the room, occupied – his arm crooked tightly around the neck of a young blonde in high heels and a short skirt, his new wife (he'd divorced the old one only last year).

I decided to wait until Mike wasn't so busy to talk to him, and ducked outside to join the smokers. Though it was still early, a woman I recognized from the Port Perry gas station (she worked the cash) was kneeling down, tossing her cookies behind the neatly trimmed and Weed-Whacked cedar hedge as people milled about, not noticing her puking as if her very life depended on it – which it maybe did, some around here do occasionally bite the big one through acute alcohol poisoning.

So I kept an eye on her – nicely, without being obvious, because sometimes you have to consider basic human dignity – as if I had a job to attend to, knew what to do while others leaned against their Jimmys and Broncos and Windstars talking about insurance and new kitchen cabinets and their kids' biology grades. Eventually she staggered to her feet, brushed herself off, and I went inside to get a beer, see how Ray was doing.

He was on the far side of the hall, twisted around in his seat at an empty table, head cocked to one side, arms crossed, eagle-eyeing the deejay, rotating his head to take in the crowd

– *gutless, spineless sheep*, I could almost hear him thinking, an accusation he'd on occasion level at me, *belonging to the old live and let live, the why can't we all get along school, the reason we're all in such trouble these days* – as usual appearing to be impressed with his own curiosity, interested only in those things for which he might be able to form a showy opinion.

Though I'd have preferred some of the hard stuff, I got myself a beer from one of the twenty-gallon ice buckets on the floor – all that was offered, that and a sticky-looking punch – and drank some of it. On the dance floor, a boy, maybe five or six, was arm in arm with what looked like his grandmother. There were couples glued together, swaying and necking even though the music was fast and loud, the women in short dresses, guys in white pants. No one fighting. I tried to see how the deejay cued up the songs but couldn't. And the noise! Not something you'd hear everyday – not this out-of-it codger, at least. I was hoping this putting in an appearance wouldn't have to take too much longer.

I looked across the room again for Ray, just as Mike Martin was passing him.

Put in a word, Ray! I thought, a hungry pang in the old gut. Here's your chance – our chance. Do it. That's what we're here for. Then we can get the fuck out of Dodge. For a second there was a roaring in my ears.

Then my hope sank. Pinned as I was on the opposite side of the hall, powerless to move, facing the ugly truth of the situation – this was Ray over there, after all. *Ray*. Nothing more nor less. And here I'd been foolishly – idiot! – hoping for more.

Christ. We should have come wearing the same T-shirt, like you see couples who've been married too long wear sometimes. Something like the words *I'm with Stupid* written on them.

And then it all unfolded as I knew it would – like I was

watching a dream I'd had countless times before, a dream of a dream. A nightmare you only remember having when you're dreaming.

Mike glanced at Ray for a second. Ray's mouth fell open into a smile, and he uncrossed his arms, sat up straight, and stuck his hand forward. Mike made a left turn and went straight to the next table that was full of people, who immediately broke into a round of "Happy Birthday." Then Mike moved on to the next table, high-fives all around.

Ray frowned and sank low in his seat, legs stuck in front of him, crossed at the ankle, and folded his arms over his chest. He looked untouchable.

I was surrounded by people, yet suddenly I felt set apart from every living soul.

At least Ray has his opinions to keep himself company.

I made my way across the floor. When I got to Ray I came around behind him, put a hand on the back of his chair. Jeez – I think I dripped some water on him from my wet beer bottle. He flinched, said something I couldn't make out.

I bent over him, coned a hand to my ear.

I said *knob*, he said. Fuck off.

I patted him on the shoulder – there, there. Like, little guy.

I finished my beer and put the bottle down on the table. He picked it up, put it down, two wet rings when he picked it up a second time. He was jiggling his legs. I leaned over him again, put my mouth right up to his ear.

You see Mike? I said.

Yeah, he said. Talking up a storm. I don't think he saw me.

Mike – with his neatly swept hair and blond beard, his big blue eyes – was working the other side of the room now, like a big-dick politician. Women hugging him, guys slapping him on the back. They were all laughing. We'd never get Mike's attention now.

He saw you, I said.

What? Ray said.

We stayed where we were for a while longer while Mike – a regular guy, upstanding in the community – pressed the flesh. When I built my new arena, maybe he'd think to send his young wife there to ride, her and her glossy in-crowd friends. Word would get around – smell of success.

What would I need Ray for? I wondered that night. No one wanted to be around him. He'd only hold me back.

Now, eight months later – the Erie finally in my backyard, the sky overhead a gash of rose against cinder, barn swallows chicking above us, a few crickets calling out and me hating this time of day, of day-night, the lonely feel to the sooted fields, my thoughts puddling with all I can't understand (the kid not around to help me out) – Ray's digging in his heels. Trying to keep me from succeeding – mixing me up.

Hope you don't find you bought a lemon, Ray says, right after he's told me about the crankcase and fucknot – the thousand things that can go wrong. That sure was a lot of money to spend on something that might never work. Though I guess maybe it's just a lot for me, and only a drop in the bucket for a soon to be bigwig. Don't think I'm not on to you. Social climber! One day you'll be too good for old Ray, huh? You and the Mike Martins of the world.

Was that a sob he choked back?

Doesn't matter – I'm so frosted that my thoughts begin to slick up like ice. Other thoughts – cloaked shapes – skate across it.

Jealous? I goad.

He starts scraping embers of rust from an upside-down steel barrel with his pocket knife.

Not to change the subject, he says, his voice shaky with

what seems like barely controlled emotion. But a word to the wise. Your *niece* –

Inside my head, now, a crackling.

He stops scraping at the barrel. He fingers the blade, seeming to regain his composure, then folds it back into itself, slips it into the leather holster he wears on his belt.

He clears his throat like he's some kind of actor.

Whoo! he says, and whistles.

I have to concentrate – again stand outside myself – to figure what's happening to me – the ice in my head crackles, a high-pitched drone, electrical.

Was that your best shot? I say – to my ears the words ring like a bell in the twilight, bright and metal-sharp with menace.

He cringes, backs away.

We're done, he says quickly. Righty-o.

Except for the manual! I call out to the scarecrow retreating fast behind my barns.

The very next morning Ray ponies up what I want. Renata drives him over in the station wagon and when I come out of the house to meet him she stays behind the wheel, not even a wave of the hand from her. Ray springs from the car, leaving the door open.

Good fucking luck, he says, almost banging the book at me. Think you'll be on top of the world soon! We'll see how you make out without me. How the mighty shall fall!

He turns his back fast.

See you, I say.

Bye-bye, he says, biting off the words. Have a good one.

Bah-bahhh, I go, fucking sheep that I am – because what I really want to do is hammer him one. Bahh!

Like I'm out of my mind. And maybe I am, I think, my courage shrinking as Renata and Ray take off – and I lug the manual fat as an overstuffed suitcase inside, get it onto my kitchen table, and turn to page one.

A couple of hours later, I'm ready to admit it – in the scour of May sunshine, the backhoe slagged on the ground and every bit of dirt and rust amazingly visible – the machine does look like less than the sum of me and my big ideas.

Do *you* think I'm crazy? I say.

Mimi narrows her eyes, which is never a good sign. Didn't get back until all hours last night from a weekend gig. I can see by her pale cheeks that she's tired. She slips a band from her wrist, reaches into her hair and ropes it.

It was supposed to be a surprise, I say lamely, wishing she could at least try to muster some enthusiasm.

Oh, she says. Really. And here I thought you'd think better than to try to surprise me any more.

Everything inside me – my plan – turns to dust.

I'm not always out to get you, I say angrily. I don't wake every morning and think, How can I fuck her up today? There's no *conspiracy* against you. In fact, sometimes I don't think about you at all.

That has never been more evident, she says, all queenly.

Nothing I do ever makes you happy, I say – spouting off, though I know it's the same complaint I have about certain others who at the moment shall remain nameless. When here I'm trying to expand my business, make some money. Money for us! And you think I'm sneaking around behind your back. With this machine? Kind of hard to do, wouldn't you think? Ridiculous! It's like you never trust me.

Trust *you*? she says.

Here we go again! I say – like I'm helpless to say. It was nothing, *she* was nothing! Why do you have to get so bent out of shape? Why do you hold on to things? You and your sorrows. Your *unrelenting* fucking sorrows.

And yours, she says, after a pause. Truly, Walker.

I feel as if she's reached inside my chest with one of her cool hands, cupped her long white fingers to my heart. Weirdly, this calms me.

Then she starts tossing her hair back and forth behind her, shoulder to shoulder.

Crazy? she scoffs, repeating my original question. I'll say. Do you even know how to run this thing? Do you think you can figure it out? That sexpot you chose to get up close and personal with must have pussy-whipped your brain to pablum.

The potty mouth on her these days! Worse than the one on the Mimi of old.

A hell-hole racket – like a swarm of locusts – starts up now in my chest. I can't feel her inside me any more. I feel afraid. After a couple of seconds, less so.

If only there were two of each of us, on two sets of tracks sliding along. We could step out of who we've become, step over to this other set. Just decide to do it, at the same time – that's what it would take. Just – close our eyes, hold our breath, reach out before somebody shows up to force our hand, and we never get the chance again.

6

THE MOON IN JUNE

I get it together, get a job. One May weekend, Mimi drives me to a nursery in Markham – fifteen minutes door to door – where I'm hired on the spot. For the next two days – without break from eight to four – I slog bags of cedar chips into the backs of Range Rovers and Lincoln Navigators, spritz banked flats of impatiens and geraniums, tend to potted-topiary doves, bunnies, and Barneys, bare-root roses, burlap-wrapped yews. Then I loiter around the parking lot until Mimi shows again, hand rammed down the throat of the Monte Carlo's horn, honking her head off.

On the afternoon of my third day of employment, the Monte Carlo's trumpet blast announces a wordless Mimi gnawing her chipped-polish fingernails, hostage to a ripper mood as she slams the car's drive into reverse and scrams out of the lot, rat-a-tatting the jumbo rust-bucket east along the pine-bordered dirt roads back to Walker's.

Before we arrive, I hear it: a raw, grinding noise. We get closer, rumbling half-unmufflered into his drive, and I realize the sound is coming from behind the arena. The horses in the front paddock skitter post to post along the fenceline. Mimi parks the car in front of the barn. We sit, the motor running – I'm not sure why – while the excavator roars in the distance.

What *is* that? I say, just to be saying something – I know full well what's making the noise.

Mimi cuts the engine and opens her door. I feel some relief, as if jittery molecules are being dispersed on the damp spring air. But the atmosphere zithers again when, instead of getting out of the car, she sinks back into her seat, lightly and quickly feather-dusts her porcelain thighs with her fingertips – her summery pink skort hiked little-girl innocently around her hips, her feet half out of her two-inch-heeled white sandals. Her knees are shiny doll-cheeks, lavender scented from skin lotion. Beside her, I feel like a sack of iron bowling balls. Loaded with material that could strike her dead.

She puts her hands to her flushed face, says, Oh my.

I try to think. All week, starting with the arrival of the machine from Ray's, she's been alternately morose and rambunctious – scant minutes ago, furious. She turns to me now, caps my shoulders with her hands, pulls me to her, drawing our heads together.

I'm so happy I could kiss you, she says.

Her breath smells like peppermint and ginger. *Happy?* I can't read her, period.

I'm so happy it's killing me, she says.

She grabs a fistful of my hair and tugs playfully.

Don't worry, she informs me. I'll survive!

She flounces from the car and fanny-checks the door shut, high heels it to the house. I get out, stand for a moment before going toward the bombast behind the barns.

Out back is still in shambles from winter's assault: the ring is a mud-curdled pit stippled with paint-peeling rails in desperate need of patching up. Thirty feet away, the half-dozen apple trees' once-festive blooms look like tattered paper party lanterns tawdry with morning-after afterglow. Torn plastic grocery bags, shreds of Kleenex and paper towel collect at the trees' bases. Jena kneels, rapt, on the ground in front of them. Joy stands several feet away, gawking.

Behold: the dance of the mechanical mastodon, grotesque reminder of every battered, lurching monstrosity ever to grace a carnival midway. The claw crabs at the ground, tears skyward with a snootful of earth. Walker – big little boy racing a dime-store horse – is in the cab.

Auntie Joy! Jena screams above the ear-splitting noise, face peaked with excitement. Don't you like it?

Quit asking me! Joy replies.

As far as I know, this is the first Walker's been able to get the junk heap running. Too bad. Now he can get started on his quagmire, which is what'll result when he gets partway through building the new arena and the old machine breaks down, and he ties himself up in other matters, and never finishes. Nothing holds his attention for long – not a single one of us.

It doesn't matter what *I* like! Joy elaborates.

The top of the machine – cab, arm, shovel – swivels above its treads. The shovel tips and unloads. Walker bows out of the cab.

Un-fucking-believable! he shouts.

Un-fucking-believable, Jena repeats slowly and loudly as she rises to her feet.

Jena, Joy warns.

When I get up for work the next morning – Joy's already left – there's no sign of Mimi in the apartment.

She's not in Walker's kitchen, either, which I see when I let myself in – though Walker is, sitting at his table, truck keys by his left hand, coffee cup to his right. He pushes out from the table and draws himself up full height, shoulders back, the warm dung-odour of Camels on him, though there's no sign he's started in with the first of his daily sixty-some-odd smokes yet.

He cocks his head to one side and cups his hand to his ear.

I'm waiting, he says. Let's hear it.

Impressive, I say. You really seemed to be getting the swing of it.

He flags his hand, imperious: more, more.

I try to smile. He has what I need right now: a way to get to work.

Nice going, I concede. Mimi seemed pretty happy about it too.

He's beaming now.

But was the engine supposed to sound like that? I say. Maybe it needs a tune-up.

It's fine, he mumbles, crestfallen. Fine.

Wouldn't that be kind of expensive? I goad. To get it fixed? I wonder how much.

He takes a pack of cigarettes from his shirt pocket, sighs, picks up the keys from the table.

Kiddo, he says. Whatever you do, don't fucking ask.

Oh, I don't *have* to ask, I rejoin.

He regards me silently for several seconds. I worry I've blown my ride, hear Joy's withering voice in my head. *Cut your nose off to spite your face, did you?*

I *sure* as hell don't know what I ever did to *you*, he drawls, finally. Been no living with you for months.

I study the toes of his scuffed boots, the uneven pine-planked floor. When I dare to glance at him again he's squinting. He looks like he's forgotten something, and is trying to remember. He opens his mouth, closes it several times, like a fish in a bowl.

You want a fucking ride or not? he says.

His face reddens as he struggles for air. I imagine a tiny silver minnow darting frantically inside him, pecking at his stomach lining, nibbling at his lungs and heart, flashing like a blade, causing the pulse to leap in his thick neck, as it does now. Taking his breath away.

Everything about him that once seemed so large – his big-gutted presence, big-smoker habit, his love of a woman like Mimi that had seemed overscaled, even his gathering up of Joy and myself – seems suddenly reduced, turned inside out.

A shock: something *I* did – touched that charged nerve within.

I'm thirsty. My mouth tastes like smoke. How could he let this happen to himself?

After work, four on the dot in the afternoon, I'm climbing back into Walker's truck. He heads straight to a used-car dealership, where on my behalf – after a quick test-drive around the perimeter of the vast, crumbling lot – he finances a very used Volkswagen Rabbit with a diesel engine, a bright-yellow mini-tank with a blue-and-red plaid velour interior.

Mad at me now? he says.

We're standing beside the car, having finished the transaction, me having read the fine print – all the print – for him. He's hunched over, fingering a dent above the driver's side wheel well.

You owe me big time, he says.

For a brief second, I wonder if he suspects I know his dirty little secret, that the car is his attempt to buy my silence – but then I decide it's not even worth thinking about. How could I know for certain, without coming right out and asking him? Which no way do I want to do, especially now. Besides, maybe he just plain and simple feels bad about poor little me – it *has* happened before.

Fine, I think, biting my tongue: you buy me a car, I'll deal.

The next day I feel up to a little meet-and-greet with the early-bird customers.

And would that be the nineteenth-century French fountain, or the silvered gazing orb for you today?

Then I spend my lunch break tootling around the back roads with my co-workers Marg and Aileen, also newly employed – Marg has been jailed once, she tells us over the Rabbit's diesel throb, for repeat shoplifting offences at Kmart, and is now trying to turn her life around. The three of us share a major stogey of a joint, swap an el grande bag of Salsa Verde Doritos back and forth, yell dim suckass things out the car window – Bite me! or, Your mamma! – while around us the industrial parks and subdivisions sport weedy beds of early-blooming scarlet poppies and pink sorbet peonies.

I get us back five minutes late, but everything is no problemo. Until, two in the afternoon, I spot Suzanne and peach-of-a-coach Kendrew, over in ornamental grasses, shoulder to shoulder, perusing the miscanthus collection – and my new-found confidence evaporates.

The older woman's hand is subtly palming the small of the younger woman's back – suddenly I'm aware of the blood flushing up my neck and into my face – who now lingeringly hooks her hair behind her ears, a slow, sensual gesture.

I try to duck behind a screen of Russian sage before they spy me – catch me with my loser face hanging out, working grunt labour and loving it – but no go: Suzanne glimpses me, glances away, pretending to be unaware of my presence for a few seconds before she drops the pretense and locks me in her sights. A beat later, Kendrew notices me, double takes, quickly distances herself from Suzanne.

Oh, *hi*, Kendrew calls out. Tanis, right?

I have been *so* busy, Suzanne says defensively as she reluctantly steps forward.

Now Ms. Peach steps toward me as well.

Nice to *see* you again, she says warmly – warmly *pointedly*, since I have sort of quit school.

Yeah, well, I stammer. You too. Thanks.

She's taller than Suzanne, in her thirties maybe, pretty in boot-cut yoga pants and fitted samurai-print bell-sleeved hoodie. Manicure and everything. Dimples – dimples you could hike all day.

Not bad for a summer job, she says, surveying the garden centre.

Yeah? I say – her small interest in me causing a tickle in my tight chest.

Suzanne – sheathed in black body-hugging Patagonia – is gazing about, too, lips curled.

Weren't you, uh, rather *horsey*? my former gym coach asks. Didn't Suzanne tell me that? Suzanne, wasn't that the link between you two?

Suzanne looks embarrassed.

You ride? I say.

Oh, the peach says, laughing. Oh, no! I'm allergic to the smelly things.

She rubs her hands together.

Well, she announces briskly, all business now. We better be off.

She glances, fake-sternly, at Suzanne.

I think we have hours' worth of plantings to keep *you* busy, Kendrew says, lecturing fondly. You'll earn your money, all right.

I follow them past the panic grass and fescue, into the parking lot, where together they load the tiny trunk of the older woman's Sunbeam Tiger with plastic pots of Rudbeckia goldsturm. I hover uselessly behind them, unable to assist, unable to wrench myself away.

Eventually peachie snaps the trunk.

Later, Tanis, Suzanne says to me. I'll *call* you.

She puts her thumb to her ear, baby finger to her mouth.

We'll *talk*, she says.

The older woman takes her leave and gets in the car. Suzanne steals a glance her way – but Kendrew appears to be distracted, bent down, fiddling with something on the floor.

Talk, I think. And what'll I have to say for myself? I got a car? – and what a car it is! Be a miracle if it lasts to its next oil change. I got a job? This: not quite a resume-builder.

Now Suzanne glances back at me.

I am *so* in lust, she whispers proudly.

As soon as I'm done with work I pull a Mimi, crank the car home lickety-split.

Jena's perched on the top step of the porch. I have a sinking feeling she's been waiting for me all day – despite the brush-off I gave her yesterday. When I'd shown up at Walker's, fresh off the lot with the Rabbit, I'd ignored her slavish ogling to jaunt around on my own instead, driving the concession roads to Highway 7 and back, past Reesor's Sod Farm to Musselman's, where I'd curved slowly around the lake to the rumble of distant thunder.

Under threat of a storm that never set, I'd driven back fast as I'd dared, scarves of gravel hanging in the rear-view mirror – driven past Walker's, south toward the city. In the cooling twilight, windows down, I found myself at the church cemetery again, where I'd turned in, sat until full darkness seeped down, then I'd dieselled back to Walker's for a little show and tell.

But Jena was barricaded away in the house somewhere, far from Walker and Mimi, who I could see carrying on through the kitchen window. Joy was already in bed.

I'd felt let down in a big way – even as part of me knew I was overreacting – like I'd stepped out of a rising elevator into thin air. The lift I'd had turned to free-fall.

I park now in the drive, and Jena ambles over.

Me likey, she says, leaning her head in the passenger-side window, eyes milky with pleasure.

Me likey too, I respond.

How fast can it go? she asks.

Fast? I repeat, stretching the moment, beginning to enjoy her devotion. Hmm.

I drum a rhythm on the steering wheel with my fingers, pretending to perform complex calculations in my head.

Well, I say. I only know I haven't topped it out *yet*.

She sucks a lolly of air in – very nice.

You brave enough to come along and help me find out? I say.

Take *me*? she says, rising onto the balls of her feet, thrusting an arm straight into the air above her head – an overeager student afraid I might choose someone else, though there's no one else around.

I cut the engine and her face pancakes.

Let's see if your dad wants to come too, I say.

But he's with *her* right now, she says. Can't I wait here? She told me, *Play outside for an hour or three.*

I'll be back, I reassure her. Then we'll go.

She crowds the driver-side door. I open it and jostle past her, cross the drive, go up the porch steps – pause, turn to see her getting in the car on the passenger side – and continue into

Walker's kitchen, where Walker and Mimi are sitting at his table. The excavator manual lies open in front of them, as well as the usual pile of bills, which Mimi is going through.

Car's running great! I say.

Glad to hear, Walker says, sounding unimpressed. Be even gladder when you start to pay me off.

Pay? I feel like my scalp has peeled loose from my head. My back teeth float.

Mimi reaches out and mock-throttles him.

That's interest-free, I hope, she says.

She releases him, then pinches his lit cigarette from the ashtray, puts it to her lips and inhales.

Nope, he says. Kid's not a fucking charity case. She's eighteen!

Come on, sugar dad, she says, smoke smearing across her mouth as she stubs the cigarette out in the ashtray.

Next month, right? he asks me.

I nod: yeah. Shift my weight. This isn't the reception I'd expected.

She runs her hands through his bushy grey hair, tugs on his creased Dumbo ears, flaps them to and fro.

Now a sick, metal-alloy feeling coats my stomach – I feel it's my fault, now, that Mimi's so unwitting. Shouldn't I have warned her about him?

You sweet ol' *thang*, she cajoles. Mr. Dee-lish! You told me you were going to be rolling in it.

Don't believe everything you hear, he teases, pulling her from her chair into his lap, causing her to hoot with fake outrage.

Yeah, I interject pointedly.

They both turn and stare at me.

Hope you're planning on working Atkins' horse tonight, Walker rumbles. Or did you forget you still have responsibilities around here?

I unlock the door to the apartment, step through the entrance, shut the door. I can still hear Walker.

Better make time for my horse too, he's saying.

Joy's in the kitchenette, slapping together a bologna sandwich with ketchup on white. She eyes me peevishly. Last night she'd refused to even look at the Rabbit.

What's with those two? I ask, hoping to deflect her attention from me – thinking I'll quickly change into my shorts and a clean tank before booting it with Jena.

A phrase Joy often uses roosts in my head.

Up and down like a toilet seat, I say chummily – trying to ingratiate myself.

You're one to talk, she says viciously. Mad at the world one minute, the next you're smelling the roses, expecting everybody else to be as well. Where've you been, anyway?

I'm working, I say. Or haven't you noticed?

So shouldn't you be at work now? she says. Or did they fire you already?

I get off at four, I say touchily. Same as you.

She tears into her sandwich, opens the fridge door and takes out a Sprite, pops the top.

Don't mind if I do, I say sarcastically.

I open the fridge and get myself a soda, open it – I can drink it while I change my clothes. I take a step toward the hallway. Joy moves to block my path.

So, your big-spender uncle has bought you a car, she vents, gimlet-eyed. Great idea! Reward you for quitting school. Never occurred to him to consult me about it. I'm only your mother!

She quaffs her drink.

I guess Walker's back in your good book again, she says. *He* can afford it.

I have to pay him back, I say, indignant.

Well, she continues, ignoring me. Maybe you can pick me up after work from now on. I won't have to rely on someone outside the family.

Can't, I say uneasily – the thought of having to cart Joy around is suffocating. I might have to stay late, and you'd have to wait for me. You're better off still getting a ride from Ida.

Oh, Joy says nastily. You've got it all figured out, I'm sure.

She's mere feet away from me, too close. I slug back some soda.

Me, he couldn't care less about, she says. Never has.

I feel a quick scrub of sympathy for her. Not true, I want to protest – then realize that I can't call to mind examples of Walker's behaviour that would disprove her claim, other than the old fallback that she's here, and not still in that one-room apartment above the laundromat. Unless I also count Walker's reaction last fall to Joy's goon guy friends. But I don't: wasn't he protecting me?

When I think of it – Joy clunking to the floor, tittering drunkenly while some slob she brought home and into bed with me slavered over what he must have thought was a mother-daughter double delight, the months of Joy crying, blaming Mimi and Walker, it never once entering Joy's head that she'd endangered me – it's apparent I'm like a doorknob to her, a cobweb in an underused corner. If noticed at all, then rarely given a second thought. For the most part, unseen.

My sympathy scabs over. I try to step around her, but she moves even closer, nose inches from mine, chest to chest: sour smell of thankless overwork, worsening, it's seemed, since she became convinced last fall that Walker and Mimi are deliberately working against her. This – *washerwoman*.

He says he's going to marry her, she continues vehemently, breath mashing against my face. That's what this is all about, his big plans. A new arena! He bought that, that thing, so he could build up his business, *afford to treat her right*, his words, I swear to god I'm not kidding.

You *wanted* them to get married, I remind her – wishing she'd muzzle it long enough for me to consider what this news might mean. Or did you, like, forget?

Again I wonder if I shouldn't have told Mimi, if now it's too late. Or if what Walker did doesn't, in the end, matter – best I didn't stir things up.

Joy draws away slightly and pauses. Then she gets up my nose again and steams on.

All the money in the world coming to him, she rails. And I'll still be paying him rent. The way they're carrying on right now! It's like I don't exist.

Suddenly my full attention snaps back to Joy. What about me? I think, something sharp in the back of my throat.

Unfortunately, I jeer – before I can press a hand to my mouth and staunch the words to come. You do. Exist.

Joy cracked, like a glass bottle, contents carbonated: tears harsh as spat tacks.

I didn't mean that, I say in a hushed voice – several seconds too late to sound sincere.

The slap is almost welcome. Like a bolt of grey cloth, pain wrapping my head like a bandage. Underneath, the enemy me, briefly thwarted. Marg and Aileen, their potato faces, rise before me, their hoots and hollers beckoning as Joy raises her arm again.

I stagger outside to the dirt path leading from the apartment. Lurching around the corner of Walker's house I can see Jena is still sitting in the front passenger seat of the Rabbit.

I reel back to where she won't be able to see me. Lower myself to the ground, sit cross-legged, head bowed.

I can feel swelling on my cheekbone, above my eye. My sinuses throb. Bruised: all of me pulled into a dense blue-black centre, above which the waning sun is a pinhole of light.

Can do, can't do, I chant inwardly, a desolate mantra.

Can't undo.

The words are knots in a widening net. I bow my head lower. Hopelessness drifts down.

A couple of days later, in a Tim Hortons doughnut shop near the nursery, I pick up a discarded classified section of a newspaper.

Once or twice, now, I've noticed Jasmine, the nursery manager, scan the job listings on her lunch break between bites of sandwich. I'm not the only one who's noticed: Marg and Aileen have, as well. It's an open secret that Jasmine's seeking new employment.

I tuck the paper under my arm, and wait for my order of six coffees and a snack pack of Timbits to be filled.

I sit in the Rabbit with the windows shut, roll my fingertips over my almost-healed cheek while I decode the columns of small type.

After work the next day, I drive back to the doughnut shop and place a call from a pay phone near the washroom. When I inquire about the job advertised, my voice pipsqueaks. The position, I'm politely informed, has been filled. The next call I make, my voice is more assured. Practice makes perfect, I tell myself each time I hang up the phone. I run out of quarters, go to the counter and offer bills for change. Maybe Walker's right: there *is* always something you can do.

I ramp up: quit the nursery for a job at a carwash with a toehold in the city, get a whacking eight bucks an hour, two more than I was previously making.

Money's honey, I throw – fling, *arrow* – myself into my new vocation. Immediately, I begin working as many extra shifts as I can, rising at five each morning – fucking-A missing Joy who's up at quarter to six – to nervously volley among the early-bird commuters for the hour-long drive. By ten o'clock at night – minimum several times a week, when I'm otherwise done by five – I'm standing, pores steamed open by the unseasonable heatwave, on the humid asphalt lot, behind me a hazy neon-lit backdrop, like some over-jazzed, tawdry spa. Then I'm jet-cruising on autopilot back to Walker's, barely able to keep my eyes open.

In the apartment's living room, Joy and I greet each other coolly: she simply picks up the remote and turns off the TV, gathers herself from the sofa and retires to the bedroom for the night. I flop into the hurriedly made sofa bed, and sleep takes me like the flu – my legs sweating the tangled sheets – leaving me feeling weaker when I wake.

Each day's classifieds perch on the passenger seat of my car, folded open to the studio apartment listings. I read them when I stop at stoplights, bring them with me into the bathroom at the carwash, comparison shopping while I take toilet breaks.

Before I even receive my first paycheque, my ears ring constantly from the noisy sudsing and buffing equipment. My hands swell from wiping hundreds of windshields and tire wells, pink across the knuckles – they look like Joy's.

Lunch rules, though. I get to sit beside the broken fax machine in the oily, dishevelled office with Karla, the manager.

She seems to have been here forever, forever fleshy, I imagine. Middle-aged, hair spazzed from too many bad home perms, her inch-long fake fingernails – stars, sequins, occasionally a rhinestone on each tricoloured oval – pointing out of her thick digits.

We order in Italian from down the street, max out on beefy lasagna and garlic bread or cheesy, sweet veal sandwiches, a couple of cans of Brio each. She ignores the ringing phone, laughs loud at my every joke. We read our horoscopes to one another from the daily newspaper, discuss the latest Hollywood shoplifting-rehab-divorce scandal – that is, I listen as she holds forth. Discounting the physical damage, the job – with its budding-friendship perk – has me *blissed*.

Until one morning halfway into my third week working at the carwash, inexplicably at first – as suddenly as turning off a tap – Karla leaves me hanging mid-sentence, staved off by a sharply pointed index finger while she actually *takes* a phone call. She works through lunch, no time to gab, straight up to her quitting time, when a mealy dweeb guy picks her up in a puce-coloured Chevette.

From a narrow window inside the wash area, I watch her leave.

Who cares, big deal, so what?

The wash ejects a white Infiniti. Soap- and dirt-dregged water drains off it in an oily rainbow onto the concrete floor. With a rag I rub the driver's side mirror. In the rectangle I catch a glimpse of myself, bitter smile clamped on my face: mirror image of Joy.

I swipe at it with my hand.

I am *not* you, I tell it.

Cheshire-cat-like, the image becomes all curved lips, neatly soldiered enamelled ridges of teeth.

What're you going to do about it? it seems to taunt.

I get a *new* new job – an even better-paying one.

I begin to drive deeper into the city, anxiously negotiating the logjammed traffic and unfamiliar routes to work as a security guard. Pretty much anyone can do it, I discover, as long as they don't have a criminal record.

I'd been hired, once again, on the spot – the paperwork for licencing and bonding commenced, assigned a uniform:

trim black pants, black shirt with grey tie, not too-uncool bomber-style leather jacket, and these big-mo, steel-toed army surplus boots.

What a little fascist! My low-risk mission? To patrol condominium parking lots, and sometimes the exquisitely landscaped private golf courses in the outer boroughs. Within little more than a week, besides my own shifts I'm covering for other guards when they want time off, find myself limp-walking until all hours – a round-the-clock, solitary graveyard – shin-splinted, foot and ankle stinging with reawakened pain.

One morning at six, I share a coffee with another guard in the parking lot of a condo complex. Hollow-eyed, shag-haired Kathy is a couple of years older than me – apparently a frequenter of bars on her nights off, a claim she backs up with an arsenal of raunchy innuendo. Several times now she's brought coffee, lemon danishes. Also, offerings from her cache of amphetamines, which are proving to come in handy for double-shifts.

I'm still feeling last night's after-effects: my scalp tingling, jaw muscles sore from repeatedly clenching them, and an hour ago the bleached dawn seemed to suck all moisture from my eyes. My lips are dry too. I've licked them sore.

After a few rounds back and forth with the Styrofoam cup, Kathy passes it to me and says, You finish it.

As I'm swilling the remnants of the coffee she says, Where to now?

Home, I say. Where else?

She takes the cup from me and crushes it, tosses it over her shoulder.

What? she says slyly. That where your heart is? Don't get me wrong. I'm just, you know. Asking.

I look at her lopsided, cautious face – used to rejection, I think, though still kind, not yet ruined. Is that what I look like? Or will come to?

Yeah, I say – gently, is how I hope it comes across, though I'm happy to mislead her into thinking I have a special, certain someone in my life.

Aargh! she exclaims. Why are all the good ones taken?

Braille-driving in the bumper-to-bumper rush hour traffic on the parkway back to Walker's – still smiling to myself over Kathy's compliment, a soft tissue of warmth in my throat – I let a pocket open between me and the Subaru wagon in front. A car from the next lane cuts in. I brake too suddenly, and the Rabbit hop-stops.

I loosen my clammy fingers from the wheel, give the car some gas, ease up on the clutch.

I try to imagine my heart, which is beating wildly. I try to imagine home. What that might be like, in a parallel universe.

A mini-van comes off an on-ramp and slows almost to a halt, trying to find a place in the seamless traffic. I let it in: good karma, knock on wood. Inside the van, in the back, are two small children, turned around in their seats. They're waving at me, convulsing with bratty laughter. Sticking their tiny tongues out.

Baby on board, a yellow-and-black sign affixed to the rear window says.

A memory stirs up.

Riding in a truck between Walker and Joy with a towering pile of beach towels – fuzzy emerald green and royal blue – on my sand-dabbed legs that are too short to hang over the edge of the seat. I'm fidgeting, uncomfortable: I have to pee. On Joy's lap, a picnic cooler. Through the open windows, the jibber-jabber of car horns, throaty complaint of buses and delivery vans, shouts lobbed and rebounded, hit-parade songs. Walker with both hands on the wheel, sitting ramrod straight, likely distrustful of the city-savvy drivers, cussing them at times – in marked contrast to the polite words brother and sister occasionally exchange, the encouraging, gracious chuckles.

Jena must not have been born, Lily not yet in Walker's life. No Mimi.

Just Walker, Joy, and me.

I press myself first against Joy, then Walker, back and forth. But my discomfort grows, a gap billowing inside, trying to push out. It hurts, and I'm about to cry.

Joy puts her mouth to my ear. *Can't you hold it?*

We must have been heading home after a day at one of the city beaches: the sun was to our left and in front of us in a tickle of gold that made me want to sneeze. I rested my head against Walker's tense arm. As if I were a receptor, the feel of the steering wheel's vibrations seemed to pass through him into me. *Almost home. Hold on. I'll get you there.*

I leave an envelope containing three twenties on Walker's kitchen table. On the envelope, in large block letters, I've written, FROM T.

I sleep heavily through the day in the empty apartment. I wake around two in the afternoon, eat some cereal while watching TV, shower. I'm leaving, dressed in my uniform, when I see Walker and daughter, planted side by side on the top stair of the porch, a small packed duffel bag and a laptop carrying case next to Jena.

She's being shunted off to her mom's again. She's crying, her eyes red-rimmed, nose like something that would squeak if you squeezed it. Walker's working a cigarette from one side of his mouth to the other.

I nod in their direction. Leg it as fast as I can toward my car, parked next to Mimi's. When Walker hails me, I flinch.

Atkins called, he says. His horse needs working. So does mine.

Wednesday morning, I say over my shoulder.

Of which month? he says.

I'll *do* it, I say, turning around and stopping – trust Walker not to mention the envelope of money, to focus, instead, on what I haven't done for him.

You know that horse is a prospect, he says, squinting against the smoke rising into his eyes.

Atkins'? I say – why does Walker still try to force me to be interested in what I've outgrown, which happens to be his whole princely domain.

He inhales deeply, takes the cigarette out of his mouth.

Ha, he says, in a slurry of smoke.

I *said* Wednesday, I say.

He's good to go, almost, he says. He would be, if you worked with him some more.

Tanis? Jena interjects in a husky voice. Can we do what you said we'd do?

Mentally, I clap a hand to my forehead: this girl who seems so out of it somehow has the proverbial memory of an elephant – here she is, more than a month later, still waiting for me to take her for a drive.

Wednesday, I say.

She smiles, sloe-eyed, an opaque blue circling the dilated irises. Behind her – where she can't see it, on the other side of the kitchen's screen door – her white cat is standing on two legs, catching its claws in the wire mesh, patiently unhooking them, catching them again. It opens its mouth and mews silently.

There, Walker says, and nudges Jena with an elbow. Told you. All you had to do was ask.

She snuffles drowsily, wipes the back of a hand across her nose, taking a fudged second to actually connect – it really is like her head's not screwed on tight, like whatever meds she's on aren't working. Or she's taking too many of them.

Maybe you'll show your cousin your new computer, Walker continues, proudly reaching behind Jena to rap the laptop case – startling the cat, who scampers off into the house. Top of the line! And tell her how you've got the Internet now. Huh? How do you like them apples! You can show her what you showed me.

Flashing the cash, is he? Like he really needed those sixty shitty bucks from me. No wonder he hasn't registered receiving them. Too bad I can't take them back.

How's the hole coming? I say to Walker, an edge to my voice – it twigs on me that I didn't notice the manual in his kitchen this morning.

It's coming, he says vaguely, ducking his head. Coming.

So, you and Mimi set a date yet? I ask – getting another dig in, this one sure to make him uncomfortable in Jena's company.

No, he says defensively – his eyes flicking toward his daughter. What's it to you, anyway?

Jena blinks slowly. What will happen to her when Mimi and Walker marry? I wonder. Suddenly I'm sorry I brought the subject up.

Where would you like to go? I ask her, my voice buzzing in my head – if only I could smuggle her somewhere safe.

Walker rubs the bristle on his cheek. I can almost hear him thinking: *Fuck* me. Torn, with not a clue in the world as to what he should do. Torn as I am.

Put on your thinking cap, I say to Jena.

She says, *I* don't know. Anywhere?

I begin to carom down from Markham to work earlier than necessary. Once in the city I drift around in the always-heavy traffic, beneath the unsettled sky, past the broody pleasure paths within the tree-filled ravines, along the streets and avenues.

On a rare weekend night off – amphetamined up and no place to go – I take the 404 to the Don Valley Parkway, ride those lazy swirls into the city so fast it's like flying, as the Volkswagen's diesel bucks against my tight jeans. I drive south, take the Bayview Extension to Pottery Road. When I get to the top of the hill I make a right onto Broadview and pull over illegally beside a fire hydrant.

I shrug off my T-shirt and don the long-sleeved white button-down I broke the bank on the day before, shopping between shifts. Using the rear-view mirror I apply Mimi's L'Oreal Sheer Moonberry *colour riche* to my lips, a little sloppy around the edges. I have my leather boots on. Is this happiness? Or what?

Everything I see seems so near: heading south now on Broadview, Riverdale Park spread below me, and on the far side, to the west – so close I can almost reach out and touch it for good luck as I swan by – the city skyline sprouts like a pop-up book.

Continuing south past Gerrard, another memory comes to me.

A white-legged Walker awkward in baggy swimtrunks, Joy curvy and young-looking in a red two-piece bathing suit – the three of us eating sandwiches, admiring the sailboats and yachts on the lake that seemed large as an ocean, as if they were put there for our enjoyment. Pointing – *there's one!* – at each blimp fish lazily breaking the surface to snack on water-skimming insects. In the distance, steel container ships – storeys high, football fields long – docilely piloted in and out of the harbour by tugboats.

A patch of sand, dominated by industrial, untouristy points of interest – loading docks and lift-bridges – that we claimed as ours for one afternoon. Where together we made a three-point, rudimentary map, each of us a corner pinning down a breezy, beach-blanket world.

Together. And yet the memory is served fried up, scrambled, singed at the edges with what's to come. The apart part.

I give the Rabbit more gas and accelerate. I'm getting the hang of carving a path between the streetcar tracks. Guided partly by memory, partly by instinct, I think I know where I am.

Following Broadview, a near-straight, gunning shot to Cherry Beach – as if the city were tipping up, emptying into Lake Ontario with its mutant dioxin-brined carp and rusty shipwrecks, the sky above jammy with planets and the wheezing of ancient breezes, the fitful coughing of the stars.

Just past Queen Street, I pull over again, head swimming.

Saturday night, and I'm still barely eighteen. Still twinned – pregnant almost – with aloneness, nothing between me and the moon but this queasy sure-slip grip of my hands on the wheel.

III

7

LICK

Love is proximity, she says. And here you are.

She butt-parks next to me, toggles her boots back and forth impatiently, slips an astonishingly cool palm over my wrist, on her fingertips chipped black nail polish. In her other hand she's holding a silver lamé evening clutch. She's smiling, open mouthed, headlights me with these brown eyes rimmed with gold – I'm like, freeze, Bambi.

For the past fifteen minutes I've been half-leaning, half-sitting, pale-knuckled, against a second-floor window casement, the glass panes above me streaked with paint. My beer bottle gripped tight between my knees as I watch the after-work crowd filter in.

I've managed to trade shifts with Kathy – having worked two weekends in a row for her, it's my turn. This is my first time here – the first time I did more than surveil, circling the block twice in my car before parking a chill-it ten-minute walk away, only to quail at the sight of the barred front window and flee.

Yo, the girl says. Oh comatose one. I *am* talking to you.

Wide face, close-cropped hair dyed an obvious white-hot, skinny knock-kneed legs poking out from a short, pleated polka-dot skirt.

Must be the strong silent type, she teases.

She swings to her feet.

I know what *you* need, she says.

We descend the metal staircase. Out across the dance floor we wend our way under a heavy salsa rain, bob and weave along the periphery under five-foot-tall trippy-chick portraits. At the stairway to the basement, we stop to catch our breath in the dimly oxygenated, turbined air. Lean against each other, share the sweetest little pant. Darling, I think: our song.

And down we go. In the basement we locate The Flesh Dress's projectile vomitorium bathroom, lock the door, stop up our ears to cries of, Fuck let me in! Gotta pee. Etcetera.

She backs up to the counter, puts her palms flat on the top – next thing I know, she's cute as a button on this porcelain perch, Calvin's knotted around her ankles. High-gloss lipstick is daubed on her chin.

We kiss, the roof of her mouth ridged and slick, hint of beery yeast, toothpaste, chocolate. A penetrating glance tells me her ass, a Pussy From Hell tattoo on the left cheek – all the news that's fit to print, *bad* news – is about to become intimately acquainted with the mirror behind the countertop.

She lifts her bony arms to embrace my head – applying a measured downward pressure.

My move – but I'm at a loss. Scared. Stalling, I taste her mouth again. Her silver clutch glisters in the sink. Her stomach is flat, the navel feathered with fine hair.

Aww, she croons. Rip the monkey hard.

And like that, I'm in.

Outside, the sky is – nothing but sky, aimlessly large. Pink-lipped through the treetops, blue-black dome curving above in this hour past sundown. She unbuttons my shirt while I turn onto Eastern Avenue. Fingers me, gutter mean and nasty, very fancy spit-wetted twists and pulls.

So when she says, Take me to Scarborough, as if ordering a cab to the kasbah and not to what I've learned is in fact a suburban desert – mile-long blocks of strip malls and high-rises, meaning her request is pretty dumb and almost ruins the mood – I nevertheless decide to give her the benefit of the doubt.

Sometimes, late at night or early in the morning when my shift is over and I'm not in any hurry to get to bed, I've driven this route back to Walker's. East on the Danforth, past the crowded Greek cafés, the 24/7 fruit and vegetable markets. Ton o'traffic. Sidewalks jam-packed: dogs towing people gabbing and shopping. Farther east, the streets begin to empty. Even the convenience stores are closed for the night. All too soon, wasteland central, where remnants of a willow-graced countryside still cling, visible in the untended summer patches of tall grass and goldenrod and Queen Anne's lace beside highway overpasses.

She drops her head in my lap, appears to lose consciousness. For a long time while I drive I touch her carefully, the ruff of bones so close to the skin as to make her seem transparent.

The street blocks lengthen. All-night buses pass going the opposite direction, the few passengers suspended, displayed in cubes of light.

She sits up.

Where are we? she mumbles.

Wendy's and Taco Bell, high-rises like concrete icicles.

Okay, she says. Next left.

A gas station, closed for the night. I park by the washrooms, around the back of the low, stuccoed building. She clambers out of the car, bag in hand, from which she retrieves a key. She unlocks a side door marked EMPLOYEES ONLY, disappears inside. Steps out a minute later lugging two large plastic watering cans, bag clenched between her teeth. Sloshes past the car.

Is she fast! Skinny, but strong as an ox judging by the ground she's covering – those cans have to weigh a ton.

I throw open the car door.

Where you going? I shout – but she's well into the grassy corner lot adjacent the gas station.

I take off in pursuit. It's hard to see where I'm stepping in the dark. I wobble over on my left ankle, arousing hackles of pain. Finally – hemmed in by a hedge, almost invisible at first, seemingly nothing more than a grey-green smudge – she stops and I catch up. She's put the watering cans on the ground, taken the clutch from her mouth.

What's going on? I gasp nervously.

She giggles, takes a joint and a lighter from her purse, gestures in front of her.

Then my eyes adjust to the dark and I see – something: the hedge, maybe four feet tall, seven feet long, is heavy thighed, abundantly breasted, clearly a woman. Boxwood, maybe. Privet, or plain old lilac well past flowering, hard to tell. Vetch – is that vetch?

The figure is reclining – one wide forearm outstretched over her chunky head, lounging on a bed of petunias beside a ditch – blurring to pure vegetation as she leafs out into the warm night air. Monumental, somehow, despite being a secret. Half-human, half-landscape. Cool green veins like spokes of summer lightning.

My mom made this, she says. Planned, planted, pruned. Before her stuff caught on with an adoring public. Now these things are in places people actually notice. But this one's neglected, poor thing. So I take care of it.

I help my date empty the watering cans. When we're finished we lean hip to hip, smoke in silence. Chubby, perfectly round droplets form, roll off twittery leaves.

So, I say. Come here often?

She giggles again. Then she stops, combs her fingers through her short hair.

What's wrong with your leg? she asks. If you don't mind my asking. I hadn't noticed you limping earlier, in the bar.

It's fine, I say. Nothing.

Oh! she says, smiling cautiously, drawing back. Touchy.

Tell me about your mom, I say.

Before she can reply I kiss her again. It's as if summer's debris – the swampy heat smells – ignites no small interest in our mouths. These – *words* in my head.

Ah: our complicated tongues.

Tell you later, she says.

Her place – back in the city proper, Queen Street East near Parliament – is like nothing I've ever seen before.

We ascend a narrow staircase painted a sticky high-gloss white. Whitewashed plywood walls rise around us steep as floes. At the top of the stairs is a door, which she unlocks and kicks open with the toe of a boot.

Inside, running the length of the apartment, is a narrow, high-ceilinged hallway with wide-planked floorboards painted the same tacky white as the staircase. Four doors line the hallway, at the end of which I can make out a kitchen with a light on. Chest-level dents mar the otherwise austere surface of the walls: fist marks? She what, punches walls?

Beyond the first door is a large living room natty in a red polka-dot wallpaper. Silver shag rug. On the two windows facing the street are roll-down window blinds painted with red dots of varying sizes. Curving from one wall is a round, red velvet bean bag chair, the only furniture. The room shudders briefly as the Queen East streetcar shambles by outside.

Next stop: a small room, its single window covered in a sheet of vellum, its walls embossed with eight-by-ten glossies of wet red things, foetal, embryonic. In one I discern – gratefully – a tiny yellow beak. Along one wall is a long metal workbench, piled with notebooks, carelessly unrolled blueprints, cables and metal switches, computer circuit boards, screwdrivers large and small, and a cumbersome, not-so-new-looking computer. Beside that, speakers, a woofer (she explains when I ask). What appear to be several battered, ancient-artifact laptops are stacked on the floor.

Look up, she says.

Sooty footprints tracked on the ceiling. From some radiate flinty red streaks that pinwheel to gold-glitter haloes.

We skip two doors and enter the kitchen. The linoleum floor resembles a pebbly beach over which shallow water gently plays, all pale blues and teal greens. In the middle of the sunburst-yellow ceiling is a door, from which a rope ladder dangles. The walls are the same yellow, from the ceiling halfway to the floor, then tiles painted violet blue take over, a number of which display, upon closer examination, astonishingly nuanced painted miniatures of ocean-themed life. Translucent jellyfish suspended in ultramarine. A red gingham tablecloth arrayed with platters of lobster, shrimp, oysters on the half-shell, paper cups of tartar sauce, a bottle of Tabasco. Sailboats racing across a glassy surface. A tidal wave threatening a beach-town of thatched huts.

The kitchen sink is scummed. Sketching pads are strewn across the Formica kitchen table. I clear my throat.

Well, I say.

She offers me a glass of water – all she has, she says.

The bathroom, next door to the kitchen, is so pink. I undo myself in front of her and pee elaborately, luxuriantly into the pink toilet. God, I think, when was the last time I peed?

She's watching intently.

What do you pay for all this? I ask.

In the almost-empty bedroom we lie down. On the wall above her futon is a hand-lettered sign: INTERFACE THIS.

Jesus. On the ceiling, another sign. This one says: SWITCH.

Wow. Next day, when I leave, it's already high noon, the sky a smoggy yellow bloat. I can smell her on me, skunky on my fingers as I walk the half-block to my car – parked illegally on Queen, a ticket on my windshield – get in and head east toward River Street. I can't remember when I work next, I'm sweating, afraid I've missed my next shift and will be fired. A streetcar pounds madly behind me – I'm jingled, jangled, a fizzy pop of exhaustion and terror – then I make a right onto Broadview.

I drive several blocks. Front Street is jammed with traffic, its sidewalks studded with the smartly dressed. All those Saturday mornings I'd drive past, intimidated – now I wait in line for fifteen minutes at the entrance to a parking lot on the Esplanade, releasing the idea of work to the winds, leering as if knowingly at every woman who walks past.

Finally a spot opens up in the lot and I park, hoof it across the baking asphalt, arrive – ages later, it seems – at the hangar-like south building of the St. Lawrence Market. Cool and dark inside. Smell of congealed blood and flowers.

Basement, first floor, mezzanine. Across the street to the northside building. Back and forth twice. Undone, I buy pell-mell, wanting everything, peering at handwritten cards labelling the never-before imagined, pointing at those I dare not try to pronounce as I blow my hard-earned wad. Endless propositions: fresh quail, lobes of foie gras. May I present heart of boar? Stiff bouquets of broccoli-rabe, arugula with edible lavender and nasturtium. A fandango of frisée. Truffles. And roses – of course, roses.

Honey, I'm home! I imagine saying.

She could laugh me back into the street – all the way back to Markham. Or simply not recognize me.

For isn't my very skin morphing? I can feel it: the nip and tuck as I stand outside on the sidewalk – overladen, gasping, eyes stinging, streaming from the thick hot wind blowing off the soupy lake, the sun spoiling like an egg in the poisonous, ozone-depleted atmosphere – in my greedy, newly emerging skin-organ, suckling, gobbling air.

Surprise, surprise: Rachel is an almost second-year art college student living on student loans who – get this – welcomes me with open arms.

Through the rest of steamy July, in her chokingly hot apartment, we cook furiously, eat, fuck, spill everywhere. When we're ready to give ourselves over to sleep, we ascend the rope ladder to the trap door in the ceiling of her kitchen, emerge onto the flat roof with its view of the Gardiner Expressway. We slumber, sweat-filmed, through the heat-jaundiced morning – wake sunburnt, seagulls squawking at us through the mid-day haze.

I manage to continue to dutifully patrol the golf courses, condo parking lots, and yacht clubs of the metropolis, working the night shift when the heat is more bearable, when thimblefuls of cool air seep through the manicured bluegrass of a golf course swale, or a rogue lake breeze at the yacht club occasionally brushes my face like damp velour.

At first, every two days or so, I drive out of the city at daybreak when I've finished my shift, angling northeast through Scarborough – manoeuvring mere blocks away from the hedge woman soaking greenly into space, secretly thriving – eventually passing increasingly rare country fields misting dawn pinks and golds to raid Walker's – scant minutes at a time, all I can stand – for changes of clothes. Within two weeks most of my stuff is at Rachel's.

On less-hot evenings, when I'm not working, the stripped-down futon on the floor is a lake, a glossy page. Late at night I leaf through her books – manifestos and monographs, whacked-out culture-war 'zines – while she levers a sketchpad across her knees and draws me: anime-round eyes, sparky jet-age outfits. Technetronic dictator, she patches these images into a cheesy video game featuring a bombshell warrior-chick whose gloriously uplifted computerized ass I kick whenever I play.

Huh! the Amazonitron goes, in sexy twenty-four-bit gutturals. Uh-hunh!

What can't Rachel do? Quite a set-up she's got, projects on the go. Paints, Play-Dohs, samples sounds with a portable DAT recorder, foraging on the street for raw scraps of conversation, a man singing in a park, a woman laughing – harvesting the bloops and scritches, the blooming orchestral topographies of daily life.

In this first flush, what's not up for grabs? I surmise love itself a polymath project that surpasses understanding. I haven't the faintest idea what she's talking about, but I swear she has the most fascinating mind.

Code talker, I think one night – fighting for breath on the bed, legs interlaced with hers, our bodies bitten by sweat, her short hair growing endlessly cellular, I imagine, between my super-sensitive fingers – as if she can read my thoughts: I'm begging you. *Break me.*

Pretty, Rachel says out the car window, as if addressing the leaves fan-dancing in the maples and birches.

I feel a hit of pride and, with it, some small yawn of yearning. I'm driving fast, and in the rear-view mirror – south, in the direction of city – I see a foam of dust. To my left, looking ahead, a red-winged blackbird perches atop a bulrush swaying in the thick wind. There's a filter of haze over the humidity-socked ravines north of the zoo, screening the Rouge River Valley, the heat-struck river. We sweep by a farmhouse, wilted blue spruce and cedars, banks of coneflowers and salvia.

But there's a sour taste in my mouth, so strong I pucker.

When're you going to ride my horse? Walker has repeatedly asked, the few times he's called the past month, paging me at work. When're you coming up?

No passalong message from Joy, no sign she's been wondering where I am, why most of my belongings are gone.

I nose the car over to the right, let a southbound black Town Car with tinted windows by. I engage the clutch and gear down to third. Second. Dread fizzes in my stomach, staticky – the white head of a dandelion gone to seed, Queen Anne's lace with its secret, blood-drop centre – at the thought of Joy, face crunching with pain in the second before she slapped me.

I haven't called to say I'm coming, that I'm bringing a friend. Maybe it's not too late to abort, head back the way we came.

You okay? Rachel asks me. If it's really bad we'll bail fast.

I'm only here because, a couple of afternoons ago, I'd made a bargain with her. I'd just been sitting on the closed lid of the toilet, watching her as she'd shaved: pits, legs, pussy – kit and caboodle, no Brazilian bikini wax for her.

I used to watch Mimi shave – when was that? A time beyond remembering. She'd prepare for a night with Walker. Soak in the tub, then depilate lovingly, curse when she cut herself. This was before waxing was the shit, laser removal the permanent solution. How one prepared, readied the skin. Mimi pulling the plug, stepping out of the tub into the towel I held open before her like wings.

After Rachel had done, she'd rinsed the tub, turned off the shower, run a cool bath. Outside the bathroom window, gulls harshed at the hazy blue sky. Already naked, I'd climbed into the tub with her, folded her face forward into my breasts. She'd reached behind her and pulled the plug. Quickly, unfussily, as the water drained, we got each other off.

I stood to get out, and she clasped her arms around my ankles melodramatically.

Whoa, there, nervous Nellie, she said.

I need to get going, I protested.

She lay back in the tub then, paddled her feet in the air, as if still in water. She put her hands behind her head to form a pillow, lengthening her lovely body. I stared: ever since I met her I've had the feeling I can't look at her enough. She'd quickly become less gaunt than when I first met her. I liked to think that I'd put some meat on her bones. Every day I'd bring home something good to eat – often something I'd never had before.

You seem to have issues, she said icily.

Useless, stupid. I stood before her – hands open, awkward, my dumb tongue heavy in its bed of white nails – unlovely. Unloveable.

Issues, I said – confounded, frightened.

She sat up, knees raised, and placed her chin on the edge of the tub.

Always running away from me, she said. You fuck me, then you're off. What do you think that says?

I have no idea, I replied, astonished by her outburst. I just –. I'm due at work in forty-five minutes. That's all. I don't know what you're expecting from me.

You never did ask again about my mom, she said querulously.

What, I wondered, did that have to do with anything? Was Rachel trying to pick a fight?

I thought you wanted to know, she continued. Aren't you interested?

I thought if you wanted to tell me you would, I managed to say back – why *this* now? I wondered, bristling.

She removed her chin from the tub's edge, laid her forehead there instead.

Don't get so defensive, she said, her voice small. It's just that I don't know if you care. About me.

Of course I care, I said, trying to mask my growing frustration – I couldn't understand what my feelings for her had to do with her mother.

She tucked her head to her knees. Now she was weeping, shoulder blades making mothlike motions.

You don't sound as if you do, she cried breathily. You sound mad at me.

I got on my knees. Took her face in my hands and raised it to mine. I kissed her wet eyes.

It came out wrong, I said. I didn't mean to sound like that.

Eyes still shut, she gave a grim smile and said, You're so distant. I just want you to know that's hard for me. I need you to give a little more of yourself if we're going to continue seeing each other.

If.

Agreed, I said, as panic cancanned in my chest.

Agreed? she repeated, sounding incredulous – I wondered if she were being sarcastic, making fun of me.

She opened her eyes then and stood in the tub, gestured for me to pass her a towel.

Mothers! she exclaimed, and uttered a mirthless, stinging laugh – I didn't know how to interpret it, interpret any of it, what she was saying, why she was laughing.

They're the greatest predictor for what a person is really like, she said. Pathetic, but true.

I know, I responded, though I didn't know – I was only hoping I was saying something she'd want to hear.

So I'll show you mine if you show me yours, she said.

Trapped: a faint sickly depression in my chest, a dead spot.

But bargains are bargains, I'd thought, placing the towel in her hands. And Rachel seemed to know so much more than I did – seemed more fully formed, more human, even, than I felt. I'd follow her lead.

So now, only days later – that dead spot vacuuming any yearning from me – I give the car more gas again, shift back up to third, even though no one at Walker's is expecting us. The road ahead simmers with heat, and boas of sunlight trail through the haze onto the fields.

Just remember, she says. Say the word, we're out of there!

I drive with one hand on the wheel. Rachel holds my other in hers. No turning back. She won't let me.

Silly bugger, Joy clucks – standing in the middle of the stiflingly hot living room, holding a jar of blueberry preserve from Marks & Spencer, a present from Rachel. Girls your age should be saving. Not throwing money around.

But I can see Joy is smitten: on her face a soft, gummy look that has nothing to do with me. *Me* she'd fixed with an angry gaze the second Rachel and I had stepped into the kitchenette – out of the blue, it must have seemed to Joy. Then she'd raised her fist in the air, shaking it at me, baring her teeth in a malevolent smile to indicate she was only half-joking.

Nice of you to call, she'd said acidly.

Nice to see you too, I replied.

Now she hefts the jar in her hand.

Why'd you do something crazy like this? she says to Rachel – who's surveying the claustrophobic living room, taking in the eye-sore furnishings.

Presents had never been much in our vocabulary. Birthdays, Christmas: a new pair of jeans, a couple of pairs of socks, some underwear – Wal-Mart or BiWay brands, instead of the Jockey for Hers I usually bought myself at The Bay – to replace what was most holey or frayed. For my eighteenth birthday, Joy had bestowed upon me a lottery ticket enclosed in a used birthday card (from Mimi?), with the words *Dear Joy* crossed out and *Dear Tanis* written in, *Sorry I didn't have time to get you a card*. And when I'd opened the card, she'd informed me I had to split any winnings with her. Nothing you'd ever think of as a real gift.

Walker was the one who came through for me: the chaps, the custom-made field boots for showing. A Steuben jumping saddle for his horse – for me to use on his horse, a present of sorts. The car, even though I owed him for it.

Jena he gave jewellery, electronics: radios and tape recorders, the colour TV that was in her room. Most recently, as far as I knew, the laptop.

Mimi got cash. Sometimes she treated Joy and me with it: fast food, silly trinkets like outrageous slogan-bearing tees, rides in the Monte Carlo she wouldn't otherwise have been able to keep running.

Rachel gives Joy a hug. When she lets her go, Joy's eyes are moist as her sweating forehead – like she'd ever react this way to me.

Wouldn't this be good on toast? Joy says, cradling the jar in her hand. Oh, I'm gaining five pounds just thinking about it.

Joy, I say sharply – eager to break up the lovefest. Where's Mimi?

I'd seen her car, parked by the barns, when I'd pulled in. Both Walker's trucks were there as well.

Joy wheels around.

How should I know! she says, then addresses Rachel again. Wish I was skinny like you. I bet you can eat anything you like and not put on an ounce.

Joy! I say between clenched teeth. Leave her alone.

She gets like that, Rachel says sheepishly to Joy.

No kidding, Joy says. You must be a saint to be able to stand her.

I thought you wanted to see the horses, I say petulantly to Rachel, who edges around Joy to give me a stale look.

I'm just talking with your mother first, Rachel replies firmly.

Infuriated, I stomp into the kitchenette. I try the door between Joy's and Walker's. Locked. I leave the apartment, take the dirt path back to the drive, climb the porch steps – ankle hurting now – and let myself in to Walker's house. Chairs neatly pushed in to the table, the oilcloth wiped clean, a couple of unopened bills off to one side. No excavator manual – I bet he's given up on his project by now.

I walk into the cool living room. The curtains are drawn. Where is everybody? Like, thanks for the welcoming squad, guys!

I cross the floor to the stairway, place my hand on the smooth painted banister. An air conditioner purrs somewhere above.

At the top of the stairs I stop and listen. Behind the shut door to Jena's room is an unmistakeable hum. I tap on the door, but there's no answer. I turn the handle and slowly push open.

She's lying on the bed wearing a long-sleeved sweatshirt and sweatpants, fuzzy slippers on her feet: the room *is* freezing. Her deaf white cat is curled between her splayed legs, sleeping as bobble-headed Jena listens to music through a set of earphones, eyes closed. I stay where I am, inventorying: the dolls and toys, the computer haphazardly shoved half under the bed, the jewellery box, the figurines of ponies and kittens.

I look back at Jena, whose eyes are now open. We lock gazes for maybe ten seconds – and I expect to see some sign of grievance against me, but it's like looking into a silvery meaningless space, an empty mirror – then she closes her eyes again, bends her leg, scratches her ankle.

I leave the room, close her door.

Re-entering the living room now from the stairs, I hear a cough coming from Walker's kitchen. I quicken my pace.

Hey lady, I say to Mimi, who's bending over the kitchen sink, running water from the faucet.

She keeps her back to me, splashes water on her face, emits a soft groan. Reaches for the dishtowel. She wipes her face, and only then does she turn toward me. Moisture felts her upper lip. She's scowling.

How's it going? I ask brightly, trying to mask my disappointment, my *annoyance* – this isn't exactly the reception I'd been hoping for.

Yeah, yeah, she mumbles crossly.

Her white shorts are creased, loosely opening where they're rolled at the cuffs. Her legs look even paler and thinner than before, her once shiny knees knobby and yellowish. Above the neckline of her white tank top is a nest of thin gold chains on the narrow yoke of her collarbone. She appears drawn, exhausted.

Trying to give myself time to think, I go to the fridge, take out a carton of orange juice. I stand, carton in hand, door to the fridge open: Mimi is blocking the sink area, above which is the cupboard where the glasses are kept.

She makes a wry face, then walks out of the room. I pour myself a glass of juice. I don't know whether to follow her, or flee.

She's sitting on Walker's couch. I hold out the glass to her, and she takes it from me, sips, passes it back up. She pats the cushion beside her. I sit, wary.

She seems only now to really notice me. She catches my eye, and her face softens. I can smell a hint of alcohol on her.

I'm so sorry, sweetie, she says. I just woke up. And here you are! Let's have a look at you.

She pauses, scratches a knee, scaly – I notice, now – with psoriasis. She stops scratching.

If I could give you one piece of advice, she says, studying her legs. It would be. Well.

You should get *that* looked at, I offer.

What I should get looked at, she says. Is my head. Why I choose to remain here of all places with that fat fucker *boyfriend* I swear I'll never know.

She rubs her knee with her hand, stops, squeezes it. Removes her hand: the kneecap is white.

With his number-one daughter, Mimi continues, raising her voice. He ignores me when she's around. Even when she's not, sometimes. It's like he's mooning over her, worrying. Do you know what it's like to be number two, always?

Now she catches my eye, again.

You must think I'm selfish, she says, lowering her voice. Going on about *me*.

It's okay, I tell her. I don't mind.

She doesn't say anything. Sighs. After a pause, her breathing quickens, and her nostrils flare.

You'd think, she says. He'd want to pay me more attention. Given his tawdry little –

Oh, I say. Ohh. Where is he, anyway?

And the money he throws at Jena, she says. Throws! When I have to beg him for smokes. Each time he buys her something, it only serves to remind me. And then, here's what takes the cake, I just have to go and shriek at her over nothing!

She laughs at herself, a scary-sounding croak.

Too much, she says.

Suddenly she turns to me, squinting. She holds my gaze for a second – pinning me.

Ohh? she says.

Then she twists her head away, puts her elbow on the arm of the sofa, drops her head to rest against the heel of her hand.

I should have known, she says, her voice flat, colourless. No matter what, in the end, you'd have his back. Not mine. Blood's thicker than water.

No, I plead. Mimi.

She's only guessing, I tell myself. Right? She can't possibly know that I know.

Your *uncle*, she says sadly – but already she's pulling herself together, head held high, drawing her shoulders back, rising from the couch and with great, slow dignity leaving the room, climbing the stairs.

I sit for a minute by myself. Reach out and with a hand skim the still-warm indentation on the sofa cushion.

When I unlock the door from Walker's kitchen into the

apartment, Joy and Rachel are side by side in the kitchenette, eating toast with preserve.

What's going on with Mimi? I ask Joy. She okay?

Okay: I could have said *alive*.

Joy shrugs, indifferent: yes, no, maybe.

Well, what happened? I press.

Who's Mimi? Rachel says.

I'd love to get her on tape, Rachel declares. From what you're saying, Joy, it'd be so *interesting*.

Joy oozes an ingratiating smile.

Let's leave Mimi alone, I say hastily.

The three of us are seated on the sofa bed in the living room of the apartment, sipping Cokes from plastic cups. Rachel's in the middle.

Do you think she'd let me interview her? Rachel ignores me to ask Joy.

Mimi'd be thrilled to tears, but be prepared, she'll scorch your ears! Joy gushes – whatever resentment she continues to harbour toward Mimi evidently eclipsed by the desire to maintain Rachel's interest.

I lean forward to glare past Rachel at Joy.

Hope you're not easily offended, Joy continues, talking to Rachel behind my back, now. Mimi's a corker!

Rachel looks to me for confirmation.

Yeah, I say – pleased, at least, to have her attention caught by someone other than my mother. You wouldn't believe the stories. The way *she* tells them.

But is she for real? Rachel says, holding her cup to her forehead. Do you think she's making some of it up? Some of those groupies were, like, rape victims. Only it was glamourized.

I raise my cup to my lips and drink.

Well, let's just say –, Joy counters, bristling a little. It's true Mimi likes to put a fancy face on things. But –

I didn't mean –, Rachel says, faltering. I think she sounds great! Former chick-with-the-band. A sexual pioneer. I mean, how cool is *that*? Well worth documenting.

Just what the doctor ordered, I say under my breath.

Rachel, with her concentration of a flea – her attention alighting on *Mimi* now. Mimi as Rachel's latest project *du jour.*

Mimi doesn't need this.

Seems you've been awfully busy lately, Joy says to me unpleasantly, out of nowhere.

You noticed? I sneer. I suppose I should be grateful.

What exactly are you doing with all your money? Joy says. Let's hope you're not wasting it.

And I would tell *you* – like, why? I say antagonistically.

Joy looks down into her Coke.

No reason, she says, self-pityingly. I'm only your mother. Wait until you're a mother one day, then you'll know what it's like. I hope for your sake you never find out.

All the things I could do – the murderous, vengeful impulses – spring to mind only to almost instantly collapse inward, a black sucking hole where my heart should be. Dense, a death star. One that's been growing for most of my life, gaining on me, pulling me down, in – in so far one day I might never come out.

Maybe if you were more of a mother, I say caustically. We wouldn't be having this bullshit conversation.

Tanis, Rachel says, frowning.

Joy crouches forward, as if she's going to lash out at me again. But instead, she makes an appeal to Rachel.

Isn't she miserable? Joy says. Always been like this.

I strut from the room, a wince of pain deep within my ankle. In the kitchenette I can hear Rachel – thank you, nice to meet you, hope to see you again soon – and am further inflamed.

I wait for her in the Rabbit. Finally she's on the drive, moseying toward me, Joy hot on her heels. I start the car.

Just then Walker comes around the corner by the barns: belly hanging exposed beneath his too-tight T-shirt, cigarette snorkelling out the side of his mouth. He hasn't shaved today. Doesn't appear to have had a haircut recently, either, judging by the bushy grey 'fro on him. Jeans stained. He used to look *normal* to me. He takes the cigarette from his mouth, rubs the back of his neck, and about-faces the way he came.

What was that? Rachel says, once she's seated beside me on the passenger seat – still gawking in the direction of Walker's disappearance.

My uncle, I say. He's –. A bit shy.

That's a plus, she says. I'd hate to see him friendly. Does he look rough or what? And you're, like, related to him?

She waves a hand toward Joy, who waves excitedly back.

You know, Rachel says to me. You said some things to her that were uncalled for. She's just a really lonely person. It makes me wonder about you.

I put the car in gear. The stick vibrates beneath my hand.

And another thing, she says. You seem to be able to move pretty fast when you feel like it. I didn't see you limp once since we got here.

I shift back to neutral, take my almost-numb foot off the clutch.

You really want to get into this? I threaten.

No, she says. I don't.

I put the car back into first, turn around, make a left onto the road. Rachel waves again to Joy, whose hand wildly gropes the air.

She likes you, I say grudgingly as I accelerate.

I like being appreciated, Rachel responds sullenly.

I speed up some more – our silence skating on the wind slushing past our open windows – then I slow the car and pull over. I look straight ahead through the windshield.

Me too, I say.

After a pause, she strokes my right arm.

Accept my apology, she says solemnly. Let's never hurt each other again.

Agreed, I say.

She snickers – nicely, is how I take it. We won't argue again today. I hope.

What's with this *agreed* business? she laughs. You are too funny.

You think? I say happily. Like, funny hee-haw?

We drive toward the city, along the dirt road framed by the trees of August: sun-sopped, fat with green, addled with heat. The wind hangs heavily in thick branches. Rachel's got her legs up on the dash in front of her. She's slid her sandals off and is barefoot, her coral-painted toenails rilling daintily like sea anemones. Young: so am I. Nothing else will ever matter, or even come close.

8

THE JET BOYS' GIRL

From inside the plane the sky looked like nothing, upending blue blank as a baby's first dream. Tin skin, that blue leaking in. Nothing to get through. Nothing to lose. Mystery. Sheen on your arm from the drooly boys. Somewhere someone's puking. And thirsty.

Before all that, you're ordering drinks, nuts, thinking Merri or Melinda will be green as fish guts – before the jet's even off the ground you're in the rear bathroom with Jimmy or Rob, doing what you do best. Later, higher still, you find crushed velveteen – purple, blue, or black – in every seat. Also, cut-out stars, the moon. Sequins, their dazzle stitching your eyes shut. Satisfaction. Give your head a shake, Mimi! – with an effort, you can detach this little lapse of consciousness from you, as if peeling back satin sheets from a bed.

Then more drinks, hits to be dropped. The plane's a tin pot banging against a hot-sink sun. Dick or Mick or Steve – the glory-boy with the curling mane – says, The bitch. He announces this carefully, very British. You're so out of it you're not sure what he means. After all, isn't the song true – love is in the air?

But what you really are is lying across the aisle, someone pressing a boot against your throat in a curious slow-time pulse as he forgets to apply pressure, then with a start remembers again.

Someone says, The stinking bitch.

(Check, check – this thing working or not?)

Wait – before I go on, let me get the order right. Say my career commenced when I was fifteen – already old, though not when you consider I'm now thirty-eight, really *old*! So I'm fifteen, and my dim mother's just ditched me in Vancouver, and it's a west coast winter raining all over me. And I'm thinking, *What* am I going to do? What's the story going to be?

A madness, a fatal flaw. Anything but ordinary – please! (Greetings, Earthlings. Ha, ha.)

Say I was hatched from a bombshell of a woman who'd torn through her early life like it was a house on fire, until the doors to all the rooms in her head clapped shut against mayhem rising like a wail. Against my commotion, even – from my infant's cries to my toddler's prattle. She'd named me Mimi, after *her* mother, an extravagant gesture, since my mother was a woman for whom the past was a vanishing point, a scrap of an old language grudgingly murmured in the ear to quiet a child. Something I remembered her once crooning me to sleep by, something odd – *shpeelt zit ah-zoy goot, ah fawks-trawt*, please play a foxtrot – a leftover from an erased world. What did she see when she looked my way? I was half her, half not – in a world where half was nothing, not one thing and not another.

By thirty my mother was easily exhausted – you could see it in the fatty eyelids and slow sorrowing lips, the rounded Barbra Streisand rear of the eternal émigré. Always moving – from Montreal to Toronto before alighting in the land of milk and honey, where she waited tables in the dining room of the

Sylvia Hotel on Vancouver's English Bay, a place of only money and no-money, grey wandering rain.

I was seven when we washed up on that shore. We lived in an efficiency in the back of the Sylvia, facing a parking lot. During the day I'd drift alone along the seawall walk in front of the hotel, too-big yellow rubber boots like boats on my feet, an umbrella with pink-and-blue poodles floating above my head while other children, in brightly coloured raincoats and pants, bobbed between sandy ribs of beach like balloons tethered to diligent mothers. The rain-scored horizon like steel wool.

At night, our windows clammed shut against raccoons prowling the ledges, eyes winking from between the vines that smothered the Sylvia's facade. Lights out, the TV on, its blue buzzing my silent mother's wood-red hair until I think she might disappear in a cathode rush.

Only fifty-seven in Vancouver today, the weatherman says in winter. Take that, Toronto!

The rustling notes, each jot of sound, pushing pictures whole into my head. Take that!

Now – slow dissolve.

I see this mostly in black and white, the occasional swab of colour – a man on stilts. He unfolds like a flower from the side door of an old van parked next to the seawall in front of the hotel. With great bows and flourishes, his oversized Stetson slipping back and forth across his small head, he mounts a six-foot-tall candy-striped bicycle.

Wind whips sand to tumbleweeds along the walk. The sky is barely spitting now, though still low and dark. It's three on a winter afternoon. In good weather, portrait painters mass like primulas along the walk near Denman Street. But on this day any stragglers have packed it in by three-fifteen. At three-seventeen the wind drops like a stone.

The man wheels past me then stops, carefully placing each stilt on the ground, leaving faint hoof prints behind him. He turns around and nods once, smiling, as if at some fabulous secret.

Beyond him I can see bluish-backed gulls rising and falling in the sky like one breath after another. Beyond them, the blue-chested mountains. For once the rain has fully stopped. The night will be clear, the sunset yielding to a sky plush with stars, the lights of the ships at anchor even now beginning to pulse above the tarry water.

He tilts his head, as if listening to the tankers waiting in the bay. A quavering wind. Impossible high notes, low notes. Laughter and applause. The clink of loose change tuning up like an orchestra. At this moment everything seems possible.

He turns his head toward me again. That same slow smile, his mouth such a miracle of makeup I think each syllable he utters attaches the newly risen half-moon to the night, as if it had been a prop waiting backstage. His teeth like polished seashells.

Through a tear in the left leg of his pink pin-striped pants I can see wood, metal, something long and cold, hard.

I asked him home for dinner. In the months that followed, my mother managed to unglue herself from her TV, revived long enough for Mr. Long Legs to win her. *Please play a foxtrot.* I felt as if I'd won her too, brought her back to life.

Stiltless, without his costumes, my mother's beau was tiny, delicate. Also, breathtakingly penniless, buying roses with money he stole from her purse while she showered. He had the heartbreak allure of the cheerfully insolvent, the seductiveness of their fugitive ease.

Mimi, my lovely girl, he'd say, slipping a slender finger and thumb into my mother's wallet. Is the coast clear?

Let the show begin! He moved out of his van and into the Sylvia with us. He brought with him a scrappy white terrier with caramel patches on its face and behind. He quelled my mother's resistance with a radiant upsweep of canary yellow, crepe-clad arms.

What's a family without a dog? he asked, standing in the doorway, cradling the squirming rag-wrapped bundle in his arms.

There was no reply. He lowered the bundle to the floor.

Released, the dog – called Alfie after the Michael Caine movie – skippered about, indiscriminately sniffing every piece of furniture in the cramped apartment as my mother peered after it, saying nothing. She looked both hopeful and afraid. In love.

The dog ran loose on the beach every day while Mr. Long Legs worked the seawall walk bestride his bicycle, floridly addressing the mothers of small children he'd take for rides, a dollar *each* direction. When a bus burst the dog at the seams one milky-white morning, entrails festooned Davie Street like streamers.

That afternoon, back in the Sylvia, Mr. Long Legs pulled me onto his lap, drummed his thumbs on my knees. He smelled of the Old Spice my mother had given him. He touched a finger to the tip of my nose.

Hey! he said, as if he'd just had an idea. Alfie still loves you.

I sat motionless as a breeze nudged the edges of the heavy beige curtains. Water sluiced through the ivy around the window. Did he know something I didn't?

After a polite moment I carefully said, Alfie's *dead*.

Mr. Long Legs drew his head away. He raised his eyebrows and opened his brown eyes as wide as they would go. He held his hands palm up and lifted his narrow shoulders.

Dead? he said, deeply shocked. You think so? No, no, no. Let me tell you something. I think Alfie's in heaven. Barking and peeing, trying to sniff the ladies.

He closed his eyes. His lips relaxed, drooping at the edges. He looked tired and sad.

Just think, he said. Heaven.

For my mother, each time Mr. Long Legs left it might as well have been for good. He was gone for weeks at a time. He always came back poorer than before. My mother would unfasten herself from the TV long enough for tears, wall pounding. What else could she do? He was a charmer – not many women can say no to one of those.

Once she ripped up his pink pin-striped pants as he stood by helplessly. When she had finished, he picked up a shred or two from the floor, held them to his face and wept, stopping every now and then to glance, grief-struck, at the craters in the wall plaster.

Suddenly he brightened. He lay the rags on the kitchen table. He took out a polka-dot hankie and wiped his eyes, blew his nose. He put the hankie away. He puffed out his slender chest and the creases fell away one by one from his just-past-its-prime brow.

I could almost hear the fresh *ka-ching* as he gazed forlornly at the pink strips on the table. His eyes were shining. He'd milk this one for sure.

What do you think *that* was worth? he said.

When "for good" came, I was twelve. It took another three years for my increasingly frail, withdrawn mother to scrape up enough scratch to return, without me, to Ontario, tail tucked between her varicosed legs.

She didn't have enough for the taxi to the airport, an extravagance she asked me to pay for with my earnings from my after-school and weekend job at Record City. Only fifteen years old, I made less than minimum wage but told myself the position was entry-level. I planned to quit school when I turned sixteen, get a full-time office job at a record company.

As I stood on the sidewalk outside the Sylvia, my mother rolled down the window of the taxi. Her face looked puffy, her drawn-on eyebrows faintly askew. Rain grizzled the beach across the street. Much of the bay itself had vanished from sight.

I'll send for you, she said vaguely. Keep yourself nice.

Did I hate her? She was my *mother*. She rolled up the taxi window, which immediately covered with steam.

Me, age fifteen – ready for the fabulous hereafter! Left to my own devices, I quickly made myself over in the image of every sulky *Creem* queen, each Bebe and Miss Pamela and Patti. Kohl-eyed, lips frosted high-glam white. If I wasn't one thing, I could be another.

Magic. All the way down the coast, I was working my way up, competing with the Fawns and Dawns and Merri Madrigals. For the L.A. record exec, who no doubt before the age of thirteen thought there was no such thing as a poor Jew. The lowly drummer with his high hats and jelly rolls. A long-tongued slender-hipped lead guitarist. Eventually a Jimmy, Mick, or Keith. *Both* Keiths. Wheeling above me, huge as constellations.

Colour this crimson for passion.

The biggest prize? To be queen for a night on some band's – any band's – private jet, the high priestess of higher love, leaving the sweet Lady Janes and Prudences of the self below, weeping in the wings.

For more than anything, this was what I craved – the *up there*, honey and smoke. The ample horizon a streak of blue beyond money and reason, glimpsed from between a guy's skinny legs, his velvet-clad butt and stick-figure bulge. Dry ice machines lisping eternity. Everything I can't quite remember – mystery, a snakeskin boot bruising my throat while all the boys love me – an A-list drug of choice.

I *never* knew nice.

Especially when those sequins in the eyes scatter, the dream breaks up, all those cotton clouds scented with creme rinse – Je Reviens – become a pure white wall, blinding.

In the bathroom again, this time alone, I face myself in the mirror, though I'm finding it hard to see. Is that *gum* in my hair?

Maybe I'm a little afraid.

And later, staring at the tarmac beneath my feet, the grain of the asphalt grits my eyes. It's not raining, but it might as well be – I'd rather be anywhere else. I feel as if I'm about to leave what's left of myself behind.

Now where *was* I? Earth to? I'll just jump right back in.

At age twenty-six, I was suddenly overripe for my chosen career. Trying to decide if Toronto's smatter of light seen from above Pearson International was the circuit board for some third-rate sound and lighting show hard-wired to my neural system or merely a sorry child's spill of beads. Was I broke! Electric with it because the truth is, poverty can elevate – that snap-crackle of fear can take you right out of your mind.

I called my mother from the airport.

Mom? Is that you?

Jerk with a briefcase bumped me. *Jerk.*

What's that? she said – then hung up.

When I walked, unannounced, into her apartment in Whitby, she cried hard. Foundation makeup shone beneath her eyes like half-moons. Her once-beautiful hair stuck out uncertainly from her head, a dry sprig of curl here, a greasy tendril there. Her nose was dripping.

Mom, I said.

Confusion's coquette, she held her arms out to me, quickly dropped them.

We'd always had this shyness, if that's what you call it, with each other. The same shyness I've come to recognize between people who've slept together long enough to find themselves in that remote place where the touching stops – each of you bedding down with the other's fantasy, someone else's breasts sliding in ones or twos across your own body as clouds might drift across the sky. Where all you are is part and parcel of these loveless moments, scorched by drink and the best – *absolutely* the best – pharmaceuticals an ace blow can buy, some guy grasping the metal bed frame to keep from falling, swaying to beat hell, bleating like a lamb, wounded bear.

These guys always have someone. Their minds are somewhere else.

(Seems Walker is no exception.)

Maybe what *I* have is this – the sins of my mother. Otherwise, how to explain the way I take leave, almost, of my senses? Papery sounds begin to rustle in my head, and my tongue flutters like a torn bag in my mouth. How can I forgive? Her, anybody. Not even the slightest indiscretion. I never thought of myself as squeamish, thought I could stomach a lot – live and let live, etcetera.

But when I stood before her that day, and she seemed at first to know me, and then to forget, I raised my hand, slapped her hard.

Where was I, indeed.

Locale is a thing to be moved through, like so much backdrop. Since I happened to be here, why not stay? This was my thinking twelve years ago. As I've said before, I was on the cusp of over the hill. And she *was* my mother – which seemed, however vaguely, to be something.

In Whitby, she delved deeper into her disappearing act syllable by syllable until she couldn't care for herself any more. By then I had a job as a manicurist forty minutes north and west in a Stouffville beauty shop, had bought an old beater in which, when the time came, I moved her out of the tiny apartment I shared with her and into the Whitby psycho home.

I took care of her! Kept myself in line as best I could, despite what that quack says. It's not as if my mother ever took care of *me*.

I entertained myself. Bit of this, bit of that. One drunken night after work, in a neighbouring Oshawa bar, I clambered on stage to screech along with the house band in front of a mostly auto-worker audience too toasted to notice I couldn't actually sing.

Here was something I could do – play the loud exotic, queen of the cross-eyed Jacks. I'd slept with the stars, hadn't I? Let my veiled past hint at marvellous futures! (So I glamourized, accessorized! Yes – I was on that plane. Rock on. Rubes!) Those horny shills lapped it up.

What a joke.

Standing up there for the first time on that puny stage, fear snaked around my throat, seancing my voice. It was perfect! Bewitching. I was giving up nothing, all my nothing years, because nothing could be everything in this nowhere place.

(Getting what you wanted? Hope so. I aim to please.)

I imagined the dull grey sounds were the ghosts of lullabies my mother never sang.

9

REQUESTS AND DEDICATIONS

Labour Day weekend arrives, unseasonably cool, starchy and clear. By late Sunday afternoon a vigorous, oaky burnish settles on buildings and trees. We promenade north along Sumach Street. Front gardens bright with marigolds bedeck the renovated Victorian row houses and three-storey brownstones of Cabbagetown.

Left at Winchester, left again onto Parliament, past the Winchester Hotel and the thrift store, turning into a café where we order double lattes with biscotti, take a table in the upstairs back room.

Rachel thrums her fingers on the table. I try to keep my mouth shut, afraid of provoking another outburst.

Several nights ago, Rachel's newly red head was buried in a magazine. I'd stood from the table, resignedly begun clearing dishes, the empty takeout containers. Hot, exhausted, hormonal, I suddenly felt overwhelmed – Rachel never seemed to lift a finger to help.

I can't do everything, I said.

She continued reading. I cleared my throat. She turned a page and cleared *her* throat in a hostile pantomime.

I took the dishes to the counter. The air seemed to be sweating, and I imagined mildew colonizing my lungs. I fought the desire to spit up. Involuntarily, without thinking, I cleared my throat again.

Suddenly she rose, knocking the chair out from under her, and pulled a major meltdown: slamming a soup bowl into the overflowing garbage can, snatching our plates from the counter before I could grab her arms to stop her. She opened her hands, and the dishes clattered to the floor, breaking.

That'll teach you, she said.

Still holding her arms I'd stared, stupefied, into her face.

Talk about passive-aggressive, she said. I never *asked* you to clean up.

Joy. That's what I'd thought. *Like mother, like daughter.*

And – and: I chalked up another to Rachel's genius for the extraordinary, reasoning that while it was true she wasn't getting out much – true she was less and less resembling the gaudy, chatty parrot I met that night in the bar, in what now seemed like ages ago – wasn't this just more evidence of her exceptionally insightful, artistic nature? Something I knew nothing about. As I saw it, my role was to nurture it along. To try not to be so inept that she'd give me the boot.

I released her arms. Chapped-looking – distressed – lips. Dark circles under her eyes. Skin waxen. Brassy cropped hair, soaked. No top, bra-less, soggy boy-short underwear.

Frying up, I thought – aware of my own feet perspiring onto the floor, the countless mornings leaking into nights, a punishing cycle broken only by weak thunderstorms, too-brief cooling periods. Little wonder we were gingery, conducting rods for a barometric-triggered unhappiness, difficult to define, stake attribution to root and cause. There was nothing to really worry about: late August had merely overtaken us, casting a restless, twitchy pall that found expression in a mounting pressure.

I would try to be less like Joy, stuck up there in Walker's Markham, where even the horses would be uppity, churlish in this weather. She'd be spending her days cleaning at the golf club, coming home to evenings by herself – tidying up the apartment, watching TV. On Sundays, her day off, she'd clean the first floor of Walker's house – the second was off-limits to her. She'd straighten the kitchen – Ajax his coffee-stained sink – vacuum his living-room rug and sofa, thanklessly, as if earning her keep. Lonely. Bitching to those within earshot, pressing them with her complaints, bitterly resigned to observing lives from which she's increasingly cut off.

Including mine, I thought with a pang: I couldn't help but wonder if Joy missed me – missed having someone to eat a Dove Bar with, leaning together over the kitchenette sink so as not to make a mess, her raunchy smell leavening the antiseptic odour of Mr. Clean as we jokingly rough-shouldered each other, jockeying for position.

Well – too bad. I wouldn't go back, bounce from one confrontation to another, shrinking inside, becoming as narrow as the world around me. As mean, if not worse.

Stop staring at me, Rachel said, interrupting my thoughts. Or *through* me. I'm right here.

I'd walked, then, down the hall to the bathroom, stood alone under the shower, compulsively clearing my throat. Things would get better soon, I told myself. Rachel would be returning to the Ontario College of Art shortly, and I found this reassuring. She'd have a schedule, course requirements, pulling her – us – slowly into the world like taffy.

I horked custardy-yellow phlegm down the drain, rinsed my mouth with needles of water, stepped out and towelled off.

I for one was ready to enter the social whirl.

First, Suzanne.

Who is late.

Nervous, I check my watch several times while Rachel and I slog through our lattes. Finally Suzanne walks in the door, poses a second in the entrance, letting her eyes adjust to the light. I put my latte down, wave, call to her. I stand.

Make a scene, Rachel says drolly. So much for your legendary sang-froid.

Then she rises too, saunters off and down the stairs where the bathroom is located. I feel self-conscious. Made of tin.

Please, Suzanne says when she reaches me. Be seated. Let's not aggravate the war wound. Don't want you limping around on my behalf.

She pulls her chair in to the table.

Is your friend always this rude? she asks.

She's my *girl*friend, I say – preposterously, grinning my head off, pride getting the better of me as, against my better judgment that I should let Suzanne figure it out for herself, I spill the beans.

Suzanne – always one step ahead, knows me better than I know myself, all these heaped-on etceteras – says, Of course she is, you big dope.

She places a hand on mine. Her face elasticizes into a sarcastic smile.

Sex haze, she pronounces. Seriously. You guys are drenched. I could see it a mile away.

Then she looks at a spot beside me: bored. I pull my hand out from underneath hers. Why did I do this? I wonder miserably, lips frozen in a painful smile. I'd called *her*, two days ago, ostensibly to say goodbye for the upcoming school year – and just what were her plans, anyway? We'd kind of been so out of touch. We'd agreed to meet – she could do downtown, she'd said, sounding blasé about it.

Now she picks up my latte, sips, puts the glass down in front of her.

It's about time you got someone, she says casually. You always were pretty backward. That's what Jackie says.

Jackie: Kendrew's first name. The way Suzanne says it – with a nonchalance hinting of deep intimacy – rocks me. But, ever the sorry ape, unable to stop myself, I continue to smile, seamed into the grinning gorilla costume Suzanne has laid out for me.

I take back my latte, gulp some. Put it in front of me on the table.

I think –, she says, tapping a finger to her immaculately hairless upper lip.

I swipe my mouth with my sleeve, try to settle myself as she picks up my coffee again and drinks, eyeing the establishment and other patrons around us. I don't want to appear intimidated by her, by how easily she seems to glide through the world – when so much feels stubborn and difficult for me. I notice she's growing her once-short hair out, uneven hanks of natural blonde coming in beneath the brittle black. As always, great posture, the lithe million-buck limbs of early ballet lessons followed by tennis and dressage.

Tomorrow, the holiday Monday, she leaves for her first year at Trent University, a several hours' drive away in Peterborough. But, Rachel – yes, my girlfriend, I think proudly – is going to art college, here in the city. By extension, that she's going to school puts a little polish on me.

It comes to me full-force now: I hate Suzanne. Hate how she says *Jackie* with so little chatty fanfare, hate the March-vacation ski trips to Austria she always seemed so unexcited about. Hate that she seems to think she knows me – someone unimportant whose friendship she discarded as casually as she might toss an unfashionable pair of jeans.

For the first time, I feel *free* to hate her, free to admit it: I don't need her any more, don't need to feel that my life is enlarged by vicariously experiencing hers. I have my own life now. I have Rachel.

What's surprising is how soothing the hatred feels – like an aromatherapeutic soak in a hot bath. Bubbles, candles, monks chanting on the CD player while this cleansing, detox hate courses below my skin – a blood disturbance, an extra beat of the heart, calming, something I can privately listen to with pleasure, at my convenience. Like having a secret friend.

Rachel joins us, no hello or anything – just swishes into her chair without pulling it out from the table, in a way that emphasizes her narrow hips, her canary-yellow pants, and tight red navel-exposing tee. Her hair is wet, spiked into tufts, as if she's put her head under the tap in the bathroom, then carelessly – defiantly – finger-combed herself without looking in the mirror: her wide cheekbones, the dramatic, dark eyebrows, thick and ungroomed, requiring no further embellishment for the strength of their impact.

Suzanne nods casually in her direction, sets to work using the last of my biscotti to scoop foam from my latte – sucks on the biscuit, showily using her tongue to dislodge sugary particles from her perfect teeth: come on! Tilting her head to one side, puffing little breaths out her nose. Then she confidently stretches in her chair, bumps my leg, which I move – and am immediately annoyed with myself for surrendering so easily to her sense of entitlement.

For her part, Rachel is acting as if she's never seen *me* before. Cruelly checked out, choosing instead to aim a faint, browsing interest at the small price-tagged paintings hanging on the ochre walls surrounding us: intense, supersaturated acrylic blues and reds, built up, scratched over, gouged repeatedly by pencil. They look like somebody tried too hard. Depressed, I slump in my seat, feeling squeaky in my skin, as if it were growing tighter by the minute. Then, restless, I hunch forward over the table, snigger nervously, hold up my empty latte glass.

Anyone for seconds? I ask.

By the time I return, triad of coffees precariously balanced in my hands, Rachel and Suzanne are going at it – sort of.

My parents own a litho by your dad, Suzanne is saying. But now he only does sculpture, right? Too bad. I really liked his earlier stuff.

Rachel cocks her head and smiles viciously. She drops the smile fast.

I pull my chair up tight to the table – too tight, an over-eager geek. I feel huge, inflated – with a sense of my own foolishness. I'd like to crawl under the table, crawl away, unseen, and never show my face again, ashamed: I'd never even thought to ask about Rachel's father. And now here Suzanne is, getting to score points.

Those images were like, so iconic, Suzanne says.

But Rachel is again studying the little paintings around us. Following her gaze, now, Suzanne cracks a snarky laugh.

Pretty bad, she opines. Tragic.

I kind of don't mind that one, Rachel says dreamily – pointing to one of the canvases.

As far as I can tell, it's exactly like the others but for the lime-green stroke down the centre.

The tension works, Suzanne allows. Like, how the primaries flurry and dissipate?

Rachel raises an eyebrow, then looks away, leaving Suzanne

high and dry – unable to impress, beached in the wake of a superior understanding, a sifting panic in her eyes – and a channel open for me.

It's got nice energy, I venture – feeling like I've leapt off a nose-bleed cliff, dived into a leaden, sink-or-swim sea.

Energy: Rachel's word, at times, for what she likes about me. For what she likes about certain books, which I then inhale.

Exactly, Rachel says, snapping back to the conversation – or, rather, to me. That's it exactly. Bravo, sweetie. Good eye!

She pats me on the head.

Hello, kultcha.

On our way home we stop at a Chinese bakery on Parliament Street south of Gerrard. Two chicken, two vegetable, two curried beef bao, and a large moon cake, which we eat out of the white paper bag, standing outside on the sidewalk crowded with crates of live ducks and roosters, row upon row of tables stocked with roly-poly fish, eyes filmy, blistered with blindness.

Rachel leans her forehead against mine. I see her doubled.

What an unevolved jerk, she says. How can you know her?

Pretty dire! I say.

I move away from her to finish my second pillowy, semi-sweet bun, vegetable. Rachel's only eaten half of her first, which is chicken. She slips it back in the bag, which she's holding. Must be on a diet or something. My pager goes off. I check the phone number: Walker.

I reach into the bag.

Who was that? Rachel asks.

No one, I say – recalling Rachel's reaction upon seeing him for the first time, last month.

I start on the curried beef – but by the second mouthful

the flavour turns pastelike. At least he cares enough to sometimes check up on me.

My uncle, I correct.

Which is it? she says, brushing a crumb from the corner of my mouth.

I finish my bun, take Rachel's half-eaten one out of the bag, and set to work on that.

Aren't you going to call back? she says, smiling wanly. Is there someone you don't want me to know about? Another girlfriend?

I wave my hand dismissively. How many languages click and vibrate through the air around us? Strings of bright shiny words I don't understand, opening, shutting like beaded curtains. The September sun is on my face. On Rachel's, a queasy, unsettled look, tumble of distrust in her eyes. People peel by, a zest of traffic. I finish chewing the bun, reach for another, which must be hers too. It's like I've got some kind of bottomless pit thing going on.

When you coming up? Walker says when I call him back that night.

Don't know.

Don't know much, do you.

In between our spare words, a telegraph of silence over the phone: short pause, long pause, long. I wonder if I have the nerve to ask about Mimi. The last time I'd seen her she'd seemed so out of it.

I've shut the office door and locked it – all's quiet in condoland tonight, and I have another three hours to go before I finish my shift.

I toe a rent in the carpet as Walker and I breathe back and forth at each other. I open and close the desk drawers. No surprises here: ballpoint pens, erasers. A TV guide, underneath the dog-eared novel I borrowed from Rachel that I've been reading on my dinner breaks.

Your mother's asking about you, he says, surprisingly. And some friend of yours.

Short breath, then a long, drawn-in breath: mine. I suck my teeth.

Then he says, Christ – and begins to hack as if through wet slag.

How much longer has he got with those shot lungs? I wonder with a stab of fear.

Hey old guy, I say. You okay?

See for yourself, he wheezes. Tomorrow.

Day after, I say.

But it's almost a month later before Rachel and I are sitting across from Walker at his kitchen table. It's early afternoon. He's been up all night and morning with a colicky horse, and his cocoa eyes are swollen half-shut – painful in appearance, red as the crimped flesh around fresh sutures. Rachel's sitting stiffly, watching him as if he were an exotic specimen, and in his shyness he hardly acknowledges her presence, merely grunting at her when we first came in.

Now he lights a cigarette, his hand shaky.

Well, kiddo, he says. So where's the Rolls?

In for repairs, I reply. I'm driving economy for now, instead. Another import, though.

Oh well, he says in a string of smoke. That Rolls is sure one piece of crap automobile. You should consider replacing it with something reliable. German engineered or something.

I begin to feel pleasantly sleepy – Walker's familiar Camel smell is dishing up a buffet of impressions: the waxy sensation of broken-in leather between my fingers, the warmth of the barns in winter, the hot salty taste of the Tabascoed popcorn he'd fix for our lunch when I was ten or eleven and we'd just returned from an early-summer ride together into the grassy fields and across the Rouge, the tops of our boots grazing the water. Jena must have been – where? At Lily's?

I lean back in my chair, stretch my arms lazily over my head in the generous fall sunlight streaming in the window, yawn.

You mean, like a Volkswagen? I ask, playing along.

I imagine laying my head on Walker's large forearm and resting: how many of my afternoons once ended this way? Snug with Walker, *Roller Derby* reruns from the 1970s on TV – trying to stay awake long enough to cheer on my favourite Fleur-de-lys skater, the nimble shorty with the black ponytail, hell on wheels.

During commercial breaks, I'd dreamily study a spoonful of translucent Jell-O salad: grapes, miniature marshmallows, and sunflower seeds embedded in lime-green cubes – Joy's doing. My mother absent, but not far: an ideal, acceptable distance.

Different from the estrangement wreaked by her being too close – close with Joy meant invasion, assault. She was someone you could love best – if at all – from a distance.

That's what I'm saying, he says – keeping the ball rolling. I believe you'd be much better off.

Funny you mention it, I respond. But I happen this very day to be taking one out for a test drive. By the way, the Erie running all right?

All right, he says.

My mistake: still holding his cigarette, he swipes his bulbous paws over his pouchy face, then rests both elbows on the table and holds his head, shaking it cumbrously from side to side. Achingly, I notice his work shirt is faded from ten years' worth of washings. The cuffs are ratty. His hands are calloused, right-hand index and middle fingers nicotined yellow. The wrinkles on his face are deep wallows. Go easy on him, I tell myself.

Rachel is starting to fidget, picking at a loose thread on her sweater's hem. She rises antsily from her chair and reseats herself, one leg folded under her.

Walker turns in her direction.

Smoke? he says, reaching toward his pack of cigarettes.

Thanks, no, she says primly – a look of repugnance on her face, a stronger reaction than tobacco usually elicits from her.

So what kind of school you going to? he demands.

Art, she replies.

Art! he says acidly.

How did you know she's in school? I ask.

Your mother said, he answers – my stomach lurches.

Should we go and see the horses now? Rachel says to me, urgingly. And then maybe your mom will arrive home?

Where's the bride-to-be? I ask Walker hurriedly – too breezily, I realize with a wince, remembering Mimi's state the last time I saw her.

Yeah, he gruffs, ignoring my question. Why *don't* you go see the horses?

I stand, and so does Rachel.

As we do, Walker leans over in his seat and allows his eyes to graze over Rachel's out-of-season cropped-pant-revealing calves and ankles, her feet in black two-inch wedge sandals, purple-painted toenails, her boy-girl bumps and curves – stretching his thick right arm, fleshy as a tongue, across the kitchen table toward her. Continuing to leer, he opens his eyes exaggeratedly wide, the black pupils pearling with a caricature lust mixed with contempt.

The colour drains from Rachel's face. I try to think of

something to say to him in warning – something rancid with an outrage violating enough to reach him on his own terms. *What's the matter? Mimi refusing to put out for you, and you can't find anyone else to bang?* But I feel flattened, one-dimensional, like a piece of sheet metal.

Walker, I say. *Where* is Mimi?

Living room, he says – with one hand putting his butt out in an ashtray, with the other gesturing us out of the kitchen. Be my guest.

Pig, Rachel says under her breath, and crosses into the living room.

I hurry after her. As usual, the curtains are drawn, and the room appears underlit. Though it's only two-thirty, Mimi is sleeping on the couch. A white bedsheet is wrapped around her, one leg protruding, a pink-pantied hip visible. Her long hair hangs in loose coils. Her skin looks tissue-thin, as if it might tear if you touched it. On the floor, beside the couch, is a glass, a quarter-inch of dark-gold liquid – rye, I can smell it now – glowing in the bottom.

Let me guess, Rachel says unkindly – apparently angry with me for having brought her here. The diva.

Although Rachel hadn't bothered to lower her voice, Mimi, in her slumber, doesn't stir. One of her arms hangs off the couch, above the glass of rye. I hesitate, then go to her, gently take her hand in mine. It feels heavy, lukewarm.

Hey lady, I whisper – fighting back my alarm.

Her hand gives a weak squeeze, then becomes flaccid again. I let her go.

I look at Rachel. She lifts her brows, twists her mouth up to one side.

I hook my fingers to the back of her neck, hard enough to make her squirm, steer her back through the kitchen where –

for the time it takes to exit onto his porch – we endure Uncle Inferno's sordid gaze.

Inside the second barn Rachel unberths a nest of kittens. They scatter, and she hops after them among the warren of stalls, stopping in amazement at the rabbity twitchings of the horses in the standing stalls, entering one after another to slip her small hands over the great round haunches and sliding thighs. I follow, afraid that any one of them, startled and surly, will boot her into eternity.

Then, still terse with me for having rough-handled her, she barely allows herself to be lead out back, behind the barns. Facing east from the sagging fenceline, we watch the handful of horses – several chestnuts coppery in the afternoon sun, the one black verging on midnight blue – turned out in the field beyond the outdoor ring.

Beautiful, Rachel murmurs. I have to admit.

Her tense body begins to relax into me. She sighs, rubs the side of her face into mine.

Looking past Rachel's head, to the north, now, I can see Walker hasn't made it far into his project: the excavator's claw lies as if dashed to the ground, and the cab is tilted at an odd angle, as if something gave way mid-motion, and hasn't been repaired.

Rachel moves in front of me, but still I keep looking toward the useless Erie.

Isn't anybody there? she says. Operator, I can't seem to connect.

But I have nothing to say to her, no response to give in return. She steps away, puts her back to me, facing the fields. The horses are grazing tranquilly, unperturbed by the visions of human malice whisking around their beautiful placid heads. The air smells of the peaking fruit from the unharvested apple and crabapple trees, a sour-sweet confection. Spiking the green fields, mustardy goldenrod. I come closer, encircle her from behind with my arms, drop my neck forward until the sides of our heads are touching. I nuzzle my jaw against hers. Kiss her hair.

What if I could see what she sees, inhabit both her and the objects of her sight, repossess them both?

I put a hand down the back of her pants. She arches her spine. I touch her with my hands, mouth at her nape. Slowly we sink to the ground, lie in a tickle of fountain grass, set amber tongues wagging.

Perhaps an hour later, when we pass back through the first barn, Jena is standing in the middle of the aisle, eyes focused on the ceiling beams. She's listening to an MP3 player, rapping under her breath.

Then she notices us, removes the headphones from her ears.

I had an orgasm last night, she says.

How long has it been since I last saw her? Two months, less? How old is she now, fourteen? She looks older, taller – has lost some of the baby fat. Her blonde hair is longer, blonder. Her jeans are tight, tighter than she used to wear them. They're turned up at the two-inch cuff, ironed-looking. She's wearing high-heeled boots that look as if they're straight out of Mimi's arsenal.

Single or double? Rachel says. Multiple? You look like a multiple to me.

This is my cousin, I say bleakly.

I think multiple, Jena says, frowning slightly in concentration.

Whizz-bang? Rachel says. Then another?

Outside, Joy squirts toward the three of us across the drive. I notice – shocked, given the state she seemed to be in – that Mimi's car is gone.

I stop. Jena, following behind me, steps on my heel. Rachel walks ahead of us, arms open in greeting.

I was just coming to look for you, Joy says breathlessly – addressing Rachel as they embrace. Walker said you were here. I'm making supper! Can't have you starving, can I?

Rachel laughs and looks back at me, says, Tanis, you are so like your mother. Both of you trying to fatten me up.

Joy glances over at me, questioningly.

Hi *Joy*, I say. Remember me?

My face stings. I feel wrathful – at least ten feet tall, and growing.

Joy can really cook up a storm, I comment venomously to Rachel.

I look at Jena, who's beside me now. She makes a face, puts a finger to the tip of her nose and pushes up.

Ew! she agrees – and plods off alone toward the house.

Joy looks aghast.

So what exactly *is* for din-din? I ask her.

See? Joy cries to Rachel. Mothers can never please.

Mother? I scoff.

You two! Rachel teases, in an attempt to mediate between Joy and me.

I lapse into sullen silence. Joy has changed her hair: a light brown with honey-blonde highlights. And her outfit, I notice, is one I haven't seen before – loose-fitting taupe-coloured pants and matching top. More flattering, softer looking, than her usual Mimi-inspired get-ups.

Don't *you* look nice, Rachel says warmly to Joy.

I pick everything out myself now, Joy replies wistfully.

And why is that? I want to say to her – didn't you drive

Mimi away, with all your complaints, especially when she needed you?

And I started going to a salon, Joy says, hands fluttering to her head.

But why should she help Mimi? I ask myself – remembering how Mimi seemed to forget all about Joy when Walker proposed. Which didn't prevent the happy couple from allowing Joy to continue to clean house for them.

Great colour! Rachel tells her.

You know, Joy says, lowering her voice confidentially. I went grey early. From worrying too much. At your age! Isn't that awful? I used to pluck it out with tweezers.

Sounds masochistic, Rachel says, chuckling.

Oh, don't do what *I* did! Joy says.

I had an orgasm last night, Jena says, trolling for attention as if rooting for truffles.

More squash? Joy asks Rachel, which she politely declines – really Rachel's eating little of the food set before her, this family feast entirely for her benefit.

Walker? Joy says and reaches across the seldom-used oak dining-room table for the serving platter.

Three half acorn squashes – baked with brown sugar and butter until scabrously charred – are left.

Just leave it, he barks.

Joy exhales noisily, picks up her fork and knife with a clatter.

Mimi hasn't returned yet, and no one mentions her. Despite her absence, with the rest of us gathered here, the meal feels holiday-ish, like a pre-Thanksgiving dinner – a holiday we've never done. Joy's gone all out in a way I've never seen before, using her mother's lace tablecloth and white dinner napkins that remain folded beside the dinner plates throughout the meal.

There's a depressingly well-done roast beef, which had been hurriedly and only partially thawed before being incinerated in a smoking oven: thanks, but no thanks. I load up instead on crispy roast potatoes, smearing them with horseradish I scoop straight from the jar. I pick at the Green Giant frozen green beans with almonds that have been nuked to near-extinction, guzzle Sprite out of a can.

Meanwhile the man of the household has settled in with an oversized plastic World Wrestling Federation freebie tumbler (Goldberg Rules!) of rye and Coke, which he guards with one paw. He hasn't begun to eat yet.

Dad, Jena says, restlessly slumping this way and that in her chair. Mom made it for me. Dad? Want to know what's in one? Orange juice. And. Um.

Jena, stop talking and eat, Joy says, and pushes the platter of squash down the table to her before turning to Rachel and sighing.

Isn't she a little underage? Rachel says.

An Orgasm! Joy says. I don't know what that woman was thinking.

Jena ponders, flips back her dirty-blonde hair, showing dark at the roots. Her eyes are rimmed with black. Purples and unclear pinks, a shimmery-white rainbow graces her eyelids up to the brows.

Walker lets go of his drink, lights a cigarette, and commences to alternate between eating and smoking.

Walker! Joy says.

Rachel observes him, smirking as he leans over the table to poke his cigarette in an ashtray from the Desert Sands Hotel in Las Vegas. The ashtray had been a rare present – bought, possibly stolen – from my father to Joy in the early days of their courtship. Growing up, I believed that ashtray represented the height of sophistication. Now, in Rachel's presence, I feel embarrassed at the memory of my early taste. Until I remember Rachel's delight at kitschy knick-knacks, the more outrageous, the better – the greater the value to the knowledgeable, ironic beholder. *Good eye!*

Walker? Joy says.

He puts his cigarette out in the ashtray.

Dad, know what? Jena says. Dad? Whizz-bang!

Jena, Joy says. Stop it. Who put a nickel in you?

She works a strand of hair around the first finger on her right hand. With the other she buttons and unbuttons the top of her Lurex-threaded top, which looks as if it's two sizes too small for her, cropped at her still-pudgy midriff.

Walker doesn't answer. Not so much as a glance in her direction as he ploughs potatoes and grey meat into his mouth.

Dad, Jena says, zippering a heart-shaped pendant back and forth on the gold necklace Walker bought at Sears for her tenth birthday – how Joy and Mimi had clucked their tongues over that, concerned that he was spoiling his daughter, but likely jealous, as well.

Dad, want to know something? Jena continues to pipe. Auntie Joy? Want to know what an Orgasm is?

We're in Walker's kitchen, where we'd left our jackets, getting ready to leave – he's upstairs, having immediately sought refuge upon finishing his dinner. Jena's also upstairs, shooed to her own room by Joy after a dessert of canned peaches.

I'm buttoning up, Rachel's wrapping a light cotton scarf around her neck, when Joy rushes in from the apartment carrying several bulging plastic grocery bags.

Here, she says, thrusting them at Rachel.

Rachel opens one of the bags. Inside are several near-empty boxes of Kleenex. She opens another one: a dozen or so less than half-full – or is that more than half-empty? – rolls of toilet paper. She looks perplexed.

They're from the golf club, I say – too embarrassed to say more.

I'm missing something, Rachel says, puzzled.

But it's simple enough: a person willing to pay twenty thousand dollars a year in membership fees wants a paradise of plenitude – wants to never run out. Instead of tossing the half-useds, Joy brings them home, cutting down on her own costs. My embarrassment tips over to annoyance at Rachel for not immediately – sensitively – *getting* it.

Thank you so much, Rachel says – still mystified but recovering her manners. How very thoughtful.

What else do you want? Joy says. Wait, don't you guys take off yet.

She disappears into the apartment, returns with yet another grocery bag.

Here, she says – pulling out a half-dozen or so fingers of individually packaged Heinz mustard and ketchup from the clubhouse snackbar. We're supposed to throw these out once they're past their expiry dates. Isn't that a waste? They're still good! Honest, I use them all the time, and I'm still here, aren't I?

Oh, my, *god*, Rachel says in the car, slapping her knee like a local yokel. Wasn't that a hoot and a half?

So far, late September has been unusually warm, and the trees by the side of the road are almost fully green still – a pinch only, here and there, of pumpkin, curry. Saffron. The beach-ball sun – gaily streaked by sunset, dust, pollution – hangs low in the sky.

I am just so psyched, she says. That was like, straight out of I don't know what.

She swivels around and looks at the back seat, covered in plastic bags.

What are we going to do with all this? she says. Junk it?

My jeans stick to my legs. My feet bake in my boots. I clear my throat until its sore. No scenic route for us this evening: I've turned right out of Walker's, north, tacking west onto the 404. Driving fast. Soon we'll be on the parkway – we're almost in the megacity now: office towers, industrial parks populated by mallards and ornamental mute swans, Canada geese. Many won't even bother to migrate south when the weather turns.

I think I'm coming down with something, I say.

Your family! she says. They're like, the goon squad.

A few minutes pass as I leave the north Toronto exits behind.

I like your mom, though, she says – an afterthought.

I put my hand on Rachel's leg and squeeze hard. Her thigh softens toward me, yielding in pain. Then she pushes me away.

I take my eyes off the road: her wide cheekbones are modelled by the purpling twilight, and her open lips appear dark, moating her mouth – I picture my calloused fingers there, digging in.

Watch out! she shrieks.

I look back at the road and brake hard. The tires squeal and the car skids in its lane. A horn blares to my right. I correct the car, back off from the SUV in front. Then, without signalling, I change out of the passing lane, accelerate past the SUV, dash left in front of it. Again I take my eyes off the road to look at her: she's clutching the door handle with both hands, her face white.

Next time, I tell her. We'll do your family.

Poured-concrete floor, brick walls painted white. In front of us, spraying spit as he squeals into a microphone, is a paunchy middle-aged sound poet. Occasionally Rachel's father, tall gaunt ascetic with long, tied-back grey-yellow hair – well-known sculptor, sometime musician, performer – stands from his metal stool and gargles into a trumpet: big bad dad performs with a free jazz ensemble once a month at the Sounding, which is where Rachel, after much goading on my part, consents to take me to meet him, partway through October.

For ten bucks a piece – I pay – we sit in the company of seven other people on folding chairs in a drafty loft. When the first set is over, Rachel leaves her chair and goes to her father.

She's lost weight recently, is almost as strikingly skinny as when I first met her – though a bit more buff, perhaps, as is visible through the clingy black yoga pants and fitted green paisley tee she's wearing, recent purchases. She certainly has a penchant for spending her student-loan money on clothes and tech equipment when the cheques come in. I cover food and utilities, and kick in for some of her rent.

What did she do before me? I wonder – and feel proud, protective, not even caring that I'm not saving a cent of my earnings – as Dad puts his arm around her bony waist and squeezes her to his side. Her shoulders stoop, and her hand flies to her face.

I wander over. Rachel introduces us, and he looks me up and down, doesn't seem too impressed by what he sees, grunts unidirectionally, turns back to Rachel and strokes her short hair, only yesterday – in anticipation of seeing her father? – dyed an intense Hallowe'en orange. I return to my seat, unnerved, wondering if coming here had been such a good idea.

Halfway through the next set, which is mostly more of same, Rachel's father walks into the sparse audience, trumpet held aloft. He stops before Rachel, cups her chin in the cage of one hand – freckled, the knuckles scraped and dry, faint scrawl of old man's hair between each knobby joint – and offers his trumpet to her lips.

Blow, he enjoins – aging asshole hipster. Go on, baby girl, blow.

Rachel shakes her head firmly, no. He swings the instrument back to his mouth and wails it as he returns to the stage.

Rachel sits beside me with her legs tightly crossed, arms twined around herself. There's a bob at the hinge of her jawline as she clamps and unclamps her teeth.

The next and last piece, billed as a concerto for three blackboards, previews with the black-clad performers – five of the seven people who've been sitting in the audience – wheeling in their instruments and placing steel buckets beside each with clenched ceremony. Rachel's father has exited, only to make a grand re-entrance brandishing a music stand and an inches-thick score.

For twenty-seven minutes the ensemble scratches fingernails, rubs erasers, thumps and clicks on the blackboards in a wilderness of sound while Rachel's father wields a white baton as if it were a beacon through all the blankety-blank-blank – though I can't tell what of this cluster-fuck, this crunchy abstract, matters.

I take Rachel's lifeless hand – a rubbery squid – in mine.

For the grand finale, the performers pick up their steel buckets and fling the contents at the blackboard surfaces. Dry heave of pastel-coloured chalk, dust.

I release Rachel's hand and clap politely. This thin woman beside me, doing the same. Above her stalklike body, her head floats, hair on fire.

A couple of nights later, I'm working a private golf club when Walker pages me.

You lech, I think, ears burning. So you want to talk, do you?

It's eleven o'clock. I've just locked the greenskeeper's office door behind me. Now I unlock it and re-enter, hit the light switch. I call, and he picks up on the first ring.

Yallo?

My head is throbbing. I'm ready to let him have it. But he beats me to the punch.

He says, Maybe you're too dumb to be, but *I'm* scared.

Ssh-cared, is how he says it: he's been drinking, consonants sloshing to vowels. My head tightens against his hurdy-gurdy, galumphing voice.

About what? I say impatiently. You're not making sense.

Shensh, he says and hangs up.

The office is loud with dial tone, flooded fluorescent light. I redial.

It's me, I say. You know –

I know, he mumbles. I know who you are.

And I have a good idea who you really are.

Not any goddamn more you don't, he says, and hangs up again.

I try one more time. *Scared.* I wonder what he means.

This is important, he declares immediately upon answering, his voice cracking slightly. Things're wrong.

He sounds sadder than I've ever heard him – I'm silent to let him continue.

There's a long, sighing pause.

Well, he says. It's Mimi.

He coughs for maybe ten seconds. I hold the phone away from my ear.

I can still see her glass of rye on the floor beside the couch, her white hand dangling inertly an inch above that amber. The last time I saw her.

I put the phone back to my ear.

There's no talking to her, he's saying. Been slamming doors. Staring down Jena, scaring her. Jena leaving the room in tears. It's been this way for months. Wanders the house at night, doing fuck knows what. Every little thing Mimi takes as a betrayal.

I wonder who's fault *that* is, I say.

So her old lady died last week, he says. I had her buried Thursday. You know, in that old cemetery down near Steeles. Christ.

Shit, I say. Poor Mimi.

Poor Mimi is right, he says. Now it's like she doesn't know if she's coming or going. Leaving or staying. Throwing forks and spoons my way or making nice with me. But she's only hurting herself.

He coughs.

Jena and me just keep our distance, he continues. Even Joy can't reach her. Mimi's even out there messing with the horses. I caught her riding one once! I'm afraid the boarders will start complaining, if they find out.

For a second, a pang clocks me. Sometimes over the years Mimi would come out to the arena to watch me jump. She'd get this look on her face, at once proud and wistful. *Better left to the experts*, is what she seemed to be telling herself.

Mimi riding! he says. Like *you* used to. If you can cast your mind back that far.

I slam the receiver on the metal desk, put the receiver back to my ear. He growls.

Tell Mimi I'm sorry, I say. Will you do that?

Might, he says.

I can hear him swallow, and then he goes, Ah, whoo! that smarts.

Thanks, Walker, I tell him. Thanks a lot.

I hang up. Go to the door, flip the light switch off. I stand like this a long time, head resting against the wall – stand for so long I feel made of straw. Dry, scratchy inside: not much else. Scarecrow. Visionless. Waiting.

Until the darkness takes shape, mounds and limbs hedging the room, a trick of the eyes: what's not there, leafing out. Eventually, an outstretched hand, moss-grown, poised to brush back my hair.

When am I going to meet your mom?

Rachel curls over on the futon and faces the wall, crushes the duvet to her nose. It's three on a November afternoon and she's been in bed all day.

Your friends? I press. Don't you have classes? Won't they kick you out?

Lay off, she says.

I put an arm around her, find her feet with mine. Her feet are freezing.

What's the matter? I say.

Lying on the futon at four this morning I heard raccoons rhumba-ing through the garbage cans in the narrow alley below, mixing it up with the tunes playing on one of the local country stations' all-night radio show, saucy tales sailing from the radio in the kitchen, plying the long hallway with spry yodels and plaintive yips, the backwash bass line that always sounds the same.

The radio's still on – we must have slept through it. Now the afternoon call-in show frazzles the air with its cornball chatter and chirpy country tunes that Walker and Joy listen to in one way, Rachel in another.

My girl. She unsheathes her mouth from the duvet.

Nothing's the matter, she says. What's the matter with you?

Christ, I think. Can't we ever have a conversation?

I sit up, lean against the wall, accidentally pulling the cover from her. She yanks it back.

You cunt, she says.

Sounds like a real nice lady, Big Dan is saying. Ella McGee, seventy years old today. Holy smokes, isn't that great.

Some of Rachel's new work – post-visit to her father – is pinned on the walls. Gouache on paper, three pieces, medium-sized rectangles.

Two similarly watery scenes: slender acrobats slipping like rain from a tent of sky, beneath which caramel-corn daddies pop and bluster.

The third piece is a self-portrait of the artist as a girlie-girl in a frothy, maximum-fem Frederik's of Hollywood white lace baby doll with matching thong: Rachel as a red-hot delectable with chest steak-knifed open to reveal a singalong organ heart pumping black-note tra-la-las around the picture's frame, a frame that here and there, in places, resembles barbed wire.

What's this all about? I want to ask but am afraid to, afraid, more than anything, of the claw of anger I feel spiking up my throat.

I suddenly feel a strange nostalgia for this moment. It's as if I'm already gone. The present is little more than a pale seed. Some day I'll look back on it – on this – from the future, one as infinite as a hall of mirrors, where the past is doomed to eternally repeat: a choked circuit stuck in endless replay. No way out.

Big Dan says, Hope you're listening up there in Pefferlaw, Ella, because this here's from George Strait, the gentleman cowboy. This one's going out to *you*.

I pat her bottom through the duvet, get up. The floor is November-cold under my feet: sends the old ache up my ankle. Dust bunnies whirl like dervishes down the drafty hallway, love me tender on the radio, messages flashing like billboards.

Come on home Sue. Don't be mad, I still love you. John please call. Thanks for setting an example, mom.

Then a commercial break, news. In the kitchen the linoleum is still tepid from the weak afternoon winter sun. I look inside the fridge for something to drink, find only an assortment of foil-wrapped leftovers, most of which by now will be bacterial cultures bizarre as school projects. I stand at the sink, drinking a glass of grey tapwater.

In the hall again I press my left hand to the wall, imagine I'm leaving an invisible escape trail. I stand in the door to the bedroom and wait for my eyes to adjust to the half-light. Rachel lies on her back on the futon, the duvet kicked off, now, despite the cold that has hardened her pale nipples. Her thin arms are behind her head, causing her body to lengthen, breasts and hip bones to jut upwards, emphasizing the bony pubis, fretted with stubble from having recently been shaved again. She draws her sharp knees up, perpendicular to the ceiling. Opens her legs, soles of her feet together, a crossbow effect.

She says, I'll tell you what's wrong. You are.

Me? I say. What's wrong with me?

Where shall I begin? she says.

But she stops there, with acrobats falling around, tearing through sheets of sky, with the rinky-dink radio man spinning the tunes and naming the names.

Big Dan says, Can our next caller identify the singer of this baby? – and a guitar strums, the airwaves grow heavy with heartache, Elvis and Hank edged as with lace by the chirpy traffic girl, the sportscaster's sarcastic *this* guy thinks he can skate – the interminable country jock blather herding the terminal distances all the way from Music City.

And the messages, piled on!

Everything will be all right, say you're sorry, love redeems.

My own father calling one day on the phone. *Spent my last three hundred. Damn nice pair of boots. Take better care of me than any woman.*

Big Dan says, Up next, Sha-ni-a. But first, how's traffic look, Colleen?

Well, Dan, Colleen says. All bunched up on the Gardiner, but then, what else is new?

Rachel's staring at the ceiling, smiling to herself.

You know something? I say – all I can think to say. You are too much. I give you everything, and all you do is take.

Feeble: I know how easily she can knock my words down. Here it comes now, her breaking ball trick, and the resulting spasm that shifts the planes and angles of our relationship. I am here. You – are there.

I give you everything, she says, mimicking cruelly.

Then her tone glides to neutral.

But how can that be? she says. When you have nothing I want?

I see: I zig, you zag, and presto – insight, a lightning bolt of understanding. Like the first time I opened her (what's this?), first two fingers, then three, pushing against her vaginal muscles – curling my hand, little bird, into her up to the wrist, my eyes closed in concentration – only to discover the frighteningly strong suck and hold of her muscles. Alarmed, I opened my eyes. Her back was arched, and red blotches stormed across her face and neck and chest, her scalp oozing sweat.

Scared me witless: in my head, white light clicking over, an annulling seizure.

Nothing! she repeats.

I shower, get dressed in my uniform, leave that cold, underheated apartment – weather, traffic reports a senseless nattering in the background – feeling simple relief.

I get in my ice-box car – frost veining the windshield – and warm up the engine. No way out. By the time I put it in first, pull away from the curb, I know I'm in with Rachel until we run our course.

Everything is us: we're all there is. Who would I be without her?

Over the next few weeks – that tailspin down into teeth-on-edge cold and darkness – she sleeps a lot. She says she doesn't feel well, she says the trees make her sad. Hours at a stretch I cradle her, as if her lightweight frame might break, while she leaks generous tears of tender gratitude – which makes me feel great. See? She needs me. I try to muster enthusiasm like a cheerleader, like someone on the sideline of depression's big game.

Nothing's wrong! I squeak. You just need to get out more.

The air around us a floating soup of night fears until nothing short of utter exhaustion, that scratchy wool army blanket, smothers us and we succumb to grey sleep.

Aren't there meds for this? Is there something she should be taking?

I worry about leaving her alone, I beg and plead.

Is there something I can do? I plaint. I mean, I feel so useless.

You, you, you, she says in a squirrelly cartoon voice. Let me tell you something. It's not always about you.

I no longer return Walker's calls.

Joy never calls.

But I catch Mimi, middle of the night one night around the end of November. I get up the nerve, place the call from the office of a condo building, playing a hunch she'll be up and will answer. She's always been something of a nighthawk.

Tiger? she says. Hey. Honeykins. I was hoping it'd be you.

Sounds bright-eyed and bushy-tailed to me: I gladly imagine her sitting in a chair in Walker's kitchen, pushed way out from the table, feet up. Painting her toenails. Smoking his cigarettes. I mean, she sounds that good. Fingers crossed.

Any new thoughts on the meaning of life? she asks.

No! I say, laughing as I twirl the phone cord around my finger.

Hmm, she says, teasing. You've always been the deep one.

Me? I ask – not sure where this is going.

The truly one and only! she replies.

Putting her hair up, glossing her lips. Removing the gloss with Kleenex, getting ready to give herself a mud facial, wafer-thin cucumber slices over her eyes. Could Mimi be herself again?

The meaning of mine, she goes on, musing. Is this. How I go to see my mother, and don't. That's it! Story of *my* life. One big mind suck.

I heard about your mother, I begin – regretting my fear of calling Mimi sooner.

I remember that day we went to see her, I say.

Ha, she says thickly. The visit that never was. Because, once again, I go and lose it. No *impulse control*. Like that doctor was ever going to let me forget!

She's suddenly quiet. I drop the phone cord and wait, rigid, for something to come to mind that I can say to her.

The lesson, she goes on, letting me off the hook. Is that you can't pit pain against pain. Hers against mine. Ask yourself this. In the end, whose do you think will outlive the other's?

I don't know, I say.

I know, she says.

After another pause she continues.

But you're smart, she says. Anyway, listen to me! The great philosopher. *Pain outlives!* And while I'm at it, let me tell you above love. It changes nothing. *Love only endures!*

She laughs.

But there's no use crying over spilt milk. Isn't that right, pussycat?

No, I say, brain stumbling to no avail for some kind of soothing message. There isn't.

Just remember, she says. And here I'm speaking from personal experience. Whatever you do, no matter how much she drives you to it, don't. And I repeat, *don't* ever raise your hands against your own mother. It's something you'll never live down.

Now I only want to get off the phone. Forget we've ever had this conversation.

Don't hate me for this, she says – her voice suddenly distant, girlish.

I won't, I respond quickly.

I'm tired, she says. Is that okay?

Yes, I say. It is.

For the first time since September, I go to Walker's. Ten o'clock, one morning of a severe December cold snap – Mimi's uncertain, lisping words from the end of our last conversation still in my ears – I bundle Rachel into the car. In our heavy coats and boots – wool scarves wrapped around our necks, ready to be pulled over our mouths against the predicted powerhouse wind chill outside – we head northeast from the city. Past crusty white fields – the few not yet sundered by subdivisions – glinting in sun. Bare red maple, slippery elm, black walnut, their branches a prim lace against the blue sky. Red pines in top hats and tiered capes of snow. Sudden blows of wind. Narcotic lines of white.

When we reach Walker's, I drive over to the first barn. His trucks are there, as is Mimi's snow-buried car. One of his dogs larks toward the still-moving Rabbit. Rachel flings her door open, and the warm musk of horse manure wells up against the cold.

Doggy woggy, she's saying. Is you a good boy?

The dog is half inside by the time I halt – hopping on its hind legs, slapping at her with his tongue. She thumps him all over with her black mitts.

Jesus christ, she suddenly says. He's soaking! What's the matter with him?

Stop, I protest weakly.

So Walker's ancient brood mare has delivered: he'd paged me last night, left a message on my voice mail – said his mare was ready, that it could be anytime now. I'd wanted to surprise Rachel – any excuse to get her out of the apartment, out of herself.

Don't touch him, I say, more loudly now – but she's already covered in blood, sloppy seconds from the wolfed-down afterbirth that's drenching the dog's thick fur.

Walker appears, coming from the first barn. He sees us and stops, puts his hands in the pockets of his work coat and stares. The dog turns and yaps once in his direction, then Velcroes itself to Rachel again, continuing to lick her face in loving strokes.

Rachel! I say.

With a loud thunk she belts the dog off her lap and out of the car. He squeals, and then, feet planted on the ground, wags his tail half-heartedly, turns a couple of circles, and lies down in the snow, watchful.

You are so controlling! Rachel splutters. Stop telling me what to do. Leave me the fuck alone.

She launches herself from the car, falls in the snow, and bangs her head on the door. I can see her knees, part of her coat. Her head disappeared.

I get out of the car, moving slowly, hoping to convey nonchalance – like, no big deal, Walker.

She's lying on her back in the snow. I kneel, pull off my right mitt with my teeth, put my hand on her shoulder. She explodes into action, twisting onto her belly, pressing her face to the white-frosting ground. She flings her arms over her head and neck as if to protect against a bear attack, an impression heightened by the hunter-style men's hat she's wearing, fastened by ties under her chin.

I wait on my knees beside her, hear Walker crunch across the drive and up the steps to his kitchen door. Wind jags snow from the nearby barn roof. Rachel labours to breathe at my feet. The dog whines and licks his paws. Finally Rachel lifts her face.

Never touch me again, she spews.

I leave her there. Inside the first barn is a staggering warmth, a nickering new life. I stand nearly doubled over in the aisle, between a set of cross ties – the feeling of nostalgia is that potent, for I've just realized that this place is already well in my past.

The barn door opens and Rachel comes inside. Tears mark her face. She's head to toe snow-caked, steak-pink where it's tinged with blood.

Tanis, she moans.

Inside my coat, my layers of wool and cotton, my long underwear, my skin tightens with cold. I turn my back to her, go to the box stall, unlatch the door. The newborn foal is a healthy-looking colt that kicks at me with spindly legs when I enter. The mare, a swaybacked thoroughbred Walker continues to try his luck at breeding each year, seems very been there, done that, and ignores me.

Here, I say to Rachel – who's outside the stall door now.

She steps carefully into the heaped straw. The foal wobbles over to gulp her fingers. I unzip her down jacket, scoop my arms inside, wrap them around her slender waist.

Love me? she asks him.

The apartment is empty. I'm not surprised – though I am when Walker knocks on the door between his kitchen and the apartment and invites us in for coffee.

We're seated at his kitchen table, mugs steaming in front of us. Rachel picks up her spoon, catching the sunlight that cuts through the window. She puts the spoon down, reaches across the table and lifts the lid on the sugar jar. Takes out a sugar cube, pops it in her mouth. She takes another, does the same.

Don't hold back, Walker says when she reaches for a third cube. We run out, I'll drive to the store. I'd hate to see you *deprive* yourself.

Well, if that's the case, Walker, she drawls. How about a wee drinkie?

Kind of early for getting liquored up, don't you think? he says, scowling.

But he scrapes his chair out from the kitchen table and stands.

What the hell, he says. I'm about as hospitable as they come.

He goes to the cupboard above the sink and gets down a bottle of rye, pours a glass. When he brings the bottle and glass over to her, she pushes back in her chair, parts her legs wide, swings them in and out: a full-frontal I-dare-you.

He freezes as if jarred out of himself.

Don't want to look now, do you? she says confrontationally. I know all about guys like you.

He squares his shoulders, resettles, seems to inhabit himself again. He holds the glass up as if taking its measure. Rachel's nostrils flare. He puts the glass down on the table, the bottle beside it. Then he's out the kitchen door and into the living room. I hear him stop.

Rise and shine, he says. Time for your close-up.

Now I hear Mimi.

What do you care? she says roughly.

Jesus! he says. Just pull yourself together. People're here.

He walks heavily up the stairs. A bedroom door opens, shuts.

Rachel dazedly tacks her attention back to me.

Hi, she says – as if relieved, as if she's just returned from an exotic journey, a radiant amnesiac: blameless, a fact nothing can ever change.

Hi, I say back – raising my right hand, giving the queen's remote wave.

Hey, she says.

The TV comes on in the living room, the volume high at first, then low. Mimi pads across the floor.

Hiya, she says, slouching into the kitchen.

I anxiously search her appearance, which seems to have deteriorated well beyond the last time I saw her. Sheenless hair pulled back into a straggly rooster tail. Clothes wrinkled as if she's slept in them a long time. Her eyes a strange glass-green. She's holding a tape cassette in her hand.

Got something for you, she says. Heard you were asking. Check it out!

The little-girl voice has vanished, replaced by her smoky, femme fatale one. A lean smile curves one side of her mouth. She looks dangerous. The feisty Mimi of old, only more. Too much, maybe.

She pulls out a chair and sits, tossing the tape onto the table.

Mimi, Rachel, I say warily as the women appraise each other. Rachel, Mimi.

Mimi leans back in her chair and taps the cassette case with an index finger. Her nails are painted cobalt blue decorated with yellow and pink stars. Despite the drafty house, she's wearing a tight black T-shirt. The overall effect is – desperate. She looks like a mock version of herself.

Here's a little heads up, for your information, she whispers conspiratorially to Rachel. I think you're going to like *this*. All about me. Whoever that is. Like *I'm* supposed to know!

She cracks a laugh.

Oh, don't worry. It's all as advertised. Everything you wanted, I'm sure.

She points to her temple.

It's all up here, she says. And now, for the first time ever, captured live on tape. On the off-chance people are finally interested!

My god, I say, incredulous.

And it's your mother you have to thank for it, she says. Surprised?

Trust Joy. Has to stick her nose in where it doesn't belong.

I guess she coughed up the recorder too, I say.

The third degree! Mimi says – putting her palms flat on the table and leaning forward. Since when did you graduate to detective? Well, I confess, officer. The recorder was Jena's. I didn't steal it or anything. I just –. Say it was a bona fide borrow, quote unquote.

She leans forward even more, elbows easting and westing.

What, tiger? she challenges. Don't you believe me?

I get up from the table.

I believe you, I tell her – deciding not to force the issue, given how aggressive she seems at the moment.

She pushes her chair out a foot from the table and turns, facing away from me.

Why don't you trot on upstairs and keep the big-yawn company? she says over her back. While your friend and I have a drink.

Walker is in Jena's peach-painted room. He's smoking, both hands on his hips. His eyes, now, are red, gluey-looking. Wrinkles canyon his face.

I'm losing, he says rawly, taking the cigarette out of his mouth.

Where's Jena? I say, heart sinking at how dismal *he* looks.

He sits heavily on the bed, where Jena's dolls and stuffed toys spoon into one another, confederates in collapse.

Lily's, I say, answering my own question. But not for good, right?

Nah, he says. Just more and more. And it's not even like Lily really wants Jena. I guess she thinks it's a way to win something over me.

The curtains are open and winter sunlight razzles the room, dilating it with light, turning the walls sherbet orange. Raucous laughter from downstairs invades. I shut the door to mute the noise.

The problem's not Lily, he says. It's Mimi.

He rises from the bed, moves to the window, looks down. Snow mists the glass.

She wants Jena out, I say.

That would be the sum total, he says. Guess I don't need to draw you a picture. She won't even try to tolerate her. A way of getting back at me. I pay every time I spend a little second or two with my daughter. And if I buy her something?

His brows draw together in a thick, dark line.

I don't suppose *you've* been much help, I say.

He starts, narrows his eyes, first in seeming incomprehension – then, as the skin around his eyes creases, in suspicion.

Then he purses his lips and whistles – a sad, wistful whoo-oo – drifts to Jena's dresser. Her jewellery box lies open on top. The pink ballerina is missing, and the quilted red satin lining is threadbare. From across the room I can see dangly feather earrings, a Brownie pin, some white buttons in the compartments in the upper tray.

I move, muscles tense and coiled, across the room to Walker, stand beside him.

I can just make out – in the bottom of the box, beneath the upper tray – a pale-blue change purse with a white felt poodle glued to its side, a gift from Lily to Jena: I'd stolen it from her once, hidden it under a pile of my socks, until Joy found it and made me give it back. I was ten, too old to really want such a childish object.

But Jena had been frantic over that missing purse, carrying on as if it were the day her mother cleared out, crying with wild abandon, a squalling passion she'd rarely displayed. It was as if she were reliving some early desolation of the spirit from which she'd never recovered.

The missing purse had reawakened her passion. She'd spasmed with tears, beaten her round little fists on her father's back, torn at Joy's arms beseechingly – elating me with a secret, thrusting guilt – until Joy happened to find the lost object of Jena's desire in the back of the socks, and hauled me in front of my cousin, tsking as I placed it in Jena's moist hand, before roughly hauling me back to the apartment.

Walker sighs and closes the lid of the box.

Poor Jena, I say – and I think I mean it, I *want* to mean it, but my voice sounds unconvincing to my own ears and, despite having only seconds ago wanted to hurt Walker, I immediately regret it.

His shoulders heave, and he looses a single, wrenching sob. I retreat, back away from him, sit on the edge of Jena's brightly coloured quilt. The sun shines into my eyes, and I shield them with my hand.

More laughter – screeching, two-toned – braids about the room.

Without turning – in a high-pitched, breaking voice – Walker says, And how about your *poor* mother? Doesn't *she* just take the goddamned cake?

For what? I say, confused.

She's out *house* shopping for fuck's sake, he says – facing me now. She's doing better than the rest of us.

I feel like I'm stuck in a revolving door, glimpsing slices of scenery so astonishing the hair on the back of my neck rises.

El cheapo Joy, he continues – his voice deepening, taking on an aggrieved tone. What did you think she was doing with her money all these years? Never spent a dime on herself, that's for sure. Or you. Nope. Been salting it away. Getting herself the deal of the century living almost rent-free here. Sure had *me* suckered.

Was she never going to let on? I think resentfully. But I also feel a modest flicker of pride for my mother. A house. It's almost unimaginable.

And then I wonder, How can Walker possibly feel used? Joy *earned* her low rent, cleaning and cooking and taking care of Jena – albeit imperfectly – all these years, no thanks, ever, from him.

But he seems to feel *she's* betrayed *him*.

She's working nights now, he says – ranting sarcastically. At a Country Style Donuts in Pickering. You ever want a sour-cream glazed or a boysenberry Bavarian cream, I guess you'll know where to go. I hear they've got a hundred and three varieties. Well that's Country Style, for you.

He sets his jaw, pushes his lips out. He's finished.

Walker, I say – floored, numb, unable to choose among the array of paths to take up with him.

What's the point? How could I possibly begin to smooth such a mad tangle?

I don't want to, but now I start to cry – a few tough crystals that break off from the inner corners of my eyes. I close them, lower myself onto my back on Jena's bed. God, *I'm* tired.

The sun streaming in from Jena's window washes my lids. For a moment I imagine I'm lying on a beach, scribbles of sand beneath me, waves of light above. I turn my head to one side, rest my cheek on Jena's colourful bedspread.

Not just doughnuts, I tell him, sniffing. Country Style's so much more. They're like, soup to nuts.

No shitting, he says gamely, with a self-deprecating smile. Since when?

I wipe my face on the spread. I can hardly believe how little he gets out. How much of his life he must live by rote, going to the same diner he has for the past thirty years. Same co-op. Bank.

I'll take you, I say – smiling a little, pushing myself onto an elbow. My treat.

The old uncle, he says – shaking his head, sticking a baby finger in an ear and popping it a couple of times. Stepping out on the town. Have stranger things been to known to happen?

No.

We both know it won't happen, that he'd probably refuse to go even if I wanted him to. He'd be too proud: like he'd ever allow his niece to show him how something's done. Never mind how he looks, I think, in his mix of out-of-date 1970s style and pure country hick clothes.

Five in the morning and the sky is lightening. A white plastic bag flaps from a snowbank, and my guard dog – a dysplastic German shepherd I'll drop off an hour from now at an east-end kennel before going to Rachel's – barks at it, nose streaking the window of the lakeshore club's dining room. I've recently progressed to canine handler – quite the step up in the world.

I pass the flotilla of Yuletide-decorated tables draped in white tablecloths, the slipcovered chairs, and enter the slop-smelling kitchen, dropping the dog's leash. He stands transfixed, nosing the complicated air. From the kitchen's cordless phone I call Joy at the apartment. No answer, no answering machine, as usual. I dial directory assistance for all the Country Style Donuts in Pickering. The dog lies down.

What's wrong? is the first thing Joy says when she comes to the phone.

Nothing, I say. I just heard something through the grapevine, and –

Ricky, she says. Save me some of that. Okay, yeah. Mustard on mine too. What is it? Tanis, are you deaf?

Not yet, I say.

Well you're not funny either, she says. Ricky, you leave my fat can alone, for the last time. What's wrong?

You talking to me? I say.

I'm on the phone, stop! she says. With my daughter, you big lug.

I pick up the dog's leash again and, his hips swinging painfully, he heels with me from the kitchen back into the deserted, Christmas-ready dining room – a ghost ship of a room. Across the thick royal-blue carpet, outside the floor-to-ceiling windows, the lake is an icy red sea, hennaed in the rising dawn.

I hear you're buying a house, I blurt out.

Who told you that? she says – now I have her attention. Walker? Bet he can't wait for me to leave. Well, he's going to have to wait until I'm good and ready, because prices are sky-high. I'm not buying anytime soon.

When are you thinking? I ask.

Snow aerosols outside. I can hear geese honking from as far away as the club's trash area, near the winterized, year-round indoor tennis courts. Soon the dog and I will have to brave the elements to check on the boathouse, where the club's members have stored their luxury sailboats for the season.

Don't *you* be holding your breath, she says, annoyed. And what do you care, anyway? Oh, *I* get it. You're going to want me to take you in. Well, well. Seems I only hear from you when you want something. My *daughter*.

My breath catches, a fish hook in my intestines, hauling up through my lungs. Blood wad. I can't get it out.

The crazy thing is, I continue to buy Rachel groceries, drive through sleet and snow to bring her lean pastrami on rye, pain au chocolat, and espresso tortes. I buy fresh-cut imported tulips in overwrought pinks and pushy reds. Environmentally correct shampoo and conditioner, microwavable containers of smoked tempeh with sun-dried tomatoes and brown rice. I worry about staph and clean her bathroom, take her to the swish laundromat off Parliament Street.

Six in the morning, six days a week, from my post at the lakeshore club – with only a shepherd for company, or sometimes an itchy, antihistamine-downing Doberman with severe food allergies – I watch the lake start to unfreeze.

On a blustery March morning – a couple of hours after my shift is over – I meet Rachel's mother.

Rachel and I pass single file along a cracked path to the tiny house in the Beaches, the front garden given over to waist-deep weeds and spindly crocuses hatched in scrapes of dirt. We trace the path around the back of the house to where a herd of cast sculptures, a flock of breasts – short and tall, fat and skinny – stipples the gravel-filled yard, another reminder of the neglected hedge woman Rachel took me to see when we first met. I'd never been there since and, as far as I knew, neither had Rachel – who is now timidly knocking on her mother's back door.

Almost instantly it cracks open: a strong, craggy face girded with high, widely spaced cheekbones, crenellated with bumpy black moles, thin hair pulled back severely. Rachel laughs nervously, shoulders hunched toward her ears.

Can we, like, come in? Rachel pipes, fake-cheerful.

It's not as if we haven't been expected: Rachel pretty much made an appointment, two weeks ago, and then called yesterday to confirm. To keep receiving her student loans, she needs her mother's signature, and a copy of her income tax return. Not only that, but Rachel – disorderly, no concept of money Rachel – is the one who, year after year, eventually gets around to preparing her mother's filings.

It occurs to me only now that – really – the girl *can* function.

If you must come in, mom says, responding to Rachel's question. Then so be it. Who the hell am I to argue?

Inside, the place is a mess, boxes of junk everywhere rendering the hallway no bigger than a crawlspace, a slivered fingernail of passage. Rachel's fierce progenitor ushers us into the cramped living room. Hand-carved wooden faces contort in the door-frame mouldings.

Sit, by all means do, she says imperiously.

At first, it's not clear where. I wander toward a butte of cardboard boxes before spotting a couch covered in yellowing newspapers. On the floor beside the couch, what looks like months' worth of unopened mail. Along the far wall is a steel table displaying mom's latest, greatest project: roadkill she assembles into motorized tableaux. Dead, damaged goods – voles and squirrels and cats – twisting serenely to music box tinklings amidst fairy tale forests of twirling, jagged blades of mirror. Above the table are three metal shelves holding an array of burlap-wrapped bundles.

Hard to know what to say. I stand awkwardly while Rachel picks through some bags of papers her mother has pulled from beneath the couch. Fortunately I remember I've brought something to break the ice, a present for Rachel's mother, a token of my esteem for her daughter: a bottle of stinging nettles and rosemary bath essence. I drag the bottle from my jacket pocket.

Really? Rachel's mother says, as I hold the essence out to her.

Well, sure, I say – taken aback by how skeptical she sounds.

Whatever possessed you? she says, then turns to Rachel, who's on her knees on the floor, up to her elbows in receipts – I'm surprised her mom *has* receipts.

I'm left holding the bottle of bath essence, arm suspended as if I'm not sure to whom the appendage belongs. Like, excuse me: is this yours?

For a second Rachel's mom seems to soften as she studies Rachel – looks almost plump, grandmotherly. Then she hardens again, and her voice scats to fury.

Go to hell! she hisses.

In an instant, the wide planes of Rachel's face appear to shift, the bones themselves appear to discombobulate then realign. She tips her head to one side, neck craned forward, fists still full of paper tickets.

Lea-ve, her mother croons. I implore you.

And Rachel, little miss roger-dodger. Repeat, mom: over and out.

We pass back the way we came, creeping out the back door, under cover of the weather, a thin pelt of weak light. We deliver ourselves to the sidewalk.

What about your loans? I ask.

Rachel shrugs.

This always happens, she says. I'll try again later this week.

I move to put my arm around her but she shoves it away. We walk back to my car, parked a block from where the lake chops the shoreline. Chip. Chip.

I turn nineteen. Joy doesn't remember to call. Walker does. He asks for Rachel's address, so he can have Jena send a card, he says.

I don't ask him how things are going. It's my birthday, why should I?

Rachel bakes me a cake, sparkler laden.

Make a wish, she tells me.

I do: for falling off the edge of the world. Crawling backwards from the wreckage of the past across smoking fields of rock, empty city streets, skyscrapers the wracked branches of winter trees. For being sick with histrionics – sick to death of our predictable suicide-chick selves. I wish we could forgive, the bad mothers ascend. Poor things: they've tried so hard to give us away! When what we are, will always be, is salt from their moon.

No other hate compares.

Early one March morning shortly after my birthday, I get up early, find Rachel at the kitchen table, chain-smoking, judging by the ashtray full of butts. She's got her refurbished PowerBook set up on the table, and several spiral-bound notebooks in a neat stack, Post-Its flagging some of the pages. She's just made a fresh plunger pot of coffee.

Everything all right? I say.

She looks different, sitting up taller perhaps. There's a vinegary smile on her face.

I'm writing a book, she says. And you're in it. Hope you don't mind.

By afternoon I've found a furnished, mouldy-smelling room for rent – shared bath and kitchen, all I can afford first and last month's rent on – in a house on Euclid Avenue. I return to Rachel's, cram my belongings into green garbage bags, line them up in the long, narrow hallway.

As I'm packing, I find Mimi's tape – the one she gave Rachel – in the bottom of a basketful of unfolded laundry. Before I leave for good, I slip the cassette – never listened to, as far as I know – into the pocket of my uniform jacket.

After I've moved my things into the car, I take the tape out and toss it in the glovebox.

They appear gorged with – what else? – refuse: I open one of the garbage bags, grasp it from the bottom with both hands, and snap upward. My clothes and what have you pour onto the floor.

I begin sorting: overly worn here, passable there. *There* isn't much.

I make a list in my head, things to buy: toothbrush, coat. A six-pack of Coke for the shared fridge downstairs.

I'm hungry. Or I'm not.

I fold a sweater, put it in the bottom drawer of the dresser. The drawer sticks when I go to close it. I jig it back open, remove the sweater. Bury my face in it. After a moment, I pull it on over my head. There's a damp spot on the shoulder – I can almost hear my mother: *Look what you've done now*. There's a blotch on the floor, over by the window: a gift from the previous tenant, I suppose. Smell of fresh paint. Like sour cream.

My *first* room: taken me all my life to get to this. I feel cindered inside. I lie on the bed. *Sheets, blankets.* I don't even have a pillow to my name. Put my hands to my throat and squeeze. I remove one hand and snug it under the waistband of my pants. Increase the pressure around my throat, until all the ancient, inscrutable stars come out on the low ceiling. I want to touch myself, but can't. Creeping, giant fronds of shadow score the walls.

Home.

Although it's spring, in sleep I see winter roads salted, flat discs of black ice levitating, rotating like tops – hear a crying shaped around them as they rise from the highway and settle among the sawtooth tops of trees. I'm half-conscious of grinding my teeth, fingers reflexing: even in my dream I know I'll be at Walker's soon enough. For the scant time being, I remain here, stolen away in the heart of my heart, a place I hardly know.

10

ERIE REDUX

I hear a noise sometime in the middle of the night, think I'm dreaming. Or maybe Jena's restless in her room. I *was* sharp with her last night. My mistake. Trying to get in between her and Mimi. And now I'm awake, thinking I might not fall asleep again.

Then suddenly it's early morning, still dark out. I get up because I'm old – the plumbing goes. I come back to bed. Mimi's long hair is spread over her pillow – she's almost peaceful-looking. I lie back down beside her, put my arm over her hip. She shifts her rear toward me, gets onto her knees. I'm sorry about yesterday. About everything. The years haven't been good to either of us, not really.

Baby, she says once – soundlessly somehow, a mute swan circling black waters that tar my lungs.

I wake up hacking. Almost light outside. I think I'll go downstairs for a smoke. When I'm in the hall I remember the noise I'd heard. Maybe I'll see if Jena's okay.

Oddly, her door is open. A few more steps – and now I see the mess.

Downstairs, I get Lily on the phone.

I guess you finally decided to join the land of the living! she says. For all your big talk about keeping Jena safe and sound, you've really done a bang-up job.

She's safe? I say.

No thanks to you, she says. Do you even know how she got here?

Put her on, I say.

I asked you a question, you shit, she says. She hitchhiked. In the middle of the night. Walked up to the main road, then caught a ride. I don't think I have to tell you what could have happened. I've been beside myself.

Lily, I say, the word falling flat – in my desperation, I don't know whether to let fly at the woman or try to calm her.

Let me talk to Jena, I say.

Why don't you have a talk with that bitch of yours, instead? Lily responds. As if she doesn't have something to do with this.

I hang up. Get a smoke, pull open the door, step outside, off the porch. Try to think about something else. And I think – of all things – about picnics. Sky with breeze and gulls, beneath which the sticky buns, ants, my old dog Gracie – her ink-spot face. Something I saw once, years ago. Before Lily. When I was trying to make amends with Joy.

The red wool blanket spread over the lumpy sand. Joy had forgotten the grapes in the car. I shuffled back up the loose rocks and bedraggled weeds to the top of the incline where the car was parked, turned around and looked down. Joy bent toward me and waved. Sunny with cloud, triangle of shadow vanishing, reappearing. I got the grapes, mashed in the back seat of the car. As I slowpoked back down the hill I could see Joy holding the dog between herself and a wrapped-up bundle – Tanis.

Say hi, Gracie, Joy said as I got closer – and the dog barked her yap off at me, though I'd fed her for years.

I put the bag of grapes, warm from sitting in the car, on the red blanket. A gust of wind lifted the edge. Joy turned toward me to say something – when I think of it now, it doesn't matter what. Something simple she did. Cloud passing over, blotting her face. My hair standing on end on the back of my neck.

Milk sours, Mumma had said, the last time I saw her. It can't keep its goodness, nothing can.

This was in the hospital. They'd let Joy and me in to see her – people *were* kind. But the kindness felt like a cold rock sitting on my chest when I saw Mumma had these machines covering her up. She could hardly speak. Seemed like she wasn't going to – a nurse put her hands on my shoulders and turned me away, Joy angry, ready to squall. From the bed, Mumma's frail voice.

Don't let the bed bugs –

Likely a smile too – knowing I knew how to fill in the blank. But I didn't say, too frozen solid inside – sheet ice of fear, knowing she was going to *die* – and ever since Joy and I left that room forever, there's been a cold shadow floating free throughout my life.

On my way back into my kitchen, I slam the door shut. The window panes rattle. The force of it stops me dead.

What an idiot I've been. Me and my big mouth. Snapping at Jena in front of Mimi.

I force myself to put one foot in front of the other – through the living room, up the stairs. Into the bedroom.

She's gone, I wheeze – sitting on the edge of the bed.

Mimi pushes the sheets off, pulls herself upright.

Is there nothing a person can do to set things straight, never a right way of thinking – A to B to C? Probably not. What's done can't be undone, not a single skinny Mimi or Margaret or Eleanor or Florette I've tried to put between each hard thing and myself.

Why should there be picnics? Whose brainchild was that?

Happy now? I ask. I guess you got what you wanted.

Mimi doesn't have much to say for herself – just uppity bullshit, like maybe Jena's at fault, or I am. Makes me feel more than worse. Enraged. At her. Myself. It's all I can do to keep a lid on it.

Until Mimi has to take things one step further. Doesn't know when to quit. But I do.

One day, she says. She's going to shred your stupid heart. You'll be sorry then. All your love, thrown in your fat face.

I tell Mimi, Get the fuck out.

She gets up, carefully, like she's something she's afraid she might drop. Gathers some clothes, puts them on in the hall – I know full well how white she is naked, and ribby, how her patch of curlies is thinning, but she doesn't seem to want me to see her now. Down the stairs, into the kitchen – after about ten minutes she's out the door. I hear her drive away.

Now I get up. Call Lily twice, no answer. I lie on the couch, sweat trickling down my sides. I'm thinking I should fix that fallen-down rail on the outdoor ring, or make myself a coffee. I should do a lot of fucking futile things.

A couple of hours swarm by, and damn if she doesn't come back – Mimi. Not exactly who I was hoping for.

She knocks on the door, baiting me – I go after her, onto the drive. I manage to keep it to shouting only. Leave her parked by the barns, return to my house. Though it's March, still cold, I shut only the storm door – wanting to keep my eye on her.

Fifteen minutes later, there's the faint sound of hooves on the drive. I look out and see – just what I need now, like a hole in head – she's mounting a horse. Mine. She must be insane.

Brazen – I'll give her that. If I wasn't so fucking fed up I'd almost have to admire it. How straight she's sitting, chin tilted up, must be Tanis's helmet jammed on her head, an old down vest she's swimming in – youthful-seeming, a childish slap-dash spirit you could almost forgive, if you didn't know what was at stake. It's like nobody ever thought to tell her she's not a child any more. There are consequences.

And this time, I won't bail her out. Won't let myself. She needs to be taught a lesson for once. She'll soon discover she can't handle the horse. As if she can handle anything any more.

I think of all the times over the years – I'd be on my knees as she lay across the bed – when I'd discover feelings I hadn't known were there, when her mouth stretched open to me and I felt I could lose myself, slip my bulk through her and disappear. A big simple man, happy in his own way as, later, I'd walk toward my chickens and horses, the crows calling tree to tree. And now I know all that's finished.

A cold wind invades through the screen. Takes hold of me.

I watch her leave. Past the March-stripped trees that rattle like spears. The weather is cool and clear, painfully bright. Even after she's gone, I watch for as long as I can bear.

How far can she have made it by now?

It's getting warmer out, a creeping mild spring fog, humid. A few minutes from my place, I start having trouble breathing, as if the air is webbed with strands of glue I'm sucking into my lungs. My eyes are misting. It seems that everything I look at – those trees, the blue car that just ripped past – is wrapped in gauze and twirling away from me like the tiny ballerina in Jena's jewellery box.

I pull the truck over.

Soon I can feel the blood leaving my brain, the swelling letting up. I've been sitting for a few minutes, when a Durango drives toward me, lights flashing in the faint haze. The guy eases alongside and buzzes down his window. He appears vaguely familiar. He has close-cropped sandy-brown hair, a snub nose that makes him look eager. He's wearing a light jacket, unzipped. From what I can see he looks trim in a Stairmaster, golf-at-the-club way – accountant maybe, or a dentist, the trophy wife out driving the champagne-coloured Lexus, getting the nails done – a way that makes me feel pissed off even more.

You own a grey horse? he says – pointing to the side of my truck.

I can feel his heater blasting. I feel sticky. He's looking at me like I'm *touched*.

There's a horse over on the Tenth Line, he says. About half a mile north of Steeles. Could it be yours?

He points again to the sign painted in black.

The ashen sky bends low, a back about to break. Rain? Wind rushes past my ear. I don't feel like myself. Or like anything. I'm no one I recognize, inside. I decide not to let on. I nod my head, casual.

A grey horse? I say. Yeah. That would be mine.

I turn my truck around. Left at the first intersection, then another left.

And immediately, from a quarter-mile away, I can see the small crowd of onlookers. I get closer, park the truck, and let myself out. I walk past a drab-green two-ton with a low flatbed trailer attached, sitting apart from the other vehicles. A man is stooped against the trailer, rubbing his face with his hands. I notice the road's pitted, uneven, in need of grading – which only usually happens once a year, in summer.

I'm trying to figure. Half-ton hauling a flatbed, heading south – a no-brainer, because it's still facing that way. Mimi coming or going? Truck's booting it maybe, maybe there's no stabilizer on it, the flatbed swinging out behind.

It's four in the afternoon – for some reason I look at my watch, wrist almost to my face, glaring.

Then I see Mimi. She's sitting off to the side of the road, legs in the ditch. Her head is down between her knees – the helmet on the ground beside her. She's hugging herself. Someone's thrown a plaid work shirt across her shoulders – there's that wind, dragging the shirt's hem to and fro. She's shaking. Blood crawls across the knuckles of her left hand. She doesn't seem to have seen me.

Farther up the road, a small knot of people stand around the horse.

For some reason, I look at my watch again.

Everything seems so still – stopped.

The stillness in my head continues, and now I force myself to look up and straight ahead, where fifty feet away my horse is standing, on three legs. The fourth dangles strangely. He's facing home.

Even from this distance I can tell he's sweating, breathing fast. For a second he starts, tries to lurch forward – a couple of women are holding the reins, and they pat his neck to calm him. A man begins to remove the saddle – undoes the girth, grasps the underpad in his hands.

Well that's that, I kind of drawl – to anyone, no one, and the words sound muffled, as if they were thumping at thick glass.

Mimi's head jerks up – she sees me. She's still shaking – knees knocking – so hard I think her bones might break. She looks old, beat up. I almost ask if she's all right. But then I have to turn away, my feelings as remote as another person's memory, the flimsy contours of a story I can't quite catch. For a second I'm awash with anger. At both of us. All that's happened.

I squat. My arm feels rigid as a board when I raise it. I can hardly bend it at the elbow, get it to sit properly around her shoulders. She tries to draw away. Useless – I remove my arm and stand, let it hang at my side.

With the most decency I can muster, I lower my voice when I speak.

As usual, I say – as if weighing in on a point well considered. You and me are just shit out of luck.

Yeah, she says. Yeah.

That's all – she puts her head back down between her knees. I return to my truck – somewhere I can sit and catch my breath, coat the nausea. Pretty much right away someone comes up to me and says they've called 911, that more calls are being placed as we speak – someone's rounding up someone to deal with this.

Sit tight, he tells me.

More gawkers show up, some with cellphones glued to their ears. Even a school bus full of kids – their foolish children's faces – until the driver gets the bus turned around for some alternate route. The wind crisps up dust and gravel. Someone in an Olds offers to take Mimi back to my place. I watch as they put their hand protectively over her head, helping her get in the back seat.

I climb from my truck, stand in the road.

A hundred feet or so to the north, there's a low bridge over a culvert where the road narrows. Mimi must have tried to rein the horse in, let the truck pass. When with an animal like that – high drive, still young – you have to fool him into thinking he's going forward, like he's going to want to do. Walk him in circles, take him off the road onto the other side of the ditch – whatever, just keep him moving.

Jesus. What did she think she was doing? No idea, probably. Reined him in hard on his soft mouth, and he fought her. Not much room for the truck to pass. A buck – the back left leg clipped metal, almost severed. Mimi ragged across the road.

Then again. Maybe the fog?

Well fuck *me*. Of course it wasn't the fog. What a stupid bastard I am.

It hardly seems possible given how little time has gone by, but now the guy with the rifle arrives in his Pathfinder. I start walking. Glance back, see the shooter following close behind.

The way people drive on these roads, he's saying, clucking. Won't slow for anything. You know, you might be able to sue this joker's ass off.

I reach my horse. He's sweating waves, neck frothed, eyes casting about in fear. Not focusing on anything, let alone me, standing beside him. The inflamed nostrils troughing open, the crests furiously mobile. I notice the saddle – goddamn if she didn't go and take my nice Steuben – has been placed on the ground, near the lip of the ditch.

I put my hand on his shoulder, and his breathing slows a little. His brown eyes are streaked with red. They stop rolling around as he looks at me. Dust panning the lashes.

Won't sleep good tonight, the guy with the rifle says – from only a couple of feet behind me.

I take my hand from my horse, put it to my nose, inhale. Dark March, winter's white disappearing through rusty dirt that's weedy, choked with roots. My throat feels stuffed. I hear the bit crunch once, twice. His left shoulder flinches.

Okay, the guy says, backing up. Ohh. Kay. Better give me some room, now.

A crack – the sky raunchy with clouds, birds – then the horse swoons down. That's it, game over. Sucker never got the chance to be good.

Nothing's worse than that. That's what really kills.

I make the right onto my drive. Before I can find Mimi – I've only just stepped inside my house – Joy turns up, fresh off her day shift at the golf club. Only a little time to spare before she has to change her clothes and leave for her second job, at the doughnut shop. Little Miss Newly Independent, in her brand-spanking Ford Festiva. She parks inexpertly by Mimi's car, over by the barns.

I come down the porch steps to greet my sister. No help, as usual – she cries when I tell her.

How could you let this happen? she says.

No, I say. That's not it.

No? she says – not really crying any more. No what?

Her face is a storm of pain and accusation. She steps closer to me and grabs my jacket front with her hands, as if she's afraid I might blow away. I try to step from her but she has me.

You let everything –, she says.

No, I say again.

She opens her hands and shoves.

When I think of all the toffee and salt-water kisses, the outings, the roof over her ungrateful head – all the things I ever did to deserve my sister's never being able to forgive me. For what? Mumma dying? For anything.

You want yes, I say – throw my arms straight out at my sides. Yes. So go for it. Give it all you've got.

She throws her arms out too.

What'll that solve? she says. Look what we have to live with now. Look what happened to your horse.

She sobs openly. I think, I could put my arm around her. But then her impatience – her unwillingness to believe such a thing as comfort is possible – causes her to rush, now, to Mimi, still wrapped in god-knows-who's work shirt, coming around the side of the house from the apartment. Joy goes to her old friend, takes her by the arm and leads her away, zombielike, back to the apartment.

This leaves me alone.

Three a.m. Thinking. How in the field out back by the Erie, my dead horse lies covered up under the apple trees. Poor prick driving the truck that hit him winched him up on his flatbed – enough men hanging around who could assist – and hauled him back here. I stayed in my kitchen, drinking – keep it coming! neat – called Tanis. I kept the lights off. Over the hours, the kitchen has become a black box. A holy hell.

I stumble outside for a smoke. Thinking how, come morning, I'd be burying my horse.

I head across the drive, enter the first barn.

Weepy with self-pity, I pause inside, consider lighting a smoke – but stop myself. Thinking of Mimi in pictures, bare and ugly as winter branches, kindling fuelling my desire for flames. Thinking I won't think any more, I make my way to the Erie.

It's morning. I'm frozen, lying on the ground. Tanis is standing over me. It comes to me slowly – I remember I'd called her. Yesterday. And she doesn't show up until now?

Well thanks a million for stopping by, I say to her.

I'm stiff, takes an eternity to pick myself off the ground. Early sunlight spangles the spring-brown grass. Soon, another month or two – weather permitting – there'll be leaves on the apple trees. At the moment, beneath them, the tarp-covered heap.

What is it? I say. Six-thirty?

Her face a sleeve, concealing what's within.

Sorry it took me so long, she says. You were expecting me, like, pre-dawn?

She's holding two Styrofoam cups of coffee. With her dark hair, she could almost be my own flesh and blood, more than my own daughter. For whom I tried – I see now I have none of the answers.

Bless your little heart, I say – take one of the coffees from her.

I get the lid off, spill some on my hand, which hurts. I notice she's kept the top on hers. I blow on the liquid to cool it.

Where's Mimi? she asks. Is she okay?

She's with your mother, I say – and the kid looks surprised, then relieved, and I realize that I am as well, about that.

Remind me, Tanis says. How was it Mimi happened to be out on the road with him?

You think this is my fault, I say.

I don't know what to think, she says.

I look at her to see if the remark was sharp, but it doesn't seem to have been. Her face remains unchanged, only sadder.

You and me both, kiddo, I tell her.

That we're linked even in this faulty way somehow manages to comfort me.

Tanis is looking at the ground. A tear falls onto the lid of her coffee.

You've got it all wrong, she says.

Then she adopts a wide-legged stance, overhands the coffee past my head. It detonates with a hot splatter on the ground about twenty feet away.

I only want to explain, make it easy, cushion her from the fact that the truth is beyond understanding.

See? There is no thinking. Believe you me. Take my word.

We had a fight, I offer anyway. I told Mimi to clear out.

Great, Tanis says. Brilliant.

I push on despite her tone.

I didn't know anything like *this* would happen, I say. Wasn't *my* plan.

After a few seconds, she points to the excavator.

Speaking of plans, she says. I suppose you'll finally get to use that thing now. That is, if it's still kicking. I guess it'll be good for something, after all.

My lungs start dry-humping my chest – as if in response, a rally of starlings rings up from the fields beyond, a call I'd gladly shut my ears to, like a message from the dead, the new ones, and the old – and then they clear and I start breathing easily.

For now, the kid's here beside me. I believe we've got a job to do.

You here to help in some way, or just to talk? I ask. Those are your choices.

Her face goes blank again. A space you can read anything into.

Help, she says.

11

NOT ONE THING AND NOT ANOTHER

I heard Walker leave the house in the middle of the night, but I never heard him return.

Buried up to my eyes in this old blanket on Joy's couch. Cold.

I must have finally slept – despite my throbbing hip. Watery March sun trickles in through the edges of the drawn curtains, onto my exposed, chilled toes.

I'm now in her kitchenette. According to the clock on the wall, it's seven in the morning. Wonder if she keeps a stash of Aspirin with codeine.

My right hand is scraped raw.

She'll be home in another hour or so.

Joy. She still has my back – I mean, when the chips are really down. Has, despite our little tiffs, since the beginning. Somehow I always felt she appreciated me.

When we first met, I'd been playing at singing – smart enough to hold on to my day job. It was one night in a bar outside Stouffville – this woman bought me drink after drink between sets. I remember now that I had a hunch she might be the first good thing to come around in a while.

Mimi, she'd said – after the fourth Jack and Coke. Now *that's* a name.

A *good* memory. Nothing complicated – she simply punched my arm and laughed through her stubby nose, as if she'd said something hilarious. She was short, roughly made up, face powder caking in the already pronounced frown lines not even a good laugh could erase. She wasn't hard to impress since she didn't seem to have ever been anywhere in her life.

Harsh, I know. Her life's been so *constrained*. Her mother dying young, her brother scramming, the foster homes – dot-dot-dot.

A friend in need. (Indeed – whichever one of us most fit the bill, then.)

So, she punched my arm and we got along great guns! And just before the bartender cut us off she gave me her phone number, saying she lived nearby, with her kid, in an apartment that was attached to the back of her brother's farmhouse. She sounded kind of proud of him. He ran a small boarding stable. Was divorced, had a daughter. Had a couple of thoroughbreds. And a name – Walker.

Now *I* was laughing! What did he think he was – some kind of southern gent?

It all was so straight ahead. A lark. How, on the following Monday – my day off from the beauty shop – I drove my Monte Carlo out to visit. Showing off her brother's assets, Joy got me up on one of the horses – and her brother came out not so much to watch as to yell.

Do this, don't do that. Christ! keep your hands down.

I almost fell off on top of him! But somehow I grasped how his unstinting bulk could be beneath me, that Walker would love me for my boys, for how I'd loved them. It was how I got to him – that I knew some of the things people do.

Twelve years later, here I am – for the time being. Everything's a mess. There's no going back again.

It began two days ago. There he was, pulling the sliding door to the arena open, tearing in. The boarder's horse shied, dancing beneath me every couple of strides to the top of the ring.

How many times do I have to tell you? Walker shouted. Christ! Don't you ever learn? At least keep your hands down.

Like he thought that was going to help. Or make me stop. When I *so* wanted to spite him, no matter if I harmed myself in the process. Legs jerking like a puppet's, I had to grab the mane to keep from falling off – even though part of me would almost have welcomed it.

Somehow I got the horse back under control.

If it weren't for you fucking me up, I said, spitting the words out. I'd be doing just fine.

He crouched as I neared the bottom of the arena.

He'd never done this before. But I should have seen it coming – I'd gone too far. I passed him and he stood, tossing oiled dirt, flummoxing my head. The horse's neck like a giraffe's hit my nose. A second later the ground pummelled my chest.

Wasn't the first time I'd been winded, sucking nothing but queer sounds so unlike singing I feared someone else had entered me. Not really painful, so much as a faceted sharpness diamonding my eyes shut. Too much *shine*, or something.

I remember that I lay on my back. When I got to my feet, Walker and the horse were gone – serves me right, I'd thought. Who'd want to stick around for this sorry sight?

I brushed myself off. In the barn I found the horse back in its stall, the tack removed. He rotated his head slightly, looking at me – like, *Who're you?*

Nobody. Apparently.

When I got back to the house, Walker was in his kitchen, seated at his table with Jena. The both of them! – leaning on their elbows, almost touching.

After a moment, Jena turned toward me. *I* wasn't going to be the one to look away! So she scraped her chair out from the table, stomped past me from the room – out the door and down the porch steps. No tears this time, at least.

Now I moved across the floor toward Walker, to the tick of the kitchen clock. Dishes drying upside down on a folded blue dishtowel, the unpaid bills in a careful stack on the table. He was looking at me, in a way I suppose he intended me to believe was meaningful. I braced myself.

You can't keep this up, he said in a low voice. Understand?

Well pardon *me* for living, I said.

You know what, Mimi? The years haven't been good to you.

What's good? was all I could reply – my mouth felt reamed with mud.

I shut the screen door quietly behind me, stepped into mid-March sunlight like ice-glare.

I found myself going back to the barn. Inside I found Jena. She was lounging on the steps to the tack room, twisting a slick strand of dirty-blonde hair around a finger, using her breath to puff up her bangs from her creamy, slightly moist face. She tugged at a ten-carat gold chain around her neck and rocked absently. Her tummy formed rolls beneath her tight T-shirt.

I nudged one step past her and sat. She pulled harder at the gold chain and stiffened, half-turned her body and hitched her head to look at me. Nothing showed in her small eyes. I leaned over and placed a finger on her wrist, tapped lightly. I felt that if I touched her harder she might break, open up to me like a fat piñata.

Knock-knock, I said – no one could claim I *never* tried to be friendly with her.

In the box stall across from us another boarder's horse rocked back and forth, gently shifting its weight.

Who's *there*? I said, prompting.

But the lumpy girl beside me was barely breathing.

Boo, I said.

No reaction. There were only the stammerings and velvety whoofs, the listing sidestep of the neighbouring horse to keep me company.

You're supposed to say, Boo-who? I told her. Like you're crying? That's how it goes.

I know how it goes, she said.

Get lost! I wanted to scream – a little advice, if she could stomach such a thing from me.

Because that's a craft worth mastering – one that allows the heart to safely grow fonder, to become a dainty memory, some vaguely remembered history of secret feints and thrusts.

Once, on a rare early visit, I glimpsed my drab, still-desirous mother roaming Whitby's bleary psychiatric home hallway, with an orderly in hot pursuit. Her fuzzy green bathrobe gaping, skinny breasts wriggling like worms.

But maybe Jena was already gone. Hard to tell. It was as if, underneath that pale-pink tee, she was some stuffed animal someone had misplaced long enough to have forgotten. She could almost be my own daughter, I thought. If she were, I'd probably treat her this way, a way I'd experienced first-hand, courtesy of *my* mother. Call it a learned behaviour. And wouldn't Jena be as callous to her own offspring?

I shoved to my feet, stepping past Jena into the aisle. I clapped my hands to startle the big animal out of his weaving. When he stopped, I stroked his nose.

Without turning I said, Still here?

How much clearer could I get?

But now she was standing close behind me. I could feel her breath coming hard on my neck. Her face, when I veered my head sharp right to look at her, was splotchy, red and white like a checkered flag. The split-ends of her hair seemed to rise and plait, vaporize almost, in the mote-scrimmed light. When she spoke, her voice was curdled, a sneer or a choke.

Still here? she mimicked. Like fucking duh. Are *you*?

I stood outside on the drive. Thought, See what I get for trying to be helpful?

I killed the rest of the afternoon soaking in Walker's stained tub, ignored all grumblings on the other side of the bathroom door. When it was evening, and Walker and Jena were silently eating dinner together at the kitchen table, I was in and out, fidgety – fishing smokes out of his pack lying on the counter, searching the freezer for ice cream, which I ate straight from the carton, sitting in front of Walker's TV. I rambled back into the kitchen to throw the container out.

Not mac 'n' cheese *again*, I said loudly. Same old swill seems to suit you both just fine.

I thumped the ice cream carton in the garbage.

Jena grabbed her plate and screeched her chair from the table, got to her feet.

Just trying to make conversation, I said.

She marched through the living room and up the stairs. Walker slumped back in his chair, punctured, like all the fight had been taken out of him. After a few seconds, I tiptoed over, stood behind him, kneaded his neck – he let me. Until Jena came back down the stairs, through the living room again, into the kitchen with her plate. Clanked it on the counter.

Dad? she demanded.

Now Walker yanked away from me.

Christ, Jena! he snapped – it made *me* jump. Beat it.

She looked dazed, then outraged, the high colour splotching back into her face.

You want me to! she bellowed. Then I will.

She stomped out of the kitchen again and up the stairs.

You just don't learn, do you? Walker said to me.

Don't think this is my fault, I said. Maybe it's hers, for once.

Shut it, he said. Or else I don't know what. You can suit yourself.

I held myself quiet.

Things don't have to be this way, Mimi, he said. But that's up to you.

He seemed so far from me then, though I was only a foot away. I couldn't seem to bridge the distance. Even when I slept upstairs with him. Slept! Hardly. I woke several times, did my best not to disturb him. Then it was finally morning – first hint of light – and he was waking *me*, getting out of the creaky bed. A bird was calling outside the window. The sheets were cool against my feet. After a minute or so, I heard the toilet flush. Then the bed creaked again, sank on Walker's side as he lay down. I kept very still.

I can almost feel his cracked hands now, running over my stomach, up and down my arms. I remember I turned, rump up.

Maybe, I'd thought. Just maybe, baby.

I remember, too, that when I opened my eyes again, later, the room was brighter with sunshine. Walker was sitting on the edge of the bed, his head hanging low, almost touching his knees. The bed frame rattled as he coughed.

Jesus, he said. Jay-sus.

He pressed the heel of his hand to his forehead.

She's gone, he said. Gone.

I unwrapped myself from the sheets and sat up. I could hear Jena's cat in the hall, trying to meow, that white noise it makes. I put a hand to Walker's back.

Don't worry, I said. I'm sure she'll be home in time for supper.

He shrugged off my hand.

I just hung up with Lily, he said – kind of honking the words out, braying them. It's serious.

He sounded as if he'd been crying, though he wasn't any more.

Happy now? he said. I guess you got what you wanted.

I had to stop myself from pounding on him.

Why is it, Walker? I said. That every time your precious daughter gets into a snit, I'm the cause?

Fuck me to tears, Walker said – dropping his head into his hands.

You think she's always so damn innocent, I said – smarting, fed up, unable to let things drop. Nobody is! Don't be surprised if one day she doesn't shred your stupid heart. Throw your love in your face.

He took a generous, *feasting* breath – I hadn't known his lungs could tolerate so much air. Then he lifted his head and turned his composed face to me – his eyes were colourless.

It was like there was glass between us, steaming up.

Get the fuck out, he said. This time, I mean it, Mimi.

So I did next what I've always done.

I get up, grab my clothes from the floor – take them into the hall where I put them on. Go down the stairs to the kitchen where I smoke, holding the cigarette high. Otherwise, my hands are empty.

Oh well.

I walk outside, climb in the car. No idea where I'm going, I drive around for damp hours, past the Reesor Sod Farms, past the Stouffville flea market, out to Musselman's Lake – a week short of spring, beneath a light, low-lying fog, a thin veneer of ice on the water's edges – along the concession roads, past brick farmhouses with crumpled barns, the new custom estate homes. I'm trying to figure out what I can still get away with.

I return, park in Walker's drive, knock softly on his kitchen door. When he comes, I turn my head away. A boarder's small bay mare stands quietly under the big maple in the front paddock, her tail swishing unceasingly. The sun comes out again, goes back in. When I glance again through the screen, Walker's looking at me through half-shut eyes, his naked belly massively overhanging his jeans. About the shape and size of a boulder. An unbudgeable man.

Give it up already! he says. I already told you.

I put my back to him and start toward the barn. He comes out of the house, then, following me onto the drive, shouting.

My tongue rasps in my mouth. I open my hands, flex them like a cat might its paws. Walker's ducks and geese barking like dogs, a dog barking. Crow. Wind in the trees.

I turn – now Walker's waving his arms above his fat head. The big bastard – still yammering!

I told you, he yells. End of fucking story.

Not exactly.

There in the barn are his dogs, sleeping in a pile of straw. There's his one good horse. I take him from his stall, put him on the cross ties, curry him. Brush him. Examine his shoes. He's perfect – quiet with me, no vices.

How'd you get such a bad rap? I ask him. You big softy.

He nuzzles me – the lips like shahtoosh, refined enough to drive a girl crazy! I pat him between the eyes, his blind spot. *How do you like me now?* One of Walker's pet phrases.

I get Walker's saddle out.

Once we're ready, I lead the horse from the barn and mount, adjust the stirrups, head toward the road. Nothing to hide! *Come and get me now, you bastard. You don't like this, then too bad*. Through the screen on his storm door, I can see Walker, moving slightly as he watches me. A rocky shelf beneath which I seem to slip along the debris of my failures.

So I took the horse out for a ride! That's all. Was that such a crime? An ordinary March day, freshly rinsed by the weak sun. There was this awesome – *sky*. Shallows and deeps. I couldn't stop noticing. Even later, when the horse gave a playful buck at a two-ton noisily driving by, hauling a flatbed trailer. *Oh, behave!* Nothing I couldn't handle. Which was *so* amazing. I remembered to keep my hands down, light on his mouth. Blue, rivering above.

(Surprise – me again. Check, check. If you're still interested.)

IV

12

BOXING NOT BINGO

Joy comes home around noon. I poke my head into the kitchen: she's removed her boots and is unbuttoning her heavy wool coat. She's lost weight over the past eight months. Her face looks waxy, melted – draining away.

Ugly, I think. She'll always seem ugly to me.

After a few seconds, she stops unfastening her coat, presses her hands to the top button, just under her throat.

He's not so good, then? I say.

You try seeing him this way, she says.

Distracted, she turns her shoulder to me.

I slouch back into the living room, fold myself onto the brown plaid loveseat from Sears, here in Joy's first house of her own. When she was finally able to buy, this past summer, a small cottage on Musselman's was all she could afford. At least it was already winterized with a half-basement, and had been recently remodelled: refaced kitchen cabinets, a new pre-moulded bath and shower unit, even some vintage-style wallpaper in the two tiny bedrooms of this aluminum-sided, nine-hundred-square-foot box shoehorned in by bikers' hangouts.

I'd taken three days off work to paint the little palace. Which felt strange. In the past, I'd sometimes laboured side by side with Walker, brushing and rolling gallons of matte over his walls, semigloss for the wood trim. And then, at Joy's, I'd finish painting in the early evening, crash at night on the living-room floor, lying in the August heat on top of a sleeping bag, in my drowsiness our *old* old apartment – before Walker – superimposing itself on Joy's newest abode. I'd fight to keep my eyes open, wishing to prolong the borderline, waking-dreaming sensation, its comforting illogic – somehow seeing not the kitchen's eggshell white I'd just spent hours applying, or the living room's pine panelling, but instead a rich salmon. And somewhere, unfixed, I remembered a framed picture of a gooey landscape, trees and flowering shrubs, Day-Glo lily beds, a path bordered with too-bright lavender leading to distant fields, grazing sheep – a primal pattern: studied, probably, since I first gained sight.

Blue couch – over there, maybe, next to the window – yes, and the feeling of being very small, swaddled too tight in grasping arms, desiring only the world of card-thin creatures – hand-fed, tame characters in a game played before bedtime.

Some fifteen or so years later, Joy walks from the kitchen into the living room. With the remote, I mute the sound on the TV.

Thanks, she says. I see you've helped yourself to the last pop.

I unmute, turn the volume up higher. She stands for a moment, watching the screen too. Then she heads toward the bathroom.

Get your feet off that couch, she yells over her back.

Ten minutes pass: I wonder if she knows how late it is.

I knock on her bedroom door.

Yes, she says groggily.

I turn the knob, push the door open: she's lying on her side on the bed, on top of the covers, still in her clothes, facing away from me. She's hugging herself.

You know, I say. I can bring a space heater in here for you.

No, she says. I'd hate to see you strain yourself on *my* account.

As I'm about to close the door behind me, I hear her turn over. I stop and wait.

I won't be cold this time tomorrow, she says. That's for sure.

I clear my throat. Within the hour, we leave for the airport, where she'll board a plane for her first vacation ever, as far as I know. She has a list to keep me occupied while she's gone: like, figure out how to regrout the tile in the bathroom, run the cold water in the kitchen sink if the temperature outside hits sub-freezing. Still, the cottage is a step up from my rented room, for a while. I can't say I'm not eager to see her leave.

Soon – if she can get herself packed and into the car – she'll be flying into paradise. An earthly, four-dimensional one. Whether she's ready or not.

Loneliness: throws you back on yourself, sometimes gets you out the door.

I know, I say, trying to sound cheerful. Lucky you.

Your old mother, she says, her voice breaking. She'll really be living the life soon.

Several nights later, in the second bedroom, the new girl's sleeping breath gives off a faint must. She's pretty – really pretty.

In two hours I have to leave to go back to work. I sit hunched on the edge of the bed, slip my hand under the girl's breast. She sighs and turns over, sealed against me in sleep.

I'd met her not long ago, on her first day of class at the Cabbagetown Boxing Club, above a daycare centre in an alleyway off Parliament Street. I was already one of the old hands – I'd been going twice a week, nine in the morning, for several months. I wasn't bad. In fact I loved boxing class, mostly because of Jimmy, the coach: five-two, weighing in at a hundred and fifteen, a former world bantamweight champion wearing Goofy sweatpants his childhood-sweetheart wife buys him at Wal-Mart. Squashed nose, mashed-gravy words, a gravity-soused bumble to his eyes.

Good morning, he'd say as we filed in. Good morning, good morning. And how are we this morning?

Then he'd order us around.

Ladies, he'd yell. Double-time skipping, push-ups, stomach curls. Speed bag, water bag, glove work in the ring. Only *you* can be a better you.

He had practical applications for what he was trying to drill into us, and he never tired of coming up with examples. He was like the old Walker – on steroids.

Girls, he'd yell. Excuse me, *ladies*. Can I have your attention please? Some guy comes walking up to you, what're you going to do? Double jab! Thank you very much, get him before he gets you, I taught my wife that. How's your mother-in-law? Double jab, one-one, one-two, hook, come back with a right uppercut. Girls, *ladies*. This is boxing, not bingo.

The new girl was several inches taller than me, had a height advantage when we sparred – she was confident enough to spar her first class! So I should have known better. Instead, I foolishly thought I'd go easy on her. After some investigatory ducks and feints, she poked out a long left hook and dinged me on the side of my masked head.

Talent! Jimmy the coach yelled, and for a second – while my vision rushed to fill the vacuum the girl's clip had caused – I felt wonky with jealousy.

After class that day, I changed out of my sweats into my jeans and a worn wool turtleneck in the grungy bathroom. When I opened the door to step outside, the girl was starting in.

I asked her to go for coffee, and minutes later we were in a café, soaking almond biscotti in a single skinny latte.

Last weekend she'd crashed a party in a new loft conversion on King Street near Dufferin – space, space, space, she was saying – and the lead singer from Fresh Sheep Kills was there, turns out they went to the same high school in Winnipeg.

Split another?

She got up and walked to the counter at the front, placed the order. Two guys came in, swollen messenger bags bandidoed across their shoulders and backs. Shapeless, oversized anoraks. Baggy cargos cut off at the knees, thermal long johns underneath. They were giving the girl the eye.

I could get "into" that, the taller of the two said.

I tried not to think of Rachel, that cocktail of craziness. I'd bumped into her in Chinatown a month earlier. She was on the arm of a dreadlocked white-guy bike courier whose vocabulary seemed to be limited to the word *whatever*.

Tonight in Joy's cottage, everything silent and sleeping at this moment: the girl's breath hovers between us as I match mine to hers, the lake outside snug in its bed of sludge, nestled safely between the weedy banks, so safe I imagine it could rise dreaming from its bower and fly. Everything possible.

I can almost forget last spring: the ground sick with early yellow crocuses, daffodils. The colour of fever. My mother standing near me, too near. Blindly, selfishly repeating words about her loss, her self – as if recent events had only happened to *her*.

She brought this on herself, Joy was saying. And who has to suffer for it?

And earlier, there'd been a wreath of yellow flowers on a stand in the tiny chapel. Too much yellow: the colour of screaming, a bright pure rage, one thin note.

Walker, glowering as he sat at the far end of a back-row pew. I kept turning from my seat in front to see how he averted his eyes from mine. I remember Joy had stared straight ahead.

The three of us there.

Four: *Hey tiger.* And a memory of a scent: clover, or banana yogurt. A sweet, smoky crumble of raspberry Camel. I never could put my finger on it.

And then, a little later, in the cemetery, Joy dares to allow her quaking shoulder to touch mine.

Girlfriend!

No matter how much.

I'd gritted my teeth and stood still, listened, forced myself to watch my mother in her grief, and thought, No matter what, I will not harm a hair on her head.

Now, in the cottage, the dreaming girl murmurs in her sleep, something I can't make out. I leave her to check on the dog – a blunt-faced male Rottweiler – crated for the night in a spacious Kennel-Aire in Joy's room.

In Joy's house: I mouth the words to myself. The fact of the matter still seems so astonishing to me. It's like we've fallen in together again, the two of us. As we were in the very beginning, though everything's changed.

I got the dog gratis recently from a family who lived in one of the condos where I work. They'd bought him at a pet store as a sickly puppy, and now that he was a year old and almost full-grown they realized their place was too small for him, so they gave him up. I've been taking him on my security rounds, keeping him at the company's east-end K9 Centre when I need to.

I'm hoping to breed him to the half-Rott bitch that

belongs to one of Joy's neighbours down the road. I met a veterinarian's assistant at the bar once, who said she could provide me with false registration papers – not exactly legal. But I could make some change selling the pups, then use that money to buy purebreds for myself.

After that, who knows?

Doesn't look like much: the road's gone to brown and grey. No green to fill things out. Probably didn't look much different then, either – more mud, maybe, a little less than now that it's almost winter. Almost the end of November. Joy due back in a few days. Telephone poles as tall as trees, taller. Expressionless totems.

I pull over. This one? Or that? Hard to recognize which is newer. No memorial.

I keep forgetting.

She didn't get very far.

Girlfriend!

I'm mad at you, I say aloud.

A car passes, and the stupid dog fires off, barking, trying to bite the glass separating him from the outside.

Then the car's gone, and the dog settles. I get eye contact with him, fixing his gaze in the rear-view. Behind his head, saliva streaks the window.

Taste good? I say.

He looks at me, uncertain, and I realize I'm being mean: there's no way for him to understand me. I unpeel the stick of string cheese lying on the passenger seat, break off a piece, turn around.

Okay, I say, his release word, and toss the cheese to him.

A snap.

Good boy, I tell him. Nice catch.

I ease back onto the road. Not many miles later, I prepare myself to drive by Walker's. I haven't seen him in months. When I do, he's standing on the grass in front of the sign advertising his stable, holding a rake in his hands, as if it were the most ordinary thing in the world – a chore, like it or leave it, has to be done – stopping in mid-motion to stare at me as I slow, something in me locked on the brink of skidding. Then I put my foot to the gas again.

For the next few days I keep thinking of this moment, suspended like a scene in a paperweight.

Carrying on.

Brutal.

Joy still hasn't called home yet.

In the morning, after work, I drop the dog off at the centre, then pick Joy up at the airport. She's tanned. Talking a mile a minute, right out of baggage claim. She's been gone ten days, and somehow her life seems to have radically changed.

Like, somehow, there's this *Ronnie* – Joy says he's a retired pressman from nearby Pickering who winters in Florida, a frequenter of the doughnut shop where Joy works.

That's why she went down south. To see *him*.

And, well, one thing led to another, and now he's convinced her to give up her cold-weather job, and return in another few weeks – on his dime – to keep him company. He wants to have some fun before he's too old!

Explains the no phone call.

She says she's saving to get a facelift.

Though Ronnie might kick in some, she adds. He wants me to look nice, I'm so lucky! Though I keep telling him, I'd be leery of all that light if I got it done. But Ronnie says you just drive to the mall early in the morning or late in the afternoon.

Dark glasses, wide-brimmed straw hat. I saw a white one in Penney's, with a red polka-dot scarf wrapped around it, perfect! With sunscreen slathered on my mug. Won't I look glamorous!

I wrestle her bags into the back of the car. Ronnie: I don't even want to know.

We both get in, do up our seatbelts.

Don't tell me any more, I say.

But it seems Ronnie is currently in Tucson attending his granddaughter's wedding.

Very rush-rush, Joy says disapprovingly, as I back out of the parking space.

Like you're one to comment, I say.

She ignores my remark. I scythe down out of the garage, pay the attendant, get over into the exit lane, try to think of Joy's face, lifted: the petroglyphs of worry lines, the rare laugh lines erased.

An avocado a day keeps cancer away, she's saying.

So now you're a health freak, I say.

And Indian River Grapefruit by the bushel! she says. But you have to eat them over the sink. Ronnie and I just love them.

On the highway, the sound of traffic doesn't drown her voice.

Things are so cheap there! she's saying. Billboards advertising vasectomies. Vasectomy reversals. We're far from the ocean, but it's waves of green everywhere you look, the rooms of the trailer done that way too.

We, I think. Well give me a fucking break. I guess he must have been mighty encouraging to her, all along. Way back here in Ontario.

I'm looking after myself, Joy says. I deserve.

Now she flips down the sunshade and checks herself in the mirror, readjusts her plane-seat-dishevelled hair.

Not bad, she says. Must be living right!

When we get to her house, she says, You won't even stay until tomorrow morning?

No, I say. No thanks. I have to go to work.

We're standing outside her front door, on the patio concrete she had laid in September. The sun is trying in vain to show. Her luggage lies between us as she searches in her purse for her house key.

I step over her suitcases, extra key in hand, and unlock the door for her. Just inside, is my packed duffel.

Looks like you can't run off fast enough, she says. You seem to think something's going to get you.

I reach and scoop my duffel by the handles. If she'd give me more room, I could turn around and leave – but she's blocking my way. I have to back up awkwardly to avoid bumping her.

You might not care about anybody but yourself, she says. And *I'll* put up with it because I'm your mother. But there's one thing I want you to keep in mind. Whatever that son of a bitch has done, or not done, he's still your uncle. You could at least try to show some consideration for him.

I lift my bag in my arms now – a bolster between me and my mother. Now a battering ram underneath my arm.

You know, she says. Sooner or later, you're going to have to forgive him.

Forgive him, I say – breathe so slowly it's like the world has stopped.

My feet feel glued to the concrete.

For having nailed the lid? I say.

Before I say more than I want to, I shake my head.

I helped him with that machine, I say tightly. When we dug that hole. Isn't that enough?

I get back in the car, humping my bag onto the passenger seat, clench my fingers around the steering wheel. She comes around to the window, which, after a few seconds, I roll down.

You're nineteen, she says, a sudden, frigid breeze shoving into her hair. A grown-up. I can't tell you anything.

She seems to have lost even more weight, and her skin drips around her jowls – presumably nothing a little surgery can't fix.

Stop trying, I say.

Maybe if you called him sometime, or went to visit, she says. You'd see how badly he's taking it.

I don't need to see anything, I say.

There's something I never told you, she continues anyway. When I last saw him, he said he has some odds and ends, for *you*. Of Mimi's. It seems that he found them recently when he was clearing out the apartment, finally. Don't expect much. She never had many things to call her own.

This is the first she's mentioned Mimi directly, at least in my presence, for months. She looks like she's really trying to keep herself from saying more. But doesn't.

I can't stand it any longer. This patched-up feeling: my skin disassembled, as if the pieces don't fit, are out of order.

Don't you even miss her? I say.

Oh, Joy says, foundering – putting a hand to her cheek as if she has a toothache. Oh!

You going to be all right? I ask, voice flat.

Some things you never get over, she says, beginning to cry.

I open the car door carefully, nudging her aside. I take my mother's arm and lead her back to the house, open the door for her, urge her in. Once she's seated in her small kitchen, at her childsized table – service for one – she stops crying, shifts in her chair, and sits on her hands. She blinks.

Without her, I say to Joy, then stop, not sure what comes next.

Joy's looking at me, expectant.

Without her, I say. You're free.

She quickly brings her hands out, pulls her coat sleeve up, shows me her watch.

I'm leaving again in a few days, she says, voice pinched with anguish and stress. I have a million things to do. There isn't time for this.

She means, this conversation.

Well, she says, recovering slightly, drawing a Kleenex from her coat pocket and jabbing it under her nose. You couldn't really trust her. But she was a stitch, wasn't she? The sun used to rise and set on her.

Then my mother smiles warily at me, and I return the favour as we decide to put the best face on things.

I only wish she could see me now, she says.

On my face, still: that rubbery, numb feeling, that familiar disconnect.

I drive away. It's the second-last month of the year, stark cold. There's no snow on the ground yet. But there's the pewter smell of snow. My blood moves sluggishly around my bones. On the outside, I feel tin-bright, electroplated.

I hear my tires whirring on pavement, sounding into the high registers, and beyond, frequencies I can't quite tune in and receive, let alone voice, myself. A silvery bracelet of frost on my rear window when I look back. *Ting.*

I'm still mad at you, I say aloud, echoey. But I don't hate you. *Promise.*

His kitchen table is as neat as ever, the buttercups and bluebells a rhythmic stylus on a November afternoon now so windlessly calm that, despite the cold, he's able to remain outside on the drive – for quite some time after I've driven past him and parked in front of his kitchen door – raking the very last of autumn's leaves, keeping to the simple task at hand.

Inside, I find the things he's set aside for me.

And later, when he finally enters the kitchen with its mismatched chairs, moves among the ordinary chores, sink, cupboard, stove, instant coffee, condensed milk, sugar, I'm more than ready for him.

Want some, kid? he says to me in a faded voice. That is, if you're still drinking coffee.

Instead of answering, I hit REWIND, PLAY.

Me again.

In the background, faintly heard beneath the magnetic hiss: tinny fair music skipping up, as from a great distance, notes heckling and jeckling like magpies over grains of sand.

I must be imagining it.

Stop, he says, and I do.

There's another one, I say. Do you want me to –

Keep it, he says.

Afraid you might hear something you don't want to? I say.

His forehead, the narrows around his eyes, the bridge of his nose, buckle. I think, You *should* be ashamed of yourself. Though the thought is cold comfort, he seems so fragile – and this, too, rankles. Like he should be stronger, so he can take what *I* want to give him.

After a moment, his face smooths.

I already have, he says. You know that.

I do: he'd told me in March – how it wasn't until the next day that they called to inform him they'd found what was left of the car. And her in it.

What you don't know, he says. And might not want to hear, is that when you were just born, and your mother didn't know if she'd be able to keep you, I told her that come hell or high water, I'd see to it that the three of us would stick it out.

He reaches to his shirt pocket, draws from his pack.

Well, he says. Didn't know that, did you? Guess it doesn't sound like much now, but there it is.

He coughs, then lights up. I'm counting in my head. I tell myself that when I reach ten, even if he's still talking, I'm going to leave.

Funny thing is, he says. *I* used to think it was something.

I've lost count. Seven, three.

The bottom has dropped out of my stomach.

You're saying I'm hard to please? I say.

That, he says. And stingy too. Like your mom.

Seems to have done wonders for *her*, I say.

Yeah, he says. Seems to have.

When I leave Walker's, I head straight for work, without the dog, late – sleepless, already into my next time-and-a-half shift that'll carry me from afternoon into next morning.

On second thought, Fuck it.

I drive south down Avenue Road, all the way to Queen, then turn right and head west, speed-baby, junkie-heart, sugar doughnut gilding my chin. Sometimes you think impossible things. An old memory playing me like a sense-defying song: one crazy night I was driving fast down the 401 with Rachel shortly before we split for good, arguing about something, when she hauled off and punched me in the head. I felt as if my skin had cracked open, something albino-rare escaping from me, a didgeridoo keening across the sixteen-lane exchange.

I park near the Gladstone Hotel at the corner of Queen and Dufferin streets.

The formerly new girl is in the bar, sitting at a small round table stocked with double drafts and a salt shaker, as if she's waiting for someone.

I haven't seen her in a while – a couple of weeks maybe.

Her black suede jacket is draped over her shoulders. She doesn't seem to have noticed me yet, turned to marble, standing here in my uniform.

Slowly, I back out the door.

My breath stains the cold December sky as I take the boat out of the shed, carry it down the hill, and push it into the water, crackling the tender, just-forming ice fringing the beach. I lower myself in along with a Thermos of rye and Coke.

It's a clear night. Satellites are out. For once the neighbouring dogs – and mine, as well – are quiet, though it's late Friday and summer-redolent memories of tunes from the far shore's dancehall fleck the wintry air.

If all went well, the litter of half-Rott to full-Rott – three-quarters? – would be due late February. How much could I charge for the pups? Two hundred a piece? Even with a large brood, I wouldn't stand to profit much, not when you consider the work and money involved in caring for them: feeding, training, vet bills, and having to endure their trusting, dopey gazes in their blunt-instrument-shaped heads. But it was better than nothing.

I shove off. The lake granite-calm, not deep.

Or: *I* could have a baby, feel it lodged inside me like a dark torpedo idling below the surface.

I sit up in the rowboat to see how far I've drifted. I reach for the Thermos and pour a drink. This time of the year, no cottage sounds chime across the water. Along the shoreline of this puddle-jump lake, where Joy's house lies, satellite dishes signal the blank, unresponding water like so many pricked ears. I replace the lid on the Thermos, pull my parka tighter across my rib-chilled chest, settle on my back, drink cupped in my gloved hands.

Me again.

I'd let the tape play through.

Then I'd stood in the darkened cottage and looked down onto the lake. It was almost unbearable: the recorder was still on – there was a complaining sound, like a mechanical toy that doesn't know how to quit, can't, not until its battery runs out. No matter what obstacle it hits.

After a while, the sound was almost like any other.

I turned away from the sliding-glass door, switched on a lamp.

Weightless and cradled now, here in my float, I eventually spot the light, though it takes a while, and I almost flip myself into the water searching for it. *Oh well.*

I pour another drink, shake out the last drops.

It was as I started to leave Walker's that afternoon, that he'd told me.

A week, Mimi. That's the long and short of it.

He said those were the last words he spoke to her.

We were both quiet for a moment. When the phone rang he got to his feet and picked up. I stayed put.

Yallo?

His body still, devotional. Then he sighed, wetly and long, before replacing the receiver on its hook.

Jena? I said.

He nodded, sat again.

A week, that's what I said, all right, he said. I wish there'd been more.

Then he said, Think you can forgive the old guy?

It was as if he couldn't think about anything else, never would. Neither would I. I noticed his hair was still bushy and thick, though drier-looking. Sapped. His eyes seemed to have receded into his head. He looked as though he'd never find his bearings again. I felt strangely light-headed. Wanted to go to him, but somehow couldn't.

Take those with you, he said, then, gesturing to the tapes, the recorder. Otherwise you came here for nothing.

After a second, I pointed to the recorder.

Isn't this hers? I asked carefully, and when he startled, I said, Jena's.

It's not like she's asking after it, he said. Is she?

He folded his arms across his chest, leaned back, legs out in front of him. Like Joy, he too had lost weight – though he still seemed huge, barrel-chested.

The big bastard.

Still yammering.

But weary, like he might slide flat out of the chair. Something heavy pulling him by the earlobes.

Pleasantly leathery, Dumbo ears, well-broken-in – I think, now, gliding in tidy circles. Mimi once tugged playfully, lovingly on them, right there in his kitchen, teasing him about wanting me to pay him back for the car he'd just bought on my behalf.

I finish the rest of my drink. Toss the Thermos cup to the other side of the boat – miss, and the cup lands in the water. I haul myself onto my knees, crawl forward, the little vessel rocking side to side. There: I pull a glove off with my teeth, reach over the edge. Got it.

Still on my knees, fingers irradiated with cold, I pause to level the boat. I remember Walker had laughed at her that time, fortressed his robust arms around her flexing waist, while she slapped at him, laughing too.

I didn't belong there. Or so I'd thought.

But there was another time, once at the beach: where was Joy? I don't remember. All I can see, suddenly, is Mimi. And then unforgivable Walker: she's shooing him from her, then noosing her slender arms around his bull neck. She wrassles him onto his side, blocking him from view. Where am I? *Here.* He's grabbed my ankle in his giant's paw, yanks. I'm ass over teakettle, as he might say. Maybe he did, then or some other time. I don't care, squinting up from my place on the receiving end, busy laughing at the sky above me, Mimi's ruby head.

She comes in closer. Is she frowning?

Kid's all right, he says, managing to horn back in. Don't fuss over her, for christ's sake. She can take it.

Now, on this small lake, I manage to get off my knees and sit again without capsizing. Pick up the oars. Better return to the house before I'm too frozen to move. If I can find it. Somehow I'm all turned around.

Tomorrow, I'll go to Walker's.

I scan the black hillside. I think of him, prismed with self-blame. I think of myself. So this is me. Not long ago I'd been up there, looking down onto the dark lake. Not exactly Walker's hell or high water. Not exactly mine. But from where I am now, it curves like an eye, once closed, now opening.

13

THE HOUR OF CHARM

When she was alive, I used to wonder what thoughts if any were in my mother's head. I'd try to imagine – if not belly laughs and raucous shouts, the able sounds of a woman fully in this world – the hope of a whisper from her, some knowledge she might like to impart.

But what?

I think, *How could you be so stupid?* Because love, in my mother's experience, was a ruinous thing, all runny pancake makeup and dimpled cooing in the late afternoon.

How could you? So much for nothing!

My mother was a rough woman, given to fits and starts. Towing me along an icy Toronto sidewalk when I was five, gripping my arm so tight it hurt. Riding a two-wheeler for the first time, when I was six, I reached out to steady myself, dizzy from the sudden spectacle of hard ground. First thing I caught was her arm. She bruised easily. It was always like this – neither of us knew what to do once we'd taken hold.

The rye's giving me a chill. Where's that blanket Joy usually keeps on the chair beside the bed? It's getting dark now.

Finally, I heard Walker return to the house, a few hours ago.

Then he was moving around his kitchen. I was in Joy's kitchenette. I took a glass out of the cupboard, set it on the counter. He came to the door, opened it. Nodded at my scraped hand. He didn't speak.

What's the matter? I wanted to ask. Cat got your tongue?

He cocked his head to one side, still assessing the damage, a grim set to his thin lips. Pity?

Don't worry, I told him. A couple of days, and I'll be as good as new.

He was no longer looking at my hand. Dead in the eyes, instead.

What he said winded me.

A week. That's it, Mimi.

A fit of air, inside me. I'm silent.

No such thing as a miracle, he said. Let's not draw this out.

Radio's on, bric-a-brackish. I don't know where I'll go, after this. Last night Joy was making promises – but now that I'm here, alone to think my thoughts, not only don't I believe, I just don't seem to have the heart.

How he loved me.

Say it was something I leaned toward, an act as simple as picking up a hairbrush. Turning on a light. The way baking soda sifts fumes in the humming fridge.

You're not young any more.

You're only hurting yourself.

That day in the cemetery, it was warm for spring, so I let the horse drink from the creek.

I'm wandering.

Turn the radio off.

I'd kept him quiet most of the ride, remembered to keep my hands down, maintain a proper seat – if only to prove Walker wrong. The dirt road was sticky. We treaded beneath rafts of cloud in an otherwise clear blue sky. A light wind scudded across brown waves of last-year's corn stalks. There was this *truck*. Heard before seen as it rumbled unmufflered, chains rattling, revealing itself, once it had passed, as a mud-caked two-ton wagging a flatbed trailer. The horse shied a little, startled. Nothing I couldn't handle.

When we got to the cemetery, I released the reins, and he cropped the winter-parched grass near my mother's grave. In the distance, city traffic chimed coolly. The tall trees creaked. I remembered that the last time I'd visited, it was summer. That as I'd driven past the neighbouring fields, a great demon baling machine was parting the blond grasses, and dust vapoured the road. My mother was leaking secrets into the earth.

Now I picked up the lathered reins, and we drifted down the low bank, where the horse cascaded his neck to drink from the creek. Above us, there were wands of dry sticks scattered about. The horse chuffed the water, rubbed his nose against a sturdy foreleg.

A breeze twitched the air. A sudden alertness in the world. I could almost hear the sleepers in their shard suits sigh damply and sink lower into the ground. I said nothing – I wasn't about to rescue the dead! – and my mother in her rattling dress said nothing back. I imagined her chattering with cold under the March sun.

I vowed I wouldn't even save her in memory. I told myself, Hold on to your hat, Mimi, whichever way the wind blows, to keep your hands from waving goodbye.

I *would* leave. Walker, this place. Poof! A common-enough magic.

There was a noise, then. The horse stopped eating and raised his head. The bit tinkled in his mouth. He pawed the ground, shook himself, flung his head higher. I snatched the reins back as a kettle of crows boiled up from the trees across the road, the thickness of their calls a remarkably dense pitch. The sound quickly died away. The birds were gone. A rotten springtime smell remained.

What what?

Only my mother, locked in the dirt, stubborn as ever. I felt as if I were peering down a well I might suddenly, sickeningly, tumble into.

I headed the horse back the way we came, north toward Walker's, away from the city – to our right, red pines, stiff-spined and elegant. In summer, I'd see mourning doves like grey silk pouched on the telephone wires strung along poles lining the side of the road.

I was thinking, That old bastard. Run to fat, not just at the belly but the brain as well, run to loud and pushy. *Get the fuck out!* And when I left? How would he make out, then?

Bridge. Ditch. Road. I reined the horse in, and he threw his head around, resisting.

For one thing, he wouldn't be sorry.

Bastard.

I shortened the reins, and kicked the horse's sides until he danced. I had to clutch his mane to hold on. Crying, fighting him.

I didn't notice soon enough the two-ton again, this time heading south – not until it was bearing down on us. Behind the truck, the flatbed swung from side to side.

We were almost at the bridge. I backed the horse onto the side of the road, sawed at the bit, trying to hold him. As the truck crossed the bridge and passed, the horse reeled out a half-turn and bucked hard, kicking metal. He nearly sheared his leg off – I saw that later.

But before that, dirt in my mouth, crumbly matter it took me a moment to recognize. My limbs came back to me one by one. Gravel and blood stippled my fingers.

I'd landed in the middle of the road – the impact with the truck had whirled the horse, and me from him. I banged my head when I hit the ground, and must have blacked out. When I came to, I was lying on the road, the driver standing over me.

Are you okay? he says.

I can barely hear him.

I get up, then have to sit immediately, legs in the ditch, head shoved between my knees, cowled with tunnel vision, the trees erased to blades of grass in black and white. I try to summon the world back, wish I could make it to the horse, but can't – I have to let everything go on without me.

I manage a glance to the side, which tells me he's partway up the road, hobbling, misshapen. Trying to make it home.

I think, This is how all creatures end.

Whatever else occurred was something I never saw. I wish things had been different.

On this faithless Markham morning, I stole into Walker's kitchen and took his Chivas. Thirsty is right. Back, now, in Joy's room in the apartment, fields and forests become the tendrils of this peeling wallpaper beside the bed, things and things like my breath in white sheets wet from so much drinking, drinking. A nearly dried-up creek. The Rouge running slowly through Walker's fields, grey horse like a ghost. Wind roams the trees until I open my mouth thinking I made the sound myself.

I have half a mind to just get in my car and go.

Any minute now.

In the cemetery it was warm. *No miracles. Let's not draw this out.*

I never went to the horse, but if I had?

I imagine myself finally reaching him, taking the reins, but they're so slick I drop them. He's not going anywhere anyway. I look down – see something wet and shiny on my boots, and in this way know I'm still here. This, more than anything, I find hardest to swallow.

When I leave him, by the side of the road, he's trembling. He's nothing I can save.

It had been an ordinary March day, freshly rinsed by the weak sun. There was this awesome – *sky*. Shallows and deeps. A glow, as if light had glanced from something hard and steeply banking. I couldn't stop noticing, all the way there. Nothing I couldn't handle. It was *so* amazing. Blue, rivering above.

This goes on forever.

ACKNOWLEDGEMENTS

Excerpts from this novel appeared in substantially different form in *THIS Magazine*, *A Room of One's Own*, *Blood & Aphorisms*, *The Journey Prize Anthology*, *Gargoyle*, and *Concrete Forest: The New Fiction of Urban Canada.*

I'd like to express my deepest gratitude to Ellen Seligman for her stunning clarity, warmth, and stamina.

I'd also like to thank Heather Sangster for her sensitive copy-editing, and Jennifer Lambert and Anita Chong for their ready assistance.

For their guidance and support, thank you, as well, to Jackie Kaiser, Jan Whitford, and Jennifer Barclay.

For her vibrant insights and big old funny bone, Kelley Aitken.

Of course, as always, my family.

The MacDowell Colony provided generously during the writing of this book, as did the Canada Council for the Arts, the Ontario Arts Council, and the Toronto Arts Council.